HER HIGHLAND HERO

Y M ZACHERY

One

Mel stared at the photograph. On the surface, it was a nice picture; the man was looking into his partner's eyes, kissing her softly on the lips. The woman rising to meet him with her eyes closed blissfully, looked peaceful and content. To complement the photo; a charming caption in which the man happily professed to have found his true soulmate, twenty-three likes and a long list of congratulatory comments.

The photograph was the very picture of normalcy and captured a beautiful celebration of the love all couples aspired to reach. The problem was that the woman in the picture was not her, *but* the man the woman was caressing, was her current partner, Jack!

Mel could hardly believe her eyes. The moment she had opened her Facebook page and seen the picture this morning. But then, she mused, if she were honest with herself, that wasn't exactly true; she'd had a feeling this was coming. Over the last few weeks their relationship had drastically changed. Jack had grown more distant and Mel, quite frankly, had become less interested in remaking plans. When Jack had started changing and cancelling plans more and more and all but stopped coming into the office for lunch, something they'd previously done at least a couple of times a week, Mel had to admit that she had felt kind of relieved. Things just hadn't been as great as they'd been at the start, and she'd begun to have a feeling that they were over which, truthfully, did not bother her. If she were honest with herself, she hadn't seen it lasting from the beginning anyway.

So what was the problem with the photo? Nothing really, except the fact that he'd beaten her to the punch and what infuriated her most of all was that social media officially knew before she did! He should have had the guts to end it with her face to face, before he took up with little Miss Prissy all over Facebook. What a Jerk!

Mel had been staring at her Facebook page for the last five minutes, fuming at the picture of her now ex-boyfriend kissing his new girlfriend – the same woman who just happened to be her new temp – now on display for the world to see. Mel snorted. *Soulmate my arse.* The pair had only known each other for a few weeks! Clarissa had been filling in for her regular receptionist when Jack had come in for one of their lunch dates. Mel knew that they had chatted a bit, but nothing seemed off. She probably should have realised something was up when he'd started asking about Clarissa offhandedly, pretending only a mild curiosity. Mel couldn't believe she had become a cliché – high profile accountant loses partner to the receptionist. She sighed.

It didn't take long for the private messages to start coming through asking Mel what had happened between her and Jack, and did she know about the new woman. Man, life had been so much easier before social media took over, no one's life was private now. Mel slammed her laptop closed. *To Hell with it!* She wasn't going to give the bastard the satisfaction of being humiliated, and she sure as hell wasn't going to give the gossip mongers more to add to their gossip mill.

As Mel sat with her head in her hands, she had to be honest about their relationship. She had not been happy for a long time. Truthfully she'd been getting fed up with his crap anyway; he was more of a woman than she was! Every time they went out, he spent more time getting ready than she did and if she so much as heard him say, *'that was hurtful'* while doing that sad pout of his one more time, she might have rearranged his perfect little nose.

Mel sat back and sighed. *Here she was single yet again.* She wondered if she would ever meet a man who could make her happy, a real man, one that wanted the same things in life that she did, one that wanted to be her equal, not her superior.

Seriously, it wasn't as if she liked being single, unlike her other single friends who claimed they were happy as they were. Deep down she wanted it all, she wanted that someone special that she could cuddle at night, someone she could talk to about anything and everything, someone who shared her dreams and, most importantly, someone she could laugh with. But, as she got older, the idea of finding that perfect man was getting further and further from her grasp and right now, the thought of going home to her empty apartment depressed her more than ever. What used to be her sanctuary had become the perfect representation of the emptiness she felt in her life.

She sighed again and, for the hundredth time in the last six months, Mel wished that Ceana was here to talk to, but the depressing truth was her best friend was back in 12th Century Scotland with her loving husband, while Mel was here, alone and miserable.

Mel remembered the last time she had seen her best friend, and it was during that visit that Mel realised what it was she wanted in love, and what she would probably never have. Ugh, just thinking about how absolutely content they were made her want to puke. It wasn't that Mel wasn't happy for them, just the opposite, she couldn't be any happier for her best friend. After all the tragedy Ceana had been through in her life, Mel was ecstatic that she had finally met the man of her dreams, quite literally, and now lived the most extraordinary life.

No it was not jealousy that drove Mel's feelings of discontent, it was just that while Ceana was happy living this extraordinary romance novel life, Mel was stuck in this shit hole, having to deal with dumbasses like Jack. Thinking about the slime-bag who had publicly humiliated her, Mel grimaced knowing it wouldn't be long before her mother saw the post and then the phone calls would start. She could just hear her mother's lecture now,

"What did you do this time? This one could have been the one, Mel! You know, you spend way too much time at work and you are way too judgemental. Perhaps if you cut the men in your life a little slack this wouldn't keep happening. I'm not getting any younger, you know, and all I want is to see you happily married before I die."

Mel loved her mother; she was basically sane and loving in all other factors of life, except when it came to Mel's love life. Mel was the youngest of three children and her two older brothers were already married with children. As the only daughter in the family all her mother's attention was now focused on getting her happily married off, at the expense of Mel's happiness. If it wasn't for her Grandma G.G, Mel would have gone insane from her mother's rants long ago. Ever practical, her grandma believed that the right man was out there, somewhere, and that Mel would find him when the time was right, and in a place she least expected to find him. Grandma G.G was just like Cee in that belief. Cee had always joked that her Mr. Right was just around the corner, waiting for the opportune moment to come in and sweep her off her feet before she even had time to know it was happening.

Of course, Ceana would see it that way, Mel mused. Ceana loved reading those romantic love stories and believed everyone should have a romantic, fairy tale-like story that she herself had been fortunate enough to find. But, personally, Mel hated those books with a passion; they weren't realistic and were too fluffy for her taste. Not only did they set women up with an unrealistic ideal of what love was, the men in them just did not exist.

No Mel was more practical than that. Give her a book that was about reality, something that had substance and truth, because that was what real life was about. She glared at her laptop; life wasn't about knights on white horses, no it was about jerks with severe attitude problems. Jerks who were selfish and wanted nothing more than a woman to pander to his every need! Life and love was a pile of horsecrap that never lived up to anyone's expectation. There was only one part of Mel's life that went the way she wanted, and that was her work life. It was why she spent all of her time and effort on her practice. Mel knew that, at the end of the day, that one truth would stay constant.

Yet, there was still part of her, deep down, that secretly hoped Ceana was right and that, one day, her very own Mr. Right would walk through her door and sweep her out of this crap hole that had become her life.

As if reading her mind, the door to her office opened without warning. She looked up, praying that it wasn't just another moron here to ruin an already ruined day, and was surprised and thrilled to see Tristan, her best friend's brother, casually stroll in. A jolt of emotion ran through her. It had been some time since she had last seen him, almost a year it would have to be.

Following the death of his best friend, Tristan had joined the army. Everyone had been surprised when he had explained his plan after Marcus' death, but they all knew it was something he had to do. Tristan had been on his second tour of duty in South America when, about a month ago, he had come home without warning. No one seemed to know what had happened or why he had come back so unexpectedly, but Mel didn't question it, she had missed him deeply and she was just glad to have him home at all.

The world just didn't seem the same without the duo of Tristan and Marcus causing trouble. Everything had seem to change that fateful day. Tristan and Marcus had always been so carefree and easy going, they were what every woman dreamed of; intelligent, good looking, athletic, but most of all, they'd had a great sense of humour. The pair of them together could put the sullenest of persons in a good mood and they had been an important part of the glue that held their little group together. That was until Marcus was murdered by a deluded 12th Century dictator who wanted to rule the world. That night, not only did he rob the world of a truly wonderful soul, he also robbed it of Tristan. The carefree nature that Tristan had built after the death of his parents left him as he was forced to bury his friend and find a new place in the world. It was at Marcus' funeral that he'd vowed never to let another person die in the name of dictatorship, so he joined the Army, and it wasn't long before he left for his first tour to Afghanistan.

Tristan walked over to her desk and Mel took the opportunity to look at him closely; he had changed since the last time she had seen him. It wasn't a physical thing that was noticeable, it was only obvious in that subjective way which came from knowing someone their whole life. It wasn't something she could even see, it was a feeling. He was harder and more aloof, something major had happened and it had stripped him of the final piece of his carefree soul, she could feel it in her bones. She continued to watch him as she came closer, trying to figure out what was missing and to her surprise, she also detected a slight limp in his walk. He did a great job of covering it up, and if you didn't know Tristan, you wouldn't see it. But she knew Tristan and she saw it, Mel wondered what had happened, but also knew instinctively that he would not tell her. Unlike the last time Mel had seen him, Tristan had shut himself off the world, and although he smiled on the outside, Mel knew that smile did not reach his soul. He was a broken man.

"Hey Midget," he said, before coming around the desk, plucking her from her seat and embracing her in a bear hug. Broken man or not, Mel couldn't deny that it was nice to have his arms wrapped around her. It made her feel like she was safe and just maybe everything would be alright. For a brief moment she could pretend that everything was the way it had always been.

"Would you stop calling me that?" She said, returning his hug. "Not all of us can be six foot, you know. Besides, my grandma would tell you that explosive things come in small packages, and I am feeling particularly explosive today, so you had better watch yourself."

Tristan pulled back slightly and gave her a lopsided grin. He had *always* joked about her height and it *always* drove her crazy. Maybe he was also needing a bit of normalcy in his life as well.

"Yeah, but there is small and then there's you," he quipped.

Slapping at him playfully, she asked, "Any particular reason you're here, or was it purely just to torment me?"

Chuckling, he let her go and moved around the desk to sit down. Deciding to get a drink, Mel walked over to the minibar that she had installed when she first opened her practice, and reached in to grab one of the many iced coffees that were always on hand.

"Want anything to drink?" Mel asked, turning to look at Tristan sideways. Mel had caught him off guard and she thought she caught the briefest flash of pain in his eyes, but it was gone so quickly she couldn't be sure. She wanted desperately to ask him about what had happened during his deployment and what had brought him home, but she knew from experience that it would be practically impossible to get him to open up about something of this calibre. *Perhaps she should offer him something a little stiffer.*

"Nah, I'm all good," he replied with a shake of his head. Shutting the fridge, Mel walked back to her desk. "How many is that today?" He asked, laughter edged his voice. Mel was in no way offended by his question as her love of coffee was no secret to anyone that knew her.

"My fifth," she answered truthfully, before removing the lid and taking a huge drink. The comfortingly familiar, bittersweet liquid never tasted so good.

"Fifth?" he choked, giving her an incredulous look, "Mel it's only 11.30am. How is it that you get any sleep at night? Surely that can't be healthy? Your blood must be made of pure caffeine!"

She had seen that look on his face many times before. It was the same one that Ceana had thrown at her over the years as she'd ask the same question. You would think they would get sick of receiving the same answer.

"I'll have you know I'm as healthy as a horse, so much so that even my doctor was surprised. And my blood is like liquid gold, thank you. I even have a little star to prove it." She said as she pulled out her 100th donation pin from the Red Cross. "Besides, it may not be good for *me*, but it *is* good for everyone else. Trust me, there would be a lot more murders around here if I didn't have it." She replied taking one more drink before she placed the lid back on and sat it near the pen holder on her desk.

Tristan shook his head, "you know, I never realised just how blood-thirsty you are."

"I'm not blood-thirsty, I just can't stand stupid people, and every day I have to deal with some of the worst, like this imbecile for instance." Opening her laptop, Mel turned it so he could see the incriminating and humiliating picture of Jack and his new girlfriend.

He stared at the picture for a moment before bursting out in laughter. He turned her computer back around. "Come on Mel, you had to know that there was no way this guy was good enough for you!"

Sitting down again, she leaned into her palms, much as she had done earlier and looked at him.

"I know Tris, I do."

"Then what is the problem?" Tristan asked.

Mel took a deep breath. How could she explain this without sounding like a whining child? "It's not the fact that we broke up. It's just that everyone else seems so happy, living their lives full of adventure, and here I am caught up in the same routine of BAS reports and CPA's, dealing with old men in stuffy suits, companies that want nothing more than to rip off their employees and jackasses like Jack. Just once in my life I would love to experience that feeling of excitement and mystery. But noooo, that's too much to ask for, apparently!"

Mel looked Tristan in the eyes hoping that he understood what she was saying. Her daily routine had never bothered her before, but for some reason she was feeling restless. The flash of pain Mel had seen before passed once more across his eyes as he answered. "You know Mel, excitement and mystery is not all it's cracked up to be. In fact, I would give anything to go back to the days when all we had to worry about was what we were going to do on Saturday night, or if there was going to be enough swell for a decent surf."

Tristan looked away from her and stared wistfully out at the ocean. The raw pain that lacerated his words broke her heart. She knew he missed his friend, but Mel had a feeling that this pain was much more than that. This pain was soul deep.

"Tris, is everything alright?" she asked. Even though Mel had feared that he wouldn't tell her, she had to ask. He looked back at her and for a moment she thought he might tell her what was going on but, just like before, he closed himself off and acted like nothing out of the ordinary had happened.

"It's nothing to worry about really, it's just this time of year you know. I miss everyone." He shrugged.

Mel knew he wasn't telling her everything, but she wouldn't push now. She would wait until he was ready, but one thing was for sure, she would not let this go, one way or another she would get Tristan to open up to her. She just hoped that when he did he wasn't too broken to fix.

"Alright then, if you won't tell me what's wrong, perhaps you will tell me what has you coming to my office today?" Before he could answer, a depressing thought crossed her mind. "Please don't tell me you need some accounting help?" She whimpered. With all that had happened this morning, her mind was on anything but work.

Tristan winked at her, "nope I'm here for something a little more exciting than that!" Mel's heart picked up with anticipation as he reached into his pocket, pulled out a letter and handed it to her. Ceana's distinctive handwriting was scrawled across the front of the envelope. Barely holding back a squeal, she reached out and snatched it from his grasp.

"Hey!" Tristan complained half-heartedly. Poking her tongue out at him, she looked down and was thrilled to see that the letter was addressed to her. "We all got one," Tristan informed her, as she continued to gaze at the envelope. Mel was always in awe at how no matter how far away they were from each other her friend always seemed to know when she needed picking up. Mel knew she should wait until Tristan left to read it, but with the way she was feeling, she needed to hear something, anything, from her best friend. Turning the letter around, she ripped the envelope open and pulled out the enclosed page.

As Mel began reading, her heart filled with happiness; this was just what she needed.

Hi Trouble,

I hope everything is going okay with Jack, and if it's not, don't worry he is not worth the ulcer. Last time I was home I told you that you would get sick of his shit. You need a real man not some new aged guy who wears more product than you do....

Mel laughed, it was just like Cee to get straight to the point. And she was right, Jack did use more product than her, in fact she'd swear that he sometimes wore eyeliner to make his eyes appear darker. What had she been thinking dating him? Shaking her head Mel turned back to the letter: -

Everything here is great, as you probably already know, so there's not much to tell you. Now on to the reason for this note, yes I have a reason, you don't think I would just write to you to discuss Jack.

No, so Katie, Caelan and Tristan have agreed to come here for Christmas this year, and the reason for this letter, not that I need one, is to say that you had better be with them when they come. Don't even think about denying me this request or I am going to come through time and drag your sorry arse back here myself. And then my husband will not be happy with either one of us, and you know that you don't want him mad at you. So, the point of this letter is to tell you that you may as well resign yourself to the fact that you will be coming. I have to go, I would have written a longer letter, but you will be here soon so there is no point is there? Besides, this way we will have heaps to talk about when you get here.

Chow baby
Love Cee.
P.S Don't do anything I wouldn't.

Looking up from the letter, Mel saw Tristan smiling at her. "Did you read it?" Mel asked dubiously.

He rolled his eyes at her. "Firstly," he started sarcastically, "no I did not read your letter. Secondly, I think I'm offended that you would even suggest it."

Grinning, she couldn't help teasing, "oh come on, we both know that if you could, you would." She was pleased to see some of the sadness leave his eyes.

"From the look on your face, I'm guessing that you have also been summoned to the Highlands for Christmas." He said with a smile.

So many thoughts were rattling around in her head. She looked down at the letter and then back up at Tristan. Ceana had to be joking. How was she going to be able to go to 12th century Scotland for Christmas? Mel shook her head, still in awe at her friend's daring. "That's pretty much what it implied, but you know that I'm not going to be able to go. I have too much work to do here. I don't know what Cee was thinking, I just can't pick up and go to Scotland, can I?"

She wasn't expecting Tristan to answer, she just needed to voice the thoughts that were running around in her head. It wasn't as if he could make the decision for her. She was just hoping he would come up with a solution. There was nothing more she wanted to do right now than pack up and leave everything behind, even if it was only for a couple of weeks.

Was it even possible? That was the million-dollar question. There was still so much work to do before the Christmas shut down and, now with the crap Jack had dumped on her, leaving would be near impossible. She could just see what the comments would be now, everyone would say that it looked she was running away, giving the impression that what he did hurt her. And that was the last thing she wanted people to think. No, there was no way she was going to let the jerk chase her out of town. She felt deflated, no matter how much she wanted to see her friend, or the thirst she had for adventure, she had her answer. There was no way she was going to be able to go.

Decision made, the wave of emptiness she had felt earlier upon finding the picture of Jack washed over her once more. Excitement and adventure was dangling in her face but her boring life was stopping her from chasing it. All she could think about was that while her friends were all in the Highlands this Christmas having the time of their lives, she would probably be stuck here dealing with the same crap she did every other day.

Mel looked at Tristan, expecting him to accept her answer, but she should have known better. Crossing one leg over the other he placed his elbows on the arms of the chair and teepeed his fingers under his chin. He gave her a lopsided smile before commenting. "Come on Mel, that's a load of hog wash and you know it, you're the boss, for Christ's sake! You, my dear friend, can do any bloody thing you want! And you *know* you want to go, so you might as well give up the fight now."

Tristan's speech opened something inside of her. He was right, she *was* the boss and she did want to go. Looking down at the letter once more she went over every scenario in her mind, but every one of them came back to her not being able to go. Looking up from the letter, she went to tell Tristan her decision, and realised then that he was leaving. He opened the door, stopped, and looked back at her. "Besides, one way or another, short fry, you *are* coming to Scotland, even if I have to drag you there myself."

Mel raised her eyebrow at him. "Is that so?" She questioned sarcastically.

He didn't react to her tone, he simply gave her a lopsided smile and added, "yes that is so, and you know why?" Mel shook her head. "Because, my dear friend, my sister threatened me life and limb if I didn't convince you to come, and I'll be damned if I'm going to face my sister alone if you aren't there. So you had better be ready to leave in the next couple of days." And with that threat lingering, he walked out of her office before she had time to argue.

Well damn, now what was she going to do? Mel looked around her boring office and thought about her life. She *had* just wished for excitement to enter her life, she just wasn't sure if she was ready for *this* much excitement. Her thoughts were all over the place. She was worried about what would happen to her practice, and also if she could handle being in a strange land with strange people. But then she remembered that her best friend would be there, and right now she needed her friend. With that thought came another – Tristan would be with her. Maybe this was the chance she was looking for, maybe being with his family would help him open up about what was going on with him.

With her mind practically made up, Mel opened her laptop and started going through her appointments, seeing what she had to reorganise for her trip. But, as her fingers started moving over the keyboard, her intuition prickled and a feeling that she was about to get more than she bargained for came over her. The feeling made the hair on her arms stand on end, and her heart began to race.

Her grandma G.G had always told her that intuition ran in the family and she had encouraged Mel to harness it. Ever logical Mel usually just brushed it off and tried to explain it away as inconsequential, but it was getting increasingly harder to do so as it tingled with anticipation and excitement.

Two

Had it really been two days since she had read Ceana's letter? It had, and now here she was with Tristan, standing beside Katie, Caelan and their son, Marcus, at the entrance of the cave, not far from Katie's home. Mel knew this cave like the back of her hand. It had been her and Cee's favourite hiding spot when they were younger.

To be fair, it wasn't exactly a cave, just two long rocks that formed an open-ended arched cave-like structure. The rocks appeared like hands that were reaching out to take hold of something; the tops of which just touched enough to enclose the cave in darkness, yet it still allowed enough light in to make them appear magical. Whenever she was here she always got the feeling that something was about to happen. What, she never ended up finding out, but it always left her feeling like there was something kind of special going on.

What she couldn't quite figure out though, was why they were all standing here, waiting. Nobody had told her much about the travelling arrangements. Not that she had expected to go by plane, but she would have liked to have known something about how they planned to go back in time. Her mind raced with all different scenarios, mainly based off of those she had seen on television.

As Mel stood by her friends looking into the cave, she was both terrified of the journey ahead, and overjoyed at the idea of going to Scotland to do nothing but spend some much-needed time with her best friend. Initially, Mel had planned to only take two weeks off;

however, the more she'd thought about it, the longer the trip became. Really, there was no way two weeks would do. Mel had rationalised the length of her stay based on the fact that she hadn't had a decent holiday in over five years and after all, like Tristan had said, she was the boss and she had a firm full of competent staff who would be fine without her for longer.

Before leaving, Mel had split her more important files between the three senior accountants and rescheduled everything else for the New Year. Then she had informed the other accountants that the office would close two weeks earlier than normal for Christmas and that gave her the full month she needed, with bonus time to spare when she came home.

So here she was, waiting, with one backpack full of clothes and anything else she needed, ready to embark on an adventure of a lifetime; her mind a jumbled mess of uncertainty and anticipation. At least she *hoped* it would be the adventure of a lifetime. Mel felt extremely unprepared for what was to come. How could she be expected to have a decent holiday with what she had on her? But one backpack was all she required apparently. At first when Katie had given her that instruction Mel had laughed, but when she realised her friend was serious Mel almost changed her mind. It felt dubiously light and empty compared to how she normally prepared for trips. She had wanted to pack more, but Katie had reminded her that this wasn't your typical overseas adventure.

"'Come on Mel, it's not like we're just going over the ocean to a country with modern conveniences.'" Katie had said over the phone the other day. She had also reminded Mel several times that they were going back in time, to a Scotland that was vastly different to the one of this period. Although curious, every time Mel thought about it she shuddered a little. If she didn't miss Cee so much, she would turn around right now and march her butt back home. What was she thinking? No flushing toilets, running water, or hot showers! They probably still used chamber pots! Just the thought of having to pee in a metal pan made her ill.

Looking over at Tristan, she saw a spark of humour enter his eyes. "Wanna tell me what has you looking so green over there, Midget?" He asked, amusement lacing his words. Mel wanted to smack his humour right out of him.

"Well, I was just thinking about how much I really hate camping." She admitted without thinking.

Katie and Tristan burst out laughing, Caelan just looked puzzled. "Lass, ya will not be camping, ya will be staying in my brother's keep." He informed her.

Mel wanted to roll her eyes at his daftness, but not wanting to somehow offend him, Mel nodded politely. After all, how did you explain to someone like Caelan, a 12th Century highlander, that you didn't like living without modern conveniences without sounding like a spoilt brat? Taking a deep breath, Mel tried to rein in her anxiety, then Tristan opened his mouth and inadvertently ruined it.

"Don't worry ,Mel, I'm sure you won't have to empty your own chamber pot." He whispered into her ear. The arse couldn't help being obnoxious. Mel got her revenge by quickly sending her elbow flying back and she felt it connect with something soft. By the quick intake of breath and the *oof* sound she heard, she would bet any money that it was his stomach. Mel grinned.

Her humour faded as all too soon it was time to embark on her adventure. Caelan looked down at Marcus, sleeping in his baby carrier nestled safely and securely against Caelan's chest, and protectively covered his head with the plaid. He nodded to Katie, "Okay it's time to go," Caelan announced and, hand in hand, he and Katie walked to the middle of the cave together, leaving Tristan and Mel no other choice but to follow into the unknown.

Taking another deep breath, Mel couldn't believe how calm Katie and Caelan appeared. They acted as though they didn't have a worry in the world. *Why would they? They had done this a million times over the last few years*, she reminded herself. Considering Caelan came from that time, there was no reason for him to be nervous; he was as cool as a cucumber.

But it was all so unfamiliar to her that she couldn't help being apprehensive. One thing she hated more than camping was surprises and the unexpected; she would rather know what to expect and to be able to plan. Mel had no idea what was waiting on the other side and that scared her more than being alone. Mel needed a boast of confidence to continue on, her mind was screaming at her to run home and stick to her boring and reliable life. Mel sneaked a peek at Tristan again, trying to gauge his reaction. She was relieved to note that he wasn't faring much better than her, his face was tinged with panic. At least he understood.

"Do we need to perform some ritual?" Mel asked when she

reached the centre of the cave, looking around at the boulders and wondering how this was going to work.

"Nay Lass, the Druid was able to set the stones up so that they open up automatically at midnight every night during the winter and summer solstice," Caelan smiled at her.

"Well, of course, how obvious." She gave him a small smile in return, even though what he said didn't make a lick of sense to her. Her logical brain was denying everything he was saying. Mel tried to calm her nerves by imagine what would be waiting for them. For some reason, all she could picture were stereotypical barbarians, like how the movies tended to portray the Scottish. Not that she had seen many movies with Scottish people to go by, and she somehow doubted that *Braveheart* was even remotely correct in *its* interpretation.

Mel decided to try and focus on another point to reassure herself that everything would be okay, and that point was her best friend. Mel doubted that Ceana would have stayed in 12th century Scotland if it was full of barbarians and unsafe for her children. While Cee was little more adventurous than Mel when it came to camping, Mel was sure that her best friend would draw the line at barbarians. That thought brought a smile to her face and Mel tried to use it to remain calm, but her mind wouldn't let up, it just kept on producing different scenarios, each one more ridiculous than the last.

Mel was brought out of her musings when Caelan cleared his throat, gaining their attention. She still didn't fully understand what was happening, but she followed everyone else's lead and took up her position beside Katie. Mel stood in the middle of the cave nervously waiting for something to happen. What it would be, she had no idea. As much as she had questioned them, Katie and Caelan hadn't gone into much detail about how they travelled through time and had decided against explaining the process to either her or Tristan, stating that they wanted it to be a surprise. They had decided that both Tristan and Mel deserved to experience the entire trip the same way Katie and Ceana had two years ago. And for that alone, she was going to kill Katie and Cee later. But that wasn't going to help her right now, nothing was going to help her. God she wished she had asked Ceana more questions about all of this over the years.

Mel was just starting to calm her racing heart, when without warning, a vortex of wind whipped up around them. Mel gasped as it grew in strength and force until it felt like she was being pulled apart limb from limb, her fleeting calmness was instantly replaced with terror. Somewhere along the way, Mel thought she'd let out a scream but it was lost in the roar of the endless vortex that would not let up.

As the wind continued to rumble around her Mel realised that she couldn't see her friends beside her anymore, everything had gone black! Mel squeezed her eyes shut and placed her hands over her ears trying to block out the sounds around her. The terror continued to build, Mel couldn't seem to ground herself no matter how much she tried. the only way she could think to describe the experience was like being a ragdoll in a tornado, only she was sure she hadn't moved. Oddly, it somehow also felt like she was still standing in the same spot.

Mel opened her eyes slowly and tried to look for her friends once more, but as it had been before, everything was still lost in a pit of endless black. She felt alone and helpless, a feeling that only intensified as the nightmare continued. Mel gave up and squeezed her eyes shut, praying for an end as the wind howled and screamed. It was easily the most terrifying moment of her life.

Just as Mel was reaching the point where she thought she would lose her mind, the roaring quietened and her world slowly returned to normal. As her ears adjusted to the low humming that had replaced the roaring of the wind, an all too familiar sound entered her consciousness. *Was it? Yes, it was a waterfall!* But there wasn't a waterfall that powerful close to where they'd just been standing. Her eyes were still tightly closed, so she didn't know if her sight had returned, but at least she finally felt like she was in her own body again.

Opening her eyes gingerly, she hoped that her vision had not been damaged permanently. As the lids rose, vibrant colours and fuzzy but distinct shapes replaced the blackness that had been there, Mel sent out a silent prayer of thanks as her eyes focused and, even though she found herself still standing upright next to Katie, she realised she was in a vastly different cave. Oh yeah, Katie was going to pay, and she was sure Tristan wouldn't stop her.

Turning to her friend, she prepared to give her hell but before she could, Mel's vision blurred once more and Mel felt as though she was going to faint. Suddenly lightheaded, Mel looked around anxiously for somewhere to rest and, with relief, she noticed a large boulder just off to her left. Slowly, on wobbly legs, she made her way over to it and sat, placing her head in her hands.

"S-shit..." she breathed shakily. She tried regulating her breathing and concentrated on getting her heartbeat under control. She would kill her friend later.

"Bloody hell, I'm going to kill you, Bata!" Mel heard Tristan curse.

Looking up at him, she saw that he looked as shaken as she felt. He was bent over with his hands on his knees; his whole body trembled with shock. The daggers he was shooting at his sister nicely summed up how Mel was feeling.

Disentangling herself from Caelan, Katie soothed a red-faced Marcus with love and sweet words until he fell back into a peaceful sleep in Caelan's arms, before she went to her brother. Squatting down in front of Tristan she brought her eye's level with his and smiled, "Aren't you glad I didn't ruin the surprise for you?" she grinned cheekily, putting her hand on his shoulder.

Mel snorted as Tristan reached out and pushed his sister over. Mel felt a little satisfaction when Katie fell on her butt in the dirt. "Next time, dear sister, don't be so considerate and give me a heads up." He laughed. Mel still detected a slight tremor in his voice and was glad that she wasn't the only one who was having trouble regaining her composure. It wasn't long, however, before Tristan had composed himself. He stood and went to help Katie up from her current position. And just like that, Tristan appeared to be over the ordeal.

Mel, on the other hand, still couldn't get her hands to stop shaking. She was taking in deep breaths, hoping to calm her nerves, when Caelan came over and knelt in front of her gently, being mindful not to squash Marcus. With the fear and adrenaline that was still pumping through her she looked at baby Marcus, who apart from a few whimpers, was sleeping soundly against his father's chest. *How the hell could a baby sleep through that?* Her heartbeat had still to reach a normal tempo and her head yet to clear from the confusion and fear over what had just happened.

"Are ya feeling okay, Lass?" He asked. Mel could hear the laughter in his voice even though his eyes held a mix of concern and humour. She swore that if he so much as grinned, the moment he got rid of Marcus, she was going to punch him. Hell, she may still do that simply because he was so cheerful.

"Hell no!" Mel replied, all joking gone from her voice. "I don't know that I will ever be okay again." This time Calean couldn't help but smile, and with it came another depressing thought. Mel reached out and grabbed Caelan's arm as she pleaded, "Please tell me that there are no more *surprises* like that one." Mel knew she probably sounded ridiculous and was overreacting, but she couldn't handle any more surprises like that, not just yet anyway. Did she forget to remind them that she hated surprises?

Katie just shook her head and continued to gather everything up in preparation to leave as Caelan chuckled. "No, I promise, Lass, that is the last portal ya will travel through while ye'r here. The only thing ya have to deal with now are hard-headed Scotsmen!" He joked. Putting his hand out, he grabbed hers and pulled her to her feet. He asked once more if she was okay, before leading the way out of the cave.

The corridor they were walking along would have cast them into complete blackness, if Caelan didn't have a torch with him. The cave they were walking through was no longer open at either end or the top, it was completely closed in. The walls were slightly damp as water trickled its way into the cervices on the floor and tiny animals could be herd scurrying along the walls. As Mel's eyes scanned the area she was in she noted that this cave was much larger than the one back home and she also noted that the rocks of the wall had slight glow to them whenever the light of the torch reflected across the water covered walls, it felt almost magical. But even though the cave appeared as though it was never ending, it didn't seem to take long before they were at the entrance, where she got her first glimpse of the Scottish Highlands.

Mel's breath caught in her throat, she had never seen anything so beautiful. Right in front of her was a waterfall so powerful and majestic that it rivalled the twin falls back at home. The colours that spiralled in and out of the water when the sun hit it just right were spectacular – she could see hues of blue, green and even a hint of yellow shimmering and dancing on the water's surface. A little of the cool spray dusted over her face as she stood there staring out around the curtain of water to see the landscape beyond. Her eyes widened at the sight of the rolling hills of green carpet that spread out before them. Every now and then, a hill or valley would be covered in purple flowers; it was simply breathtaking. They were no longer in Australia, or the 21st century, that was for sure. No tall buildings, cars or paved roads marred the beauty of the countryside in front of her.

As she stared down across the landscape beyond the waterfall, Mel now understood Ceana's love for this place and why she had raved on about how cold and industrialised the world they lived in had become. Still in awe, Mel smiled her first genuine smile since this trip had begun. She was glad that she had come after all. This was going to be an adventure she would never forget.

Hearing noise behind her, Mel realised that the others had started to make their way down the winding path. Inhaling some of the cleanest air she had ever smelt, free from the smog and pollutants of home, Mel followed Tristan, Katie and Calean with one last look at the massive, beautiful waterfall in all its power, promising herself that she would return here before she went home.

As she walked down the winding track, her mind was racing with anticipation and bewilderment. Now that she was here, things felt real. She couldn't wait to see Cee! Mel had so much to tell her. Even though Ceana had been home six months ago, it had been a quick visit and, between work and family, they hadn't been able to catch up like they'd wanted to. Despite the letters they wrote to each other, they were only able to get them to each other when Caelan went home, so by the time the letters reached her, they were at least six months out of date. The letter Tristan had given her had been the first one Mel had seen in a while. Besides, letters were not the same as seeing each other, there were just some things one could not put in a letter. A loud piercing whistle brought Mel out of her contemplative state and on gazing down at the open field where the sound had come from, Mel realised four highlanders were waiting for them at the bottom of the hill. She froze, uncertain of who they were. *Friend or foe?*

Three

From her position on the mountain, Mel could tell that they each held an air of masculinity about them. Standing beside their horses with their arms crossed casually over their chest, they wore plaids wrapped around the lower body and across the front, leaving their chest half-bare. *Maybe Braveheart wasn't that far off?* Mel thought to herself. Even though Mel could not make out much of the highlander's features from this far she could tell that the first three highlanders looked as though they were ready for anything, but it was the fourth who caught and held Mel's attention as she descended further down the path.

Unlike the other three, this one possessed an aura that portrayed him as a formidable force. He was at least half a foot taller than the others and just as wide. But there was not an ounce of fat on him, no, he was made of sinewy muscle and, as he stood there watching them, her intuition screamed warning bells at her. It was the same feeling she'd had back in her office a few days ago. Something was telling her that she had to run far from this man. But no matter how much her intuition screamed at her, Mel stared back down at him with open curiosity, uncertain of what the tension she was feeling meant.

Her eyes continued to roam his muscular body, but her attention was brought back to her group when a piercing whistle sounded beside her as Caelan returned the greeting. Nervous excitement filled her as she realised that this was the welcoming part and Mel was uncertain if she was happy that she would get to see this brute of a man up close, or if the feelings rushing through her were something else entirely. Either way it would not be long before she got her answer.

As they approached the party waiting below, Mel's eyes continuously found the giant and each time her heart started beating like a runaway train until finally she was unable to take her eyes from him. He *was* handsome, she realised, after the initial shock had worn off. He was tall, taller than Tristan, and that was no easy feat. But this guy was easily at least a couple of feet taller, and the width of his shoulders! There were no words. In some ways, his size reminded her of a modern-day bodybuilder, except somewhat stronger and more brutal. His shoulder-length hair was a deep, dark auburn colour, and a small breeze playfully whipped its curls around his face, adding to his wild aura. As it blew in the wind, the sun would occasionally reveal lighter shades and, as stupid as it sounded, all Mel could think was that women would pay a fortune to have his hair colour.

As she was staring at the giant, superb specimen of a man, Mel's foot hit something on the ground and propelled her forward, straight into Tristan's back, causing him to stumble with a cry of surprise. Mel flushed and glared at the offending root as if it was the root's fault that she hadn't been paying attention. *How embarrassing.* Mel couldn't bring herself to look back up at the group waiting for them below now, thinking for sure they'd be laughing at her. Here she was in front of all these gorgeous men and she had made an arse out of herself. *Good first impression, klutz!* She thought dejectedly.

Mel hated that one flaw about herself, it wasn't as if she was naturally clumsy, but on occasions she had this bad habit of getting so entrenched in a thought or, as with now, so focused on something, that she forgot to check her surrounds. She had lost count of how many poles she had walked into, or how many steps she had missed because she had been so fixated on what she was reading or saying.

"Hey there Short Fry, there's no need to push me, we'll get there quick enough." Tristan protested, trying to pry his shirt from her fingers.

Groaning with embarrassment, she let go of Tristan's shirt – she must have grabbed it instinctively – and looked up at him. Trying to save the situation, she gave him a death stare right before giving him another, more pointed shove to get him moving again. But he wasn't budging. Mel knew that the only way she would be able to get him moving once more was to explain herself.

"Perhaps I wasn't rushing, maybe I was trying to push you over the edge." Mel glowered. Tristan shook his head as he allowed her to push him along. Thankfully, he didn't ask her what she had been doing. What would she say? *"Oh you know, just ogling those muscles down there."* Yep that would have given him food for fodder.

As they continued their trek down the winding path of the cliff, Mel didn't look at the highlander again, until they were right in front of them, then she couldn't hold it off any longer. Flushing with embarrassment, Mel moved to stand beside Tristan and took a deep breath. When she finally found the courage she'd had earlier, she raised her head and looked at the men in front of her.

Her eyes collided with the very intense green eyes of the giant she had been ogling earlier and she lost her train of thought all over again. Mel was caught up in the beauty of his sparkling eyes and could think of nothing else until she noticed the laughter in them. Her intrigue was quickly replaced with anger? Annoyance? At least something similar to it. *How dare he laugh at her!* she thought bitterly. Mel would bet this hunk never had a moment of embarrassment in his life!

The more he continued to stare at her, the angrier she got. *What right did the jerk have to make judgements about her?* Mel could feel her anger rising, and she wanted nothing but to storm off and leave the jerk behind. Then common sense prevailed, Mel realised that she was once more overacting. But the longer she looked at him and the twitch at the end of his smile, the more her fury built. *What was wrong with her?* Mel couldn't get her head around her anger; never had she experienced such an explosive reaction to a guy she'd just met.

Her emotions were all over the place. Mel knew that her reaction was completely irrational, but no matter how much she tried to psychoanalyse the situation, it didn't help how she felt. Right now, she was feeling that the best option she had was to run in the opposite direction.

Thankfully, Katie interrupted Mel's train of thought when she ran to the mountain of a man, hurled herself into his arms and was immediately engulfed into a bear hug. "Hey Ham, how are you going? I have missed you!" Katie said as she pulled away.

Mel heard the giant groan. "Och, Katie, I really wish ya wonnae call me that."

Mel was still trying to get her head around the soft, fondness that had replaced the laughter in the giant's eyes as he looked down at Katie, when Tristan stepped forward and offered his hand. He obviously knew who this hulking giant was. Mel just wished someone would fill her in.

"Don't bother trying to talk this woman out of *anything*. Trust me, after years of torture, I finally learnt to just go with the flow."

The Scotsman snorted at Tristan's advice as he shook the proffered hand. "So ya advice Lad, is to let the lass get away with everything?" He asked, winking at Katie.

"Exactly! At least until you can get revenge." Tristan grinned as he nudged his sister fondly.

The Scotsman chortled and whacked Tristan on the back, causing him to wince slightly. That wince gave Mel some satisfaction. Shame on Tristan for not introducing them and explaining to her who this man was. Mel knew she was being unreasonable, but the uncomfortable feeling that was settling inside of her was making her irrational, irritable and confused. Mel folded her arms across her chest as she impatiently continued waiting for Katie to introduce her, but before she could, the giant turned around to give orders to his men.

Expecting to be at least acknowledged, Mel watched in wonderment as he walked away once the orders had been given. *Now that was just plain rude.* But then Mel found she couldn't hold on to her indignation for long. Her mind was soon on other things as she watched him go about his business. *Man, the guy had a nice butt!* Even though he was wearing a kilt, she could tell that his arse would be as muscular as his legs. His back rippled with every movement he made and as she stood there watching him, she was struck with the urge to run her hands all over his body.

Mel gave herself a slight shake. *What was wrong with her?* One minute she was thinking of him as nothing but a rude jerk then she was drooling over him and wishing she could take him to bed, which sent her into a mild panic. She had all of these emotions running through here and she'd only just met the guy! *Get a grip on yourself!* Mel scolded herself.

"Well Short Fry, are you ready to start our adventure?" Still staring and lost in her thoughts, Mel gave a startled yelp as Tristan grabbed her from behind.

"Bloody hell Tristan, would you warn a person before you do that?" She snapped. Mel immediately realised her mistake. Tristan raised one eyebrow and gave her a mocking smile. "What's gotten into you?"

"Nothing," she answered back a little too quickly.

His eyebrow crept up a little higher. "Sure, and I'm Batman." He grinned.

Mel just stared him down, not giving him the satisfaction of embarrassing her further. Thankfully, he got the hint, raising his hands he backed up in defeat. As the laughter left his eyes Mel felt bad that she had taken her mood out on him and she relented. "I can't wait to see Cee!" She offered as she smiled at him. It was not a lie, only a half truth, but mentioning her best friend brought back the elation she had felt earlier, and just like that, her exhilaration was back.

Mel opened her mouth to ask Tristan what he had wanted, when three horses were brought over for them to mount and she stopped, staring in admiration for the beasts in front of them. She loved horses, had ever since she was little, and in front of her was the most beautiful horse she had ever seen. Its whole body was pure white except for its legs. From the knees down, along with its mane and tail, were ebony black in colour and the contrast between the two colours was striking.

Reaching out instinctively, she ran her hand along its white muscled flank and was pleased that it did not shy away. The softness of the horse's skin told her that the animal was well cared for, and she smiled to herself as the horse moved its head around and nuzzled her shoulder, as if letting her know that it liked what she was doing.

"Her name is *Seodag.*" A heavily accented voice whispered close behind her. Mel did not jump this time, she knew instinctively that it was her giant. As a masculine hand shot past her to run along the horse's flesh, higher up from where Mel's hand was currently resting, Mel caught the flash of a ring sitting on the hand's pinkie. Normally she wouldn't have noticed it, but the jewel seemed out of place on the highlander. As his arm continued to rest on the horse her heartbeat picked up and her body tingled all over.

Trying to focus her mind on something other than the man

behind her, she whispered, "what does it mean?" Mel was not sure why she had whispered, but she felt as though it was appropriate. As Mel waited for him to answer, she tried to say the Gaelic name he had used, but it just didn't roll off her tongue the same way it did his and it came out sounding something like 'seadog' instead.

Mel was surprised that he had been able to sneak up on her. She briefly wondered what had happened to Tristan as well, she had been so entranced with the mare that she had not felt the Scot approach her and was surprised that he had moved so quietly. He was so close! She could feel him pressed against her back and she knew she should tell him to back up, but the warmth that surrounded her from his body was intoxicating. Mel was literally wedged in between the horse and the man. It left her feeling as wild as the countryside around her. Her heart began racing again and she was having difficulty catching her breath. Instinctively, with almost a mind of its own, her body leaned back against his own hard one, and the moment her body touched his she could feel his muscles rippling around her.

A shiver of pure lust ripped through her body, and Mel could not remember the last time she had felt lust this strong. It almost felt as though her very being relied on him touching her. The feeling only intensified when he bent down and placed his lips right next to her ear. "It means little jewel, *Breagha.*" He whispered, his warm breath tickling her cheek, before he walked away, leaving her even more flabbergasted than before.

Four

❧

hat is wrong with me? Hamish wondered as he walked away from the strange new lass. He had never felt so drawn to anyone in his entire life but he didn't have time for the passion that he was feeling in this moment. No, his life revolved around being Laird, fighting and keeping the family's secret safe. That was what he was built for.

After the death of his father, Hamish had learnt the truth behind what and who he was, and it had changed his life and purpose forever. The power that his family possessed had been the reason his mother had been killed and his baby sister sent away, it had destroyed his family. And now, it was his secret to protect. Hamish had sworn that he would never allow anyone else to use the power that his family possessed against those he loved.

He loved his sisters and brother, and although he would love nothing more than to have his own family, he would never allow anyone else to get that close to him. This way, he'd reasoned, no-one could hurt them through him, and as a bonus the power would die with him and so he kept a part of himself locked tightly away, even from those he loved. It was a lonely life, but he believed it was necessary. So far, he had been able to keep people at a distance, and he wanted to keep it that way.

So what was it about this lass that had set his blood on fire as soon as he laid eyes on her? The moment he had seen her coming down the narrow path of the mountain, it was as if his body screamed for her attention. He had been waiting with the rest of the welcoming party for the group to come down from the cave He'd been looking forward to seeing his sister and meeting his new brother, so volunteering for the journey had not been a chore.

At first, he was just focused on Katie. As a familiar face, it was good to see her again. Every time she went back, he missed her, and he looked forward to the times when she would return. He was especially looking forward to meeting his new nephew. Hamish had spent most of his life as an only child, and the life he had led living in the woods, hiding from a madman, made him glad that he had. It had been a surprise to Hamish at how swiftly his sisters had wormed their way into his heart, now he could not imagine his life without his family.

As he'd watched Katie, his eyes had been instinctively drawn to the young man that was following her. He'd known straight away that it had to be Tristan, Cee's other brother, and Katie's twin, the two could be identical if it wasn't for their sex. Tristan was only slightly shorter than himself and weedier than your typical highlander, but Hamish still sensed a strength surrounding the man; a strength he intuitively knew came from having been in battle. The young man carried himself as though he were a warrior, and as though he carried the weight of the world on his shoulders, Tristan had seen things, only those in battle knew.

Tristan was virtually the male version of Katie and the way he joked with Katie eased Hamish's mind about the upcoming meeting, Hamish knew that he would get on fine with the lad and that there was nothing to be worried about. Then, almost inexplicitly, the hairs on the back of his neck stood up as the sensation that someone was watching him ran through his body. His first instinct had been to scan the area around them to make sure that there were no traces of his enemy.

This had been commonplace for Hamish and his men as hostilities had been rising between the MacDonnell clan and others over the last month, but there had been no sight of anything suspicious and some of the tension left his shoulders. But the feeling of being watched only intensified, there could only be one place that it was coming from. Looking back up to the party his eyes once more travelled along the people making their way down the cliff. And there he found the source of his unease when his eyes collided with the last member of the group and it took all his warrior training to keep his emotions hidden.

Despite sharing the oddities that came with future travellers, the woman behind Tristan was easily the most beautiful creature he had ever seen. She was striking and had stood out from any woman he had ever known, even at a distance. Hamish's heart beat picked up as she'd approached closer, and when she was near him he saw long, dark sable hair that cascaded down her back in a riot of curls. Even though it was tied up, it was still long enough to reach her hips. It was lusciously thick and looked like a chocolate waterfall. Hamish's eyes moved from her hair to the strange outfit she wore, it was similar to the odd one Ceana had worn when she'd first arrived in Scotland two years ago. But, on this woman, it had made his mouth go dry and his cock stand to attention underneath his kilt, in that moment he was thankful for the room that his kilt offered him. The last thing he needed was for his men to see how this woman affected him.

His eyes continued their appraisal of her clothes, the blue material of her trews hugged her legs and hips so tightly that he could see every movement the muscles of her legs made. The centre of her trews also perfectly accentuated the curve and dip of her womanhood, and his cock twitched again. Needing to regain focus he moved his eyes from the part of her that was tantalising him, back towards her face. But her top half wasn't much better, the shirt she was wearing just as tight as her trews, and when she had lifted her hand to move a piece of hair out of her eyes, he was rewarded with a glimpse of her luscious body. It took everything Hamish had to keep his emotions in check, he had almost lost his composure at the sight of her ivory skin begging him to taste her. Hamish moved his eyes from her body and moved them up to her face, it was then he was surprised to see that shad been staring at him just as intensely and, as her eyes remained on him unashamed, his heart cried out with unadulterated possession.

No one had ever looked at him like that before; he knew women wanted him, but it was only because he was laird. This woman however, couldn't possibly know that, and yet she'd been staring at him, openly, intensely, with a need that matched his own. Hamish wondered briefly if she'd felt the same pull he was feeling, he wanted the moment to last forever, but it was broken when she stumbled straight into the back of Tristan. Hamish's mouth twitched as he watched the exchange between the pair, it gave him great pleasure to know that he rattled her. As he continued to watch the exchange it came to him who this lass was, it had to be Mel, Ceana's best friend, there was no other person it could be. Ceana had talked about Mel non-stop all last week and from the stories she told, Hamish knew that Mel was a spitfire. While most highlanders would have been surprised at the way her and Tristan acted towards each other, he wasn't; he'd learned years ago to adjust to the odd ways in which these 21st century lasses spoke unabashedly, and he'd learnt that one should never underestimate a woman in the 21st century.

Hamish gave a slight chuckle as he watched Mel push Tristan back into walking, but to his dismay the lass kept her eyes down the rest of the way, she did not look at him again, and he felt a keen sense of loss. He'd been left hoping she would look up at him again, but the connection had been broken, until she was standing right in front of him and couldn't avoid him any longer.

Hamish held his breath waiting for her to meet his gaze and when her eyes had finally met his again, another bolt of lust had struck him. His groin had grown even harder and he'd had to resist the urge to reach down and relieve the growing pain. Embarrassed at himself for his lack of self-control, Hamish tried to get his mind on other things, he was half-surprised that his cock hadn't lifted his kilt with how stiff it was. Hamish tried to get his mind on other things to relieve some of the tension, but all he'd been able to think about was how her trews didn't leave much to the imagination. They appeared to be painted on and he'd briefly wondered how much difficulty he would have removing them. As Hamish looked at her and wondered what she would look like naked withering around in his he saw a flash of defiance enter her eyes. He briefly wondered what had brought about the look and with a grin, he'd wondered what the lass would think if she knew what was on his mind.

Hamish moved he eyes from her own and continued their path down her body, adding every curve to memory. He followed the gentle swell of her breasts to her neck then up over her face, until his gaze had once more collided with hers, what had surprised Hamish was to see that the defiance that had been there earlier had been replaced anger, and could swear it was directed at him.

What Hamish couldn't figure out though was why, he hadn't even met the minx, and yet she was fuming. Hamish had been sure to keep his emotions under control and his perusal of her had been done in a way that she wouldn't have even known he had done it. But, the longer they stood there watching each other, the angrier she'd become, that made him think that perhaps she had noticed him staring. Hamish knew he should be sorry, but he couldn't muster the feeling because he was not sorry for taking in all of her beauty. Hamish had the sudden need to hear her voice, he wanted to see if it was as sweet as her body, he prepared himself to greet her and ask her if something was wrong when Katie threw herself into his arms, and greeted him with the name she was so fond of; a name that made him cringe.

Hamish had tried everything he could to discourage his sisters from using the name that likened him to a barn animal, but one thing he had come to learn over the last two years was that when his sisters got something in their heads, it was nearly impossible to change their minds, and that name happened to be on that list. Once Katie had finished with her greeting, he turned his attention to his brother, it was good to finally meet Tristan, but it also gave time for Hamish to gather his thoughts. It was during this time that Hamish decided he would like to introduce himself to the lass in a more private manner, he did not want their first meeting to happen while she was full of anger. Hamish could not explain why it was important that she like him, but it was. With that in mind Hamish turned from the group and ordered his men to get things ready, and set about organising his own horse.

Minutes later Alec brought *Seodag* over to him, although Hamish had his own battle mount, he had a personal connection with this mare. It had been bred from his mother's favourite mare and his father's prized stallion for Ceana. It was why Hamish chose the name *Seodag;* it meant little jewel and that was exactly what this horse was.

Growing up *Seodag* reminded him that a little jewel was out there somewhere waiting for the day that she could come home, and with that in mind Hamish took it upon himself to raise and care for the horse as a present for his beloved sister.

Of course, when Ceana had come home it turned out that she was not a fan of horses and while she loved *Seodag* she had pleaded with Hamish to give her to someone who would treasure her as was intended. Hamish had finally agreed and so he had brought her along with them today intending to give her to Katie. But the moment his eyes had rested upon the lass, his heart sang out that this lass was a jewel and he decided he needed to see the lass riding his horse. Before he could change his mind, he instructed Alec to give the mare to the lass, while Hamish wanted nothing more than to give the horse to Mel himself, Hamish knew that if he got close to her in this moment he would not be able to control himself any longer .

Hamish watched at Alec presented Mel with the horse, and the pure joy he saw on her face had him heading to the pool at the bottom of the waterfall. Hamish knew he needed the sharpness of the ice-cold water to cool down his lust. Stripping out of his kilt Hamish dove head first into the cool pond and swam from one edge to the other, by the time he finished and walked out of the water, he was once more in control of his emotions.

Picking up his kilt Hamish ran it over his hair and body before once more placing it around his body. He turned and took in the waterfall for a little longer, making sure that he was in full control of *all* of his emotions.

But Hamish soon learnt that the icy-cold water would only provide temporary relief; the moment his eyes found the lass again, his lust was back in full force.

Hamish found her standing beside the mare, mesmerised. Her hand was running lovingly across the horses flank and Hamish sensed the love she had for the animal. It was the same love he had and only a true lover of horses appreciated one the way she was. As he continued to watch her run her hands over the flank of *Seodag* an image of her running her hands over him in the same way flashed in his mind and it affected him as no other image ever had. Hamish needed to be close to her, and of their own accord his feet made their way towards her.

Uncertain, and with an unfamiliar timidness, he quietly approached her, he was loath to interrupt the serene mood she seemed to be in. But as he neared her he found it harder to keep his presence a secret, she was so close he could breathe in her scent, a scent that was intoxicating.

For the first time in his life Hamish was unsure of what to say, so he decided to introduce her to the mare. Leaning down so that his lips were close to her ear he whispered, "Her name is *Seodag*," as he reached forward to pat the horse, trying not to startle her. Hamish had half expected her to move away from him, but his heart sped up when she asked, "What does it mean?"

Hamish closed his eyes and resisted the urge to groan when he was rewarded with the husky sound of her voice, when he didn't answer right away she tried to repeat the unfamiliar sounds with her untrained tongue. A smile played on the corner of his lips at her attempt of his accent.

Hamish continued to stand behind her and pat the horse and for a moment, she succumbed and leant instinctively back into him. This time he did groan softly, he couldn't help it her closeness sent fire through his vein and almost instantly, an overwhelming need to know everything about the lass filled him. Hamish knew in that instant that he was going to have to watch himself with this one. This lass could bring all the well-constructed walls he had around his heart crashing down, and that was bad not only for himself, but for her as well. He had barely spoken two words to her, and yet she made him wish for things he could not have. That was dangerous.

"It means little jewel, *Breagha*," he answered her, before turning on his heel and once more heading to the icy-cold water of the falls.

Five

Finally, they were on their way, Hamish led the group with his second in command Tamhas, while Alec and Morgan brought up the rear with Caelan, who still had baby Marcus. Hamish noticed that the bairn was strapped to his father's chest with some 21st Century contraption that looked akin to a torture device, the quietly sleeping bairn didn't seem to mind though. Even though Katie and Ceana had been teaching Hamish all about the 21st century over the last two years, he still found himself confused with most of it.

Katie, the lass and Tristan rounded up the group, they rode in the middle chatting away as if they hadn't seen each other in years. Every now and then, the sound of the lass's laughter would reach Hamish's ears, the deep husky sound washed over him, like warm scotch, the sound did little to quill the lust that was raging through his body.

It was going to be a long ride home.

It was a day and a half's ride to Kessan's land; a day and half of pure torture, he thought to himself. Hamish's keep was only another day's ride from the McKinnon keep, and although he loved seeing his sisters Hamish wished he was home now. There was no place Hamish liked being more than his home, after the death of his father, the McKenzie name had been restored and Hamish had been finally able to claim his keep and clan honour. From that moment two years ago Hamish had spent most of his time rebuilding the castle to its former glory, he wanted to make his father and his clan proud warriors once more. With that in mind Every time Hamish was away from home, he missed it.

The keep was filled with memories from his childhood; he had been seven and ten when his mother died, and his sister had been sent away, he still remembered what it had been like before that, he had been carefree and loved. But it would never been like that again, is mother's death as a young lad, and his father's death a few years ago at the hands of their enemies still left a bitter taste in his mouth. If only he had known about the power that ran in his family back then, he could have prepared better, trained better. Done *something*.

Instead, he had only found out about it when his father died. Hamish remembered that he had felt such rage and helplessness at not being able to save his father, and that he had somehow trigged the magic within him, not even his father knew he had it.

Now it was all he could do to keep that magic under control. While he spent a little time learning about his powers, Hamish hadn't been trained to cope with the full power of it yet. He wasn't sure he would ever have full control, but what he did know was that he couldn't let the power rage like he wanted to.

To let it was dangerous, if Hamish had learnt anything from Kendrick it was that power led to people wanting to kill him and use his magic for themselves. That made him – and those around him – a target; it would be like McKenzie's reign of terror all over again.

For Hamish that meant letting go of any ideas he had about the lass. He was destined to spend his life alone, battling for those who couldn't protect themselves, love and family were not on the future for him.

Hamish turned his from the lass and what he would do once he arrived back to his own keep, he was going to forget about the lass and get back to the job of catching those that had been raiding his land and disturbing the villagers. He knew exactly who was behind the trouble that had been plague him, and when he caught them, they were going to pay.

At first, the raids had been relatively harmless, nuisances really; a few sheep and cattle went missing once a week and occasionally the thieves would take a horse. But, about two weeks ago, the raids had become more serious. The bastards who were behind the trouble raided one of the crofter villages and razed it to the ground.

Young lasses had been raped and several men had been killed trying to protect their family and their village.

On alert, Hamish's men noticed the smoke and had ridden down to the village to offer aid. By the time they'd arrived, the bastards had escaped, though not before leaving a message for Hamish with one of the young lads. The poor lad had trembled as he'd told his Laird their threat-laced warning, that the war had only just started.

The thieves had claimed that they were paying Hamish back for interfering in their lives. It was then that Hamish knew it had to be the Macintoshes, they were the only clan that currently held a grudge against him.

Last year, Hamish had discovered that the MacIntosh Laird had been selling information about Scottish clans to the English army. When Hamish had confronted the laird's excuse was that, when the war came, he planned to be on the winning side. Hamish couldn't stand traitors; half of the lowlands were already under the power of the English and he would be damned if he would allow the Sassenach bastards to take away their highlands as well.

Hamish had taken the information he had and went to the other lairds, in retaliation, the Macintoshes had been exiled and were now outcasts. Hamish didn't feel sorry for them; they had chosen their path, and now they were going to die by his hand for harming his clan.

Hamish did not fear the wrath of the highlands as he had supporters and knew there wouldn't be any resistance from the other lairds. Once he got the group safely to Kessan's keep, he was going home to deal with this mess.

The last thing he needed was this attraction, an attraction so strangely powerful that it scared him. For the first time in his life, Hamish was going to run. Turning, he looked at the lass once more, oh, how he wished it was otherwise. The lass had spirit and she wasn't scared of him; something he wasn't used to. Maybe that was what had attracted him to her? The lass was bolder than he expected; he had anticipated her upbraiding him for being so bold in his approach, but she didn't.

Instead, he'd felt a shiver run through her body as she back slightly into his warmth. Hamish didn't think she'd been aware that she had even done it, to him it had felt as though she belonged there. Hamish closed his eyes as he let the memory of her scent wash over him, she had smelt of roses and musk. A scent that brought with it the overwhelming urge to kiss her until she melted into him. Shaking his head in disgust at his lack of control, he turned and kicked his horse into a faster pace, the sooner he got away from the lass the better off they would all be.

Six

As the afternoon wore on, Mel looked around and realised that there was still nothing but rolling hills around her, and wondered where they would be stopping for the night. The group had yet to pass any small towns and she didn't notice any inns in the tiny villages they did pass. *The giant wouldn't make them ride through the night, would he?* But, no sooner had that thought entered her mind, the leading party turned off sharply to the right and headed towards a glen. Mel was getting ready to complain but her breath caught in her throat as they entered the small clearing, it was absolutely magical. Surrounded by a ring of trees, the glen had a small river that lightly trickled over rocks before flowing into a pool below. The grass was so green and lush that, once Mel dismounted, she immediately removed her shoes and walked around, enjoying the feel of the soft grass cushioning her feet underneath. As she stood there, allowing her cramped legs to gain some feeling back, Mel looked around her and committed every last part of this place to her memory, she wanted to make sure that she never forgot it.

This place was beautiful; *this* was the adventure her soul had been craving. Mel continued to take in her surrounding and was so enamoured and charmed by them she didn't hear Katie walk up behind her.

"Hey, wanna come and have a wash?"

Mel started, what was with everyone sneaking up on her today. Turning around with her hand on her heart, she glared at her friend.

As was typical her look had no impact on her friend whatsoever, instead Katie simply smiled and joked, "What has you so jumpy?"

"I'm not jumpy!" Mel snapped back, even though she knew it was a lie. Of course she was jumpy, she was in a foreign land, with people she didn't know, what did they expect.

"Uh huh," Katie replied sarcastically, letting Mel know that she didn't believe a word she said.

Mel rolled her eyes before looking back at Katie, it was then Mel noticed she had a towel wrapped around her neck and soap in her hand.

The words Katie had spoken finally sunk in and as much as Mel wanted to wash up, she had a bad feeling about what that entailed. Taking a deep breath Mel asked, "Where?" hesitantly, somehow knowing she wasn't going to like answer.

Katie laughed, "where do you think, Mel? In the loch, just there." Mel followed the line of Katie's finger to the water's edge and her heart lurched.

Mel looked at the enormous pool spread before them as conflicting emotions ran through her. More than anything, she wanted that bath; she was sweaty and itchy from the day's riding and Mel knew she smelt of horse and sweat, such an appealing combination of aromas to be sure. But Mel wasn't sure she wanted to dive into that open lake, especially with strange men close by. Mel stood there for a few minutes more as the battle of what to do waged itself inside her mind, but in the end the need to feel clean and human again won out over her anxiety, so giving into the need she followed Katie down to the water.

Mel stood by the water and watched as Katie stripped down to nothing and dove straight in, Mel was going to leave her undergarments on, but decided she would rather not sleep in the wet garments all night. Stripping down to nothing Mel followed Katie's lead and jumped straight in, she broke the top of the water gasping. The water's crisp chill prickled Mel's skin and her teeth chattered at how cold it was, grabbing the soap from Katie Mel moved to the edge were she could quickly wash herself. Mel didn't waste any time washing herself and getting out, she didn't want to stay in long, despite the beauty of the place, not only was the water too cold for her, she didn't want to run the risk of someone catching her, someone like the highlander who set her blood on fire.

Soon Mel and Katie had finished washing and had dried and

dressed themselves. Then they made their way back to camp, Mel had just entered the camp area when one of the highlanders she didn't know walked forward and handed her a plaid.

Mel was about to ask him what it was for but he had disappeared, she turned to Katie instead.

"What is with everyone just walking away." She asked disgruntled. "I mean what am I meant to do with this."

Katie let out a laugh as she took it from Mel. "It acts as an extra layer to keep you warm at night." She offered.

"So what I just wrap it around my shoulders or something," Mel asked before Katie could say anything else. Katie laughed once more and shook her head, then she took the time to show Mel how to wrap it around herself to keep warm.

Mel offered Katie a smile of thanks as she took the plaid back and followed Katie's instructions. She had to admit, she hadn't expected the piece of material to add as much warmth as it had, and as the sun continued to set below the horizon Mel got the feeling that she was going to need it. The chill from the night air and her still wet hair was indicating that tonight was going to be cold.

With the plaid wrapped around her and Mel's hair once more tied up she was once more feeling human, with that a feeling of contentment washed over her as she sat down to observe all the activity that was buzzing around her.

Everyone was busy doing something, Katie and she were the only women in the camp, so Mel enjoyed watching the highlanders flex their muscles. After watching two Scotsmen effortlessly erect some kind of tent, she looked for Hamish and Tristan and wasn't surprised to find them off with the horses; they were deep in conversation. *No doubt they were catching up on getting to know each other.* Mel smiled to herself, she knew Tristan would have been happy having a brother, hopefully having another male in the family would benefit Tristan. She knew he missed Marcus a lot; they all did.

Tristan was cooing too baby Marcus in between his conversation with Hamish, and Mel was once again comforted knowing that Marcus' namesake would live on through that little man. Mel's heartbeat skipped a beat however when Tristan handed Marcus off to Hamish as he left the campsite. Watching Hamish scrutinise the tiny tot brought a smile to her face, the man looked so out of his comfort zone having the babe just thrust upon him. She grinned at his expression, she couldn't' help it, but it didn't take him long to readjust, and once again the man was playing havoc on her emotions.

Once Marcus was happily nestled against his shoulder, Hamish stood up and walked over to a group of men setting up another tent, in that moment she caught a glimpse at what kind of father the man would make, and it made her heart wish for something she knew she had no right wishing for. This man was dangerous.

Tearing her eyes from the happy scene, Mel looked around the camp, where fires were being built, and hunters were coming back with food, it then finally dawned on her that they would be camping here the night. *Oh, just fantastic. So much for no camping*! And just like that her contentment from moments ago washed away.

While she sat there in horror everyone else seemed calm, as though they were happy to be where they were. The highlanders seemed the most at ease in nature, as though they enjoyed being in the wilderness. Mel sighed, it was stupid to think anything else, she supposed they'd be used to roughing it, but what Mel couldn't understand was how *anyone* could find pleasure in camping, *period*.

No matter how many times Mel had tried it, she always came to the same conclusion, she hated it with a passion. In fact, camping had been a major bone of contention between her and Ceana growing up. Ceana loved it, whereas Mel was more a five-star hotel kind of girl. Mel felt that there was nothing worse than sleeping on a bed that, more often than not, went down during the night or having showers in shitty little cubicles with toilets so close that everyone knew what you were doing.

An involuntary shudder went through her body as Mel remembered one particular camping trip. Somehow on Easter three years ago Ceana had convinced Mel to go camping with her, she had promised it would be fun. But it turned out that over one thousand campers were at the camp grounds and it only had one amenities block with six showers and toilets for each gender, and let's just say, not everyone possessed the same hygienic standards as her, or any kind of hygienic standards for that matter. On top of that campers were allowed to bring their dogs, so Mel had spent her time trying to avoid dog shit and listening to dogs fight and bark all night long.

That had been the last camping trip she had ever taken. Right then and there, she had decided that camping was unquestionably not for her. Ceana had been disappointed of course but was open to compromise, Ceana did the hotel thing with her once a year and, in return, Mel went 'glamping' with Ceana.

Glamping was as close to camping as Mel got, and the site had to be in a five-star campsite, then at least she was guaranteed a clean toilet block. With thoughts of her best friend Mel wondered what Cee would have said about her camping out tonight. Just thinking of her best friend made her smile; they were almost there, Caelan had told her a couple of hours back that they would reach the keep by mid-afternoon tomorrow. Soon everyone was finished with their chores and were sitting around the fire eating and laughing. Mel sat beside Katie and Tristan and happily chatted catching up on all aspects of their lives, occasionally she felt as though someone was watching her, but chose to ignore it. Overall the night had been pretty amazing, and as Mel lay in her tent that night, listening to the unknown animals of the night, and the highlanders that were on watch walking around, Mel had to admit to herself that tonight her camping trip hadn't been so bad, and as she drifted off to sleep her dreams were filled with images of what was to come and a certain highlander

Seven

The next morning, Mel woke up and was happy to see that she hadn't dreamed her day yesterday, she was still here and the Highlands were just as magnificent as they had been yesterday. But as easy as she had fallen asleep, she had not stayed that way. Mel was glad she didn't have a mirror handy after the rough night she'd had. Her neck ached and every part of her body felt like it had been run over by a car. With a groan she cracked her back. Mel would have given anything to have an air mattress to sleep on last night, even one that went down would have been better than laying on the hard ground.

Soon the camp was rustling with activity as everyone got ready to depart, and after breakfast the group was back on the road, heading to their final destination. Mel was glad that they only stopped once to have lunch, so that Katie could feed an increasingly restless Marcus, and were now ambling across the open lands. Although she was eager to see her friend, she didn't mind the pace, Mel had to admit she was thoroughly enjoying riding through this glorious land, untouched by modernity. The air was fresh and crisp, filled with the scent of heather and, with every breath she took, she swore she could feel her lungs detoxify from the smog and grime of her time. It was an incredible feeling, one that she was not looking forward to losing when she went back home.

Mel looked out over the field where the purple flowers dotted the landscape, the hills that they were riding over were covered in a carpet of green and purple. *Magical!* That was the one word that kept on playing over and over in her head, no other word came close to describing how it felt and looked.

"We're almost there," Katie said beside her, she was carrying Marcus but Caelan was close by in case Katie needed him, it was how it always was. Mel smiled wistfully at the couple, she hoped that, one day, she could experience the same kind of love that both Ceana and Katie had found, it was the kind of love that defied logic and time.

"Look." Katie's voice brought Mel back to the present. Katie pointed ahead, and when Mel followed Katie's finger she found that she was looking at a castle that appeared to be rising out of the hills. It was the most spectacular building Mel had even seen. The stone walls and turrets reached to meet the sky and were framed by the blue ocean which spread out behind it, a far cry from the ruins and dilapidated state of the castle relics in her own time.

Unlike their own modern dwellings at home, this one appeared as if was part of the landscape; as if Mother Nature had intended her to be there.

"Is that really your home?" she asked Caelan in awe.

"Sure is Lass," he answered, pride evident in his voice.

Mel turned her head to look at him, and the look on his face

matched his tone. Not only could she see the love he had for his home, she could hear it and feel it, and Mel once again understood why Ceana loved this place. If it wasn't for the lack of modern amenities, Mel had to admit that she could fall in love with this place too. But she suspected it was a little too primitive for her tastes and Mel was sure that, after a month without running water and modern plumbing, she would be well and truly ready to return to 21st Century living.

But, for the next month, when in Rome! She compromised, and with that mantra in her mind Mel decided that no matter what came her way she would do her best to try and enjoy every minute of her time here.

They continued to ride across the hills and the closer to the castle they got, the freer Mel felt, it was the strangest sensation. It was as if she had no worries, here she didn't have to think about being professional, or about what people would say about what happened between her and Jack. There was simply no 21st Century expectations. No clients looking to her for answers, or her mother harping on her to keep up appearances, and especially no questions about how she had lost another boyfriend.

The only thing she had to think about was the fact that soon Mel would be with her best friend again and she knew that around Ceana she could be herself. With that thought, her mischievous nature reared its ugly head, and she smiled, why wait? Turning slightly in her saddle she looked over at Katie and Caelan.

"Caelan, this land is Kessan's right?" She asked projecting an air of innocence. Katie saw through her innocence though and groaned, she was the only other person besides Ceana who knew what the look in Mel's eyes meant. Caelan hesitated when he heard his wife's protest, Mel had to admit he was a smart man, but he still answered. "Aye Lass, it is." He said warily.

Mel offered him a smile, "So, in theory, we should be quite safe on this land. I mean, no highlanders are going to come out and attack you on your own land, are they?" Mel asked offhandedly.

She was trying to give the impression that she was only mildly curious. Though of course, she knew Katie wasn't buying it for a second.

"Aye," he replied after a slight pause, but the dubiousness was still in his tone, but after moment a smile spread across his face "The only thing scary on this land Lass, is Hamish!" he said with a grin and a nod to the big man ahead of them. Mel heard the giant up front snort in response, but that was the only indication he gave that he was paying attention to their conversation.

"Thanks," she said to Caelan as she turned to Tristan. "Hey Tris!" she said in a singsong voice.

"Oh God, help us now," she heard Katie pray.

Ignoring her friend, Mel looked at Tristan and waggled her eyebrows, not wanting to waste any time putting her plan in motion. Mel almost laughed when he raised an eyebrow in return, waiting to see what she had to say. They had always been a bad influence on each other and they were both competitive, neither one wanted to let the other one win, and it was that combination that Mel was relying on to get him to be her partner in crime. "Yeeees?" he answered.

"You up for a little wager?"

Mel watched as his whole demeanour changed, he was sitting a little straighter in his saddle, and a twinkle entered his eyes. "What did your devious little self, have in mind?" he re-joined eagerly.

Just from his change Mel knew this was going to be good for him, he needed a little laughter and fun in his life, in fact so did she. As they'd ridden along, she noticed that Tristan had been slowly pulling into himself, and the closer they got to Ceana, the quieter he had become. While Mel had sworn that in the next two weeks, she would do whatever she could to put the smile back on his face and hopefully uncover what was wrong, she needed to find ways to achieve this. And right now, she had the perfect opportunity to achieve both missions.

"Well, let's say that if I was able to beat you to the keep, you would have to be my slave for a week, which includes answering every question I ask." She paused to give him time to consider it, but it was taking him too long and Mel was worried that she had blown her chance, then inspiration hit her. She knew a sure-fire way to get him to compete, "as well as give me your signed Kelly Slater board!"

Tristan's eyes rounded, Bingo!

"Come on Mel, you know I can't give you that. It's my prized possession. And besides, you don't even surf!" He sputtered.

"So, I might want to learn." She re-joined, he was right of course, she had no intention of surfing or actually taking the board, but the look of disbelief on his face was priceless.

"You? Surf? Yeah right." He mocked, "For one thing you hate anything physical like that and you would be too scared of sharks." He added.

Mel relented, she would give him that. "Ok, well how about this then, if I win you will still be my slave, and you still have to answer *all* my questions. But instead of your surf board, you are not allowed to have sex for a month. And, if at any time you fail in any of these, *then* I get your board." She retorted with a grin.

Tristan wasn't looking so smug now, in fact, he was looking a little green. She could see him weighing up what chance he had of winning, and she had a sneaking suspicion that he was going to bow out. So, Mel did the one thing she knew would guarantee him accepting. She insulted his manhood.

"Oh come on, don't tell me big tough Tristan is scared that he can't win a race with wittle owld me?" She mocked.

The sparkle in Tristan's eyes disappeared, his back stiffened even more and Mel could have sworn she heard him growl. In that instant, Mel knew she had him. Men were all the same, there was nothing a male couldn't stand more than having his manhood questioned by a woman. Worked like a charm every time.

"Fine it's a deal, but in return, *when* I win you have to be my slave for a month. As well as do my tax free of charge for the next two years"

Mel snorted, "Is that the best you got. Easy." But she should have known better than to mock him. As the evil smile spread over his face, Mel had the feeling that she should have kept her mouth shut.

"*And* you have to go on a blind date with someone I choose!" He grinned widely at her.

That made her pause for a second, Mel's mind tried to picture which of his friends he would set her up with, and there were some that made her stomach drop. But in the end she decided it wouldn't matter who he chose to set her up with because it was only one date, and she didn't plan on losing.

Laughing, Mel realised that she had a secret advantage that Tristan had probably forgotten about. She had been riding horses since she could walk, there was no way he was going to win.

"Deal," she said, reaching out shaking his hand.

"Now get ready to lose, sucker!" Mel taunted, as she readied herself for the race.

Tristan was doing the same when Katie's voice interrupted them, "Um, guys, I don't think this is such a good idea."

"Since when has that ever stopped us, Katie?" Mel shot back, giving her a cheeky grin.

Katie just shook her head and looked at her brother. But he was not going to be much help to her either, as he was dead set on paying Mel back for her comment and that was exactly what Mel had hoped for. Katie once more looked at her, "Nothing I say is going to deter you, is it?"

Mel simply winked at her. "All right Tristan, are you ready?" She said, turning back to him. She didn't wait for his response, instead she kicked her horse into action and shouted.... Go!"

She heard Tristan's bark of laughter as her horse shot into a gallop and sped past a bunch of astonished highlanders towards the castle. Throwing her head back, feeling the air tug at her hair, Mel whooped out loud. *This* was the life; she hadn't felt this free since her younger days spent at her grandparents' farm, where she got to be herself. Leaning down further into her mount's back, Mel urged it on faster. As the horse flesh moved underneath her, Mel felt one with the horse, she was simply remarkable. Mel felt a kindred spirit in her; and she hoped she would get to ride her again while she was here.

Galloping faster, Mel's hair came loose from the rough braid she had put it in this morning and was now flying out behind her. And that's how *she* felt, she felt as if they were flying across the green fields as one, free and unburdened by life.

As Mel galloped on she could hear the hooves of Tristan's horse pounding behind her. Her heart raced along with the hooves of the horse knowing that he was gaining on her, but she was not done yet. Giving her horse another sharp jab she sped across the green hills even faster, not daring to distract herself by looking back. Mel was going to win this race. Nothing was going to stop her. She had never felt as alive as she did right in this moment and she never wanted the feeling to end.

Mel raced on over the fields heading closer to the village that lay at the bottom of the hill before the castle, it wasn't until she neared the village that she slowed down. Mel had told Tristan that the first one to the keep would win, but it wasn't until now that she realised they couldn't go racing through the village; she didn't want to hurt or scare anyone. Mel smiled at the advantage she had just gained, she knew he would have to slow down too, so she wasn't too worried about her losing any ground she had made up.

By the time she got to the village entrance, her horse was barely at a trot but she could still hear Tristan coming up on her at speed. *Would he put people at risk just to beat her?* She wouldn't have thought so, but Tristan was a different man and she had to stop forgetting that. Now she wasn't sure what he would do.

Mel stopped her mount and turned to face her opponent to see exactly what he had in mind, but before she could turn around fully, she was yanked from her horse and placed roughly onto another. It had been so quickly executed and with such force that the wind had been knocked out of her. Breathing heavily and turning to give Tristan a piece of her mind for cheating, Mel came face to chest with Hamish instead and froze. *What the hell?* Mel's heartbeat was racing for a whole different reason know, and her mind had turned to a muddle heaped. It took her few minutes to gain control of them.

When she finally gained control of her senses Mel prepared

herself to about to ask him what he thought he was doing, when her eyes met his green ones she lost her train of thought once more. Hamish's eyes did not hold the laugher they had the day before, instead his eyes were burning with fury and, as she regained her bearings, she realised that his whole body was rigid.

He was furious but she couldn't, for the life of her, figure out what his problem was. He should have realised that she wasn't going to go speeding through the village. *Surely he didn't think that lowly of her?* Mel knew she should have been apologising or explaining herself, but she felt anger and indignation instead and was now just as furious as he was. How dare he manhandle her like she was a small child, who the hell did he think he was? If he thought she was going to listen to anything he had to say, he was deluding himself. Even if she wanted to Mel couldn't talk to him, partly because she knew that if she opened her mouth she would give him a piece of her mind and she was not about to give him the satisfaction.

Mel folded her arms and angrily faced the front, fuming over what had happened, and somewhere between being dumbfounded, angry and humiliated, she numbly became aware of Tristan speeding past them. Mel could do nothing but watch on as he raced towards the castle, his horse kicking dust in its wake and leaving her behind, but not before she'd gotten a glimpse of the huge, mocking smile on his face, and her rage and humiliation rose to boiling point.

At first, Mel thought he was smiling because of what had just happened but, as she watched him ride confidently up to the keep, she realised that Hamish had cost her the bet. All she could do was watch as Tristan rode through the gate to victory. Mel groaned and hung her head, thanks to the brute behind her, she'd lost the edge she needed to get Tristan to open up, and now she was going to be subjected to being his slave and going on a date with one of his friends. Mel could only hope that he picked one of the decent ones.

As for the man behind her, he was about to learn that he had messed with the wrong woman, he may be accustomed to treating highlander women like this, but she was not going to stand for it. Once they were off this horse and out of arms' reach, she was going to give the giant an earful and she was going to make him pay for losing the bet, he had just made himself an enemy, one with a very long memory.

Eight

Hamish knew the lass was angry with him, but at this moment, he didn't care. He was glad she was keeping silent because he needed time for his heart and temper to settle down. Hamish had to admit that while they had ridden across Kessan's lands he hadn't been paying full attention to the group behind him. His thoughts were on making sure that the group remained safe and that no enemies were lurking nearby. Even though they were on safe land, with the Macintoshes out for his blood, he wasn't risking anything.

It was for that reason that he was left just as stunned as his men when she'd ridden past him as if the devil himself was on her tail. It only took him a second to regain his instincts before he took off after her. *What the hell was she thinking?* Didn't she know that she could have broken her neck racing across unknown lands like that? Not only could she have injured herself, she had also put his beloved horse in danger. It didn't take much for a horse to become spooked and, if *Seodag* had fallen in a hole and become seriously injured, he would have had to put her down. That thought alone set his blood to boiling once more.

Hamish knew that *Seodag* was more than capable for the race, but she didn't know that, and she wasn't at all familiar with the countryside or the horse.

Nevertheless, although Hamish was angry with her, he couldn't help but admire her riding ability, and when she'd bent lower over the back of the horse, her experience in riding shone through, which was a small mercy.

Hamish's heart raced once more as he remembered that during her ride she had given him a perfect view of her arse and as he raced after her he had to admit that it was a sight to admire. He could not get the image of her bent over the horse with that hair blowing out wild and untamed behind her, out of his mind. Hamish had to admit that the image showed that she could almost fit into the wilderness that was his home.

As Hamish remembered the image of her on the horse it was replaced with a flash of her naked, leaning over him while she rode him to climax. Shaking his head, he cleared the thought out of his mind and had spurred his horse into a faster pace. By the time he had caught up to her, she had slowed down near the village. His rage, adrenaline and instinct pumping, he grabbed her from her horse, deposited her on his, and that was how they entered the keep.

Thanks to her silence Hamish had begun to regain control over his body and thoughts, but he could sense that she was still seething and angry with him. Not worried about the lass' wrath, Hamish slowed his mount and came to a complete stop just behind Tristan.

"I must thank you, brother." Tristan grinned and turned to Mel, "I must admit, I thought you had me, but as it is all the time, luck was once more on my side. I hope you are ready to attend to my every need and whim." He joked and, just to rub it in further, he added with a satisfied smirk, "and I will make sure I have *lots* of tax work for you to do when we're home."

Hamish didn't understand most of what Tristan had said, and he wasn't sure he understood what was happening. What he did know though, was that Tristan's words only seemed to fuel Mel's animosity towards him. Hamish still was not sure on what they had been doing in the first place? He had been too far ahead of the group, so he had missed what had set off the race across the fields. But Hamish was certain that it had all been the lass' idea and he was going to get to the bottom of her madness right now. Hamish lowered himself to the ground and reached up to help Mel of the horse, but she slapped his hands away, her angry, glowering, expression unwavering as she dismounted herself. Hamish had expected her to rile at him, instead she spun around on Tristan so fast, it made his own head spin.

"Oh no way buddy, the bet is off, there is no way I am holding up my end of the bargain. The only reason you one is because that oaf interfered, in fact I beat you set him up to you didn't you. I don't know how you did it but you cheated!" She fumed, voice raised and angry. Hamish took offence to her calling him an oaf, and he was just about to defend Tristan's honour but Tristan beat him to it.

Tristan shook his head a small smile playing at his lips, Hamish had to admire how he didn't let her anger bother him. "No Mel, I don't think so, you didn't specify how we should get here, just that the first one who did won, and in this instance, that was me! But as to your other claim, I in no way enlisted Hamish's help, but I sure am glad he intervened." With that Tristan winked at Mel then sauntered off to wait for the others to catch up, whistling as he went.

Hamish folded his arms across his chest and waited for the lass to turn her anger on him, he was not going to be as pleasant as Tristan had, not only had she endangered herself and called him an oaf, she had also called into question his honour. Highlanders did not cheat, well this highlander didn't. He

Hamish didn't have to wait long, it had only been a minute since Tristan left when Mel inhaled sharply and faced him, all her anger now directed solely at him. But, instead of giving him an explanation that he had been waiting for Hamish was surprised when Mel starting riling at him, just as she had Tristan.

"Thanks a lot! I would have won if you hadn't interfered, and I had reason to win too. What is it with you men thinking you have the right to interfere in our lives. Tell me, did you deliberately aim to piss me off or is it just a natural ability you have?" She snapped.

Hamish didn't answer her, momentarily unsure of what to say and that seemed to make her angrier, which Hamish didn't think was possible. When Mel marched forward and shoved him hard, with little to no effect, it took everything he had not to smile. Hamish had to give her credit, while he was much taller and more solid than she was his size didn't stop her from showing her anger. Hamish had to admit that her lack of fear excited him, it also worried him, he got the feeling that Mel was used to getting her own way, and her in the highlands that could lead to trouble.

Hamish was once more left in surprise, when Mel turned away from him and started to stomp off, but he had news for her, they were not finished with their conversation. The lass had just ignited his own temper, no one told him what to do. It wasn't often that it came out, but when it did those around him usually fled. Grabbing her arm, he spun her around so she was facing him again, he had expected to see some fear in her eyes, but they were filled with same defiance he had witnessed yesterday.

"Och, let's get one thing straight Lass," he snapped back. Hamish was surprised at himself for letting her get under his skin. "I doona' care where ya come from or who ye are, ya will no' put yaself, or my horse, in danger again do ya hear me?" He practically barked.

Hamish had hoped that the mention of *Seodag* would have calmed her, instead her face turned even darker as her anger bubbled over, now her eyes flashed with fury. Ripping her arm out of his grasp, Mel took a step forward and stood so close to him that he once more picked up the scent of roses that clung to her body, as it had yesterday his cock twitched of its own accord, his lust was coming back in full force, it mingled with his anger, causing an all-consuming need to have her.

Mel's finger jabbed sharply into his chest as she spoke venomously, "do not tell me what to do, you... you... barbarian! You may be used to using your size to intimidate people around here, but I am not one of these people. I will not be controlled. Not by you or by anyone! Do you understand me?"

The last statement was said with so much resentment that he half wondered if someone had tried to control her before. Hamish was not completely oblivious to reading between the lines but he refused to back down and, by the looks of it, she wasn't budging either. They were staring daggers at each other, her eyes were the colour of rich chocolate, heat suffused her face, bringing a red tinge to her cheeks and her chest was rising and falling with each angry breath. The image was intoxicating, she looked like a warrior goddess and before he knew what he was doing, he grabbed her and pulled her up against him.

Momentarily grateful that the others had yet to reach the keep he seized a handful of her hair, Hamish tilted her head back and crushed his lips to hers. He waited for her to hit him, push him or let him know in some other way that she wanted him to stop but as she had been doing all day she surprised him once more. Mel grabbed two handfuls of his own hair, holding it so tightly he was amazed she hadn't ripped any out, and pulled him closer, their bodies were now pressed tightly against each other, Hamish could feel every curve of her body press into her. Growing he pressed his tongue against her teeth, he was instantly rewarded when they parted and allowed his tongue access. Their coming together was wild, and he wanted more.

Tilting her head back just a little more, he wanted to taste every corner of her mouth, so he deepened the kiss and was satisfied when she moaned deep in her throat. Regrettably the sound broke through her passionate haze and before he knew it she was ripping his head back forcefully with the fistfuls of hair she still had in her hands.

Looking down into her flushed face, he watched as her eyes transformed from being dazed to snapping pure fire at him, "Let. Me. Go," she demanded forcefully.

Hamish knew it was a ridiculous request, she was the one that still had hold of his head, but he did not wish to anger the lass any further, Hamish dropped his hands from her hair, letting her know that he wasn't going to resist her, and waited for her to do the same.

"Don't ever do that again." She fumed, giving his head one last yank, before dropping her hands to her side.

Hamish noticed that her chest rose as she inhaled angrily, he wanted to kiss her again, but before he could grab her Mel turned away and started to march away. Hamish was once again gifted with the sight of her arse, wrapped in her tight trews. Hamish wanted to say something that would bring her back, he loathed to lose any time with the lass.

As though she could read his mind Mel paused and turned back towards him, he was half expecting her to rile at him once more, instead she marched forward and gave him on last hard shove. Hamish stumbled slightly, still off-balance from the emotions that were running through his body from the kiss.

The lass had a spirit within her that he envied, his body was on fire and his cock was so hard it was almost painful. Hamish had to get a grip on his emotions and fast, this was ridiculous, he had never reacted to any kiss like this before. He enjoyed kissing, but his emotions rarely went beyond that basic enjoyment of it.

But here was this lass form the 21st century and after just one day she had his whole body burning with such an intense need that he didn't know how he was going to be able to keep his distance from her for the next few weeks, but what he was sure of was that keeping his distance was imperative.

Hamish watched as she marched away from him towards the

keep, her fists balled at her side and he realised that she had just given him an order, whilst ignoring his warning. Hamish knew that he should just let her go, get on his horse and go home, but the warrior in him could not let her leave without having her promise that she wouldn't do something that stupid again, as much as he didn't want to admit it, he felt a protectiveness towards the lass that he could not ignore.

With determination in his stride, Hamish marched right after the lass, he caught up to her just as she was entering the castle and had to grab the door to stop it from swinging back in his face. Hamish vaguely noticed that the others in the group had finally caught up to them and were also inside. But he only had one thing on his mind, Mel.

"One more thing Lass," he demanded following her inside. His voice was strong and steady, it did not betray the passion and anger he was feeling but Mel was already half way across the foyer and did not hear him, or chose to ignore him. Either way he was not about to let her strong will scare him, it was about time she realised that she was now dealing with highlanders, not the meek, mild males from her time, and things were done differently here. Raising his voice to gain her attention he spoke once more, "My warning from before Lass is no' to be ignored, here in the Highlands *ye* will do what I command of ya or you will have to face me, ya ken."

Hamish let the threat hang in the air as he the door slammed shut, stopping her in her tracks. They were standing in the main hall now and he knew the others were staring at them, while he hated to be the centre of attention he was not willing to let this go. Flicking his eyes around the room quickly Hamish realised that Ceana and Kessan had also entered the room, but he didn't care, at the moment Mel was the only one who held his attention, and he was not going to back down. Thankfully, it didn't take long before the lass spun around to face him. He had half expected her to scream at him from where she was, but once again she surprised him. Hamish almost smiled when her eyes filled with fire and she marched back to him, she was now standing toe to toe with him, battle ready. Hamish was fascinated with the way her chest rose and fell with each furious breath she took. Her chocolate tresses were still in disarray from their earlier encounter, some of it curled along the side of her face. Her eyes, which reminded him of a rich dark whisky, narrowed, and a picture of what she would look like riding him flashed before his eyes.

"You overbearing, misogynistic Scotsman, do not threaten me. I am not one of your simpering highland misses that will do whatever you say, *and* I am not your problem so back off!"

Mel's furious words brought Hamish back the present and he had to look away from her as she was shouting her tirade. She was so full of fire and spirit; his soul sung out for fulfilment. Rarely had anyone, especially a woman, found the nerve to stand up to him, let alone bark orders at him, it was refreshing. It had been so long since Hamish had felt this kind of excitement and it made him want to taste her again. Without thinking his hands started to move up towards here, but then he remembered that others were in the room, so he changed his course and ran his hands through his hair instead. Taking a steading breath Hamish glanced up at his surroundings where he caught Ceana staring at him and the Mel. A small smile was playing at the corner of her mouth and he wasn't sure he liked the way her eyes were narrowed on him. He had to think of a way to defuse this situation and fast.

Hamish winked at Ceana letting her know that he finding this encounter nothing more than a then his way to assert himself, the last thing he needed was for Ceana to get any wild ideas. This was nothing more than Hamish showing a young lass how the highlands worked. But while Hamish could lie to Ceana and everyone else, he could not lie to himself. While it was true that Mel needed to understand her the way the highlands worked, part of him had wanted to see the fire within her again. Hamish gave Mel a dismissive glance, knowing that would anger her further; "Och we will see Lass," he challenged before turning abruptly to properly greet his sister.

Nine

Mel lay in her four-poster wooden bed, studying the designs woven into the canopy. The bed was truly extraordinary; she had never seen or felt anything like it, it was as though she was floating on a cloud and Mel was in no rush to move. Mel hadn't expected that 12th Century Scotland could be this comfortable. She loved how the material enclosed her in the bed, draping around her, closing out the world and creating her own private haven.

When Mel had examined the material the night before, Ceana had told her that it was created from a mixture of silk and animal hair. Mel should have felt disgusted knowing she was touching hair from a dead animal, but she couldn't seem to dredge up enough concern to care, it was the most extraordinary bed she had ever seen. The underlay of the 12th Century mattress was filled with wool, and then a layer of feathers sat underneath.

Mel had expected to sink deep into it, but surprisingly it held firm, and was one of the softest mattresses she had ever slept on. Before travelling here, Mel had spent night awake imagining sleeping on mattress made from materials such as pine needles that would poke her all night, but she couldn't remember the last time she had slept so well, even considering the events of the night before.

Gazing towards the ceiling, Mel thought about last night; it had been a blur of emotions and excitement. One minute she had been excited about the freedom she had been feeling, then anger, mixed with lust replaced that emotion, and then, when she had seen Cee, everything changed, excitement once more came to the forefront.

Hamish and his dictates had been all but forgotten, planting a smile on her face Mel had rushed forward to greet her friend and everything else faded into the distance.

From that moment forward, Mel found herself swept up in a rush of activity and excitement. It started with an incredible dinner, during which Tristan had taken great pleasure in letting her know, in front of everyone, that her slave duties would start tomorrow, and ended with Ceana and herself sequestered in the corner of the main hall. Mel and Ceana had spent hours catching up on all the news while the others chatted and got to know Tristan better.

Mostly they had talked about Mel's ex-boyfriend and about Ceana's impending pregnancy, news that her son had so eloquently spilled in front of everyone as soon as they had arrived. Mel couldn't be happier for them, no one deserved the happiness they had found more than Ceana and Kessan, they had beat not only time, but also space to find each other. As Mel continued thinking about her friends and what they had talked about, her thoughts turned to the Scottish giant.

As thoughts of him filled her head, she could almost feel his lips on her own, and she was surprised to find that her anger with Hamish hadn't gone away. Mel was baffled by how fast and strong her emotions became just from the thought of him. She had thought that once she was away from him, and after a good night's sleep, the anger would dissipate. But every time she found her mind wandering to him, some of the anger would return. She couldn't believe his nerve! *How dare he think he could tell her what to do!*

But Mel had to be honest with herself, there was something else there besides anger too, she'd felt it stirring from the first moment she laid eyes on him, but she wasn't ready to acknowledge it yet, afraid of what it might mean.

Life was funny, even if Mel had tried, she was sure that she couldn't have found someone more opposite to Jack, to have feelings for. Mel snorted, what was wrong with her, there was no in between when it came to the men in her life, they were either complaining, whining and more feminine than she was, or were over-dominant, brutish and oozing in masculinity and authority. And yet no matter what type of man she dated they all ended the same way.

Mel wondered if her mother was right, perhaps it was her,

maybe she *was* the problem. Was she too picky? Or did she have a neon sign on her forehead that said, '*Jerks apply here?*'

Was it too much to ask for a man that had looks, smarts, a sense of humour and one who would be comfortable just letting her be herself? The way life was going, Mel would be lucky to get at least one of those things, never mind all four, and the last point seemed to be the killer.

What was it with men being insecure with an independent woman. All the men Mel had dated over the last few years had either complained that she was too work-orientated, too uptight, or too free. They all wanted something from her but could never make up their minds what that something was. And, they never liked that she earned more money than they did and always expected them to be her priority. *Men sucked.*

Mel sighed, while she hated them sometimes – point in case the Scotsman downstairs, she knew that she wanted one of her own. Just one that would treat her like she wanted to be treated and cherish her for her, not boss her around like the Scottish jerk had tried to do! She hated him with a passion.

Just thinking about Hamish set Mel's pulse racing, well, okay, she didn't *hate* him as much her brain wanted her to think she did. If her body had its way, she would go downstairs, throw herself at him and show him just how wild and uncontrollable she really was. It was that kiss that made her want to eat him alive.

That kiss!

It had been nothing like anything she had ever experienced! Mel was used to the typical soft, coaxing kisses, kisses that were supposed to be romantic and loving, but turned out to be more like she was drowning. Man she hated those kisses, most of the time it felt like she was kissing a slimy frog, trying not to gag on the tongue that they were trying to shove all the way down her throat.

But Hamish's kiss were nothing like that, his were more of a take charge and consume you kind of kiss. Jack certainly didn't kiss like Hamish.

Hamish's kiss was the kind of kiss that possessed you, it was a son of bitch, raw sexual kiss; a kiss that let you know exactly what he wanted. Mel groaned as she imagined his lips against hers and that electric jolt that had taken possession of her control. It left her breathless and as she lay there remembering it her body hummed with that same passion it had yesterday, and it practically screamed for release. Mel buried her head into the covers and tired not to scream, man she needed to get laid.

After her she had gotten control of her thoughts and body, Mel decided she should probably get up. While she wished she could lay here all day, Mel didn't want to miss any of the time she could have with her best friend. With the thought of seeing Cee again she threw the covers back, climbed out of bed and dressed. Mel prayed that with any luck she wouldn't see that dammed Scotsman at all today, or tomorrow. She needed time to rein in her emotions and, if luck was on her side, she would get the time she needed to come up with a plan.

Heading down to breakfast, Mel tried to focus on what she was going to do today, but her mind kept on replaying the kiss. She couldn't switch it off. As she turned the corner to enter the dining hall Mel noted that Ceana was already there and she was with a young woman Mel didn't recognise.

"Hey, didn't you sleep well?" Cee asked taking in her dishevelled appearance as she came up to hug her best friend. In that moment Mel wished that her best friend didn't know her so well. It was hard to keep things from someone who knew you like they knew themselves. Mel decided to ignore her friends question and simply walked forward and embraced her.

"God, I've missed you." Ceana said hugging Mel tightly. As much as Mel didn't like hugging people in that minute she felt at home in her friends embrace and was not in any hurry to end it.

"Feeling's mutual," Mel commented returning her hug. Ceana pulled her forward and offered her breakfast. Mel's stomach rumbled at the smells that were emitting from the smorgasbord of food to the side of the room. While there was a lot of food Mel was not familiar with, all of it smelled wonderful and if was anything like the food she had eaten at dinner, Mel knew it would taste as good at it smelt. But there was one small problem, Mel was not interested in eating.

"Come on Cee, you have known me practically all my life. Since when do I eat breakfast? I will just have a coffee though, if you have any." Just then, a terrifying thought hit her. She grabbed Cee's arm.

"Please tell me you have coffee, Cee. Because if you don't you can just send me home now." Mel could hear the whiny tone of her voice, but she didn't care, there was no way she would get through the next month without coffee, especially if she had to be Tristan's slave, and deal with an overbearing Scottish hothead.

Cee just stood there, laughing at her while shaking her head. At first Mel thought her friend was shaking her head no, as in 'no we don't have coffee,' but the next words out of Cee's mouth brought a rush of relief over Mel.

"Of course we have coffee! Come on Mel, I have known you since we were five, do you really think I would invite you here and not have coffee on hand? I happen to like the people who live here." Ceana quipped as she headed to the side table to pour Mel a steaming hot cup. Mel wasn't even concerned with how it would taste, she just knew she needed her coffee fix. It had been hours since her last one, and Mel could feel her body start to crave it. Mel looked at the young woman who was standing there, watching them, wondering who she was and how this must all look to her. Ceana must have caught her look as she finally introduced the pair.

"Mel, I would l like you to meet Thora, my sister-in-law." Cee said as she poured the coffee.

Mel was half listening to her friend and watching her pour the coffee when Thora came forward and curtsied in front of her. "It's nice to finally meet you," Thora greeted her warmly. "I have heard so much about you in the last two years."

Mel turned her attention to the young woman in front of her. She was beautiful, but with brothers like hers, Mel wasn't surprised. Thora had the same colouring that Kessan had, but her jet-black hair tumbled in a riot of curls to her waist. Half of it was swept up with a white bow, which gave the young woman an air of innocence. Thora's eyes were the same deep ocean blue as Kessan's too, but on her, the combination of the dark hair and deep blue eyes was astonishing.

As Mel continued to take in the young woman, she had marvelled at how regal she appeared, she was almost flawless, apart from the small scar ran the length of her eye, nothing marred her skin. Mel briefly wondered how she had gotten it, but thought it was probably rude to ask, she would have to remember to ask Cee later. But overall the scar did little to detract from her beauty, rather it seemed to only add to her allure.

"I hope it was all good," Thora joked.

Thora smiled at her, it took a moment for Mel to remember what she was refereeing to. Once her mind caught back up with the conversation she smiled.

"Well most if it was." She joked winking at Ceana who was heading back towards them.

Thora laughed and Mel realised she hadn't been at dinner last night. She was about to ask where Thora had been, when Ceana came around the table, holding out a cup of coffee. Thora forgotten, Mel grabbed the cup and breathed the rich aroma in. While it smelt a little different to the flavoured coffees she was used to drinking at home, it was still coffee and it smelt divine.

"Hello, old friend." She sighed before taking a sip, savouring the warmth that spread through her body as the bitter liquid entered her system.

"Oh come on Cee, you know you shouldn't support her addiction." Tristan remarked as he came into the room and saw the cup of coffee in Mel's hand.

"What are best friends for, if not to help you with your addictions?" Mel shot back with a happy smile on her face as she felt the familiar heat and comfort of the cup in her hand.

Mel was just about to ask Tristan if he wanted her to get him anything, when she noticed the slight colouring that came to Thora's cheeks as she looked over at him. Mel wasn't surprised in the least, growing up with Tristan, she was used to the way women reacted around him, and she was sure that Tristan probably hadn't even noticed. Tristan shook his head, sat down at the table and reached for some fresh bread that someone had placed there.

Mel watched briefly as he spread some butter on the bread, Ceana joined him at the table and Mel decided to do the same.

"Are you going to come and have some breakfast?" Ceana asked Thora as she continued to stand.

Mel watched Tristan closely and saw a slight smile on his lips as Thora answered.

"Och, nay thank you. I have some work that needs to be done." And with that the young woman quickly left the room.

Mel continued to watch Tristan and she was certain she saw a flash of disappointment enter his eyes before it was gone and he turned his happy smile to her and Cee.

Mel narrowed her eyes at him briefly. But when all he did was smile she wondered if she was seeing things that weren't there.

Mel took another sip of her drink as Cee turned to her brother, "So what have you been up to?"

With that Tristan proceeded to fill Cee in on what he had been doing since he last saw her. Mel got the feeling that he was only telling them about half of the truth, but she was happy to let it go as their laughter filled the dining room. Mel finished her last sip of coffee as Tristan finished telling them one last tale.

Mel was considering getting up and getting another coffee, when Cee spoke.

"Do you guys want to see the rest of the castle?" Ceana asked excitedly.

Mel was torn, while she wanted nothing more than to see the castle she wanted another coffee. She looked at the pot longingly as Tristan spoke up.

"Sorry sis, I have already promised Katie I would spend some time with her after breakfast. But perhaps later? Maybe you could help me come up with some great ways to torture Mel while we're here. Did she tell you that she has to be my slave for the next month?" He asked wickedly.

Mel's eyes shot back to Tristan and narrowed, trust him to rub it in.

"Yeah, what in the world is going on with you two?" Ceana laughed.

"Nothing, I would have won if there hadn't been interference. But you know your brother, he takes his wins anyway he can." Mel answered bitterly as she stuck her tongue out at him.

Tristan took it all in his stride and just chuckled as he got up, kissed Ceana's cheek.

"I'll leave it up too Mel to fill you in on all the details." He said as he left the room to find Katie, his promise that he would find something for her to do later following him out the door. Mel flipped him off, before Ceana turned to her.

"So do you want to tell me about it?" she asked laughter underlying her tone.

Mel narrowed her eyes on her best friend, "what do you think?" She asked.

Ceana put her hands up in surrender before changing the subject.

"What about you?" Ceana asked turning her attention back to something else. "Do you want to see the Keep? And while we are at it you can explain more in depth about Jack the Jerk."

"Hell yes!" Mel replied jumping at the chance to get her mind on anything else, she was eager to see the rest of this amazing place, but she was also eager to have some more alone time with Cee. Even though they had spent time together last night there hadn't been much privacy to tell her all the important things. There was so much Mel needed to tell her and so much advice she needed. Mel rose, finished her coffee and then walked out of the main hall, arm in arm with Ceana, telling her all about the race to the Keep.

"Mel, have you noticed something seems off about Tristan?" Cee asked once they were outside in the courtyard.

Mel stopped walking she could hear the concern in her friend's voice and knew that Ceana had sensed what she herself had been feeling. When Tristan had been filling them in on his time in the army, Mel had the same sensation that she'd had back in her office, he wasn't telling them everything. Something bad had happened to him in South America, she just knew it, something inside of her was telling her that he was not okay.

There was nothing specific that she could put her finger on; all the stories he had told them had been entertaining and amusing, but at certain times when he spoke about his SAS team, an intense sadness passed over his eyes and edge entered his voice momentarily, before he guarded himself and continued with the story he had been telling.

"Yes, I noticed it now, but I also noticed it when he came to deliver your letter; he seemed different, more subdued. Something's up alright," Mel answered sadly. She knew that he had been part of a Special Air Services team for the army, but no-one knew exactly what their duties involved or what horrors they had seen.

"Do you think I should ask him about it?" Cee wondered, she was looking nervously around the courtyard as though she was afraid they would be caught conspiring.

Mel felt for Ceana, she herself wanted nothing more than to

force Tristan to tell them what was going on, but she knew it would not get them anywhere.

"No. I think that when he is ready to talk to you he will come and ask you for help." Mel answered after a moment's thought.

Ceana nodded, a sadness that Mel felt entered her eyes. "He used to be so open and trusting," Ceana said sadly.

Mel agreed, Tristan used to be the carefree and open one of their group. In the old days anyone of them could have ask him anything and he would not have hesitated to tell them the truth. But since the death of Marcus, Tristan had changed. Mel could only watch as he gradually became closed off from those around him.

At first it had been little things that had changed about him, but his distance and closed-offness had only gotten worse over the years, especially since his last tour. Sadly, Mel had a feeling that they were losing him and that soon they would lose him for good. She could see that there was no way he was going to tell them what was wrong unless he was ready, and she knew that if they tried to push the matter he would only close up on them for good.

"I hope you're right, Mel; I really hate seeing that sadness in his eyes. He hides it well, but I know it's there."

"You noticed it too?" Mel asked.

"Yes, and I hate it," Cee answered.

Mel had to agree, she hated seeing any of her friends in pain,

but in this moment, there was nothing they could do, they just had to wait until he was ready for their help. A shroud of sadness engulfed their happiness. Cee wrapped her arm once more through Mel's and they both walked in silence as they continued to walk through the bailey, each lost in their own thoughts.

Mel was trying to come up with another plan to get Tristan to open up when Ceana abruptly blurted "enough of this gloom and doom, tell me about what's going on with you!" she demanded.

Putting Tristan out of her mind for now, Mel was glad to finally have the opportunity to tell Cee about her life, from the weird clients she had, to her family and finally, Jack the Jerk. They spent the next hour laughing and gossiping about what was happening back home. Ceana still got a kick out of her brother's antics, Mel on the other hand wished they would grow up a little. But it was the stories of her clients that got the most laughs out of Ceana.

"You aren't serious, are you?" Ceana asked as Mel told her

about one client that had asked her how he could write off his wife and two girlfriends as a tax deduction.

"What is he a pimp?" Ceana had asked Mel.

"At least I could claim that as business expense." Mel had quipped back bringing more laughter from Ceana. It seemed that her best friend thought it was funny that Mel had just spent a frustrating week trying to explain why he couldn't claim a luxurious holiday he had taken girlfriend number two on, as a work deduction.

"I seriously don't know how you do it." Ceana had commented.

Mel wasn't sure either, some days were harder than others. "It's not easy I can tell you. If it wasn't for client confidentiality, I would \ring Mrs Paton, and let her know what was going on." Mel said, disgust and humour lacing her voice.

Mel went to say something else about Mrs Paton probably having her own side piece when she realised that Ceana had stopped in mid-step during their conversation, and now that her focus was not on Cee, she looked around, observing for the first time that they were walking along the rampart of the castle. The view from up here was magnificent. As Mel looked out over the rolling hills she could swear she could see to the cost.

"So, what happened with Jack?" Ceana asked drawing Mel's gaze back Ceana and their conversation. Mel knew that Ceana had been working her way around to this question, in fact Mel was surprised that it had taken her this long. Taking a deep breath Mel prepared herself to explain the whole ordeal again. Last night, Mel had only given Ceana a quick rundown and left it at that. She was not ready for the whole dining room to hear about her humiliation. Thankfully, Tristan, Katie and herself were the only ones in this century who knew what had happened. Mel turned to face the rolling hills once more and was getting ready to tell her friend about Jack, but the image that greeted her had her losing her train of thought.

The sight that was before her was awe-inspiring; she had never seen anything like it, she was not sure how she had missed it before. Down on the hills just below were a bunch of men in the field training; a blur of swords, plaids and burly Scotsmen. Her lips parted in surprised admiration, it was a sight to behold that was for sure. Then, one man in particular caught her attention.

Hamish!

There he stood in the centre of crowd, wearing nothing but his kilt. He appeared to be in the processes of trying to kill Kessan! Mel cringed as Hamish sword clashed with the metal of Kessan's and with every blow that Hamish landed on Kessan's sword, Kessan landed an equally brutal one back. Mel could hear the brute force of the impact from where she was standing, yet neither man appeared to feel the blows, instead they battled even harder.

Mel stood there gaping, Hamish's body was glistening with sweat and every muscle, from his arms to his legs, strained with each blow. As she continued to watch his body contract and contort with each hit of his sword her mouth went dry, and her pulse started beating rapidly, sending butterflies shooting to the pit of her stomach. This was beyond ridiculous; how could she be so aroused just by the mere sight of him? It wasn't as though she had never seen a gorgeous man before, and on top of that sweaty men were a turn off to her.

So what was it about this particular one that drove her wild?

"They're something else, aren't they?" Ceana whispered in her ear.

It was enough to break Mel from her gawking, and shaking herself from her stupor, Mel turned to see her friend eyeing her husband with the same lust-filled stare she was sure had been in her own eyes only minutes before.

"If you say so," Mel said off-handily, trying to be nonchalant hoping that Cee didn't see through her facade to how much Mel wanted her brother. While Mel felt comfortable sharing almost everything with her best friend, Mel was not sure she was ready to share this. Mel shrugged as she walked off hurriedly, but her ploy didn't work, she heard Ceana snort as she increased her stride to catch up with her.

"Come on, Mel, don't give me that bull. I know that look on your face."

"I have no idea what you are referring to." Mel tried as she started heading down the stairs and back into the bailey.

By now Ceana was right behind her and she wasn't giving up. "Come on Mel, you can't fool me. It is the same look you had when we were in university and you saw Robbie Curtis for the first time."

Mel finally made it down the uneven stairs into the bailey before she turned to answer Ceana, she needed to be on solid ground for this conversation.

"Yeah, and look where that got me, I ended up dating a moron who had more brawn than brains! And to make matters worse, he sucked in bed! And it has been all downhill from there let me tell you."

Mel could see that she had shocked her friend with her brazenness. Mel had given up trying to deny anything, what was the point, Ceana would have eventually gotten out of her. Mel had simply had enough between Jack and Hamish, she was mad at the male population. Mel had expected Ceana to say something, but as she looked at her, Mel was annoyed to see her friend standing there trying her hardest to control her laughter.

"Oh, go on laugh, you might as well, laughing about these things has been the only way I have remained sane over the years." Mel informed her. She was going to let Ceana say something, but the moment the truth had left Mel's mouth there was no holding back the waterfall of emotion that came pouring out. "I mean for God's sake, if I hear one more male tell me that I hurt his feelings, I am going to slap him so hard into next week that even his mother won't be able to find him! Not to mention, the lack hazard love making, I mean whatever happened to a good ol' hard and fast romp, why does everything have to be slow and sensual. Sometimes a girl just needs a good fuck."

With that last bomb Ceana lost her composure and broke down into a fit giggles.

"Oh poor Mel, ever so unlucky in love." Cee teased.

"You have no idea. Cee. The guys at home are getting less and less appealing by the minute. Do you know how hard it is to get excited about sleeping with someone, when all they want to do is talk about their feelings? Let me tell you, you can't. It's been so long since any of them have even turned me on enough to *want* to have sex, let alone actually having it. I may as well become a nun!"

Even Mel could hear the desperation in her voice this time. She hadn't meant to just blurt it out like that, but she was beyond caring at this point.

"Come on Mel, be serious," Cee said still laughing.

"But I am." She answered with just enough sarcasm in there to let her friend know that she was dead serious. And it got just the reaction Mel was hoping for. Her friend no longer looked amused, she looked shocked.

"How is that possible? You've been dating Jack for the last year." Cee asked, astounded.

For a brief moment Mel felt as though she should probably feel embarrassed, but then anger filled that void. No she would not feel embarrassed over something that was beyond her control, and Mel knew that there was no way in this world that Ceana would judge her, so taking a deep breath Mel spilled her heart.

"Where to start," She sighed, "first that little dirt bag told me that he liked to take things slow, and that he never slept with anyone in the first six months. His excuse was that he wanted to get to know each other on a deeper level so that when we finally did sleep together, we would have more of a connection."

"No way!" Ceana gasped.

"Oh yes, and then, once the six months were up, whenever we came close to doing it, he would suddenly become self-conscious and complain that *he* didn't feel attractive enough, or that the timing wasn't special enough" She snorted derisively. Ceana was still gaping at her. Mel wished that she was making this stuff up, but it was too ridiculous not to be true.

"And don't even bother to ask me if I'm serious again, Cee, because I am. Although, he didn't seem to have any trouble boning little miss temp the first chance he got!" Mel spat bitterly.

"Oh Mel." Ceana breathed as she placed a hand over her open mouth. Mel could feel tears building in the back of her eyes, not because of Jack the Jerk, but because she felt her friends sympathy for her, and that was something she didn't want anyone feeling for her. Especially not over someone like Jack.

Mel shook off the feelings that were overwhelming her and continued on with the story.

"Yes, according to Facebook the other day, they're madly in love despite only knowing each other for a few weeks. Damn Cee, what's wrong with me? Every man I meet either turns out to be a wimp or so full of himself that there is no room in the relationship for the two of us." Now she was sounding downright pathetic even to her own ears, but she no longer cared. Mel just wanted a man who would be a man and let her be herself at the same time.

"There's nothing wrong with you, Mel," Cee chuckled and put an arm around her shoulders, "you're just an acquired taste that's all." She teased.

"Oh geeze, thanks bestie, you make me sound like an STD. It's no wonder men run screaming from me."

Ceana burst out laughing, bringing the light-heartedness that had been there earlier back. "Don't give up Mel, I'm sure there is someone out there that *is* man enough to handle you." Cee said with a grin.

Mel sighed, she prayed that her friend was right, but she just couldn't see it happening for her. "At this point Cee, I would be happy just to have a *willing* man, in fact I would consider jumping anyone's bones, that's how horny I am." Mel groaned in frustration.

As she stood there thinking about what she had just confessed to her friend Mel felt the need to get out of there, she needed to do anything but stand here and talk about her sex life, it was only adding to her depressive state. Mel hadn't meant to reveal all that to her friend, but once the dam had been broken it was impossible to close back up. Turning on her heel Mel prepared to make her getaway, but just like every other moment in her life, this one was not going to go her way either. No instead of making a clean get away Mel had run right into the other thorn in her side, Hamish.

"Of course, you had to be here," Mel said under her breath, dropping her head forward. Mel heard Cee coughing, covering up a laugh and was considering all the ways she could punish her friend later.

Ceana should have been helping her out of this situation, but instead she found joy in it. Mel flushed with embarrassment as the last moments of their conversation came rushing back. What timing! Groaning, Mel closed her eyes briefly hoping the Scotsman would just go away, but when she opened them it was to find that he was still standing there, silent as usual. Mortified, Mel realised her hand was planted firmly on his chest where it had landed when she braced herself from the impact.

Mel wanted nothing more than to leave, but looking at her hand on his chest was the wrong thing to do. Her body once more betrayed her, and has it had when she watched him battle on the field she felt her throat go dry and her composure leave her. All that muscle in front of her made her knees go weak and Mel couldn't have stopped her hand from moving even if she wanted to.

As Mel's hand slid along his sinewed body, gliding easily over the muscles, everything around her seemed to fade away and her entire being was focused on the man in front of her. She ran her hand over his pecks, through the coarse hair of his chest, from one to the other. It skimmed over the nipples, and she was pleased when she saw them harden. Moving slowly, Mel brought her hand back to the centre of his chest then slowly made her way down his body until she reached his rock-hard abs.

Mel was fascinated at the way the muscles rippled underneath her hand. There was not an ounce of fat on him, she thought admiringly. As she continued to run her hand over his abs, Mel had the urge to run her nails over his ribcage and was excited to feel a shiver run through his body.

Her mind and her heart were at war with what to do, she knew dimly that she should stop but, for the life of her she couldn't; his body fascinated her. Her heart and hormones won out over her head she continued her slow journey until she reached the band of his kilt. Never in her life had she felt such a raw need to see a naked male's body, and never in her life had she felt so bold and powerful. Mel could not explain what this man did to her.

Running her fingers along the edge of his kilt, she idly wondered what would be underneath. Would he wear underwear? Or was this another part of Scottish life that the movies got right, was he as bare as the day he was born?

Mel continued to run her finger along the edge trying to decide what to do next and, before she knew it, her hand was back in the centre of his body, right in front of her, right above the part she wanted to feel most. Swallowing, she contemplated ripping his kilt off. Mel's tongue darted out of her mouth as she slowly slipped on finger below the waist line, her heart beat picked up. Mel was feeling heady, and before she could stop herself another finger dipped below, this was thrilling. Mel was getting ready to throw herself at him, but before she could go any further his hand snaked out and caught hers, effectively breaking her from her trance.

Looking up at him momentarily stunned, part of Mel realised she should apologise, but the pure lust she saw in his eyes prevented her from saying anything. She couldn't seem to find the words she needed, so Mel decided to do what she had initially considered doing, she ran instead, something she was becoming good at it seemed.

"And on that note, I will be going!" she said hastily as she spun around and headed straight for the castle. Deciding that she was not to be trusted around the Scotsman she decided she was going to lock herself in her room, Mel concluded that she wasn't coming out until Hamish had gone home! What was wrong with her? The man made her absolutely nuts every time he was within her vicinity. Point in case, what had just happened. As Mel rushed past her friends and towards the keep she couldn't believe what she had just done! Mel hoped that her friend would just let it go, but she should have known better.

"This conversation is far from over!" Ceana hissed at her with far too much glee as Mel stalked past.

"I have no doubt," she replied sarcastically, before she broke into a run, face burning, and Ceana's loud laughter following her.

Ten

Hamish had just blocked another staggering blow from Kessan's sword, and was preparing to respond with his own attack, when his man Morgan interrupted them.

"Laird, a messenger from home is waiting in the hall and he says 'tis urgent." Hamish didn't wait for any more information, he placed his sword on his back where it belonged and started off the field.

"I will keep the men training." Kessan informed him, Hamish turned and nodded his thanks before he continued towards the keep. Before Hamish had come to the McKinnon keep at the behest of his sister, he'd left his commander in charge at home with strict instructions to contact him if there was any trouble. The tension that had been rising because of the attacks was reaching a fever pitch and Hamish knew that Iain would not have sent someone out here unless something major had happened. Iain was more than capable of handling anything short of trouble, up to and including war. But Hamish knew his commander would wait for Hamish's command before he took control of that too.

With his mind on what was happening back home Hamish had been heading to the stables to wash up, he hadn't bothered fixing up his plaid to cover his chest. Rounding the corner of the wall that would bring him into the bailey the first thing that drew Hamish's attention was Mel's voice. Stopping dead in his tracks; Hamish could not help but listen to what his sister and Mel were talking about. From what Hamish could gather, Ceana and Mel were having a heated discussion and Mel seemed to be upset. Hamish was not sure what the conversation was about and found himself in an awkward position, he loathed to interrupt their conversation, but he needed to get to the hall.

Deciding that it was more important to get to the hall, Hamish tried to make his way quietly to the stables but he was brought to a stop when Mel's last comment reached his ears – *'a willing man?'*

Shocked at the brashness of the topic, he couldn't believe what he was hearing, surely Mel was not complaining about the lack of sex in her life out in the open? It just wasn't done in this time; lasses didn't go around complaining about stuff like that!

Feeling like an untried lad, Hamish couldn't breathe, his veins sung with passion as a million thoughts played out in his mind. As image after image ran through is mind of what he would like to do to her as her 'willing male' his body hardened. This lass was wreaking havoc on not only his mind but his body too. It was only just now that Hamish realised he was standing just meters from the stables fantasising about what he would like to do to Mel, instead of dealing with clan business.

Even more so now Hamish knew he should stay away from her and, with her words still fresh in his mind, he decided he would wash up and head straight for the keep, he needed to find out what was going on at home in order to get his mind of the beguiling lass.

Hamish started walking once more, he was hoping that he could get to the stables without either lass noticing him, but he had only just made it a few steps into the bailey when Mel threw her hands up and spun around, smacking straight into him.

As he had the day in the glen, Hamish was again assailed with her scent which sent his emotions and body into a frenzy. At the rate he was going, if Hamish didn't start to get a hold on his reactions to Mel he was going to be walking around with a permanent hard-on.

As he continued to stand there with Mel plastered up against him, Hamish didn't know whether to feel ashamed or amused. Hamish became aware that Mel's hand was on his chest and he was expecting her to pull away from him, but she didn't. Instead, she remained there muttering to herself, Hamish knew he should try and focus on getting away from her, but the warmth of her hand on his body was making it impossible.

Looking down Hamish was about to ask her if she was okay, but he lost his train of thought when he noticed that she had her eyes closed. Hamish admired her as she stood close to him, so close in fact that her breath blew across his chest, raising the hairs there. The image that she presented him added fuel to the already burning fire within.

Hamish continued to stand there and watch the young lass, and it wasn't long before she opened her eyes, she appeared dazed, it was almost as though she was in the same trance that Hamish found himself in. Hamish continued to stare into her eyes, hoping that she would give him some kind of sign that she wanted him.

Hamish watched in fascination as he saw her eyes turn from dazed to confused as she realised her hand was still on him, a small pang of regret passed through Hamish as he realised that soon she would be removing her hand. But Hamish should have known by now that this lass was far from predictable, and he was grateful for that.

To Hamish's great delight, instead of removing her hand Mel started moving it across his chest. Hamish knew he should have stopped her, but he couldn't; the feeling of her hand moving across his body reminded him of the fantasy he had had the first day he saw her. Swallowing a groan, his body twinged with anticipation as her hand continued to explore his chest, but it was nothing like the anticipation he felt as her hand travelled lower, across his abs to finally reset at the top of his kilt. Hamish breath hitched when one of her fingers slipped below the lip of his kilt, reaching for what waited below. Hamish's cock twitched as if begging her to take it in her hands. Hamish couldn't take it any longer, he decided that he was going to have this lass one way or another.

Business could wait, the only thing on his mind right now was sating the lust Mel had provoked. Without thinking about the consequences Hamish grabbed her hand intending to drag her away, but the moment his hand touched her his sanity returned. Hamish finally remembered that his sister was standing about a foot behind them, there was no way he could do what he had been considering doing with his sister standing there. While Hamish was a barbarian, and sometimes forgot that he no longer lived in the forests hiding, it was not a side of himself that he wanted his sister to ever see.

Hamish closed and took a deep breath, trying to rid himself of the disappointment his body was feeling. While Hamish would have liked nothing better than to follow through with his plan, he somehow didn't think his sister would appreciate him dragging her best friend off right in front of her. Hamish was not naive enough to believe that Ceana would not know what was going on, she was married to a Highlander after all, and he had lost count of the amount of times Kessan had dragged his wife off to tend to their needs.

But Hamish knew that even though his sister now lived in 12th Century Scotland, she still possessed her futuristic view's on what was acceptable behaviour and, he speculated that view probably didn't include the ravaging of her best friend in broad daylight, in a barn no less.

Hamish decided that this would have to wait, and he was just about to release Mel's hand, but the heat and need in her eyes were making it difficult to find a sense of civility. While the warrior in him screamed out for satisfaction, the civilised side of him kept his lust in check. With his civilised side in control at the present Hamish decided he would apologise and walk away, but Before he could, Mel seemed to gain some sense of her own.

Hamish watched as a slight blush rose up over her cheeks, which only added to her appeal, and then the fire was back in her eyes. A small smile played at the corner of his mouth as he watched the realisation of what she had just done cross her face.

Mel didn't waste any time thought, she reefed her arm from his grasp and was practically running back to the castle before he could utter a word. Hamish continued to watch her, even after his sisters slight cough tried to gain his attention. Hamish knew that he should explain his behaviour to Ceana, but he couldn't quite take his eyes off Mel, and if he was being honest with himself he wasn't even sure where to start explaining this to her.

It was only after Mel had disappeared inside that the spell was broken and he could face Ceana. Hamish braced himself for the onslaught that was sure to come, he was expecting his sister to warn him away from her friend. Hamish wasn't going to listen of course, after this little encounter no-one was going to keep him from experiencing all the fire he had seen in the lass's eyes.

While he loved and respected his sister, Ceana was just going to have to get used to the idea that what happened between himself and her friend was none of her business. Folding his arms protectively across his chest, Hamish turned to his sister and prepared himself for a lecture.

"She's pretty incredible, isn't she?" Ceana asked, as she came up placed a soft kiss on his cheek.

Hamish was baffled, he had been expecting Ceana to warn him away from her friend, or at least try and offer some kind of warning. The last thing he had expected his sister to say, was that her friend was incredible, if he didn't know any better he would say that Ceana was trying to get him to seduce her friend. Hamish shook the absurd notion from his mind, there was no way that Ceana would do that.

"Och, aye," he replied cautiously, making sure to keep the emotion out of his reply. He could have easily have lied, but he knew Ceana would not believe that and it would have only raised more questions.

"I knew you were a smart man, Ham!" His sister laughed, before slightly punching his arm.

Hamish narrowed his eyes on his sister before he faced her fully and folded his arms across his chest. Something was not right here.

"What, are ya no' goin' to tell me to stay away from her?" Hamish asked still trying to figure out what was going on.

His question only seemed to add to Ceana's amusement, "Mel's a big girl Ham. She can look after herself, she doesn't need me or anyone else fighting her battles. As for you though, all I have to say is good luck." And with that last cryptic comment hanging in the air, Ceana gave him one last hug before she left him standing in the bailey, trying to process what the hell had just happened.

A few moments passed before Hamish shook his head clearing it from all the confusion. He gave up trying to figure these women out and, remembering that the messenger was still waiting for him in the keep, he realised that he'd been wasting time. Cursing his own stupidity, Hamish headed into the stables, washed up and put on a clean shirt before he made his way into the main hall.

Eleven

Putting all thoughts of the lass out of his mind for now, Hamish tried to focus on the matter at hand. Pushing his way through the doors, he entered the main room of the castle and saw that Dougal, was waiting for him. This could only mean bad news; Iain had sent his second in charge, something he wouldn't have done unless things at home were bad. Hamish strode over to the table and poured himself a dram of scotch, he had a feeling that he would need a drink for this, he could feel it in his bones. Drink in hand, leaning against the table Hamish nodded for Dougal to begin, and downed his drink as the young lad began to speak.

"Laird, another village has just been attacked. We were able to stop the bastards afore too much damage was done, och and like last time, they got away."

Hamish cursed in Gaelic, this was the second attack in one month; the bastards were getting bolder! This was not good.

"Iain wanted me to find out what ya wish him ta do." Dougal added.

Hamish took a minute to think, and while he was formulating a plan Kessan came through the door. With still no plan in mind Hamish took the opportunity to fill Kessan in on what had been happening. His brother in law asked a few questions, before he helped Hamish formulate a plan. While Hamish had been bread to be the laird, with all the trouble that had followed his family all his life, he had only had the chance to practice what he had been taught for two years, thankfully Kessan had been doing this a lot longer.

"Och, alright Dougal tell Iain to set up patrols around the remaining villages and to let me ken if anything else happens. Offer aid to any of the villagers that need it and send some men down to help them repair the damage." Hamish ordered. Kessan nodded his approval as he filled both his and Hamish's glasses.

"Also tell him that I will be home on the morrow. There is no need for me to stay here any longer; I can return here when 'tis needed." Hamish added. He was torn, he wanted desperately to stay here and get to know the lass better, but his clan came first.

"Laird, there is no need for that, Iain said to tell ya that, if ya planned to come home, not ta. We will manage another week without ya. He just wanted to check with ya on what yer orders were ta be."

Reluctantly, Hamish nodded his understanding. While he wanted to be at his keep to help, he also knew that a highlander's pride was easily insulted when it came to matters of war. Hamish knew that he would insult Iain if he went home now and under minded his ability. Commanders were expected to be able to look after things while the laird was away, and his presence now would only undermine Iain's authority, and Hamish could not do that to his loyal friend. Iain had been by his side from the moment they were young lads, and he had stuck by his family during the darkness that had seen them lose everything.

Hamish placed his hand on Dougal's shoulder and nodded his understanding.

"Och, when ya leave, Dougal, take some of my men with ya to help with the village and the patrol." Kessan offered up as a compromise. Hamish offered Kessan a nod in appreciation, at least Iain would have the manpower he needed to keep his clan safe.

"Och, thank ya laird." Dougal bowed in acceptance then turned to Hamish, "Is there anything else ya want me to tell the commander?" Dougal asked.

Hamish thought on it for a moment before he added, "nay that is all for now. Let Iain know that I will send someone to him if I think of anything else." He gave permission for Dougal to go get a fresh horse, and to round up some of Kessan's men. Dougal gave his thanks and left the room.

"What are ya gonna do about the Macintoshes'?" Kessan asked Hamish after Dougal had left the hall.

"Simple, I'm going to kill whoever is behind the raids. With any luck that will send a message to the rest of the outlaws." Hamish replied, venom lacing his voice. There was only one thing he hated more than taking a man's life, and that was a traitor. But Hamish would not hesitate taking the life of the person responsible for this trouble, no self-respecting highlander would ever hurt women and children. With that through in his mind, Hamish finished his ale, then headed for the door.

He needed time to think about what the best plan would be for capturing the outlaws. It was hard to know what the right move as, sometimes being laird was a pain in the arse, he wasn't only responsible for his own life, but he was responsible for every member of his clan.

One wrong move could not only end his life, it could end in the deaths of people who depended on him; not just his men, but women and children as well. People he had known all his life. Right now, he needed a better plan, then watching and waiting, they needed to get ahead of the outlaws.

Hamish knew that sending men out to the villages to petrol the boarders would not stop the bastards. No, all it was likely to do was make them determined to come after him sooner. And, if he were honest with himself, he couldn't wait, Hamish would rather they attack him than his clan, if anything he was going to relish bathing in their blood. It would be the sweetest revenge for all the women they had raped, children they had killed and damage they had done.

But, he needed to come up with a plan that would allow him to leave here, the last thing he needed was for them to make trouble here. While he wanted revenge for what the bastards had done, Hamish had to make sure that his family was unharmed in the process.

With plan after plan forming in his mind, Hamish walked through the door and out into the bailey, he headed back to the stables and saddled his horse. Hamish needed some space and time, trouble was coming, and he needed to be ready.

Twelve

M el still couldn't believe she was here, she had been having so much fun with Ceana and the gang, so much so that two weeks had already flown by and she was, surprisingly, in no rush to go home. The only bummer that was facing her now was that Tristan would be leaving tomorrow, unlike herself, he had only opted to stay for two weeks.

"Do you really have to go?" Ceana was asking him for the hundredth time at dinner.

Mel could understand her friends dismay as she also wished he didn't have to leave, spending quality time with everyone over the last few weeks had been a balm to her soul. Being here with them all had felt like home and it was as if everything was back to the way it should be, just like it had been when they were younger, carefree. Mel was not only going to miss him, she was worried for him, her instinct was telling her that the moment Tristan left, she would never feel that way again. Her gut was telling her not to let him go, because one he did everything would change.

"You know I do Cee; I have to get back. I leave for duty again in a couple of days," he said.

Mel was surprised to hear anger enter his voice, and when she looked at him closely she could see that there was a fire in his eyes which matched that anger. Mel's intuition started running wild once more and she got the feeling that he was not telling them everything. In fact she wouldn't mind betting that for Tristan this wasn't just any ordinary tour and it had to do with whatever was bothering him.

Over the last couple of weeks, both her and Ceana had tried to get answers out of Tristan, but every time they brought up the subject of his last mission, or why he had come home early, he managed to avoid answering, and now time was running out and Mel was sacred that she would never get the true story from him.

"I know, it's just that I miss seeing you." Ceana sniffed with moist, teary eyes. Tristan looked at Mel and shook his head at his sister's behaviour. Mel smiled back, it was so unlike Ceana to be this emotional, but since she had been away from her brother for so long, they understood. Plus, the pregnancy didn't help.

"I don't remember her being this sooky when she was pregnant with the twins," Tristan joked as he playfully tickled Camden who was sitting in his uncle's lap.

Mel laughed when Cee's daughter jumped down from her father's lap, where she had been happily eating her dinner and ran too where her brother and uncle were playing. It didn't take long for Cara to scramble up to join her brother on Tristan's lap. Tristan looked momentarily surprised to find himself holding both twins and Mel smiled as she watched the three of them wrestle and joke around.

"Uncle Tris, mummy is right, why can't ya stay with us a wee bit longer?" Camden asked.

"Och aye," Cara followed, "Papa make him stay." She pleaded, throwing her little arms around Tristan's neck as she turned her big green eyes on her father. "Och and maybe ya can get Uncle Cal and Aunt Bata ta stay as well; that way we can play with Marcus." Cara had turned towards Katie who was feeding Marcus and gave Katie, her trademark puppy dogs eyes, when she added the last bit. Katie, much like the rest of the woman in the family were immune to such a look and Mel was not surprised when Katie laughed it off.

"Oh God, do you hear that accent Mel? Even my niece and nephew are starting to sound like barbarians." Tristan piped in while winking at her.

Mel laughed once more as a piece of bread flew across the table and hit him in the head, both children joined in her merriment and giggled hysterically. They were the most adorable things Mel had ever seen and she was struck by how much she truly missed them all. Her laughter soon turned to melancholy as she realised that she was missing out on a large part of her best friend's life, the way it was going Mel was going to miss out these cherubs growing up.

"What was that for?" Tristan asked, feigning hurt.

"That was for insulting my husband, and for leaving too early, you jackass." Ceana glared at him through wet eyes.

Setting the children back on the floor, Tristan stood up and walked around to join his sister on the other side of the table. Mel could see the love in his eyes as he took Cee's hand in his. "I promise, Cee, once this mission is over you will see a lot more of me," as he spoke with his sister, Mel noticed that the determination was back in his voice. While that determination eased her concern a little, Mel couldn't shake the feeling that something bad was coming their way. Ceana, on the other hand, was placated for the moment, but Mel knew they would go through the same process again tomorrow.

An hour later dinner ended and everyone went about their usual nightly rituals. Katie and Caelan with baby Marcus headed outside to go for a moonlight walk, Tristan went to bed, Kessan and Hamish disappeared to discuss clan business and after putting the kids to bed, Mel sat with Ceana, enjoying a rare moment alone with her best friend. Mel had expected Ceana to start talking Tristan, but tonight she guessed her friend need a distraction from everything that was going on.

"Tell me more about Jack." Ceana asked as they got comfortable in the chairs by the fire.

Mel rolled her eyes, "what more do you want me to tell you, I practically spilled my guts to you today."

"Come on Mel I need something to cheer me up." Mel considered Ceana for a moment more then decided to do just that. She went ahead and told her best friend some of the more outlandish moments she'd had with Jack over the year they had been together. By the end of her stories Ceana was in fits of laughter, Tristan's impending departure all but forgotten.

"How the hell did you last this long with him? I would have shot him months ago."

"You know Cee, I ask myself that question all the time." She said honestly. Ceana opened her mouth to reply when Thora entered the dining room.

"Och sorry, I didn't mean to interrupt you." She apologised. Ceana gave her a smile as she got up to hug the young woman.

"You don't have to apologise. Did you need something?" Ceana asked. Mel was once more reminded how much Ceana had grown since moving to the highlands, she supposed it had to do with the fact that her friend was married to a highland Laird and with that came the responsibility of the whole clan.

"Well, I was just goin to ask ya for some advice, but I can come back later." Mel watched as Thora wrung her hands in front of the dress. The young woman looked nervous and although Mel could tell that Thora wanted to stay and talk to Ceana.

"Don't be silly." Ceana waved her hand. "Sit, perhaps Mel may be able to help too." She added, letting Mel know in her subtle way that she wanted her to stay.

Mel gave Thora a warm smile, she liked the girl, even though she hadn't spent that much time with her, and unbeknownst to anyone Thora had just given Mel the perfect opportunity to change the subject from what was happening back home. Quite frankly Mel didn't want to discuss home anymore, as all it was doing was reminding her that soon she would be back there having to deal with it all again.

"I would be glad to help." Mel said with sincerity giving the girl the opportunity to decline. When the Thora sat down across from them, Mel added. "Besides, I am an excellent advice giver. How do you think Ceana ended up so smart?"

Ceana snorted. "Don't listen to her Thora, *she's* the reason I ended up in trouble half the time." Thora laughed, Mel was glad to see the girls shoulders relax a little.

"Now tell us the problem," Ceana urged, once Thora had taken her seat.

Mel watched as Thora's eyes darted around the room to make sure that no-one else was around, she then leaned forward in her chair and spoke just above a whisper. "Och, well, If I may be so bold, I was wondering if I ken ask ya a question about men."

"Men?" Ceana asked in surprise. Mel had to cover her smile with her hand at her friends reaction. Of course the young woman wanted to ask about men.

Thora nodded. Mel continued to smile as she watched her friend shift in her seat a little before swallowing and asking.

"What exactly do you wish to know."

Whatever Mel had been expecting Thora to ask it was not what came out of Thora's mouth next. "I was wondering if you could explain to me how ye got Kessan to stop thinking about the job and notice ye?"

The blush that stained Thora's cheeks told Mel that she was a little nervous and had never had this frank of a conversation before. *Man these highlanders really were old school.* Ceana shot Mel a look begging her to help, but before either of them could answer, Thora rushed on, "I am normally not so bold, but I doona have anyone else I can talk to aboot this, after all tis no' like I can talk to my brothers. Could ye imagine what they would do to the lad."

The dejection on Thora's face had Mel remembering the times she had tried to talk to her own brothers about her love life. Yep, she felt exactly where the girl was coming from, a and Mel's brothers were from the 21st century where it was normal for a girl to sleep with a man before marriage. Just picturing how 12th century highlanders would react brought a chuckle to her lips.

"No I suppose not; I can just see the vein popping out on Kessan's head now." She added.

Ceana hit Mel lightly on the shoulder. "Not helping!"

"Sorry." Mel said trying to keep a straight face and failing miserably. It did however help Thora relax some more, the young woman smiled at Mel.

"Who, may I ask, is the gentleman you wish to gain the attention of?" Mel questioned. She had asked the question not expecting an answer of course but she had not been expecting the reaction she'd gotten either.

"I would rather no' say," Thora blushed once more. Mel's curiosity was sparked, and the sparkle in Ceana's eye indicated that Cee was just as curious to find out who he was. For now though Mel decided to play along and give the young woman advice, at least she might be able to help one highland woman become more independent.

"Alright then, do you have reason to believe that this gentleman has feelings for you?" Mel tried.

"Aye, but he is stubborn and refuses to listen to reasons. He has his mind set on getting himself killed and I don't know how to stop him." She answered unhappily.

Mel didn't miss the love and worry that filled the girl's voice when Thora talked about her mystery man. Mel was once more filled with a longing to have that kind of love. How was it possible that this young woman who was barely out of the schoolroom had found what she had been trying her whole grown life to achieve.

"In that case, the best thing to do is to tell him how you feel.

Perhaps if he feels the same way he will give up on the mission. It's time to remind him how much you mean to him." Ceana advised.

Mel looked at her friend, of course she would know what to do, she had won Kessan's heart after all. Mel thought about her friend's relationship and everything Ceana and Kessan had been through and then it hit her, turning to Thora Mel added "give him something to live for Thora." Ceana nodded in agreement.

Thora sat contemplating what they had said for a few minutes, Mel thought she might disagree but when he smile spread across her face Mel knew they had helped. "Och, thank ya, for yer advice ya have given me much to consider." Thora stood up and offered them both a slight curtsy.

"No problem! You are now my sister and you can come to me for anything anytime." Ceana offered as she too stood and gave Thora another hug. Thora then wished them both a good night before she headed off into the darkened hallway outside of the dining room.

"I wonder who the lucky highlander is..." Ceana spoke thoughtfully after Thora was well and truly out of earshot.

"I haven't a clue, but you had better tell me when you find out!" Mel said, also curious now as too who would be stupid enough to mess around with the laird's sister. Whoever it was had to be as bold and brave as the young woman was. It took a lot of courage to pursue something that was not easy, and Mel only wished that she had the strength to do the same one day.

Thirteen

After Thora left, Ceana and Mel went back to chatting about anything and everything, loath to have the night end. Currently, Ceana was telling her about all the mischief the twins got into.

"I swear Mel, I never realised how hard it would be to raise

children in the 12th century. Some days I feel like I am losing control and that my children will turn into heathens."

"Really, compared to what we have to deal with at home? At least here you don't have to worry about them being victims of the modern day troubles like drugs, kidnappings or bullying." Mel was not naive enough to think that 12th century Scotland didn't have its issues, Mel was just trying to put some perspective in her friends life to stop her from worrying about the future.

Ceana sighed. "I know that, but while I don't have to worry about the issues of the 21st century, I do have to worry about other things."

"Surely they can't be that bad?" Mel asked with humour lacing her voice. She half expected that Ceana's worries were doubled by the pregnancy. She was just feeling a little overwhelmed Mel was sure.

"Oh you think so do you? Well let me tell you how the other day Camden thought it would be a great idea to see if he could pick up his father's sword. A sword mind you that is twice his size and sharp enough to pierce a man's armour. I almost had a heart attack. All I could picture was him dropping it and chopping off his foot."

Mel could just picture the little imp trying to become just like Kessan. Camden might only be four-years-old, but in his heart, he was a tough warrior just like his father. Mel smiled as friend rubbed her belly. "Some days I would kill for some 21st century luxuries like cartoons, especially on rainy days. And what makes it worse is every time I think about what I will have to give up with this baby I cry. For God sake Mel I'm not going to have access to disposable nappies and wipes." Ceana sighed. Mel know her friend was being overdramatic, but she played along anyway.

"You know there *is* an easy solution." Mel joked.

"And that would be?"

"You could come home." Mel quipped.

Cee laughed, "I'm sure my hubby would love that." Cee had

told Mel of Kessan's struggle in the modern-day world and she knew it be the last thing Kessan would want. He was a true-blue highlander, and this was where he belonged, which unfortunately meant that this is where her best friend belonged, because if Mel knew one thing to be sure it was that Ceana would never leave Kessan.

After they joked a bit more on what Ceana could do they continued to talk for about another hour and as much as Mel wanted to continue into the night she could tell that Ceana was tired. For the last half an hour Cee had been yawning non-stop, and Mel knew that she wouldn't go to bed, unless Mel went first. While neither of them wanted to disrupt their time together, Cee needed her sleep, so Mel being the best friend that she was did the only thing she could. Exaggerating a yawn, Mel stood, stretched her arms above her head and pushed out of her chair. "Well I'm going to call it a night."

The relief in Cee's eyes at the thought of going to bed almost had Mel laughing once more. Mel waited until Ceana stood, then she gave her hug, thanked her for the night and headed up to her own room. *God she had missed this.* As eh climbed the stairs she thought back on the weeks she had spent here, while Mel had been going on with her normal life, she hadn't realised how much she had missed seeing Ceana, Katie and Tristan every day until just now. It had become so much a part of her life over the years that she didn't comprehend how important it was until they were gone. And this month had been the first time in over two years that they had all been in the same place at the same time.

As Mel wandered down the hallway to her bed, she reflected fondly on all the good times they had spent together over the years, from night singing karaoke to days spent at the beach. Memory after Memory flooded her mind, but Mel was abruptly brought out of her musing at the sound of arguing voices. At first they were quiet but as she continued walking down the halls, more quietly than before, they become louder.

She didn't know where it was coming from until she was right on top of the arguing voices, only then did Mel realise the argument was coming from Tristan's room. Mel had never heard Tristan so angry and she couldn't fathom who would be yelling at him, Katie was still with Caelan and she had just left Ceana down in the hall. The intrigue was killing her, edging closer to his door Mel tried to make out what was going on, but the voices while loud and angry, where muffled by the thick timber of the door.

Mel knew she should probably just continue onto her room, but she stood there staring at Tristan's door debating whether she should interrupt and see what the problem was. It only took a few more minutes of listening to the argument for Mel to make up her mind, reaching out for the door she was getting ready to knock but was surprised, when it was yanked open.

Mel was stunned to see who was standing on the other side of the door, it was last person Mel thought would be there. But there she stood in the doorway fuming. Thora had her back to Mel and was facing into the room, so she didn't see her standing there. Mel could not see Thora's face but one thing was clear, from the tone she was using as well as her demeanour, Thora was mad.

"I willnae let ya do this, Tris!"

"There is nothing you can do to stop it Tor, please understand!" Thora tensed and balled her hands at her side in anger, "Damn

ye, ye pigheaded Sassenach!" Thora added a few more words in what Mel assumed was Gallic before she furiously before she marched out the door and in the opposite direction, still not noticing Mel, who had now taken a step back to give them some privacy.

Mel stood there gaping after Thora's retreating back. She wasn't sure what shocked her more; the fact that Thora had been in Tristan's room, their lack of formality with each other, or that the sweet girl Mel had talked to just hours ago, had just as much of a temper as her brothers. Whenever Mel had spoken to Thora over the last two weeks, she had seemed so meek and mild, obviously not!

When Thora had disappeared out of sight Mel turned back to the doorway and realised that Tristan was preparing to shut the door before he caught sight of her.

"I hope your life insurance is up to date." She joked trying to lighten the chilly atmosphere.

"Bite me Mel!" He snapped.

Mel was surprised at the defensive tone she heard in his voice, in all the years that Mel had known Tristan he had never let someone's good natured ribbing get to him, especially not hers. As Mel stood there trying to figure out what was going on flashes of incidents over the last two weeks involving Tristan and Thora started to make sense.

On one occasion, Mel had entered a room where Tristan and Thora had been talking, they'd stopped, stepped back from each other and looked awkwardly at her as she approached. Mel hadn't thought anything of it at the time, but now she also remembered the slight blush that spread over Thora's face, and Tristan had acted as guilty as Hell.

That wasn't the only time they had acted strongly either, on rare occasions neither of them joined in group activities, instead they had disappeared claiming to have needed some alone time . Something was definitely going on here, then the conversation that had occurred downstairs not two hours ago hit her. But it wasn't what Thora had asked them that bothered her, no Mel remembered how worried Thora had been about Tristan and his so called mission he was on and Mel's instincts kicked up again causing her alarm.

"Tristan?" It was a simple question, but he knew what she wanted.

"It's nothing Mel, seriously. You have nothing to worry about." Tristan would not look at her, he simply stood at the door holding the door knob and looking at the floor. She could tell that he wanted her to leave, but she could not do that.

Giving him a dubious look, Mel tried again. "It didn't sound like nothing." When Tristan still didn't say anything anger swelled up in her and she took a step forward placing her hand on the door to make sure he could not close it on her. " I swear Tristan, if you don't start talking now, I am going to go and tell Ceana what just happened."

"How about you mind your own damn business." He spat as he

finally looked at her, what happened next though surprised Mel even more than the fight had. Tristan placed his hand against her shoulder and shoved her out the door before slamming it in her face. Mel stood there in shock, she was not sure if it was from his

harsh words or the fact that he had pushed her out of his room. Mel had never known Tristan to be that rude, but as she stood there trying to comprehend what had happened and why he would be so defensive more of the conversation from earlier came flooding back. Mel did not hold back, grabbing hold of the door knob she reefed open his door and simply marched into his room, she was not going to wait for him to deny her entry again. "Oh no you don't buster. You have five seconds to start talking or I'm going straight to Kessan!"

Mel should have been worried by the anger that came over Tristan's face when he turned around to face her, but her own anger was too high, she just couldn't let this go. Tristan had to be the man Thora was talking about just a few hours ago. The idea of them together however was not what horrid her the most, it was what Thora had said about him. Thora had stated that man she loved had his mind set on getting himself killed, and that Mel could not let go!

"Nothing is going on, Mel." He tried again, but seeing that he wouldn't look at her told her he was lying, instead he started to pack his bags.

"Try again," she fired back vehemently, walking to the side of the bed and grabbing his bag so he could not pack it.

Tristan sighed and finally looked at her before he spoke. "Look Mel, it's over ok, I am going home, and I will likely never see the girl again. So, you see there is nothing to be concerned over, and there is no reason you should get *Kessan* involved, all it will do is make her life Hell when I am gone."

Mel couldn't believe that he thought she was upset about his and Thora's relationship, the girl was old enough to make her own choices. "For Christ sake Tristan, I don't give a damn about you and Thora, what I give a damn about is you trying to get yourself killed!"

Tristan 's look of regret turned to a look of shock and Mel realised that he finally understood that she knew what was going on. Tristan let out a sigh and sat back on the bed, before looking back at her, he looked so defeated. Mel didn't know how to help him, she didn't know how to get it through his thick skull that he had people who would do anything for him, and she was one of them.

"Thora told you, didn't she?" he asked dejectedly.

Mel only felt a little bit of regret for revealing the girl's confidences, but she needed a way to get through to him and this had been the only way she could do that. Mel was sure that Thora would forgive her if it meant that Tristan was safe. Still Mel wanted to help the girl out as much as possible, and so she told him the truth.

"Look don't be mad at Thora, all she did was ask for some advice on how to get you to notice her. She never mentioned any names, she only mentioned that she wanted to stop someone she cared about from getting themselves killed. It was only after the fight I just witnessed that I put two and two together."

Tristan nodded wearily, "Mel, I know you are all concerned about me, but you all have to realise that this is something I have to do." Mel was about to ask him what exactly that something was, but before she could held his hand up to halt any more questions than continued. "Before you ask, I can't explain what that is right now as it is still too painful to think about, let alone talk about. But I need you to understand and accept that I can't let this go, so please don't ask me to!"

Tristan had finally let down some of his guard and the pain that she saw in his eyes was soul shattering. Whatever had happened on his last mission had finally broken the last innocent piece of Tristan that was left. Walking forward Mel pulled his head close to her body and hugged him.

"I can't stop you, can I?" she asked on a broken whisper.

Tristan didn't answer but she felt him shake his head. Tears pricked the back of her eyes, she tilted his head back gently so that she could look into his eyes, "then promise me you will stay as safe as possible. Do not do anything unnecessarily dangerous to get yourself killed."

Mel watched as he considered what she had asked, and it wasn't until he nodded that she let out the breath she had been holding. "There is one other thing, I *will* be telling Ceana about this." The last thing Mel wanted to do was make Tristan mad again, but this was not a secret she could keep from her best friend, and he shouldn't have expected her too. Mel could see that he wanted to argue with her, but he just nodded.

"Could you at least wait until I'm gone?" He pleaded.

Mel was of two minds, she hated keeping anything from her best friend, but telling her would only cause her to worry and cause a fight between the siblings. With Tristan going off to battle his demons, the last thing any of them needed was for their last words to be ones they would regret. No good would come of her telling her just yet.

"Fine, but I'm not doing it for you." She spat at him.

"Liar" he said weakly. "Now get out of here so I can finish packing."

Mel released him and reluctantly walked to the door. "Mel..."

She stopped and turned back to Tristan and for the first time in days, he looked like that young boy she had known.

"I love you, you know that, right?" He said as he looked at her earnestly.

Mel's heart broke a little for him. "Yeah, I do Tris, and please remember that there are people here who love you too and would be shattered if anything happened to you, me included."

Mel moved back to him, Tristan stood this time and she hugged him close once more. Her intuition alarms were ringing loudly, the bad feeling that she was feeling was telling her that this was going to be the last times she saw him, and yet there was nothing she could do. "Please stay safe." She pleaded once more before she left the room, tears now running down her face, her heart heavy.

Mel practically ran to her room and as she entered, she sent up a silent prayer to anyone who would listen to keep him safe. Then she curled up on her own bed and cried herself to sleep.

Fourteen

The next morning came quicker than Mel wanted it to, she had not gotten much sleep last night as her dreams were filled with nightmares of Tristan's death. Mel spent the morning having breakfast with them while trying to keep up her happy appearance, then all too soon Tristan was leaving. Currently they were all standing out in the bailey saying their good byes, Tristan grabbed his sister in for one more hug and he held her close while she cried. "Can't you just stay for a couple more weeks?" Ceana pleaded.

Tristan laughed lightly. "Cee, we have been through this, you know I can't," he said giving her a kiss on her cheek. The twins were next: they were crying, wanting their uncle to stay, but once he had given them one final kiss, with promises that they would see him soon, they forgot their tears and ran off to see what Brodie was doing with the horses.

Katie came forward then and gave him a quick hug, their goodbye wasn't as emotional as Cee's, Katie probably believed that she would see him when she returned home, Mel hoped that Katie was right. The burden of her secret still encasing her heart, Mel wanted to shout the truth out to Cee and make her stop him from going, but she knew that it would do her no good. It would only cause more turmoil; Tristan was determined to leave and Ceana was in no condition to handle any more stress. When it finally came to her turn, Mel couldn't believe that he was going to go through with it and that she couldn't do a damn thing about it. She let her anger out the only way she could, balling up her fist Mel punched him.

"Ouch, what was that for?" he asked warily. Mel could see the worry in his eyes as he silently begged her to keep his secret.

"That's for leaving me you lout. You were meant to stay here with me; after all, you are the only other outsider here. Not to mention you're also making me go through that hell of a portal by myself." She said grumpily as she pulled him in for a hug. Mel wanted to rage at him for making her worry about him and his mission as well but she knew she couldn't.

As Mel hugged Tristan she felt him let out a small, relieved breath before keeping up the charade, "I'm sure you will be fine Short Fry, besides just think you now have two weeks free again since you won't have to be my slave anymore" He joked returning her hug.

"You had better remember your promise. If you get yourself killed, I will hunt you down and kill you again," Mel hissed in his ear so that no-one would hear her as she hugged him tighter not wanting to let go.

Tristan gave a short snort. "You realise how illogical that sounded don't you?" he teased.

"I'm serious Tristan. Don't make me regret this."

Tristan pulled back and looked her in the eyes so she could see that he meant what he said. "I promise Mel; I will try to come home in one piece." He whispered in a low tone. Mel wanted more, but she knew that was the best she would get out of him.

"You had better go before I do something stupid, please stay safe," she ordered him, holding back the tears as she let go of him. Tristan gave her a curt nod, as he stepped back. Mel had expected to see him get on his horse and leave right away, instead he stood there looking quickly around the Bailey. When a look of disappointment passed his eyes, she realised that he had been looking for Thora. It was only then that Mel realised she was the only one that hadn't come to see him off.

"You had to expect this Tristan, she cannot in good faith send you on your way as though it doesn't matter." Mel said as she placed her hand on his arm.

Tristan looked at her with sadness lacing his eyes, "you seemed to manage." He half-heartedly joked.

"It's different and you know it, it's not easy for me to do, so I can only imagine how hard it would be for her."

Tristan thought on that a moment before he nodded his head. "Please tell her I am sorry, and look out for her."

Mel simply nodded letting him know that she would do as he asked. Tristan took a deep breath before he finally moved away and mounted his horse. With a huge smile on his face, that Mel was convinced was just for show, Tristan gave one last wave and then followed Caelan out of the bailey towards the waterfall. And just like that, Tristan was gone, Ceana came up to stand beside her as they continued to stare at the gates, just hoping he would come back. But he didn't

"I am so glad you aren't going home yet. I could not have handled both of you leaving today." Ceana sobbed as she pulled Mel in for a hug.

Mel returned the hug, needing to feel her friend's arms around her. "I'm glad too, Cee, I really am." As the words left her mouth Mel was surprised to find she actually meant them.

She wasn't ready to leave this place yet and face reality. Mel had been shocked at how much she'd quickly become used to life here. Apart from the lack of plumbing, everything else was magnificent. She loved the fresh air, the wilderness, the people, and even Hamish was growing on her. Over the past week, Hamish had been involved in many of the gatherings and activities that Ceana and the others had organised. During that time Mel had gotten to know him a little better, and what she had come to learn was that she was not as opposed to him as she'd first thought herself.

Thankfully, they'd both managed to rein in whatever that initial spark had been and had started to interact more with each other on a social level. There were still moments of course where the spark would decide to rear its ugly head and make her rethink everything. Like occasionally Mel had been startled when she caught him looking at her with something she could have sworn was raw lust in his eyes. The frustrating thing was Mel was not sure if it was lust or not as he'd mask it as soon as their eyes met. Mel was not sure she wanted him looking at her with luck, because the problem was she had often found herself staring at him longingly when she thought no one was looking, and if the two of them let that lust rule them they would end up in a whole world of trouble.

Who was she fooling? She knew it had to be her imagination

playing tricks on her. After all, why would this magnificent highlander be interested in her? Mel shrugged it off and decided that those first intense moments had been nothing more than her own humiliating lack of control. It must have been triggered by the unfamiliarity and shock of travelling to a different time and world, she reasoned to herself, desperate for an explanation.

Time travel sickness? Portal lag?

After all there had only been the one kiss and that godawful embarrassing moment in front of Ceana. Mel had been so embarrassed after that and she had dreaded seeing him again, but thankfully, he never approached her about it and he had been courteous to her ever since; almost like it never happened. Mel was convinced more than ever that whatever it had been was going, even if the times they'd found themselves together often involved over twenty other people if he had wanted to make a move he would have found a way. While Mel had decided that there was nothing there she still admired him.

"What do you think?" Cee asked bringing Mel back to the present. Mel had no idea what Cee was talking about, her mind was a mess. She wondered if she had done the right thing. Should she have let him leave? Should she have done more to stop him? What he ended up getting himself killed, how was she going to explain that to his sisters? With all the emotions from the past week mixed with the guilt she was feeling Mel needed some time alone, in the past two weeks, she hadn't had much of that. Mel could feel her body filling with stress, and she felt a minor panic attack coming on.

"Cee is there a quiet, safe place I could go outside of the castle for a few minutes alone?" She asked her friend, desperate to be anywhere but here.

"Is everything ok?" Cee asked, her voice filled with concern. Mel felt guilty for making her friend worry, she hadn't meant too, but the need to be alone was overwhelming her.

"Yes, of course it is, please don't worry, it's just that in the last two weeks, I feel as though I have constantly been surrounded by people, most of whom I don't know. You know me, when it comes to crowded places, sometimes I get the feeling that everything is closing in on me and I just need a few minutes by myself to think." Mel was pleased to see the look of worry leave Ceana's eyes, but was surprised at the look that replaced it.

"I know the perfect place!" Cee replied with an overly enthusiastic grin.

Was she scheming? *Cee often got that look when she was up to something* her intuition warned her. Confused for a moment, Mel dismissed the feeling. It was probably just her imagination anyway, she'd been reading too much into expressions lately and besides, what did she have to scheme about? Cana was oblivious to Mel's concern and just kept on talking "If you head down that path just beyond the gate and walk about a kilometre out of the village, you will come to a very private glen with the most wonderful little river that feeds into a pond. It is very secluded and peaceful so it should provide you with the privacy you want." Ceana was pointing towards a patch of trees off in the distance that did indeed look private, it was perfect.

Excitement was once again rushing through Mel's blood. She couldn't to get some alone time and consider everything that had happened since she had arrived. It would also give her a chance to formulate a plan for telling Ceana what was going on with Tristan. With that in mind Mel took a step away from her friend towards the gate, but an afterthought had her stopping in her tracks.

"Will I be safe there?" Mel asked, trepidation in her voice. Yes she had been out into the village with Ceana many times, in the past few weeks, but this would be the first time Mel would be alone in the century. "I mean, there are no wild animals that will try and eat me or anything is there?" Mel realised her question may have sounded a little stupid, but what did she know about 12th Century Scotland? They could be using wolves as pets for all she knew.

Ceana laughed. "Oh, there are *definitely* no wild animals down there."

Mel was momentarily suspicious again at the humour she heard behind her friends tone. Mel once again wondered at her game, there was something in her tone and her mood had picked up. Obviously, Ceana found something amusing and Mel was determined to find out what that was, but not right now. Right now, all she wanted was some peace and quiet and the glen was beckoning to her, everything else could wait an hour or two. Giving Ceana a quick hug in thanks, Mel started off towards the village; her step a little lighter, her mind a little clearer. Maybe today wouldn't' be so bad after all, maybe it might just surprise her.

Fifteen

Ceana watched her friend go happiness once again filling her heart. Once Mel was out of sight, a mischievous smile spread across Ceana's face, she knew that she would have hell to pay when Mel returned, but right now, she didn't care. Just thinking of Mel's question about wild animals made her chuckle. "You should be more worried about the wild man down there." Ceana commented to herself. She knew she should have probably felt a little guilty about sending Mel down there with no warning, but she was sick and tired of seeing the lonely look in her friend's eyes. Besides if she left it up to the two of them, Ceana would be waiting another century for them to realise what she had known form the start, they were meant for each other.

"What has you smiling?" Her husband asked as he came up from the stables to give her a kiss. Ceana sank into Kessan's kiss and lingered on his lips a little longer than she should have. Even after two years of marriage Ceana was in awe at how this highlander was her mate. Never in her wildest dreams could she have imagined a more perfect partner in life. And that was all she wanted for her friend, someone who would cherish Mel the way Kessan cherished her.

"Why you, of course, my dear husband." Cee answered him sassily. Kessan snorted, she should have known she wouldn't be able to get anything past her husband.

"Cee, Lass, I ken when ye are up to mischief. And right now I would say that ye knee deep in it." Ceana laughed, she couldn't help it, he seemed so serious. Her poor husband was still getting used to her ways, and what he called mischief she called ingenuity.

"Whatever Trevor," she replied, "I'm up to nothing of the sort, I am just glad to have my friend here." She hedged. Ceana smiled as her husband narrowed his eyes on her, she loved that he knew her so well.

"Och, we will see," he said, giving her a kiss before he walked away into the keep.

"Oh yes we shall," Ceana breathed. If things went as planned and she got her way, Ceana would bay happy like this for days to come as she would have her friend here a lot longer than just another two weeks more weeks. Giving the direction Mel went one more glance, Ceana decided she would just have to wait and see what happened. With that in mind she turned on her heels to follow her husband inside, she didn't need to make it obvious that she was plotting and if she was still standing here when Mel came back, that would positively give the game away.

Sixteen

As Mel wandered through the village enjoying the freedom of being on her own, she was again struck by the simplicity of life here. Everyone was busy, and yet, they all appeared content. Kids ran free chasing animals, playing games, or helping their parents, oblivious to the dangers that surrounded them. They were safe, they didn't have to worry about drugs, guns or anything else that plagued the youth of modern society.

She wasn't naive enough to think there were no worries or fears in this time, but it sure seemed like nothing happened as often as it did back home, it seemed as though every other post of Facebook lately had been of a missing child, or some crime that had been committed. Too Mel it seemed as though the more sophisticated the world became the more dangerous it brought with it.

Strolling down the road, she took in all the little markets and shops, so different from those back home and yet the same. They sold goods that ranged from cloth and jewellery to animal hides, but it was the bakery at the edge of the village that had her stopping. The wares of this little stall smelt wonderfully warm and enticing and she decided she would get a few bannocks with honey to eat while she lazed by the pond.

Bannocks had become her favourite food in the last two weeks. Unlike the modern day mass produced breads at home, the bread here came in all different flavours; they almost reminded her of the scones her Grandma G.G made. Mel preferred the brown ones that were full of fresh fruit and nuts – not a preservative or additive in sight. When you mixed this with the fresh, untainted honey collected right in the fields out back, it was divine.

Grabbing her treat, Mel paid the baker and then continued onto the glen, her pace a little more hurried now that she was away from everyone else. Mel couldn't wait to see just how peaceful the glen was, she was looking forward to settling down on the grass and enjoying her treat in peace. As Mel drew closer to the glen she hoped it was as beautiful as the one they had stopped at on her first night here.

When she entered a thick forest of trees, moments later, she wasn't disappointed. Ceana was right, it was just perfect; the trees formed a large, dense protective circle that she had to walk through but, as she followed the path further into the forest, it started too thin out. With only a few steps more Mel found herself in the middle of her own private oasis.

To the left, a small creek flowed and cascaded over rocks and boulders bubbling cheerily; it was such a peaceful sound that Mel was instantly transported back to the Firefly Hideaway. Owned and run by Ceana's family, The Hideaway had a creek very similar to this one where Mel had spent hours basking in its tranquillity, escaping life's problems. Unexpectedly, tears formed in Mel's eyes as she was assaulted with the worry over Tristan and the relief of finally being alone.

After the craziness of the last year, this was exactly what she needed, Mel was finally going to be able to relax and Mel had the growing sense that she had just come home and the longer she stood there the more she wondered how she was ever going to leave this place. If it wasn't for her family back home, she just might be tempted to stay.

Walking deeper into the glen, Mel closed her eyes and took a deep breath, letting the sounds and smells wash over her. The musky aroma of the heather that dotted the bank reached her nose, it was a subtle scent which allowed her to breathe in deeply without getting a headache. She would have to remember to consider getting a candle in this scent when she got home, that way she could keep the smell of the highlands in her house always.

As she continued to stand there with her eyes close she could hear the wind rustling through the trees, coupled with the water cascading over the rocks and all the stress just left her body as she relaxed, taking in the tranquil sounds of nature. Mel loathed to move just yet, but a noise from the pool behind her brought her eyes open. Mel turned, heart racing, slightly panicked to find out exactly what disturbed her peace.

Ceana had promised her that there were no wild animals in the area, but how could she be sure. It wasn't a completely ridiculous idea; wild animals were unpredictable, Mel's imagination started to run wild with what types of animals could be in the forest, she looked back at the path and considered leaving, but the call of privacy stopped her from leaving. Turning back towards the pool Mel readied herself to confront whatever animal was there, but the moment her eyes collided with the deep green of Hamish's, she instantly wished it were a wild animal. As he continued to stare at her Mel couldn't move, all she could do was stand there and stare back.

Hamish had obviously been bathing; but now he stood on the bank with only his plaid wrapped around him, water still streaming down his chest from his wet hair. And, just like the last time she'd seen him thusly dressed, she became aware of her heart pounding and her blood rushing though her body. Mel felt her face turn warm and her mouth dry as every nerve in her body screamed out for his touch.

"What are ya doin' here Lass?" Hamish asked when Mel continued to just stand there and stare at him. His voice sounded far away and, as he pushed his hand through his wet hair, Mel tried once more to regain control of her thoughts, but he wasn't helping as he moved nearer.

"Um, Ceana told me that no-one would be here." Mel babbled, hoping that by talking she could keep her hormones at bay. While she was talking though she realised that Cee had said there were no *animals*, she had said nothing about underdressed men! Mel was going to kill her best friend when she got back to the keep. Looking back up the path, Mel tried to judge how quickly she could make her escape, but she didn't like her options. The only choice she had was to wait it out until she could politely take her leave. "What are *you* doing here?"

Mel continued to look everywhere but at the half dressed man in front of her, but when Hamish didn't answer her straight away her eyes were drawn back to him. Mel's heart beat picked up once more and she decided that the best course of action was to make her escape after all. She didn't want to go, but he had been here first and she couldn't very well ask him to leave.

"I'm sorry I bothered you," she said awkwardly, hoping he couldn't see how much his presence unnerved her. Mel started to inch her way towards the path, hoping that he would not stop her. Her eyes never left him, but thankfully he didn't make a move to stop her, instead he stood still, appraising her, silent and pensive. If she had been an irrational person, she might have even said that he was stalking her, like prey.

"What have ya got there?" Hamish asked, breaking through the silence that was starting to unnerve her. Mel tried to focus; her mind on what he was saying by following Hamish's glance, as she stared at the cloth in her hand she remembered the forgotten delicacies.

"Lunch!" Mel replied a little too loudly, relieved to have a distraction from the gorgeous man in front of her. Mel was just starting to get her heart rate under control, but her breath hitched when Hamish started walking towards her once more. Unlike the last time however this time she didn't move, she couldn't have if she had wanted to, her feet felt as though they were clued to the ground. All Mel could do was watch as Hamish stalked towards her, and before she knew what was happening, Hamish was close enough to reach out and pull the cloth-wrapped bannocks from her hands.

Mel should have protested the loss of her treats, but she was too enamoured of the man in front of her to say anything, Mel was a smart woman and yet this man left her speechless. On opening her package a wide smile spread across Hamish's face, that smile sent the butterflies in her stomach into overdrive. A small dimple appeared in his left cheek and it was driving her to distraction.

"Mmm, my favourite!" Hamish cooed as he pulled out one of her honey covered bannocks and took a bite.

Mel just stared up at him silently, watching his jaw work as he ate the bannocks, but when his tongue darted out to lick a drop of honey from his lips, a soft groan escaped her. Mel shot her eyes to the ground as her cheeks scorched with heat, she hoped to God he hadn't heard her. Mel continued to stare at the ground for a few minutes more, but when the silence got to too much for her she dared a quick, embarrassed look into his eyes, but as usual they didn't reveal anything.

Mel had a feeling that he was trying to put her at ease, but watching him eat that morsel of food had the opposite effect. Now that they were alone, all her well-built self-control had departed, but unlike earlier in the week there was no-one else to focus on but him. Mel couldn't believe that she had thought the spark was gone, who had she been trying to kid when she told herself that she was over her attraction to him? When had simply watching someone eat turn her on? She might have been trying to kid herself these past few weeks, but she could no longer do that. Not when all Mel could think about right now was how she wished *she* was that bit of bread he was devouring. Mel body hungered for the same amount of devotion that he was currently showing his fingers as he licked at the excess honey.

He, on the other hand, must be thinking that she was completely nuts. Who wouldn't? After all, Mel wasn't doing or saying anything other than just standing there like an idiot staring at him agape as he ate. *Not creepy at all, Mel!* Embarrassment crept in again, Mel needed to get a hold of herself and fast, before she really made a fool of herself. Shaking herself out of her stupor, Mel turned to leave, as much as she wanted to grab her bannocks, she wanted to get away from him more, she would just have to get some extra ones on her way back to the keep. Mel had only turned slightly however when he stopped her in her tracks, offering her the last piece of the bannock he still currently possessed. This was it, it was crunch time; she either took the bull by the horns or turned tail and ran. Mel continued to look at the treat, and as the honey ran down his fingers she knew she should run, but the moment she looked back into his eyes and saw the challenge there, her fate was sealed.

Pushing all reservation aside, Mel leant forward and took not only the bannocks into her mouth, but also his fingers. Moving closer to him, she grabbed his wrist to stop him from pulling away so that she could get every last bit of honey. The saltiness of his fingers, coupled with the sweetness of the honey played havoc on her senses. Mel couldn't look at him yet as she was worried it would remover her courage. Without thinking she rolled her tongue around his fingers, taking her time before she gave one final lick and released his hand.

Mel took a moment to gather he senses, running her tongue around her lips she removed any of the sticky morsel that remained. Once she felt as though she had her courage Mel lifted her head and looked into his eyes to gauge his reaction to her boldness. But whatever Mel had thought to see was nothing compared to what was there, Mel was undone by the pure lust that radiated from them. As that lust reached her body she could no longer deny her need for him, forgetting everything she had been thinking and just letting instinct take over, Mel reached up grabbed a fistful of his hair and smashed her lips to his.

Mel could not deny the passion that was running rampant in her body anymore, she no longer cared about anything but the man in front of her. Her body pressed firmly against his and she could feel the water that was still streaming down his body seeping into her dress, but she didn't care. The only thing she cared about now was the taste of him. He tasted like the bannocks she had been looking forward to eating, full of fruit and honey. As Mel kissed him the intoxication of honey and him sent her sense into overdrive, she held her breath dreading the moment he would end the kiss. However, it wasn't long before he dropped the cloth with the remaining bannocks, wrapped his arms around her, and deepened the kiss. Mel sent up a prayer of thanks to whoever was listing.

Mel groaned, she had forgotten how good it felt to have this man's arms around her and his lips on hers. Their bodies were so close she could feel his heartbeat pounding in his chest. Mel had never felt hot need like this before, it was as though every nerve ending in her body was on fire and with every touch, her blood ignited more. No matter how Mel tried she couldn't seem to get close enough to him, Hamish must have felt her need as his hands snaked underneath her arse and lifted her so that she could wrap her legs around his waist. The moment her core connected with his hard cock, they both moaned in unison, Mel gripped his hair in her hands harder and kissed him like it was the only thing on earth that would save her.

Mel was lost in the feeling of him, but when she felt him start walking causing his cock to rub against her core, everything around her faded away, all that mattered was this man and what he was doing to her. As Hamish continued to take more steps his lips never left hers, they had become fiercer, almost devouring. Mel had both her hands planted in his hair, she knew that she was gripping it tightly, but she couldn't seem to make herself relax, and with each thrust of his tongue and rub of his cock, she was brought closer to the brink of a climax.

Mel's breath was partially knocked from her body and into his when her back pressed into a tree as he thrust his hips forward, effectively pinning her between his body and the rough bark. Moaning, she dropped her head back until it too, rested against the tree's surface, she was eager for him and wished that he would hurry up and take her. Mel could feel the warmth gather between her thighs, and yet she still wanted more! She was just about ready to beg when he pulled the top of her dress down over her breasts, lowered his head, and took one into his warm, wet mouth. For once, she was glad for the simplicity of 12th Century clothing, and that she had decided to forgo the complicated underwear that had been laid out for her on the first day, never had she been more grateful for that decision!

As Hamish continued to work her breast Mel wasn't sure how much more she could take, she was in ecstasy! Having been so used to the selfish love making style of men at home, she had all but resigned herself to never finding a male who would show her true pleasure. This was nothing like anything she'd ever experienced! Hamish was now moving between both breasts sucking, pulling and nipping at her nipples, sending an intense combination of pleasure and pain shooting through her. Mel was lost to her emotions, she was trying to regain control over her body, her pleasure was instance and she worried that she was going to come right then and there!

As Mel continued to try and gain some control she dimly became aware that he had lifted the hem of her dress and was slowly moving his heated, roughened hands up her thighs to her core. Mel moaned at the sensation, how was he able to do what he was doing, Hamish was still working her breast with his young and mouth as his hands made their way up her legs and together, the combination was exhilarating. Mel didn't know what she wanted, she wanted him to speed up and slow down all at the same time, and in that moment yearning anticipation completely overwhelmed her senses.

The only thing Mel *was* sure of was that if he didn't take her soon, she was going to explode right there in his arms. Digging her fingers into his scalp while pushing her pelvis forward into his groin, Mel silently urged him to give her more. Hamish gave a slight chuckle as his hands moved higher up her thighs, he was so close Mel could almost anticipate what it would feel like to have his fingers inside of her. Her breath caught as one of his fingers reached her core, and when he brushed it against the wetness that was there, her heart stopped for a moment. She had been right, making love to this man was going to be exquisite, Mel waited with anticipation for more, but when he just held his fingers on her thighs close to her core but not touching Mel could have screamed with frustration.

What was he doing? Lifting her head up to see what was going on, she was greeted with his shocked expression.

"Where are ya undergarments Lass?" Hamish asked, his voice hoarse.

"What?" Mel asked confused and disorientated. *Why the hell was he asking her about her underwear?*

Then his question and confusion sunk through to her lust filled mind; a small impish grin spread across her face. "I never wear them." She replied saucily. It was only half a lie; after all Mel had never worn them *here.* Hamish groan was satisfaction enough for her.

"Och, I'm glad I dinnae ken this before," he replied before he began kissing her once more. But this time it was different, as his lips pattered hers, and his tongue entered her mouth, Hamish sunk three of his fingers deep within. In that moment, Mel could no longer hold back, as his fingers continued to spread her wide, and the damn of a yearlong drought was broken, her world exploded.

Seventeen

el had climaxed two more times before Hamish withdrew his fingers; she had to admit the man knew what he was doing. As Mel's head contend to lay against the tree trunk she willed her heart to come back to normal. Then she felt him move her slightly before he moved his kilt to the side, and before Mel had a chance to prepare herself his cock was at the entrance of her core, ready to replace his fingers.

Hamish stood still positioned at the entrance of her womanhood, waiting patiently. Mel briefly wondered what he could be waiting for, but as she looked into his eyes she could see him searching them for something. It took her few minutes to realise that he was waiting for her permission.

Mel removed her hands from his hair and ran them down his body, a small smile spread across her face as each of his muscles twitted under than her administrations. Mel took her time exploring his body until her hands were able to grab his firm buttocks. As her hands rested against the tight muscles a seductive smile spread across her face and Mel winked at him right before she braced her back against the tree. With intense satisfaction, Mel gripped his arse a tighter and pulled him forward, successfully planting his cock deep within her. That was all the permission Hamish needed, thankfully the highlander began to grind his hips against hers, effectively removing and reinserting his thick manhood insider of her over and over again. Throwing her head back, an animal-like moan rose from deep inside Mel as Hamish continued to withdraw and then re-enter her with strong forceful movements.

As Mel continued riding Hamish against the tree, Mel was happy to note that her Scotsman was no simpering gentleman, no, he was a soul shattering warrior and he made love like he fought, powerful and strong. As Hamish's movements became more forceful Mel's nails sunk deeper into his back, urging him on faster, and Hamish drove deeper within her, until she couldn't hold on any longer. Throwing her head back, Mel screamed as her body pulsed around him, she didn't have to worry about being quiet as there was no-one around to hear her. Hamish joined her with his own roar moments later, spilling his seed deep into her womb. The feeling of his warm seed entering her and his cock pulsating deep within her sent Mel cascading over the edge once more.

For several moments neither of them could move, and so they stayed linked together as one, braced against the tree in a glen that was their own private haven. Mel cherished the feeling of Hamish still inside of her, her body still pulsing around him. Mel was pleased to note that she had been able to get Hamish to let down his warrior exterior, no longer where his emotions hidden from her. A small smile played across her lips as she listed to his rapid breathing, Hamish also still had his head down against her shoulder and she could feel his heart hammering against her own chest.

Feeling bolder than she ever had and loathed to lose this connection, the playful side of her took over. Leaning her head to the side a bit Mel took his earlobe into her mouth and gently nipped it. She was pleased to see gooseflesh instantly rise up upon his skin as she ran the lobe through her teeth once more.

"You know, I could get used to this," she whispered as she let go of the lobe. To get her point across she moved her body against his letting him know that she was ready for round two.

"Aye, so could I Lass, so could I" he purred into her shoulder moments before she felt him harden again. His burr sounded thicker, more intense which ignited her senses, once more. But his growing erection was what made her hot and ready for him once more. Mel couldn't believe that she was prepared to go another round so quickly, but never had she experienced sex this incredible before. Never!

Looking down at Mel's flushed face, Hamish found it hard to gain any sense of control over his emotions. He was still reeling with all that had happened since the lass had interrupted his swim. Earlier in the day when Hamish had come down to the glen to bathe, he hadn't expected anyone to interrupt him, but now he was glad that she had. Hamish had known that the lass was bold, he had seen it the first day they had met, but never in his wildest dreams would he have expected this kind of boldness from her. Since the day in the bailey Hamish had spent days making sure to keep his lust in check, if only he had known then how powerful their love making would be, perhaps he wouldn't have waited.

Mel had defiantly surprised him that was for sure, when Hamish had first challenged her, he hadn't expected her to accept his challenge, in hindsight he should have known, as he had seen her competitiveness with Tristan. At first Hamish had only wanted her to stay and talk to him, but when she had taken his fingers in her mouth, an image of her doing that to his cock had his body humming with such raw lust that he had to fight with everything he had to let her take control. That hadn't lasted long however, because before he knew what was happening, she had attacked him in the best kind of way. Just thinking about the way she had purred and melted at his touch had him getting hard again.

Lifting her head up so that she was looking into his eyes once more, Hamish started moving against her, igniting the previous fire that had yet to dwindle.

This was paradise.

As the moans began to escape Mel's mouth Hamish began to move faster and harder and was pleased when her body started to respond again. Hamish watched as Mel's eyes misted with passion and ecstasy, but he couldn't watch for long as the ecstasy he was seeing there brought him closer to reaching another climax, and he wanted to make sure that she climaxed at least once more before he joined her. Hamish could feel her core tightening, and as her moans became more intense and her body moved faster and harder he could feel his release building. Hamish was not sure how much longer he could hold out, but when Mel moaned signalling to him that she was ready he began to let the tension build. They were almost there, he could feel it, Mel's core tightened around his cock and he was sure she was getting ready to explode. That was until a loud whistle sounded through the trees, followed by a voice that broke through their haze of passion.

"Och Laird, I'm truly sorry to bother ya, but Iain is waiting at the keep and he says it is urgent!"

Hamish groaned, as Mel halted their love making mid thrust. He had expected to see embarrassment lace her eyes when he looked at her, instead he found humour. Mel covered her mouth with her hands to cover her moan as he moved inside of her once more before he pushed her hard against the tree effectively pinning her there, as he felt her core tighten around her he groaned and dropped his head on her shoulder, he couldn't be certain but he was sure she was doing it on purpose to drive him crazy. "Can I kill him?" Hamish asked her, not even lifting his head from her shoulder.

Mel giggled; flustered at the interruption, "You had better go." She stated as she started to wriggle against the tree. Her movements however only managed to keep the fire burning and the reluctance he heard in her voice had him not wishing to lose the contact.

"Aye, I had best" he agreed, but didn't move. As much as Hamish knew that he had to go and see why his commander was here, nothing seemed as important at finishing with the lass. Mel's core once more tightened around him as he moved slightly to the left, and Hamish could no longer control his actions. Lifting his head Hamish looked deep into her eyes as he thrust forward, reminding her that they were still joined.

"Are ya sure ya want me to go Lass?" He said moving one more time, making sure that she felt him all the way to her womb. Mel dropped her head back against the tree, closed her eyes and moaned his name. Hamish moved a few more times before he leaned forward and took her breast in his mouth.

"Don't stop" she replied in a hoarse whisper, grabbing his hair once more. Hamish started driving into her with more force once more drawn into the haze of their lovemaking.

"MacDonnell!" Alec's voice interrupted again with more urgency this time. Hamish let out a curse at having forgotten that they were no longer alone. Giving Mel an apologetical glance he removed himself from inside of her. At first Mel had tightened her legs around him trying her hardest to keep him there, but when Alex cleared his throat once more Mel reluctantly unwrapped her legs and lowered herself to the ground.

Hamish looked at her and was in awe at the picture she presented. Her hair was in disarray, and her cheeks were still flushed from their lovemaking. Hamish smiled when he noticed that her breasts were still free from her dress and before he could stop himself he bent down and took one in his mouth, where he sucked it hard before he took possession of her mouth one last time. As he kissed her deeply Hamish took the time to right the top of her dress, but even though she was probably dressed once more it didn't help to curve the passion he was feeling for her.

"We will finish this later Lass," Hamish ground out against her lips before he turned and headed for the path.

The last thing he wanted to do was leave her alone in the glen, but the fact that Iain was here had finally penetrated his lust- filled brain, this could only mean bad news. Hamish stopped and looked back at Mel, and was pleased to see that she was watching him leave. Her eyes still held the passion from lovemaking and her chest rose and feel with the quick breaths. It took everything Hamish had not to re-enter the glen and finish what they had just started. If it had been anyone else but Iain that had called for him, Hamish would have ignored the summons. But Hamish knew that this was not a summons he could ignore, not with the Macintoshes stirring up the villages. Damn those rouges to Hell, now he had another reason to kill them, giving Mel one last wistful look, he issued a demand to her.

"Stay and enjoy your peace." He said, before turning and heading up to the keep, his lust now replaced with urgency.

Eighteen

M el stood in the centre of the glen, dazed and wonderfully content. *How she was meant to relax after what had just happened?* She looked longingly to the place where Hamish had just left, hoping briefly that he would come back even though she knew he wouldn't. One thing that Mel had learnt over the last two weeks here was that clan business came before anything else. Mel thought back on what she knew had been happening with Hamish's clan just knowing that his commander was here meant that something had happened. It didn't help matters that Alec's voice had been filled with urgency when he had called out to Hamish.

Mel knew she should have felt embarrassed that someone had come upon them during lovemaking, but the bliss of the moments she had spent with Hamish overruled any kind of embarrassment that she would have felt. Nothing and no-one could take away the good mood she was now in.

Trying to decide what to do, Mel noticed the forgotten cloth bag on the ground, it installs brought with it images of Hamish's wet body. Taking a deep breath to slow the lust that had just re-entered her body, Mel went over, picked up the bag and then sat by the pool to eat the rest of her bannocks. Her body was still tingling from the aftermath of their lovemaking and a small smile played at the corner of her mouth.

Mel's smiled deepened as she took a bite of the delicious honey-soaked bread, the reminder of what he tasted like when she kissed brought a moan from deep in her throat. *The man certainly knew how to make a girl happy,* she thought giddily. But Mel's happiness was short lived, as she ate her bannocks, image after image of what had just happened rushed through her mind and with them the reality of what had just happened hit her. Not only had Mel slept with a stranger from another century, she had just slept with Ceana's brother, a brother she had only just connected with and she was leaving in a couple of weeks. And to make matters worse they hadn't used protection, something Mel had never done before.

"Aww shit!"

Hamish reached the edge of the forest in no time, Iain being here concerned him, he would not have come here himself if it wasn't serious. Hamish was just about to rush up to the keep when he caught sight of Alec leaning against one of the trees, a small smile playing at the corner of this mouth. Hamish knew that Alec would not say anything about what he had seen, as highlander men did not question their Laird's about such matters, but it didn't stop them from enjoying their Lard's discomfort. Hamish couldn't blame the young lad, he would have acted the same way if he had found Alec in the same position. Stopping in his tracks Hamish turned towards. "Did Iain say what it was aboot?" Hamish questioned Alec, hoping to get his mind back onto the business at hand.

"Nay," Alec replied.

Nodding at the warrior, Hamish decided that he'd wasted enough time, he proceeded to move past Alec and then stopped.

"Mel is still in the glen, stay close just in case there is trouble." He ordered. Alec nodded and then retreated into the forest. Hamish knew he was probably being paranoid, but with everything that was going on Hamish was not willing to take any chances. Content that Mel would be safe for now, Hamish continued to the keep at a faster speed, and when he entered the main room, both Iain and Kessan were already deep in discussion.

"Iain," Hamish nodded. Iain didn't waste any time in getting to the point. One of the reasons Hamish had chosen him to be his commander, even though he was younger than most of the men in they can, was Iain's ability to keep a calm head in situations such as this. His youth did not hinder him in any way, Iain had a no-nonsense type of personality and he believed strongly that everyone deserved a fair chance. However, Hamish liked that while he was fair Iain also believed in a swift and quick punishment for those found guilty of wrongdoing. He did not sit back and just let things happen, he made them happen, he was a true McDonnell warrior.

"The Macintoshes are up to something." Iain stated simply.

"How do you ken this lad?" Kessan asked from beside the hearth, but Hamish put his hand up to stop any further questions. While, Hamish had nothing but respect for his brother-in-law, this was MacDonnell business and he would hear the all of it before he started questioning Iain.

"Explain," he directed Iain.

"Och, about four days ago there was another raid on the village to the south of the keep, the patrols were able to stop them before they could do any real damage, but they were still able to steal some of our livestock."

Hamish nodded indicating he wanted more.

"We thought that would be it for a while, much as it has been over the last few months, but in the last two weeks, there have been five separate raids, one every other day, and then nothing for the last four." Iain said, a frown marring his face.

"And this makes ya think they are up to something?" Kessan asked.

Both Hamish and Iain looked at him with astounded looks on their faces. "Och brother I think ya starting to think like a modern man and not a highlander." Hamish quipped. The look that Kessan gave him promised all sorts of hell when this meeting was over. Hamish ignored Kessan's look and answered him instead, "Aye, I agree with Iain, most likely they are up to something."

"Och, but that is not all Laird, one of Laird McKinnon's men heard the bastards saying that it was pointless raiding the clan if you, MacDonnell, weren't there for them to kill. Forgive me Laird, I ken I was only meant to come here if it was important, but this sounds personal and I thought you should ken the whole of it." Iain apologised.

"*Faigh Muin*" Hamish swore, he was in no way mad at his man from bringing him this news, if anything it only added to Hamish's own suspicions on how far the bastards would go to get to him. It was time for him to put his plan in motion.

"Iain, I need ya to go back to the keep and send all of Kessan's men back here. From what I ken gather, Macintosh will be coming after me now and our men can look after our villages." Iain didn't need any more prompting and left immediately to do his Laird's biding.

"Kessan, you should probably start doubling the watch around here, I have a feeling the bastards are going to try and attack me here." Hamish deliberated, turning his attention to his brother-in-law.

"Do ya really think they will be brazen enough to try to get to ya here?" Kessan asked.

"Aye, if they really want me, they will try and get to me anywhere you ken it," he nodded. While Hamish knew from a highlander's point of view that this was what they were planning, he also knew if for sure thorough his powers. For days now they had been warning him of impending trouble, and Iain's words had given them credit. Hamish of course could not explain that to his brother-in-law without giving away his secret and so he went with logic.

"They are after revenge," Hamish offered as a way of explanation and that was all that needed to be said. Both men knew that when a highlander was out for revenge they would stop at nothing to get it, and unfortunately this was where they believed they were going to find it.

Hamish knew that had to get away from here, because there was only one person they would think to go after, Ceana. Everyone in the highlands knew his sister was back and how much she meant to Hamish. As an added bonus, by going after Ceana not only would they getting revenge on Hamish they would also be paying McKinnon back for his role in outlawing them.

Hamish would come up with a plan once he knew that his family was safe and, to do that, he would have to lure the rogues away from McKinnon land, but leaving McKinnon land also meant leaving the lass. Disappointment filled Hamish as he headed for the stables, he prepared to fill Iain in on the rest of the plan. Before he left for home. Hopefully they could stop the madness before someone he loved was hurt, and then if he was lucky he could get back to enjoying his time with a beguiling 21st century lass. Hamish just needed to keep his family safe fist, because it was the only way the Macintoshes could get to him.

If only he'd known then how wrong he was.

Nineteen

❧❀❧

Mel sat on the banks of the creek, running her hand through the beautiful clear, cool water. She tried to think how she was going to tell Ceana about Tristan, but every other thought came back to the highlander who had just rocked her world. This was useless there was no point in staying down here if all she was going to do was daydream Mel thought to herself, it was time for her to go. Mel looked around the glen and let out a sigh of regret, maybe she could stay for five minutes more. Closing her eyes Mel lay back on the grass and listened to the water lapping over the rocks. But a sound that shouldn't have been there had Mel opening her eyes once more and rising to a seated position.

"Hamish?" She called out quietly hoping it was his returning from whatever business he had to attend too. But when no answer came Mel started to worry. The urgency of Alec's earlier command had her worried, but after a moment she settled back down. Mel doubted Hamish would leave her here if there was any danger to be found. Although Mel lay back down on the grass she could not shake the feeling that someone was there.

Maybe it *was* Alec?

Mel sat back up and spoke once again trying to control the tremor in her voice. "I hear you Alec, you might as well come out and join me." She said without even turning around to face where the noise had come from. Mel didn't actually have any idea if it was Alec, she was just hoping that it was him and not some wild animal.

To her surprise, Alec walked out of the forest to her right not the direction that had originally caught her attention. Mel glanced back to where she'd heard the noise, and saw a shadow of movement between the trees, she looked back towards Alec to see if he had seen the shadow but he was as stoic as Hamish usually was. Mel shrugged, it was probably just a bird, or some other animal, if the man standing before wasn't concerned then why should she be. Trying to forget about the shadow and her intuition which was screaming at her that something was not right, she turned her attention to Alec.

"Sorry, I didn't mean to disturb ya." He apologised. While his apology sounded sincere Mel noticed that he seemed uncomfortable being in the glen with her alone, never once did he look at her and he was constantly looking around as though he wanted to be anywhere but with her.

"Is everything alright?" she asked, trying to put the highlander at ease.

"Aye." Alec nodded and then went back to surveying his surroundings. Mel wasn't sure if that was his cue that he didn't want to talk, or if he was just being rude. Either way she decided that she would head back up the keep now. The glen just didn't seem the same without Hamish and Mel no longer felt like being here without him.

Standing up Mel brushed the grass off of her dress then started to walk towards the row of trees she had first entered. She wasn't sure if she should tell Alec or if he would follow, opting to leave it up to him, Mel didn't say another word.

She was halfway across the glen however, when his words stopped her, she turned and face him once more. "If I may request on thing of ya Lass."

Mel didn't bother answering she simply nodded letting him know it was okay to ask. "How did ya ken I was here?" He asked puzzled.

Mel looked at him inquisitively, the truth was she hadn't known; it was just pure luck on her part. If the noise hadn't drawn her attention Mel never would have called out to him. She thought about messing with him briefly, but his confused look had her thinking better of it.

Mel pushed a stray strand of hair behind her ear, then answered. "Well, to be honest, I didn't." Mel almost giggled at his astounded expression, instead she explained further, "I heard a noise, but I thought it came from over there," she said pointing in the direction she had seen the movement earlier. "You were the last person to be here and since Hamish had left and there shouldn't have been anyone else here, I took a wild guess and assumed it was you."

Alec gave her a grin, but didn't move any closer to her. Instead, he stood at the other end of the clearing, feet braced apart, hands cupped behind him, eyes continually scanning the area, it was then she came to realise that he was not uncomfortable being with her, he was simply on guard.

"You guys don't relax much do you?" Mel asked. While she had asked the question out of curiosity she found that she really did want to know all about highlanders, especially one in particular.

"Nay Lass, if ya relax out here you end up dead." He answered honestly. Even as he answered her question Alec's eyes were roaming the area, watching for any threat that may be viable. Mel remembered Hamish doing the same thing whenever she was in his presence, it was as if they expected to find danger lurking around every corner. The feeling of trepidation that had been bugging her all day crawled up her spine once again but she tried to ignore it.

"Blah, that sounds boring and deadly," Mel answered as she paced in the glen. That comment brought Alec's eyes swiftly back to hers and the look that accompanied that was one of astonishment.

"Ya make no sense Lass."

"How so?" Mel asked, deciding to sit back down on the ground. If she was going to have a long conversation she might as well stay. Mel would have asked Alec to join her but she was doubtful that he would oblige and so she sat with her legs off the side with one hand on the ground ready to state her case.

"If it is 'deadly' as ya say, then how can it be boring? Ya make not a lick of sense when you speak like that. For 'tis the danger we face daily that keeps us alert. Highlanders live for a good fight, 'tis what makes us feel alive and 'tis why we train so often, and that cannae' be boring." he answered openly.

Mel dared not laugh at the authority she heard his voice, she didn't think he would appreciate her humour, especially not when he had sounded so serious on the subject. Mel admired his gumption to defend his options, but it was his facial features that intrigued her. For the first time since she'd met the highlander she saw his face light up as he talked about fighting and danger like it was going for a walk in the park. Never had Mel met anyone that got excited about facing danger, she had to give it to them, these highlanders had balls.

"I see your point, Alec, but isn't that same danger you talk about, the reason why many of you die young?" Mel pointed back logically not ready to give up on her own point. It wasn't often she found someone who could have a good debate with her.

Mel valued having serious discussions with anyone that could match her, so much so she had been a part of the debating team at school. Of course that same passion for debating was one of the things that drove her friends batty. In the end they gave up debating with her, because they never won, and how could they really. Mel was always the voice of logic and reason, even in situations she knew she couldn't explain, such sitting by a glen in 12th Century Scotland, her logical brain devised some way of explaining it.

"Ya only die young if ya no good in battle Lass." He replied, just as logically.

Mel laughed; she couldn't help it. It was nice to finally meet someone who was willing to battle wits with her, and with logic no less. Mel was just about to throw back a rebuttal back at Alec to really get the party started when a flash of metal caught her eye, moments before a man burst into the clearing.

Mel didn't have time to react, but thankfully Alec had not let his guard down during their conversation and had drawn his own sword, launching an attack. To her horror, even before she could scream the two men were locked together in a ferocious battle, swords clashing violently. Alec was a decent fighter and he was holding his own, they just might get out of this alive Mel thought to herself. That was until two more sword-wielding highlanders entered the clearing.

Now outnumbered, Mel had a bad feeling that this wasn't going to end well, that nagging feeling she'd felt all day was no screaming at her, she guessed the shadow hadn't been a bird after all. Creeping to the edge of the clearing on her hands and knees Mel to stay out of sight, she didn't want to go into the trees alone as she wasn't sure what she would find there. So keeping her mouth shut and hiding behind one tree as much as she could Mel sat watching the two men fight while deciding what her best move was.

The battle seemed to go on for ever in Mel's mind, even though she knew it had to have only been minutes. Alec held the three men off as long as he could, somehow managing to stand his ground.

Mel was so engrossed int he battle in front of here, trying to decide what to do that she didn't see the two other men come up behind her.

Before she knew what was happening they grabbed Mel by the arms and reefed her to a standing position. Her shocked yelp distracted Alec, a distraction that cost him dearly. When Alec turned to see what was happening, one of the intruders brought the hilt of his sword down hard onto Alec's head with a sickening crack. Her heart thudding wildly, Mel watched in horror as Alec crumpled to the ground, and while Mel continued to stand there and stare at them the second man who was standing above him angled his sword ready to sink it straight into Alec's chest for one final blow.

Mel screamed, the piercing sound had her captives covering their ears and before they had any inclination of her intent, she rushed forward, knocking the man with the sword to the ground. She didn't believe for a second that she could get the better of him but because Mel had caught him off-guard, he fell to the ground, stunned his sword falling out of his hands and away from Alec. Crawling back to the highlander who was lying unconscious on the ground, Mel positioned herself so that she was draped over his body. Mel knew that she was probably putting herself in danger but she didn't care, she vowed that she would protect him with her last breath, there was no way she was going to let them kill Alec without a fight.

As Mel lay over Alec's body all she could do was wait and see if they would kill her too. She had no idea why these men had come into the glen to attack them, but she wasn't about to ask. Mel eyed the man who had knocked Alec out, daring him to come any closer. She knew she didn't have much of a chance against him, but she was willing to give it everything she had. For a brief moment Mel considered trying to get Alec sword, but that thought better of it, the darn thing would probably be too heavy for her anyway.

While Mel kept her eye's on the man in front of her, intent on keeping Alec safe, she didn't hear the brute that came up behind her. Before she knew what was happening, Mel was picked up roughly and tossed over his shoulder, effectively knocking the wind out of her lungs. The force of her ribs hitting his shoulder not only took her breath it also sent a wave of dizziness shooting through her and by the time Mel had time to get her bearings her captor had started marching out of the woods in the opposite direction of the keep.

Mel had to think quick, lifting her head she scanned the area of the aftermath of the battle and, with some satisfaction, she noticed one of the attackers laying on the ground not far from Alec either unconscious or preferably dead. Then her eyes found Alec, he was still lay unmoving, the ground around him soaked in blood, and it was more than obvious to her that *he* was dead. Tears flowed down her cheeks at the brutal sight, Mel didn't know what was happening or why it was happening but what she did know was that she couldn't let these men take her away.

As Mel tried to figure out what to do she was reminded of her favourite talk show. In one episode, the police told women for all over the world to remember one thing in the event of a kidnapping. That advice was that they were to do everything they could to avoid being taken to a second location. Because once that happened the likelihood of someone ever finding you was near impossible, and that had never meant more than it did in this century. Mel knew that if she had any chance of being found that was exactly what she had to do.

Taking a deep breath, Mel prepared herself to let out a scream and fight with everything she had, she wasn't sure who would hear her, but she needed to give it a go. Closing her eyes Mel opened her mouth, but as if aware of her intentions the brute who was currently carrying her lifted her up and slammed her stomach back into his shoulder, effectively cutting off any noise she had planned to make. Gasping for air Mel slumped, once again short of breath and out of options, these man planned to kidnap her and it didn't look like she had much options but to go along with it for now.

What was she going to do? How was anyone going to be able to save her when no-one knew what had happened? And they would never know, because she knew in her heart that Alec was dead. No-one could survive the loss of that much blood, not without modern day resources. As the brute walked further thought the trees panic overtook her, and her vision started to blur. As her body was continuously slammed into the brutes shoulder a blinding pain ripped through her skull; the events of the afternoon were becoming too much for her to cope with and, as blackness engulfed her, an image of Hamish's face was the last thing she saw before she blackout fully.

Twenty

"Ya cannae' expect me to sit here and do nothing!" Kessan argued once again. Hamish sighed, they had been having this discussion for over three hours now. When Hamish had come back from the stables to inform Kessan of the plan that he and Iain had devised he had hoped to be on his way long before now, but Kessan was proving to be as stubborn as ever.

"Aye I can," Hamish replied moving away from the table. He headed over to the side of the room to get a stiff drink, it looked like he was going to need something stiff to help him get through this conversation. While Hamish loved his brother-in-law and understood Kessan's need to help family, the last thing Hamish needed was to put his sister through worry. Kessan needed to be at home with his family right now, and Hamish needed him to stay here and make sure his sister and the bairns were safe. Hamish just needed to get Kessan to see that without insulting him. Taking a long gulp, Hamish looked out of the window across the field as he thought about what he would say.

"Kessan, ya have two bairns, another on the way, not to mention a wife and clan who need ya here. The Macintoshes are my problem and I will deal with them!" He pointed out trying to get through the Scot's thick skull.

After the last time Hamish had stopped the raid and killed a few of the Macintosh men he had hoped that the highlanders would let the feud go. But he should have known better, they were desperate and they weren't going to give up until he was dead. What the

Macintoshes hadn't counted on tough was Hamish will to fight back, they had sorely underestimated him if they thought he would just sit back and let them have their revenge. If the Macintoshes thought that Hamish would just sit around and wait for them to strike, they dinna ken him very well at all.

"Ya still have no' told me ya plan yet!" Kessan pushed.

Hamish finished off the rest of his drink before he faced Kessan once more.

"Och, tis simple brother, I plan to go hunting." He said savagely, slamming the glass he was holding onto the table. Kessan threw his head back and let out a boisterous laugh as he walked over and pounded Hamish on the back.

"I should have ken better than to have doubted ya. Fine, if I can no' join ya then take as many of my men as ya need." Kessan offered.

Hamish nodded in thanks, he was going to take Kessan up on that offer, he had given the Macintoshes more than enough opportunities to change their minds, but they had refused. If it was a war they wanted, it was a war they would get, this time though he would not leave any of the bastards alive, this feud was going to end here.

With everything settled with Kessan Hamish planned to go and finish getting everything ready. He was planning to head out in the morning to begin their hunt, he just hoped that nothing happened in the meantime. The Macintoshes had crossed a line coming after his family and they were going to pay for it. Hamish thought about everyone and loved and what he had to lose if his enemy came here, it was then Mel's face flashed before his eyes. Just the thought of leaving her made his blood boil, he finally had her right where he wanted, and now he had to go. He knew it would be the last time he saw her as he doubted very much that this would be settled before she went home. And even if it wasn't, Hamish knew that, while the Macintoshes were out for blood, he had to keep his distance from everyone, and that included the bold lass who set his blood on fire.

Thinking of her brought back the memories of their last encounter only hours before. The thought of her riding his cock had hard once more. He knew he had a lot to prepare, but as he was probably never going to see her again Hamish decided that he needed to make time for her. After everything they had shared today Hamish could not leave without saying a proper goodbye. Giving his brother a hearty pound on his back, Hamish turned and started to make his way out of the dining hall, he needed to find the lass now, nothing and no one was going to stand in his way. Nothing and no-one but his sister that was. Hamish was momentarily halted when his sister walked through the door.

"I hope I'm not interrupting, am I?" She asked as she walked over to greet her husband.

"No Wife, our meeting is finished." Kessan replied looking at Hamish for confirmation.

Hamish nodded in answer as Kessan pulled Ceana into a tight hug and gave her a proper greeting. Watching them made his heart ache for something he knew he could never have. While Hamish's heart sung out to find a mate, the last thing he ever wanted to do was burden his bairns with the power that had been given to him. Unlike his sister, his power was stronger and more intense; and because of this he had decided years ago that this power would die with him.

"Well I best be going," Hamish said clearing his throat to gain their attention.

Ceana smiled at his awkwardness, "Not before you give me a hug." She said walking over to him and wrapping her arms around him.

Hamish's body tensed as the sensation of his sisters love poured through him. Even after all this time, Hamish found that he was still slightly uncomfortable with displays of affection. Having lived the latter part of his life, with only his father as his companion, in the wilderness of the Scottish Highlands Hamish was not accustomed to affection. While his father had loved him, he had also taught Hamish to be tough and ruthless, it had been the only way to ensure his survival.

The problem was that sometimes it was hard to shake the roughness that made him who he was, even around his family. Over the past two years Ceana had been helping him change slowly, but he was still a work in progress. A certain sable haired minx may very well have been able to chip away the last of his resistance, but with the threat now imminent Hamish would never know. While there had been no awkwardness in the intimacy he had shared with her, Hamish still felt as though he could not let her in fully, not knowing what he knew about himself.

Hamish was just about to pull out of Ceana's embrace when she abruptly pulled back from him and searched the room, before her eyes shot back to him and she asked, "Where's Mel?"

Hamish swore that she possessed the power to read people's thoughts, but he wasn't going to give her any indication that he knew where her friend was or what she was talking about.

"I doona ken Lass, I have no' seen her since this morn." Hamish hedged, eyeing his sister curiously.

"Hmm, I thought she would have come back with you." Ceana replied offhandedly as her eyes searched the room once more. Hamish looked at Kessan who had a small smile on his face before looking at his sister, speculatively. She was so focused on looking for her friend that he did not think she had realised her slip up.

"What do ya mean Cee, why would she have been with me? I was down at the glen, which you knew." he replied as mildly as he could. It wasn't long before he was rewarded with just the reaction he wanted. Ceana's cheeks turned a deep bright red as she realised what she had just inadvertently revealed to her brother. He couldn't wait to see how she dug herself out of this mess.

"Um, I just thought you might have seen her on your tracks that's all." Ceana backpedalled faster than a horse galloping at speed, and with a cheeky grin she returned to her husband's side.

Hamish wasn't buying any of what she was saying; something was going on here and everyone was in on it but him. Ceana had somehow known that he'd been with Mel that morning, and he wouldn't mind betting that his sister was up to her meddling matchmaking tricks again, only this time they were directed at him. Hamish briefly wondered if Mel was in on it too, but just remembering how shocked she had been to find him in the glen had him thinking otherwise. Hamish would have to remember to have a word with his sister about his meddling late as she did raise a good question. The lass should have been back from the glen by now, and so should of Alec. Hamish knew for certain that Alec wasn't back yet as the Lad would have checked in with Hamish the minute they returned. An ominous feeling washed over him, and the hairs on the back of his neck bristled in warning.

Twenty-One

❧

Storming out of the hall, Hamish headed for the keep; if Alec were to be anywhere he would be in the warrior quarters with the rest of his men. As he reached the keep though, a noise and commotion met his ears; one of Kessan's men was yelling for the gates to be opened. With the briefest sense of relief Hamish headed towards the gates hoping that he would find Alec and Mel. Instead, Iain rode through at an urgent pace with two other horses in tow. Alarm now overtaking his senses, Hamish couldn't focus to process what he was seeing, and it wasn't until Iain stopped in front of Hamish that he finally recognised the man draped over one of the horses.

Alec!

Ceana gave a distressed cry as she came out to meet them, Iain informed her that Alec been unconscious the entire time since they'd found him collapsed at the edge of the village. Hamish gently helped Iain get Alec down from the horse and then carried him carefully into the keep where Ceana could tend to his wounds. The deep, bloody gash on the back of his head which still had blood trickling from it worried Hamish, that coupled with the fact that Alec was still unconscious didn't look good for the young lad. After taking him inside and placing Alec on the bed, Hamish turned and walked past Iain and Kessan and headed back out to the keep. He didn't need to say anything, Hamish knew that Iain and Kessan would follow him and he didn't stop until he was standing in front of the other horse, which, to his satisfaction, had an equally injured Macintosh draped over it.

Anger flared through his veins and Hamish was glad that Alec had gotten in some of his own blows before he fell, but knowing that he did fall meant that something had happened to make him fight, and knowing that Mel had been in the Glen with Alec told Hamish that whatever had happened involved Mel.

"Where did ya find this one?" Hamish asked Iain, without once removing his eyes from the man. Hamish's anger was flowing through his veins and he wanted nothing more than to rage at the man in front of him, but he also knew that he needed to act like the cool headed laird he was.

As he waited for Iain to answer Hamish walked forward and lifted the man's head needing to do something with his hands, it was then he realised he recognised the bastard. It was Samuel, the Macintosh's second in command, and his being in bad shape meant that there had been a fight. His clothes were covered in blood still flowing from a wound in his chest and, from his pallor, Hamish could tell that it wasn't going to be long before the man bled to death. What worried Hamish the most was that he knew the Macintoshes never rode alone, and that meant that there were more out there. Hamish vowed that no matter what he would not let Samuel die until he found out as much information as he could, and Hamish would find out everything even if he had to keep Samuel alive to do so.

Hamish wasn't going to waste any more time waiting for Samuel to come around, he had to find out what happened to Mel, the longer he waited the more danger she was in. Without giving it another thought Hamish went to the horses' trough and filled a bowl that had been nearby with the dirty water from within, then without hesitation Hamish threw the dirty stinking water into the Macintosh's face. Samuel came awake spluttering and cursing.

"Where is the Lass?" Hamish enquired when the man came up spluttering. It was clear the Macintoshes had her, Alec would have protected her with his life and, considering his injuries he had sustained, he had done just that. Now it was up to Hamish to find her and time was running out.

"Go to Hell MacDonnell!" Samuel spat back, venom filling every word.

Hamish fumed; he was in no mood to deal with this scum, Mel's life was in danger and Samuel was wasting their time. Grabbing a handful of the man's hair, Hamish dragged him off the horse and rather than remove his hand even as the man fell to his knees, Hamish used it to reef the man up higher so that he could drive his fist into the wound at his side. With satisfaction, he noticed that Samuel lost more of his colour as a scream of agony ripped from his throat. The Macintoshes had no idea what they had just unleashed, Hamish was out for blood and he wouldn't stop until every last man that was involved was dead.

"I am only going to ask you this one more time." Hamish hissed into Samuel's ear. "Where. Is. The. Lass?" He enunciated each word menacingly. Samuel understood that he was going to die, painfully if Hamish had anything to do with it, and utter fear entered Samuel's eyes brought had the bloodlust in Hamish's veins running wild.

"If I tell ya, the Laird will kill me," Samuel uttered miserably.

"If ya doona tell us, I will make ya wish yer Laird *was* the one killing ya!" Kessan roared as he pushed himself forward.

When Samuel didn't answer, Kessan spat malevolently. "Ya realise that ya Laird has taken one of my family members and *that* I will not tolerate?"

Indecision played across Samuel's face as he thought about his options. Finally after deciding he only had one, Samuel began speaking, "He will no' care that she is ya family, Laird. Macintosh will no' give her back without a fight. Och, nay knowing that she is part of the McKinnon clan will only add to her allure. Ya see Laird, now that we ken that the Lass is not only one of your family members, we also ken that we hold the MacDonnell's hoore! And that is more valuable than my own life" He coughed out snidely and triumphantly.

Hamish was taken back, how in the hell had they found out about Mel and himself? Macintosh must have been watching them earlier, it was the only way they could have known. Hamish was fuming at himself for not having checked the area more thoroughly, the bastards must have been lying in wait trying to catch him unaware. Now all he could do was make them think they had made a mistake, it was the only thing that was going to save Mel's life. Trying to gain the upper hand again, Hamish denied the allegations. "Ya laird is no' only a traitor he is also an idiot if he thinks the Lass is connected to me in anyway. Ya better hope that nothing happens to her, because if it does ya ken that I will eradicate every Macintosh in the highlands! Now tell me where she is!" Hamish demanded.

Fury erupted in the pit of his stomach as Samuel connoted to hold out. He was mad at the Macintoshes yes, but he was also furious at himself. With all the danger around Hamish knew he shouldn't have left her alone! Hamish thought for sure that the lad would tell them what they wanted to know but he wasn't so sure now. Even though he could see the fear still lurking in his eyes, the bastard straightened his shoulders with as much dignity as he could and stammered with a nobility that Hamish might have admired if he wasn't wanting to the kill the man, "I will no' betray my Laird."

The lad's words sank in and horror ripped through Hamish's body. Roaring uncontrollably, Hamish let his rage out in full force. Hamish punched the lad so hard Samuel's neck snapped back, instantly rendering him unconscious. Hamish tried to bring forth his powers to help in calming his nerves, but as they usually were when his emotions were all over the place, they were absent.

He was through wasting time, he had to do something, and wasting time on Samuel was not getting them anywhere. Turning towards Iain, Hamish gave his order, "Keep him alive any way that ya can. If even a hair on Mel's head has been hurt, I want the pleasure of gutting this bastard myself!" He barked hoarsely before he headed to the barn.

All that mattered now was finding Mel, he had to get out of here; his mind was going crazy with guilt and images of what was happening to Mel. He should have stayed with her or at least made her come up to the keep with him. Picking up the pace, Hamish ran the rest of the way and had just entered the barn when Kessan's voice stopped him.

"MacDonnell what are ya gonna do?" Kessan asked.

Hamish didn't bother stopping to look at his brother-in-law, he made his way to his horse and started to saddle him up. The truth was Hamish didn't know what he was going to do, he didn't have a clue as to where they could have taken her or how he was going to find her. Macintosh was not a stupid man; he would have had a plan, and he would have covered his track well. At this point Mel could be anywhere in the highlands.

"I doona ken," he replied harshly. "What I do ken though is I have to do something. I will go down to the glen and see if I can figure out which way they went. Hopefully then I can try and understand what they have planned." Hamish could see that Kessan wanted to argue, but he wasn't in the mood to listen. Turning to his commander, who had been coming up behind Kessan, Hamish added. "I need ya to stay here and get the men ready in case there is war, or in case the bastards return. Tell Morgan and Tamhas to be ready within the hour, they can come and help me scour the surrounds. Send someone to inform me at once when Alec gains consciousness. Hopefully he heard something of their plan afore she was taken."

Hamish didn't wait for Iain to respond to his commands, he turned on his heel and mounted his horse, the anxious feeling in the pit of his stomach was only increasing the longer they took wasting time. Hamish knew that if they did not reach Mel soon; they would have no chance of getting her back alive.

Twenty-Two

Mel was freezing, she moved restlessly once again trying to bury herself deeper into her dress. She had her feet tucked up underneath the heavy material and had also wrapped the plaid material that Ceana had given her, tightly around her arms and upper torso. Ceana had given her the plaid to wear so that all in the highlands knew that she was part of the MacKinnon clan. It was meant to protect her, although it wasn't doing a very good job of it right now. *Why couldn't these men follow the same rules as everyone else?*

Mel longed to be back at the keep right now with her friend safe and warm, having a magnificent dinner and joking about the day's events. She hadn't even been able to tell Ceana about Tristan or Hamish for that matter. Mel had thought that telling Ceana about her two brothers was going to the hardest thing she had to deal with today, well she had been wrong on that.

To make matters worse, the snow that had been steadily falling for about an hour and a half was starting to melt its way through Mel's well-constructed barriers, and as her captors had bound her feet and hands before they went to sleep themselves, just added to her misery. Mel was sure that the ropes were slowly burning their way into her flesh, and she could feel the sting as blood seeped from her chaffed wrists.

Mel sobbed quietly as the reality of her situation sunk in; she didn't think she could be any more miserable, until her teeth started chattering. She was exhausted and normally she hated letting her weakness show, but Mel was hoping that at least one of the vulgar men surrounding her felt pity for her and would give her something extra for the cold. But as the cold air continued to rise around her and her tears feel down her cheeks, their snores sent Mel's spirits plummeting even further into despair. *How had her day turned from heaven to hell so fast?* One minute she had been experiencing pure bliss in Hamish's embrace and then the next moment she had been flung over someone's shoulder and taken prisoner, while an innocent man lay dead after trying to protect her. *Poor Alec.*

Mel shuddered at the memory of his lifeless body lying on the ground as his blood continued to flow out around him. Mel had never seen a dead body before, and she wasn't sure she would ever be able to get the image out of her mind. Mel had tried to stop the criminals who had her from causing Alec any more damage, but unfortunately the damage had already been done. The enemy had struck Alec so hard across the head that he had crumpled to the ground instantly and the amount of blood that had been seeping out into the grass from the wound he had sustained could not have been a good thing.

Mel was not sure if it was the sword that had caused the damage, or if Alec struck his head on a rock as he landed. Either way, something had caused Alec to bleed out and die, and it was all because he had been trying to save her. Tears filled Mel's eyes as she remembered him laying so still on the ground, she hadn't meant to get the young man killed. He shouldn't have tried to protect her. Mel's tears fell harder as her teeth continued to chatter, she wondered if she would get any sleep tonight.

Hours later, Mel still hadn't gotten any sleep, and it didn't look as if she would any time soon. While she lay on the cold hard ground shivering, Mel decided to put her sleeplessness to use. Thinking about all of the men she'd encountered within the last twenty-four hours Mel endeavoured to catalogue as much about them as she could. Maybe that way if, by some miracle, someone saved her she would be able to provide them with some kind of information on these criminals. She didn't know what type of legal systems they had in 12th century Scotland, but what she was sure about was that Kessan would make these men pay somehow.

Mel looked around and noted that some of the men in question were awake now, talking between each other as they took up guard duty. Mel tried to listen to what they were saying but they were talking too low for her to catch anything important and there was not quite enough light to get any real facial details on the men. Mel closed her eyes and opted for just listing to them talk, hoping that they would let something slip. About an hour later Mel gave up trying to follow their conversation, the bastards intentionally spoke in nothing but Gaelic and based on the fact that they had been deliberately ignoring her the entire time she wouldn't mind betting they were under orders to do just that.

As Mel lay on the ground pretending to sleep she tried to figure out why these men would have taken her. She didn't know anybody in the highlands and as far as she knew Ceana and Kessan didn't currently have any enemies. Thinking about enemies the conversation Mel had overheard between Hamish and Kessan's, after her humiliating encounter with Hamish, came flooding back. Mel hadn't meant to overhear their conversation, but she had been coming down the stairs to find Ceana and had caught Hamish informing Kessan that he was going to go after the Macintoshes for the raids they had done on Hamish's clan. Mel had stopped on the stairs to let them finish, as she didn't want to interrupt, and to be honest she wasn't quite ready to face Hamish either. That was why Hamish hadn't seen her when he had stormed out of the castle. Mel had seen him though, she still remembered the look on his face, it was the first time that Mel realised that this quiet highlander was capable of murder.

With the conversation still in her mind, Mel had an epiphany. That had to be it, these men had to be the Macintoshes Hamish had been talking about, obviously they had mixed her up with someone else, perhaps they thought they had kidnapped one of Hamish's clan members. It all made sense to her, she had been in the glen with Alec after all it would have been and easy mistake to make. Mel's hopes rose, if she had figured it out it wouldn't take Hamish long to figure it out either. But Mel's hopes plummeted just as quickly as they had risen when she realised that while Hamish might figure out *who* had her, he still wouldn't know *where* they were taking her. Burying her head deeper into her plaid, Mel cursed herself for ever coming on this trip. Seriously, what had she been thinking?

"For Christ's sake, I may as well be camping, and I hate camping." Mel mumbled to herself as she once again tried to get warm.

"And to make matters worse, I don't even have a bloody iced coffee to help me cope!" she mumbled again.

Mel knew that she was being ridiculous, the last thing that she should be worrying about was her lack of iced coffee, but while it might have seemed ridiculous to others, to her it was a way to get her age up. Mel was hoping that her anger would generate enough heat to start warming her, but no such bloody luck all it seemed to do was bring forth how miserable her situation really was.

Mel continued to mumble about stupid highlanders, and men who thought they had a right to take whatever they wanted. She was just getting wound up when the highlander closest to her threatened, "shut up 'hoore afore I gag ya," right before he rolled over and resumed snoring.

Mel fumed silently to herself, not only could she not get warm now she couldn't even bitch about the situation. It was hopeless, she thought bitterly, no-one was going to find her out here. There were no GPS, no phones, no way to follow her, as far as Mel was concerned she would become one of those missing person cases that were never solved. Oh, what she wouldn't do to be back in her apartment, wrapped up in a blanket, watching *Supernatural.* With that last thought, Mel buried her head deeper into her arms and cried herself into a restless, painfully cold sleep.

After Mel had finally drifted off and had gotten a few moments blissful peace, she was woken abruptly by a boot being kicked viciously into her ribs. It didn't take her long to wake, and she yelped as pain lacerated her entire side.

"Wake up hoore, we have to get movin' afore this storm hits any harder. I wanna be outta Scotland before ya man realises ya gone!"

Mel rubbed her eyes with one hand as the other held the side that had been kicked. It took her a minute for her sleep addled brain to catch up with the words that had reached her ears. Mel looked up to see the tallest of the highlanders standing over her with a menacing look on his face.

During their mad dash across the countryside yesterday Mel had surmised that he seemed to be the one in charge. This menacing looking highlander was the one that had shouted out the orders when they had stopped and, as the night wore on, she noticed that the men always referred to him when they had questions about what to do. If anyone was going to be able to help her it was this highlander, Mel would have to start using her charm.

Groaning, Mel rolled over and noticed that her hands and feet had already been released. She stretched, hoping that she could gain some feeling back into her limbs, but it didn't help, instead it only added to the ache in her body. Mel felt awful; no doubt she was going to end up sick from this, her nose had already started to run as it was, and her head felt foggy with an oncoming headache. That was the last thing she needed, it would only give the men something else to be angry at her about, as if she could help it.

Sitting up gingerly, Mel looked around to see if there was any way she could escape, but six burly men sat around her and she had no doubt that if she did try to escape, they would make her already miserable life even worse. Her bones creaked and her muscles protested the movement as they were stiff from sleeping on the cold, damp ground. The way she was feeling, Mel wouldn't be able to move fast enough to stage any kind of getaway before they caught up anyway. It was hopeless.

Mel sighed when her body started aching, but it was replaced with her stomach lurching when a disgusting bowl of something that resembled food was shoved in her face.

"Eat and be quick aboot it!" The highlander snapped.

Looking down Mel saw what could only be referred to as slurry. Smelling it, she thought it might've been porridge, but in no way did it look like porridge. There was no way Mel was taking any chances with eating it, she wasn't hungry anyway and she doubted whether her stomach could even handle food. It was so knotted she suspected that if she did try and eat something she would end up throwing up.

"I'm not hungry," she said forcefully when she noticed the man glaring at her when she hadn't taken the bowl from his hands. If Mel had thought the man would simply move away from her she was wrong. He was set on getting his way and there was nothing Mel could do.

"If ya think to starve yaself hoore, think again, I will force feed ya if I have to!" he sneered. "Now eat!" he roared.

Mel wanted nothing more than to pick the revolting meal up and throw it in his smug face, but she knew that would only gain her more punishment and right now she had to preserve all of her strength for when an opportunity for escape presented itself. Telling herself she needed the food, Mel picked up the spoon and forced herself to eat. It wasn't easy, with each mouthful she took, her body rejected it and she had to force herself not to gag. If she ever got home, she was never complaining about her mother's cooking again!

While Mel sat and ate, she tried not to think about what crunched horrifyingly unexpectedly between her teeth every now and then. This was probably how all her friends felt when they had to eat her cooking she mused, trying not to smile. Once she and Ceana had been making pizza and Mel was left in charge while Ceana had to go and help Katie with one of the cabins. By the time Cee had returned, the pizza was as hard as a stone, not even throwing it at the ground could break it. Another time they had almost burnt the house down, when the chips they had been cooking splattered oil onto the stove top.

After that Mel gave up trying to cook, most of the time she ate at her parents or got takeaway. Tears started to flow down her cheeks as Mel thought about her friend. She knew Cee was probably worried sick about her and she would give anything to see her face one last time. Mel wished that Cee was here with her, she knew that her friend wouldn't be waiting for the men to kill her. No Cee would have been fighting the whole way. Thinking about her friend gave Mel the courage she needed to keep on going; she focused on what Cee would do while she tried to finish her food. Mel would be damned if she was going to die out here with these brutes.

Mel had eaten about as much as she could take, she placed the bowl on the ground beside her, pulled her legs up to her chest and rested her chin on her knees. She sat there wondering what was going to happen when the leader stood. She was half expecting him to come over to her and yell at her for not finishing her meal, but instead he yelled, "Move out!" And just like that, everyone around her prepared to leave. Rising stiffly to her feet, Mel took one last look at the way they had come hoping that, while the men were busy, she might be able to make a run for it.

The moment she laid eyes on the trail, however, her hopes plummeted. The snow that had been falling all night in a steady flow covered the trail completely and she could no longer see the difference between trail and uncharted land. It had also covered any tracks that had been left behind, eradicating any hope of escape or rescue. Turning away, Mel wiped angrily at the fresh tears that began to flow down her face and stormed stiffly over to her horse and mounted it before anyone thought to get near her. Taking one last look back towards home, she cursed.

"Fine!" She fumed, straightening her back a little more, "I've never needed anyone to save me before, so why start now?" With a new fire in her soul Mel urged her horse onward, following the men as slowly as possible.

She didn't care that snow now covered every part of the landscape, obscuring the dangers that lay beneath, Mel was determined to find a way to escape. For now, she would follow the bastards acting as docile as possible. But once her chance for escape came, she would take it without hesitation. For the second time Mel was thankful for her riding lessons, or that they didn't seem to suspect her capability, otherwise they mightn't have given her a horse to herself. Their ignorance may just be the thing that saved her.

Twenty-Three

M el wasn't sure how long they had been travelling for, but she had a feeling they were getting closer to their destination judging by how the highlanders had picked up their pace. Mel was going to have to try something soon or she was afraid she would miss her chance. The further she got from home, the harder it would be to get back. A deep-seated feeling in the pit of her stomach was telling her that if they made it to their destination, her life would never be the same, that was if she still had a life. With escape solely on her mind, Mel almost missed her opportunity. While her mind had been focused on what she was going to do, the man who was meant to be watching her had rode forward to talk to their laird.

Mel could only assume that because they were away from her family it would deter her from trying anything stupid. Mel was glad that they didn't know her that well. Looking around again, she noticed that the other four men were quietly talking in front of her, paying her no attention at all. They had just given her the perfect opportunity! Taking a deep breath, Mel turned her horse around as quickly and quietly as she could and without warning, she kicked it in the sides spurring it into action. Mel thanked God that this horse was a warhorse and not some mule, it had strength and speed, everything she needed for a successful getaway. As Mel and her horse raced away from the group she had no idea where she was going. But that didn't slow her down, she'd rather take on the mountains of Scotland than continue down the path these highlanders were taking her.

As the ground sped away under the hooves of her horse, she hoped that the highlanders wouldn't notice her disappearance for a while. But to her dismay, it didn't take them long to give chase and she soon lost her advantage. Mel could hear the pounding hooves of the men's horses behind her. Fear surged through her as the pounding hooves drew closer, but she didn't let it take control of her, instead it encouraged her to go faster.

"Please dear God do not let me fall off," she begged out loud as she kicked her horse harder, gaining herself some more speed.

Mel had a fast horse now all she had to do was stay ahead of her captors long enough to lose them then she could slow down and try and figure out how to get home. But time seemed to stand still, no matter how fast she rode, the men slowly closed the gap and before she knew it, Jacob, the mountain of a man who had been originally assigned to watch her was beside her, lifting her off her horse in one foul swoop, fury mottling his face.

"Noooo!" Mel screamed, using the opportunity to punch, kick and bite with all her might, but it did her no good. All it endeavoured to do was amuse her captor.

"There's no point tryin' to escape, Lassie." Jacob laughed into her ear as he turned his horse around and headed back to where the other men had stopped to wait.

As they neared the group Mel's fear mounted, the leader jumped from his horse and stormed angrily over to them. Mel flinched and tried to brace herself for what was coming, and before Jacob even had a chance to stop his horse, the angry highlander grabbed her by her arm and roughly ripped her down from the horse. He did it with such force that the horse shied away and almost unseated Jacob. Mel wished it would have as she would have gotten some satisfaction to watch the oaf land on his arse. But unfortunately, the brute righted himself before he landed in the dirt.

While Mel sneered at Jacob, she was too late in realising that she should have been paying attention to the highlander who had a grip on her arm. Because before she could react, the man's fist connected with her face causing her head to snap back and a blinding pain to radiate up through her jaw. Never in her life had she ever been hit, and she had to say she was grateful for that, it was not something she would recommend to anyone.

"Ya stupid Sassenach bitch! Do ya ken, what ya could have cost me?" The man screamed at her.

Spittle was flying wildly from his mouth, some landing on her cheek. His face was a mottled, ruddy red and Mel could see the vein in his temple throbbing, even his men were weary of his anger, each of them finding something else to do. Mel however couldn't leave, she had to sit and listen as he ranted and raved about how she had cost them precious time. He warned her that if the Duke was at all unhappy with having to wait for them he would put the blame exactly where it lay, with her.

Mel didn't think he had meant to let it slip where they were going, but she was happy that he had. While she hadn't been able to escape, at least she now knew that they were heading, they were heading to England. The thing that now worried Mel was the Duke himself. If a man such as this fearsome highlander feared the Duke, what did that mean for her. While the knowledge of where they were going should have calmed Mel, it only intensified the ever-growing pit in her stomach.

Through the haze of pain, Mel tried to recollect herself, escape hadn't worked and now she decided to try a different approach, "I'm sorry, look you don't have to do this." She tried reasoning with the highlander. When he just looked at her with more fury than before Mel took a deep breath and tried again. "It's not too late you know, no harm has been done you could just take me home and I will make sure that McKinnon and MacDonnell know that this was all just a misunderstanding." She pleaded trying a different tactic.

Mel hated begging to anyone but she knew that her smart mouth would only make this situation worse, these guys had no gumption about hitting a woman. She had briefly hoped that if she could calm him down enough, she could talk some sense into him and make him see the logic in what she was saying, she was not sure who was giving the orders, but maybe she could make this man see the sense of giving her back.

But mentioning Hamish's name was a mistake and only increased his fury, "nay Lass, ya will no' be going home! Those bastards are goin' to pay for what they did to my clan." He fumed, his face turning an even deeper shade of red. "Especially the MacDonnell!" He sneered in her face. "Now get up on ya horse and doona make me chase ya again, or I will end ya myself." He said, venom dripping from every word.

Damn not only was this man in charge of this group, he was the actual Laird of the Macintoshes, and that changed everything. From what Mel could gather, this man had it out for Hamish bad, and there was no way he was ever going to go back on his plan, not when it involved giving Hamish what he wanted. Without another thought to her, the Laird strode back to his horse and mounted as Jacob put her back on her horse, this time staying firmly by her side. Hopes of escape dashed as they once more headed in a southerly direction. Mel knew now that there was no-one in this group that would help her, her only hope now lay with the Duke. Hopefully there was be someone at the estate who'd be willing to help her, and if not, she would have to figure it out herself.

Twenty-Four

"Damn, bloody, stupid snow." Mel cursed to herself. It had started falling again not long after they had recaptured her, now her entire body was soaked through, AGAIN!

Mel usually loved the cold, but not when she was stuck outside in it or while a river of melting snow cascaded down her back. Even Ceana's plaid was soaked through, giving her no protection from the cold whatsoever. Man, what she wouldn't do for a nice steaming hot shower right about now. Mel could just imagine the hot water tumbling down her back, replacing the freezing cold water that was currently there. Mel was lost in her bubble of misery when something solid smacked her in the head followed by a sharp "Here!"

Braden, she thought it was, had tossed a heavy piece of tartan at her. Letting go of the reins with one hand, she quickly grabbed it before it fell to the ground. She had no wish to beholden to any of these louts for anything, but she was not stupid enough to cause her own death because she was stubborn either. Stopping her horse, Mel looked down at what she was holding and gave a silent prayer of thanks when she noticed looked as though it was a dry plaid.

Without wasting time, Mel wrapped the dry tartan around her as best she could. It was not completely dry, but it still offered her more warmth than her presently soaked clothes. Continuing to wrap the plaid around herself, Mel tried to arrange it so that no more snow could seep into her already soaking wet dress. As she went to tie it in a knot at her neck to seal it tight, a brilliant idea came to her.

Grabbing the extra bit of tartan that was hanging down her back, Mel proceeded to wrap it around her wet head, but the minute she brought it down near her face, the smell of wet horse and dirty sweaty unwashed man assailed her senses.

Gagging Mel dropped the tartan back down to where it had lay before, there was no way she could keep *that* stench near her head What was wrong with these people, Mel thought bitterly, she had dealt with rotting fish better smelling than this piece of clothing. *Hell, didn't these men ever bathe or wash their clothes?* A small rivulet of water ran down the side of Mel's face from the melting snow in her hair and she decided to try once more to cover her head. Perhaps she could manage to place it far over her head enough that the material covered the majority of her wet hair, while keeping the smell up wind. For what seemed like hours Mel tried all different ways to position the tartan so that it gave her the most coverage without making her sick, but it didn't seem to matter how far back Mel placed it on her head, the smell was so overpowering that it wafted straight into her nose, practically burning its hairs.

Taking a deep breath Mel let go of the tartan one final time and let it hang back where it had originally been. She just couldn't do it, she would rather put up with melting snow in her hair and on her face than try and breathe that toxic odour in. The best Mel could do was wrap the odorous material around her neck and try and tuck it into her dress. Mel was sure she would have to burn the dress when this was over, there was no way she ever going to get the stench out of the fabric. Thankfully, this stopped most of the water from continuing down her back, and the little bit that did run down her face was not that unbearable and, while Mel still occasionally got a small whiff of the pungent odour, it was tolerable enough to put up with so that she could be more comfortable.

As they rode on, Mel kept looking for another opportunity to escape, but it never came and within the hour, they arrived at a huge mansion sitting in the middle of green, rolling hills. The landscape here confirmed her suspicions; they were no longer in Scotland, while the Scottish highlands had rolling green hills, they were not this manicured and gone where the purple flowers she had come to love.

This had to be the estate of the Duke. At least they were not taking her to some dark, dank hole where she would probably have to share a room with rats, Mel thought bitterly trying to comfort herself in anyway. Then again who knew what was going to happen, this Duke still could put her in a room with rats, she thought miserably. While part of her still clung to the hope that someone here would be willing to help her, the minute the wide fresh doors opened all her thoughts of help vanished. There was no way anyone would go against this man just to help her; if anything, this man standing in front of them would be able to do anything he wanted to her, and no one would lift a finger to stop it.

The party Mel was riding with stopped the horses in front of the house and dismounted, she was not going to follow, she was not going to let them give her to this man willingly. That had been the plan before Jacob grabbed her arm and dragged her off of her horse and with him as they approached the entrance. Mel struggled feebly to free her arms from his clawing grasp, the wanted nothing more than to run away from the horrible man who held her captive. But soon found herself face to face with what she could only describe as evil, and Jacob no longer seemed like a bad choice.

The man standing before her was well-built and in his mid-30's, he was quite handsome, he kind of reminded Mel a little of the famous British actor from *The Rite*, but that was where the similarities ended. There was no kindness in this man's eyes, in fact there was nothing there at all. Much like his emotions, the man's eyes were empty and devoid of any emotion, until they flicked over to her. Mel took an involuntary step backwards when her instinct raged at her; the pure sadistic pleasure that entered his black eyes was terrifying. Mel had hoped that it was just her mind playing tricks on her, but the smirk that appeared on his face when he realised she was afraid of him only imbedded in her mind that this man was sicko of some kind.

Mel didn't need any evidence to the contrary, she had seen that look many times on the face of modern day psychopaths back home. The ones who derived pleasure from hurting others, ones that she had met in the flesh and seen in all the true crime shows. Mel might not have known this man, but what she did know was that this man was going to bring her more pain than the highlanders ever could. Mel tried moving further away from him, but Jacob still had a hold of her arm, so when he walked forward she was forcefully dragged with him, until they were standing right beside Macintosh.

"Here's the Lass we promised ya!" Macintosh answered with a

little too much glee in his voice for Mel's liking. Her skin began to craw when the Duke's eyes widened and his creepy smile widened.

"Where is our gold, Sassenach? I would like to be gone from England as soon as possible, ya ken?" Macintosh demanded.

Mel turned towards the laird, trying to reef her arm from Jacob's grasp as she went, but he was not giving her an inch. Mel hated pleading with the bastard who had kidnaped her but she would rather take her chances with these highlanders than the monster standing on the porch above them.

"Please you cannot leave me here, you know you can't! I will pay you double what he is asking!" Mel beseeched, she didn't know how she would get the money, but she was sure that Ceana would help her out.

Mel's hopes were dashed when the laird laughed at her, he really had to have hated Hamish for him to have knocked back that much gold. Macintosh strode forward until he was in front of her, his nose almost touching hers. The smell of his breath was almost as bad as that of the plaid that was wrapped around her neck, and it took everything she had not to gag and offend this man more than he already was. "I doona care how much ya can pay Lass. I just want the pleasure of watching ya Scot's face when I tell him ya dead. Money cannae' buy that!" He spat at her.

Mel couldn't breathe, she had been right in her assumptions earlier this was to get back at Hamish! The kicker of it all was that she was hardly his woman, in fact she barely knew him! *Maybe that was the key to getting her freedom!*

"But you have it wrong! It's not what you think, I barely know the man. He will not care what happens to me, so you see, your plan will not work." She tried reasoning again, but it fell on deaf ears.

The Duke paid the Highlanders' their money and then watched helplessly as they returned to their horses, they were going to leave her here and there was nothing Mel could do.

"Wait," She heard the Duke command. Hope rose in Mel's heart but just as quickly as it had risen it was taken away.

"Do not go too far, I may have need of you again." The Duke commanded.

Mel watched as anger crossed the Laird's face, and it became clear to her that the Laird didn't like the Duke any more than she did.

"Do no' be thinking to tell me what to do, Sassenach. I will no stay in this stinking country one more minute then I have to!" Macintosh scoffed.

The anger that spewed from the highlander has Mel assuming that the Duke would back down. But that was not the case, instead he took a step closer to the stairs and smiled. "Oh I think you will because if you don't I will be telling MacDonnell exactly who stole his woman." the Duke threatened.

"Ya dare to bribe me?" The laird fired back.

"It's not a bribe, it's a warning."

Mel watched the indecision play across the laird's face, she stood silently praying that Macintosh would take offence to the Duke, take her back and come up with another plan.

"Och okay, I will give ya two weeks, no more. If I haven' heard from you by then I will return home. Until that time my men and I will stay at a small village just across the border. I wonnae send another minute on Sassenach land!"

The Duke gave a nod; and Mel could do nothing but watch helplessly as the highlanders mounted their horses and left. They had really done it, they had left her in the hands of a madman. Turning around Mel faced the man that she knew would become her tormenter. Though she tried to hold them back, tears sprung to her eyes, she couldn't help it, she was exhausted and Mel had never felt more helpless and alone than she did right now.

Mel finally understood how Ceana must have felt the night Adrian had beaten her to within an inch of her life. Thinking of her friend and what she had been through that night gave Mel courage, just like Ceana had she would go out fighting. One of the lessons Mel had learnt from Cee during that ordeal was to make sure that your tormenter never knew how scared you were, that only give him more pleasure and, in turn, more power.

With Ceana's voice in her heard telling her to be strong, Mel straightened her shoulders, lifted her head a little higher in defiance and prepared herself for battle. She might die here, but one thing was for sure, Mel was going to die fighting. There was no way she was going to let this devil kill her without gaining a few injuries of his own.

Twenty-Five

Mowbray's smile faded as he looked at the most beautiful woman he had ever seen. He knew she feared him, he could sense it bubbling under the surface and it turned him on like nothing he had ever felt. But the little bitch was going to try and defy him; he could see it in her eyes as she stood boldly at the bottom of the stairs.

He knew the exact moment she had decided to fight him, when the highlanders had left the young woman's shoulders had slumped and tears had filled her eyes, now here she stood proud and strong. Mowbray almost laughed out loud, he had seen this kind of behaviour before, he has seen it in every single woman he had broken.

This woman would be no different, if she was hoping that by defying him he would back down, she was in for a rude shock. The Duke of Norfolk never backed down from anyone or anything, he was going to enjoy breaking this beauty indeed and it was going to start now.

Mowbray walked down the stairs until he was standing close enough to reach her and yet he was still above her. Without giving her an inkling of what he had planned the Duke reached out grabbed her by the hair and reefed her head back at a painful angle. He knew he had hurt her; he could see the tears lingering just beneath the surface, tears that she wouldn't allow to fall. As he continued to watch her fight back her fear, Mowbray had an overwhelming urge to smash his fist in her face, but he knew that patience was the key here. He would let her have her pride for now, it wouldn't last long, and when he finally had this woman where he wanted her, he would savour his victory all that much more.

Leaning down so that his eyes were level with hers, Mowbray began his torment. Letting the smile that he had been hiding cross his face he sneered, "I am going to enjoy breaking you bitch." Mowbray's pleasure increased as he felt a shiver run through the young woman's body. She might be able to hide her emotions on her face, but she couldn't hide her bodies reactions.

The Duke couldn't wait for tonight when he would have his first taste of this beauty, it would also be the first time he got to inflict some pain on her as well, the pain he liked to inflict. Mowbray knew she was going to fight him, and he welcomed it; the more they fought the more his pleasure intensified, and right now that pleasure was the only thing that was keeping him from becoming fully unhinged.

Twenty-Six

The fear that ran through Mel's body was overwhelming. She had expected the Duke to at least be subtle in the way he was going to treat her, but she should have known better. Why would the psychopath need to hide what he was if he had no reason to?

Right now the Duke had her hair in a tight grip at the base of her skull and he had let her know straight up that he planned to break her. Well, she had news for him, Mel didn't break easily, and right now Mel was about to give the Duke a taste of the 21st century. Leaning back a little Mel positioned her head so that she spit right in his face, just as her brother's had taught her too in a fight. They had always explained that if she couldn't reach his groin to do damage, spitting in her captors face was the next best thing to getting her release.

Mel watched as the big loogy that she had just hocked sailed through the air and landed in the middle of his eyes. Thankfully it got the reaction she wanted, unblinking she watched with some satisfaction as he slowly reached up to wipe it off his face. As was predicted Mel briefly gained her freedom when he let go of her hair; Mel took a step back putting some distance between herself and her new captor. She breathed a sigh of relief when the Duke turned his back on her to walk away, it may not have been elegant, but Mel was happy that the Duke now knew where she stood.

Mel relaxed and tried to regain her strength, she briefly thought about trying to escape but when she looked out at all the open hills she realised that she wouldn't get far on foot before he caught up with her, for now she would have to bide her time. Mel took a deep breath and walked up the stairs, she had no choice but to follow, the only problem was in doing so she had let her guard down.

It was the worst thing she could have done, because before she could brace herself the Duke turned back around and backhanded her so hard that she stumbled backwards and would have fallen down the stairs if he had not grabbed her by the arm, painfully pulling her back to him.

Mel cried out as pain radiated down her arm. "You little whore." The Duke spat at her. "The next time you think about doing that, remember that I alone control your life here and I alone can make that life as miserable as you would like. I will let you have this one, but you had better learn quickly that you are now my property and I will do whatever I please with you!" The fury in his eyes made Mel tremble. "Do you understand me?" He raged when Mel didn't answer quick enough.

"Yes," Mel answered dismally, she knew the best option for herself was to answer but she was not going to give him any more than that. For now, she would play the docile lamb but eventually he would learn that he would have to kill her before she succumbed to him. Satisfied for now, the Duke turned around with her arm still in his hand and dragged her into his house, a house that was to be her very own living Hell.

Mel didn't know how much more of this she could take, she had been in the Duke's house for one week already and no-one had come to save her. Thankfully, she had not had any more run-ins with the Duke since that first day despite his promise. Mel didn't think it was from lack of want, it was more because that first day she had arrived the Duke had been called away on business and he had yet to return.

Mel had been thrilled at the time, thinking that she would have a chance to escape, but the guards that were strategically placed all over the property soon dashed that hope. Every day was another lost chance of escape and every day that the Duke was gone had her nerves on edge because she knew that any day now he would return, and she knew without a doubt that he *would* come for her. Mel remembered well the sneer that had been in his voice when he threatened her, and it was only a matter of time before he made good on that promise.

As part of her routine, Mel was made to clean the kitchen, while others would have cared, she didn't. Mel used the time to try and desperately plan a way to avoid the Duke's advances. The kitchen was enormous and dirty, and her hands, more used to accountant work than physical labour, blistered from the less than effective 12th Century cleaning equipment. Nevertheless, Mel had 'settled in,' as he had put it, and she was dreading her first encounter with the Duke.

As thoughts of what he might have had store for her ran through her mind, Mel scrubbed hard at a greasy spot by the cooker and swore at it when it didn't come out. Mel was taking her frustration out on the floor when Elise, one of the other young maids, entered the kitchen carrying the linen that she was preparing to wash.

Mel jumped swearing, everything about this place had her on edge. She flung down her scrubber, moved forward and assisted the younger maid, while Mel knew that her job still needed to be finished, she need some company to get her mind of the Duke. Grabbing some of the linens from the top of the pile Mel followed her outside to the tubs. Elise and Mel had become close allies and she was fond of the girl, she was also grateful that she had someone to talk to.

Elise was a small, petite blonde who had only just turned twenty, she had told Mel that she was only eighteen when her father, once a successful businessman, put their family into the Duke's debt and all that he had to offer as payment was Elise. Mel looked at the young maid and realised that soon she would be much like her if she didn't get away. During the day, Elise was degraded to the role of maid, while at night the Duke sexually and physically abused her. Mel had never seen firsthand knowledge of this, but she didn't needed it because when she looked at her friend closely she could see flashes of scars on her arm as she bent down to pick up a dropped towel.

The pain that this girl must go through nightly made Mel sick, grabbing the girl by the shoulder Mel held her tight. Elise flinched as Mel gently pulled back her sleeve and revealed the extent of the wounds. Mel shook her head as sadness filled her, she could not let this happen to herself Mel thought bitterly. And she could not in good conscious let it keep continuing to her friend. "Elise you have to fight back," she pleaded.

"Please Mel, just let it go," the girl whimpered. "You haven't been through it yet, you don't know what he is capable of, especially when it comes to disobedience."

Mel hated feeling so helpless, but she knew her friend was right, what right did she have to give someone else advice on a subject that she knew nothing about. Slamming the towel into the buckets of water that were used for washing, Mel started to wash the towel. She continued doing this pulling the towel out and then pushing it back into the water running it up and down the washing board so vigorously that her fingers started to ache. Mel would never ever complain about washing again! What she wouldn't do to have her automatic top loader here, or a dishwasher, or even *Spray and Wipe!*

Mel knew she should just let laying dogs be, but the misery she saw on her friends face had Mel adding, "Elise, you can't just let him continue to beat you. I don't care if he comes to me, in fact, I wish he would then I could show him what it is like to try and abuse someone who isn't afraid to fight!" She spat angrily.

Even though Mel had said the words she knew deep down it wasn't quite true, but she'd had enough of anxiously waiting for the creep to make his next move. Mel didn't want her friend suffering anymore either and if that meant she had to fight the duke to her safe, then she would. A sinister laugh came from behind them, causing the hairs on the back of her neck to rise. Mel froze in shock not waiting to believe it, but when she turned to see the Duke walking back into the house, that sickening smile on his face she knew she was in deep trouble. *Shit! How long had he been standing there?* Swallowing the lump that had formed in her throat, Mel turned back to her friend who had an equal look of horror and fear on her face and tried to calm her nerves.

"Oh, Mel what have you done?" Elise asked her voice trembling.

Mel felt sick, he was home and now all the pent-up anxiety and emotion of being trapped here and waiting for the inevitable finally bubbled over. Mel gagged as bile reached the back of her throat and before she threw up into the washing Mel rushed to the side of house, she promptly losing her lunch into garden. As she sat there heaving what was left of her empty stomach into the garden, her anxiety exploded and all the signs of a panic attack brewed. This could not be happening! The Duke thrived on disobedience and pain, no not only had Mel given him exactly that, she had also bragged about it to her friend. Instinctively Mel knew that her punishment was going to be a lot worse than before, she would be lucky if she got out of this alive.

For the rest of the day, her nerves were shot and her mind was a jumbled mess of thoughts and emotions, Mel was finding it hard to focus on her work properly. The earnest sympathy and fear in her friend's eyes only made the situation worse. But as Mel cleaned up from the evening meal she rationalised that whatever as going to happen was going to happen regardless of what she had said, the only difference now was, at least she knew the when it was going to happen and that gave her time to prepare, and prepare she would.

As Mel finished her evening chores and walked resiliently up the stairs, determination grew inside her with every step she took. The fear was still there, but she refused to let it rule her, she was the master of her own story and tonight the Duke was going to learn that same thing. "Let him bring his worst," Mel murmured. She was not going to sit back and let this happen, she was hell bent on fighting him with everything she had and that was exactly what she would do. Mel just hoped it was enough.

=

Twenty-Seven

S itting on her rough maid's bed with her back against the wall, a far cry from the comfort of Kessan's keep, she listened nervously for movement outside her door, and as the night wore on, her resolve weakened slightly and her hope that he wouldn't come increased. That hope was dashed when heavy footsteps abruptly thudded down the hall, this was it, it was time for Mel to fight.

Sitting forward on her bed Mel waited, heart in her mouth, to see if they would stop at the room next door, but they continued on and she knew with a heavy heart that the duke was coming for her. Taking a deep breath, and offering up a prayer of strength and guidance, Mel pushed herself off the bed and placed herself at the farthest end of the room on the other side of the bed, using it as a barrier. Then she waited, listening as the footsteps slowed and then stopped outside her door.

This was it! Mel tensed as the handle of her door turned, slowly at first, then the door was thrown open, smashing against the wall with a loud bang. There he stood, a menacing smile on his face, Mel knew that he had thrown the door open purposely, hoping to catch her asleep and off-guard. One advantage to her!

Smirking back at him, Mel rebelliously stood her ground, silently daring him to make his move. "I see you still have not learned your place, whore." He sneered

Mel saw red, she was so sick of everyone referring to her as a whore. "Call me whore one more time dipshit and you will be the one learning a lesson," she said, trying to mask the tremble in her voice.

Mel knew her mouth was going to get her into trouble, but it went against her nature not to stand her ground. Ceana had taught her that when people were angry, they made mistakes, maybe if she made the duke angry enough he would storm off like he had last time. Unfortunately for Mel, it seemed like her plan wasn't going to work as well she'd hoped, instead her defiance this time only seemed to make him happier and more alert.

"Oh, I am going to enjoy breaking you." He purred as he took a step closer to her.

Now Mel really did feel like prey, her plan had backfired, w while she had hoped for anger and irrationality she ended up with pleasure instead and she didn't know what to do with that. Mel could deal with angry and irrational, but calmness was unpredictable and dangerous. Mel needed to get out of here and now, out of this room, this place, but most of all this century!

Mel waited to make her move, her eyes never leaving his face, until he started making his way around the bed. As the distance increased between him and the door, Mel couldn't wait any longer, she hurled herself over the bed and ran for the exit. Heart hammering and adrenaline coursing through her veins, she had almost reached the door when his body hit her from behind, sending her plummeting to the ground. She screamed, her body landed with such force against the floor that pain radiated up her entire body.

The force of the landing had also knocked the breath out of her and before she could think about what to do, the duke turned her around and pinned both her arms above her head, using just one of his hands to hold her captive. *He was strong but her will to survive was stronger.*

Mel's blood ran cold when the duke calmly, deliberately and slowly pulled a knife out of his boot; her fear was real now. Mel tried not to squirm, choosing to show defiance instead of fear, when the knife sliced her dress down the front bearing her entire body to his gaze. A trickle of blood formed where the knife had bit into her body, and Mel knew that if she didn't act soon she was going to end up as broken as Elise was and that she could not bear.

Undergarments were not allowed here; Elise had informed her of that rule when she had first handed Mel her clothes. It was so that the duke had easy access to them whenever he wanted. Now because of that Mel was completely exposed to his lust filled eyes. Mel made the mistake of looking up as he inspected her, and found that he was looking at her as if she was nothing but a piece of meat. The gleam that came to his eyes when he saw the trickle of blood running down her ribs was truly frighting, it was all she could do not to shrink back inside.

"Oh yes, I am going to enjoy ravaging your body." He purred running his tongue over his lips. Mel shuttered and didn't think it could get any worse, that was until he leaned forward and ran the tip of his tongue up the side of her face. Mel felt his cock swell in his pants, as slick line of saliva remained where his tongue had been. The bile began to rise in her throat as her fear almost overtook her, but then her fighting instincts kicked in again and she decided that it was now or never.

Taking a deep breath, Mel braced her feet on the floor, and bucked him off over her head. This time, she *had* caught him unaware, Mel was rewarded when the duke was thrown forward and, as he rolled off her, he lost his grip on her hair. Mel didn't wait around to see what he would do, rolling to her side she quickly sat up and planted her feet against his chest, shoving him forcefully into the wall across the hall, where he sat temporarily stunned.

Taking advantage of the moment, Mel bolted out of the door which was still open from his previous entry and ran down the hall. She continued to run even as a bellow of rage followed her from behind, Mel ran faster than she had ever run before, but it was still no use. She felt like minutes had passed, but it was only seconds before he had her hair in his hands once again. Ripping her head back roughly the duke pulled her back so forcefully some of her hair ripped out of her scalp and a scream escaped her mouth.

Surely someone had heard her scream and would help her? As the seconds ticked by, Mel realised no-one would come, because everyone was too scared to do something. No they would simply sit and their rooms and listen to the screams that broke through the silent house. Mel knew without a doubt that this would happen, because while he had been away the duke allowed his guards some entertainment with the maids and they took full advantage of his generosity.

The other people who resided in this house would no more help Mel than they had any of the other girls, Mel had to face the reality that she was alone and she couldn't depend on anyone else but herself. New anger and desperation fuelled her, reefing her head forward with as much as force as she could Mel tried to detach his hand, but it was no use, instead he only tightened his iron grip more. Mel continued to struggle as he pulled her head back and slammed it into the wall across from her.

The force of the blow brought blood to her nose, Mel's head instantly started spinning and her stomach lurched as the urge to vomit became stronger. Mel tried to get free when the bastard began to drag her back to her room. Mel couldn't let that happen, she knew that once he had her inside of that Hell hole would all be over. Taking multiple deep breaths, fighting through the pain that was still thrumming in her mind, Mel tried to get her eyes to focus and her head to stop spinning, she need to fight. As her equilibrium came back, Mel quickly spun around in his arms, throwing him off balance; he was clearly not used to anyone fighting back.

When she was free of his grip once more Mel closed her fist and threw all of her weight forward, punching as hard as she could. Mel was overjoyed when her fist connected solidly with the side of his head, it was not hard enough to do any real damage but it was hard enough to gain her a brief moment of freedom. But the moment didn't last long before she could run – she was still shaky from the concussion – the duke grabbed her by the arms and forcefully shoved her back into the wall, once again stealing her breath.

"Fine you little bitch, if you like it rough I can play rough. If you wanted me to take you right here in the hallway for all to see all you had to do was ask!" He snarled.

Reaching down, the duke ripped the remains of her dress completely from her body. Now Mel stood in front of him naked as the day she had been born, shivering from the cold, fear and exertion. The duke was not finished with his torture however, reaching forward he grabbed her around the throat and lifted her slightly off the ground. He had just enough pressure on her throat that she could still breathe, but still enough that with each breath she took it became a challenge to breathe.

Mel felt panicked, her asphyxiphobia was kicking in and it was robbing her of any clear thought. Mel had always had a fear of suffocating since she was little after she had almost drowned in a pool and here she was decades later, in a foreign land and her worst fears coming true. With each breath she took Mel fought the rising panic rushing through her veins. Her mind raced trying to figure out how to make him release her, but as she gasped and struggled, her mind became more frazzled and her sight dimmed.

If she blacked out now, at least she wouldn't remember what was to come.

As the blackness crept in a sharp pain ripped through her chest and brought her back to reality. It took her a moment to work out that the duke had grabbed hold of one of her breasts and began roughly palming it, while pinching the nipple between his fingers. Mel's eyes watered as the pain his administrations was causing intensified, surely it couldn't get any worse than this? But even as that thought crossed her mind, Mel watched in horror as he slowly placed his mouth around her nipple and bit down on it, before dragging his mouth back pinching the nipple harder between his teeth, drawing blood as he did so. Mel screamed in agony, she couldn't help it, she had never felt pain like this!

Mel was sickened as he raised his head looking her level in the eyes, the satisfied gleam that rested there repulsed her. "That's just the beginning, whore!" he spat savagely, spittle flecking her face.

Rage licked at her senses, she could not let this monster ruin her, she would not let him take away the one thing that was hers to give. Drawing on every ounce of willpower and energy she had left, Mel leaned her head as far back as she could and then butted him right in the nose. *Damn that hurt like a son-of-a-bitch!*

While the pain that radiated through her skull was intense, it gave her immense satisfaction when she heard a crack and the sound of breaking bone. It thrilled her to no end to know that she had caused him as much pain as he was causing her. *Take that, you pig!* She cheered inwardly as the Duke screamed in pain and dropped to his knees. As he fell his hold on her was lost, unfortunately Mel had been too high off the ground to anticipate the release and she too feel to the ground beside him. Mel looked over at him and a small smile of triumph spread across her face as she watching him bring his hands up to his nose to staunch the flow of blood.

Panting and gulping in air, Mel sat on the floor when he looked at her, and what she saw sent shivers of intense fear down her spine. There was nothing but pure rage in those eyes now, no ounce of human decency or any sign of sympathy, just pure unadulterated animal rage. Mel tried to back away, but the wall behind her stopped her retreat, this was bad, this was really bad. Mel could only watch on as he rose to his feet and approached her, never taking those eyes off of her, calculating his next move, stalking her like the pray she was.

Then the Duke attacked, grabbing her by the hair he yanked Mel off the ground and laid into her with such fury that it took all her willpower not to black out. Mel could no longer hold back the tears as blow after blow hit her ribs and her stomach, each one with more force than the last. Mel screamed out as she felt one of her ribs break, if he kept going he may just do more damage than she could handle. Thankfully though, once he had sated most of his anger, he stopped and simply glared at her.

Mel watched his chest rise heavily with exertion and anger, she had a feeling he wasn't through with her yet. Mel felt as though every bone her body had been broken, and she could see blood dripping on the floor from where she wasn't sure, what she did know was that her whole body was shaking with pain, fear and adrenaline.

The duke obviously liked what he saw, he looked at her with pure evil in his smile, before he once more grabbed her arm and started dragging her down the hall, towards the stairs. At first Mel was glad that he was going in any direction but her bedroom, but when he spoke a new fear entered her body. "Let's see you fight after this bitch." He spat.

Mel had no idea where he was taking her until they reached the basement, where rows of cold stone cells waited. Without pausing the duke pulled her to the last one, opened it, and tossed her in without a second thought. Mel's bruised, naked body sang out in complaint as it struck the hard-dirt floor. Without another word, the duke slammed the door to her cell shut and walked away without even a backwards glance.

Relief at being out of his grasp overwhelmed Mel until she had time to take in her new surroundings. There was nothing in here, not even a bed to lie on. The room was cold and dark; there was no windows, no coverings on the dirt floor and no light, and a scurrying sound in the corner caused her to freeze. Rats! It had to be rats!

With a heavy heart, Mel wondered if this was the place where she would meet her end, with only the rats to know of her fate. Perhaps head butting the duke wasn't the smartest idea she'd ever had, Mel thought miserably. Mel hoped that the duke would come back, but as the realisation that she was going to spend the night in this cell sunk in Mel did the only thing left to do. Rolling herself into a ball, as much as she could, Mel wrapped her arms around her legs and buried her head deep into her lap as she wept.

Her cold, exhausted and broken body started shivering uncontrollably as the cold from the dirt floor seeped into her body, and as Mel lay there praying for the end, she truly did believe that the duke may have been right, this just might be the thing that broke her.

Twenty-Eight

M el was so cold her body was finally numb to all the pain, she was sure she was almost hypothermic. Mel had gotten very little sleep during her stay in the cell, but was so tired, she no longer cared about anything. As she lay on the floor bleeding, Mel wondered what was happening at home, would Ceana be looking for her, did any of them even known she was missing, and if they did would they ever know what happened to her.

An immense sadness engulfed Mel as she realised that her parents and her grandmother might never see her again. As Mel thought about those that cared for her, her mind drifted to Hamish, the strong Highlander who had stolen her heart.

Mel found herself wishing that she'd had more time with him, she had been so stupid fighting the attraction that had been between them, and because of that stupidity she would miss out on finding out if that was something there. If only she'd given into her feelings when she had first met him, then maybe Mel could have at least enjoyed him for a little bit longer.

Mel was grateful that she had at least experienced that wonderful mind-blowing moment in the glen and as she imagined the warmth of his embrace her body began to warm a little. But the warmth went as quickly as it came, and as the cold one more seeped into her bones Mel closed her eyes and prayed, for the hundredth time, that she would get out of this mess alive and if she didn't, Mel hoped that her death came swiftly.

Mel lay on the cold hard ground, not knowing what time of day it was, the only thing that was constant in her cell was the sound of the rats scarring back and forth. Mel didn't know how long she had been in the cell when she heard footsteps coming down the hall right before the slammed open. She didn't need for anyone to tell her who was his, the duke's dramatic entrance told her everything she needed to know. Mel pulled herself into a tighter ball trying not to move, she hoped that he would see her pathetic state and just leave her as she was. But it was not to be, the footfalls drew closer before she was wrenched up brutally from her position.

Mel's body screamed out in agony at abruptly having momentum forced through her limbs. She had been laying in the one spot trying to stay warm for so long that her body rejected any kind of movement.

"Arsehole," she croaked out. Mel was beyond caring what he did to her anymore, all she cared about was denying him every chance she got.

"I see your manners still have not changed," the duke growled. Mel should have taken his tone as a warning, but she didn't see how he could do any worse than what he had already done, expect kill her, and that he would not do. The day he had thrown her into this cell the duke had given away his plan, he had told her that he wanted her to break, and as Mel lay shivering on the ground, she realised that, no matter how far she pushed, him the duke would not kill her until he saw that plan to fruition. He was not a man who liked to lose.

"Go fuck yourself!" She snarled in answer. She would have spat on him once more, but Mel's throat was dry from lack of water and she had to settle with her scathing remarks.

"Oh, little one, I prefer to fuck *you,* as you so nicely put it." He mocked as he pushed her violently up against the wall, and prepared himself to enter her. Mel cringed, only just realising now that he was as naked as she was. Her mind was so busy trying to better him it hadn't taken in that little fact. So this was his pitiful plan? He thought to weaken her enough so that she couldn't fight him! Well Mel had news for him!

No way was she ever going to allow this pathetic animal to defile her body, she didn't care how much pain it cost her, Mel decided that she would fight him until her dying breath if she had to. Mel summoned up as much strength as she could and let out a roar. She didn't hold back, using everything she had Mel punched, she kicked, and she bit, she was a like a wild animal who had been cornered. Mel put everything she had into gaining her freedom, she could hear him cursing her, but she didn't care. As she fought Mel felt her nails connect with his face, and her feet with his shin, but it wasn't until her knee connected solidly with his manhood, that any real damage was done.

Mel allowed herself a smile of vindication as he went down, gagging and raging.

"YOU WHORE!" he screamed at her, flecks of spittle and blood spraying from his teeth.

"Yeah, yeah, yeah, you've already said that," she scorned. "Is that the only insult you know?" Mel knew she was not strong enough to make her escape. She also knew that he would only take pleasure in hunting her. Instead, she squared her shoulders and prepared herself for the fury that she knew was coming.

"Oh, I know a lot more than that you bitch, and you are going to be sorry you ever tried to play this game with me." The duke sniggered breathlessly as he hoisted himself up.

"Go ahead, give it your best shot!" She stated as she stared him down, "but be warned, I will fight you with everything I have until you kill me." Mel said with more bravado than she felt. Mel cringed at his menacing look, maybe she shouldn't have challenged him so thought weakly after the point, and as he continued to stare at her Mel wondered if she had pushed him too far.

"Oh darling, I promise you that what I have in store for you is going to be worse than that and by the time you return, I will have you *begging* for death." He laughed.

What the hell did he mean by that? Return, return from where?

Before she could ask any questions, the door the cell slammed shut and she was once again forgotten, left alone in the darkness of a cattle with only the rats to ponder her fate. *When was this nightmare going to end?*

As the hours ticked on, Mel's nerves were stretched to breaking point. No longer did she try and get some sleep, instead she paced her cell waiting for something, anything to happen. The fight with the duke earlier had renewed her adrenaline and desire to live, she refused to lie back down and be at the duke's mercy when he returned. But when he door finally did open Mel was surprised to see Elise enter. Hope flared in Mel's heart, maybe she had won after all, but the moment she noticed that Elise was crying that hope was put out like a candle in the night. Elise's eyes were red and weepy and she looked at Mel with such sadness and pity that Mel felt nauseated all over again.

"Mel why couldn't you just leave it alone and accept your fate?" Elise pleaded as she took Mel back up to her room.

As Mel followed along behind her friend, she thought about that question herself, but the reality of the situation was, Mel was not wired that way, she had been born and raised in an era that did not accept this kind of behaviour and neither could she.

"Elise, it's not in me to just let someone hurt me. Where I come from, woman are taught to stand up for themselves against behaviour like this." Mel answered, trying to get the girl to understand.

Elise turned pitying eyes on her. "But you are not at home now Mel, now your fate is sealed and no-one can help you, especially anyone from home." The words that came out of Elise's mouth were filled with pity, and as she handed Mel a clean dress, she gave her one final hug before she walked out of the room, softly closing the door behind her.

Her friend's hug and words did nothing to quill Mel's panic, folding the dress out and putting it over her head, Mel cursed as she once again wondered what the future held. The Duke was unpredictable and now she had no idea what to prepare for. *Damn stupid temper.*

Mel had always been told that it would get her into trouble someday, she just didn't think it would be this kind of trouble. *There was no point in backing down now,* whatever he had planned for her Mel would deal with the same way she dealt with everything else in her life, one day at a time. Mel was grateful for the dignity of being clothed again, and with apprehension, she started to pace the room as she waited for him to come and get her, she knew it wouldn't be long.

Twenty-Nine

he bitch was going to pay. No-one insulted him! Mowbray fumed as he stormed into the woman's room, he grabbed her roughly and was pleased to see her wince of pain. He had hoped that her night stay in the cells below the castle would break her, but she had connoted to fight. Even now she looked at him with that infuriatingly defiant look, but that look wouldn't last for long.

Mowbray took great pleasure in knowing what was in store this bitch and he was going to enjoy every minute of her pain and torture. After his humiliation at failing to conquer her himself, he didn't care what it took to break her, as long as she broke; if he was lucky, Mowbray would get to witness the moment she broke. He could feel his excitement throbbing just at the thought of watching every inch of her spirit break inch by inch, nothing was going to give him more pleasure than that. Except maybe for the moment he brought her back here where he would punish her until she begged for him to take her.

Mowbray loathed to let anyone else sample her fire first, but it was time she learnt that there were worse men out there than him, and the place he was taking her too was the perfect environment for that.

"Where are you taking me?" She asked resignedly, as he dragged her out of the house and deposited her into his waiting carriage.

As much as Mowbray loathed to talk to her at the moment he wanted to see the fear back in her eyes. "Somewhere where you are going to learn manners and obedience!" he gloated.

Mowbray's pride was still sore over her last insult to his manhood, and it took a great amount of control not to slam his fist into her smug face. Slamming the door of the carriage shut, Mowbray decided to ride up with the groom until his temper had cooled enough to deal with her, she needed to be somewhat presentable when they arrived at their destination and in his present state, Mowbray was not sure he could keep his rage under control.

It took them a full day to reach the little town of Blightingham, on the edge of his county. Mowbray had ridden with the groom for most of the day, after which he spent the rest of the time in the carriage. The highlander's whore refused to acknowledge his presence and he was fine with that. Mowbray took the time to study her intently, his eyes watching for the moment she realised where she was going. He got some pleasure watching her stare miserably out the carriage's small window as they entered the town and pulled up in front of the *Red Scarlet*. His pleasure grew the moment realisation struck and fear and trepidation rippled down her body. Her eyes opened and her mouth formed an *o* of shock as she finally came to terms with what her future held. Turning to face him for the first time since he had joined her, the raw fear she no longer hid from him caused his whole body to tingle with lust.

Nothing turned him on more than the smell of fear on a woman. He had never understood where it had come from, but ever since he could remember, nothing brought him more pleasure than watching a woman writhe in fear and pain. The truth was he couldn't have sex without those emotions present, he gave up trying anything else long ago and learned to embrace it. At first, Mowbray had felt shame and guilt, he had thought he was the only one in the world who had these pleasures, so in the beginning he had kept it to himself. His younger days had been miserable trying to hide his true self.

By chance though, he had been coming home from London at the end of a season one year, and happened upon the *Red Scarlet*. This house of disrepute catered purely to men with his taste and here he learned that many of his peers were just as depraved, if not worse, than himself, and he felt alive for the first time! During his years here, Mowbray had learnt from the best and discovered how to elicit as much fear and pain as he could in new and innovative ways. That was why he had brought the little bitch here, here she was going to learn what real pain and punishment were, and his body was tingling with such pleasure that he almost came right there in his seat thinking about all the things he and his peers were going to do to her lush body. Once more his world made sense and Mowbray knew beyond a doubt that this woman would pay.

Thirty

Horror crept over her as Mel stared at the dilapidated building beside them. *He couldn't be serious? The bastard was going to sell her to a brothel!* Mel turned away from the house of horrors and turned her gaze back to the duke. All the pent-up rage she'd been carrying across the journey bubbled over and she was prepared to let it loose, how dare this man think he had the right to sell her.

Mel stopped and reconsidered her actions when she recognised the look of pure pleasure she saw on his face. The disgusting creep, he was getting off on this! Mel was about to say something about his depravity, but before she could get a word out, a blood-curdling scream sounded from somewhere in the building. Mel recoiled as he shivered once more, licked his lips and closed his eyes as if the sound of it filled him with pleasure.

Demented, this man was truly demented. Mel would give anything to take him home to the 21st Century, to modern day law enforcement, or a modern day shrink. But thinking about home only reminded Mel that she wasn't in her time, she was out of her depth in 12th Century England with a demented man and there was nothing she could do about it.

From what Mel could tell it didn't even look like there was any law enforcement to be found in this small, middle of nowhere town. Unadulterated fear gripped her, and Mel had an overwhelming need to run, to escape, to be anywhere but here. Looking around she tried to calculate what her rate of success would be, but as another scream rent the air she decided to Hell with statistics she needed to take a chance.

Diving for the door, Mel opened it with the intention of fleeing, but now sooner had her body made it half way out the carriage door the devil himself grabbed her before she could get away. She would never take freedom for granted again, she thought as she stared up at her future. Before she could do anything else Mel was pushed out of the carriage where she fell to her hands and knees. Her hands burned from the rough dirt road and her knees ached from the force in which she had hit the ground. Oblivious to her pain the duke picked her up and threw her over his shoulder before he toted her towards the house of disrepute as if she were nothing but a sack of potatoes.

No matter how much she fought, the monster didn't loosen his grip this time, he was too focused on getting Mel inside of her new prison. Screaming didn't seem to help either, and before Mel knew it, they were inside, the door shutting behind them with a resounding, ominous click. Mel started kicking and punching the duke which saw her deposited roughly on the floor in front of an elderly, busty woman who wore nothing but a corset and see-through skirt. The woman leered down at Mel, her yellowed teeth glistening, her eyes gleaming, eyeing Mel as if her next price had come to town.

Mel leapt up and grabbed the woman by the arm, hoping she could get her sympathy. "Please, you have to help me!" Mel pleaded, though she knew it was a long shot. "This man has kidnapped me from my family; I don't belong here!"

Whatever hope she had of the woman helping her disappeared when she put her hands on her hips and laughed. "Well, you weren't wrong Mowbray, she does have a lot of fire in her," the woman sneered as she contend to stare at Mel.

Reality struck as Mel looked at the greed permeating from the woman in front of her and, just as it had the day the highlanders dropped her on the dukes door, Mel's world came crashing down. Just as she had the first day she met the duke Mel knew without a doubt that she wouldn't find help here. The sick feeling in her stomach intensified.

"I did warn you that she was going to be a handful, Claudette." The Duke smirked.

"Oh baby, I am sure it is nothing I can't handle."

Mel listened on in horror as the two of them discussed her like she wasn't even in the room.

"Now you know the deal, work her hard, but no-one is to taste her unless I am here to see it. I want the pleasure of watching her beg for mercy." Mowbray informed Claudette as he handed over a bunch of gold coins.

So this was what he meant by punishing her? The bastard was going to allow men to have their way with her and beat her under his watch until she could take it no more! This was how her life was going to end, shock infused every inch of her body and mind. Looking back at Claudette, she was sickened by the amusement in the woman's face, *didn't anyone in this century have an ounce of humanity?*

"Oh honey have no fear," the woman purred seductively at the duke, "I will have her broken before the end of the week. Then she will be begging for you!"

All control left Mel, tears welled in her eyes and started to fall down her face. It was becoming all too real and all too much. How had her life come to this? She was the owner of her own accounting firm, she had friends and family that loved her and, apart from a few dating dramas, her life was great. All she had wanted was some excitement in her life, and now she was in the hands of a madman, not knowing what was going to happen next.

Tristan was right; excitement wasn't all it was cracked up to be, she should have been happy with her plane boring life. Mel felt sick, she just wanted to go home, why hadn't she left when Tristan had? As another blood-curdling scream rent the air, Mel's mind finally snapped, she felt numb, her vision swam and the world went black. The others payed her no mind, continuing their negotiations as she fainted to the ground, lost in a world where nothing could hurt her.

Thirty-One

Hamish kicked his horse once more, urging it on faster, he needed to get to Mel *now*. Enough time had been wasted trying to find out what had happened to her, and every minute more he wasted was another minute Mel was in danger, Hamish had been making good time, only to be interrupted by a snowstorm that caused them to lose half a day's journey.

At first, Samuel had refused to tell them anything despite the threats of torture and then actual torture. Showing surprising resilience the highlander wouldn't betray his Laird for any of it. While Alec had gained consciousness about three days later, he couldn't tell them much more than what they already knew. It had been a full week of agony and torture before Samuel finally broke and told them everything, including where the Macintoshes had taken her.

Hamish's blood had run cold when Samuel informed them that the bastards had planned to sell her to the Duke of Norfolk. Everyone knew about the Englishman's depravity; the stories of his cruelty had reached to the northern most part of Scotland. If Samuel was telling the truth and Mel was at the dukes mercy, Hamish was going to do more than kill the Macintosh, he was going to eradicate anyone who had a hand in this and then some.

Hamish had brought two of his best men along, Tamhas and Morgan, Kessan had tried to get him to take more, but Hamish knew that more men would have hindered rather than helped. Hamish also had another reason for leaving his mean behind, he wanted to make sure that his family was left well-armed and protected in his absence, he didn't need anyone else to worry about or slow them down. His own mood darkened at the memory of his sister's face when they had finally found out what happened to Mel.

Ceana had been crying when he and his men ha left, her utter heartbreak only added to his already growing fury. Her sobbing plea still rang in his ears. *"Bring her home Hamish. Please bring her home it's all my fault!"* Hamish had tried to reassure his sister that he would do everything he could while also blaming himself. Hamish knew that if he had brought Mel back to the keep with him that day, she'd still be with them safe at Kessan's Keep. Despite her matchmaking, Ceana could hardly have known that the Macintoshes would strike, but *he* should have been more prepared for any attack, no this was not on Ceana it was on his head.

Hamish cursed himself as he kicked his horse harder, he had let his guard down and revealed his weakness, something he had vowed never to do. Moments earlier they would have found him bathing alone, instead they got the vulnerable, 21st Century lass who was completely unprepared for anything the 12th Century could throw at her. As Hamish rode on he hoped and prayed that she was still alive, Ceana had lost so many people in her life Hamish knew that losing Mel would break her.

Hamish's anger surged at the thought of what was happening to Mel in the hands of the Duke. Kicking his horse harder, Hamish raced on towards the Duke's estate; it had already been two weeks since she had been taken, a lot could happen in that short time.

Mel groaned as she climbed into bed, every muscle in her body ached and screamed out in misery. She had spent the last two days being primed, as Claudette at called it, to receive her first client. Mel felt humiliated as she thought back on what being primed meant. This was a house that catered to the lowliest of scumbags, and that meant Mel had to learn to tolerate whatever was thrown at her. In the last two days, Claudette had had her beaten with all types of different weapons.

Most of the damage had been done to her ribs and torso; it wouldn't do her business to have the girls she wished to sell looking battered and bruised. After all Mel still had to look attractive to the men that were going to a bus her, not to mention the idea that the customers wanted their women looking untarnished, even though they themselves planned to beat them. The Duke himself had explicitly asked Claudette that Mel be in somewhat decent shape for his return, it was ridiculous.

Today had been particularly brutal, not because she needed to learn anything new, but because Mel had dared to ask Emerald for assistance in escaping, that had not gone over well for either Mel or Emerald. Both girls had been severely beaten and humiliated by the other girls and then they had been made to scrub the floors of the empty rooms until they glistened. At first cleaning the rooms didn't sound so bad, Mel would have taken that over the beatings anyway, that was until she looked at the rooms closely.

Each of the rooms she had cleaned today had been caked in the evening's aftermath and Mel could only imagine what the dark stains underneath her scrubbing brush had been. Those dark stains haunted her memory as flashes of what might have caused them tormented her mind, especially knowing that sooner or later, someone would be cleaning up after her. Mel's skin crawled in disgust.

To make matters worse the death stares Emerald had been shooting her only added to her misery, not only had she lost her chance to get out, she had also lost her only friend. Mel had known that Claudette had used Emerald as an example to the other girls, she hadn't done anything except listen to Mel. It didn't matter though, Claudette's plan had worked, now none of the girls would even talk to Mel let alone help her. She had lost any chance of making an ally or friend in this hellhole, Mel was once again alone.

Closing her eyes, Mel tried to will away the pain so that she could at least get some sleep. There was one small mercy for being so broken and tired, it didn't take much before her body finally gave in to sleep, and as had been her ritual for the last two weeks the last thing Mel remembered before she blissfully faded into nothingness was Hamish's face. If only he would come and save her.

Thirty-Two

Finally! Hamish felt relieved as the edge of the Duke's estate came into view. Slowing his horse down, Hamish moved over to an outcropping of trees, and positioned himself so that he could see all of the estate. Here he could inconspicuously observe who was coming and going without drawing attention to himself. While Hamish wished to rush in storm the place he knew that doing so would only put Mel in more danger.

Dismounting his horse Hamish positioned himself in the outcropping of the nearby trees; Tamhas and Morgan joined him not long after.

"Do ya see anything Laird?" Morgan asked as he pulled abreast of Hamish.

"Och yay. The bastard has guards placed all over the grounds." What's the plan then?" Tamhas asked joining them.

Looking at his men Hamish answered. "I am going to sneak in and see if I can find her. You two wait here, and be ready for trouble ya ken. I will give the signal when the coast is clear."

Both of his men nodded before they too went to find a place to bunker down. With his men waiting Hamish made his way quickly and quietly to the back of the house on foot, sword raised ready to fight. He had no idea who he would run into, but Hamish was not taking any chances, he would kill every last person here if need be to find Mel. Rounding the last corner, Hamish came face to face with a young maid and froze. Startled, the young woman dropped the basket of clothes she had in her hands and opened her mouth to scream.

"Doonae' fuss yaself, Lass." Hamish quickly hushed her. He had laced his voice with a bit of druid magic hoping that it would be enough to calm her. He never liked to use that kind of power and didn't wilfully abuse it, but sometimes it was necessary. Hamish didn't have to wait long before he could see it take effect, he could sense her fear starting to ease, until her eyes flicked down and saw sword. As they had when Hamish had rounded the corner her eyes widened again and she looked at him with new shock.

Hamish cursed himself for being a fool and slowly lowered his sword. He smiled awkwardly at her. He didn't know if the Duke was home or where Mel was and, if the lass screamed, all hell would break loose and he would lose his advantage. It had been hard enough to sneak past the guards as it was and the last thing he needed was for their attention to be drawn this way. "Please Lass, I willnae hurt ya. I am just needing some help," He tried again.

Thankfully the woman gave up on screaming and ran her trembling hand nervously through her hair . "H-how may I be helping you, Gov'ner?" She asked with a tremor in her voice, eyes nervously darting around them.

Hamish cringed inwardly at being labelled with a Sassenach title, but he didn't have time to debate the merits of Scottish and English distinctions. Taking a good look at the woman, he realised that she was a pretty, little thing. Grimly, he also noted the fading bruise on the side of her face, as well as a cut above her right eye, and sported bruises and scars up her arms. A spark of rage ignited inside him and Hamish hoped the Duke was here so that he could kill the bastard. *What man in their right mind found pleasure in hurting women and children?*

This girl couldn't be any older than Katie, he thought desolately. Men like Mowbray sickened him, they had no honour and no compassion, they deserved to wiped off the face of this earth, the certainly didn't deserve to look after such a sweet young lass. In that moment, Hamish decided that he was not going to leave the lass here, no matter what else happened, he would save at least one person's life today. Hamish didn't answer her, instead he let out a whistle that only his men would recognise.

"Who are you?" the young woman fearfully asked once more, eyes wide and confused. She hadn't moved and, even though she kept looking around to see if anyone was coming, she still hadn't screamed, Hamish took that as a good sign. At times like these, he was grateful for his magic.

Hamish felt bad for ignoring her but he wanted to make sure that his men were nearby before he told her anything. It was a defensive move, this way if anything happened he would be able to get her out of there fast, he didn't want to risk scaring her off. After waiting long enough for his men, Hamish proffered his hand. "Tis okay Lass, I'm a friend." He offered, in hopes of keeping her calm, then taking a chance, he added, "*Not* the duke's."

The dubious look she gave him told Hamish she wasn't buying it, so he tried another tactic.

"Och tis the truth. I'm not here to cause trouble, I'm simply looking for a young lass that was brought here aboot a week ago, she's a friend of mine..." Hamish didn't get to finish what he was saying the girl lost all her timidness as she grabbed the front of his shirt, clutching it tightly in both fists. Hamish was certain that he wasn't going to get any answers out of the girl, she was probably scared that Mowbray was on his way. Hamish looked around to see if his men were coming, he needed to get her out of here now. But the young woman had other ideas because she started shaking him as she pleaded, "You have to save her!"

Hamish's eyes darkened, the young woman now had his full attention. "What do ya ken?" He asked urgently grabbing hold of the tops of her arms to stop the shaking. The maid appeared dazed for a minute as she tried to decide how much to tell Hamish. Then, between gasps and sobs, everything spilled out in rapid succession as Hamish tried to make sense of it all.

"She tried to fight him, I warned her not to but she wouldn't listen!" She wailed. "God I wished she had just listened! I wish Mel had listened" The panic and sadness in her eyes at the mention of Mel troubled him.

Hamish tried to calm her down with soothing words, his pervious magic was no longer working. But the lass ignored him, instead she continued with broken sobs. "I should have stopped him! I should have helped, but I was so afraid. I didn't want to go back to the dungeon, it's so cold and dark down there and there are rats. But I should never have let him take her."

"Is that where he has her Lass?" Hamish asked impatiently, while his heart broke for what the girl was telling him, Hamish needed to find Mel. He needed to know if she was still inside or if the Duke had taken her someplace else. Hamish prayed for the first one, but his hopes were dashed when she shook her head.

"No, if only it were that simple. I'm sorry." She whimpered and broke down into sobs once more. Hamish pulled her gently into a hug, awkwardly trying to soothe her but as his arms encased her the maid became hysterical again. Grabbing at his arms, she began to shake him. "Why aren't you doing anything? You are running out of time! You must leave now; the Duke took her to Blightingham about three days ago! You have to find her; you have to save her. NOW!" She shrieked as her nails sunk even further into his flesh.

Hamish's heart sunk and he balled his fist to his side. He knew exactly why the Duke had taken Mel to Blightingham. The *Red Scarlet* was a well-known house of disrepute that allowed all sorts of depravity to happen underneath its roof, and it was common knowledge that Englishmen frequented there to revel in beating women and from the stories he had heard, it was the happy hunting ground for the Duke. The young woman was right; he had to get to Mel now. As Hamish looked around for his men once more, cursing their tardiness he prayed that Mel was still in once piece when he found her.

Hamish knew Mel was strong, but no-body was *that* strong. *Where the bloody hell were his men?* Putting his fingers to his mouth he was just about to let out another shrill whistle when Morgan rounded the corner. "Sorry Laird, the guards have figured out we are here. We took out two of them quietly but one escaped and headed across the field, it wonnae' be long afore the others realise what has happened. Tamhas is preparing the horses, we have to go, *now!*"

Hamish stared back at the young woman and realised that she had gone deathly pale. "Y-you have to g-go." She stammered. "He will be here soon; he isn't far. The other guard would have ridden to warn him. If the Duke catches you here no one will be able to save Mel, and she is all that matters."

Hamish swore. So much for his advantage, if the Duke found out that Hamish was here before he found Mel, there was no telling what he would do to her.

"Get her out of here," he ordered his man as he peeled the young woman from his shirt, before thrusting her towards Morgan.

"What, no, wait, you can't take me! You have to go and save Mel!" She cried in fear as she clutched on to his arm again. Morgan came forward and gently pried the young woman's fingers from Hamish.

"Shhh, it's okay, Lass" Morgan soothed. "We will no' harm ya, doonae worry aboot Mel, Hamish will save her. What's say we get out of here ourselves?"

The woman looked up at Morgan's eyes and nodded, and even though she was scared, Hamish was relieved when she finally agreed to go with his men. Morgan grabbed her hand and the three of them made their way across the lawn, back to the tree line where Tamhas was waiting with their horses. Hamish was glad that the young lass was not fighting them. "Take her to Ceana." Hamish ordered as he mounted his horse.

"Doonae worry Lass, my sister will look after ya, no harm will come to ya while in our custody." He promised, before he kicked his horse into action.

Hamish did not look back towards his men, he simply headed out of the forest towards the west. Before long he was galloping across the countryside, praying that he still had enough time to get to Mel before it was too late. As he rode on, he vowed that when he had her safely home, he was going to hunt down the Macintoshes and the Duke and make them pay for what they were doing to her, they had no idea of the fury that he was about to unleash on them.

They were going to rue the day they messed with Laird MacDonnell.

Thirty-Three

It took Hamish a day and a half of hard riding to reach the small town of Blightingham, although you couldn't call it much of a town. He rode down the street towards the stables, passing only a few small markets as he went. There were no authorities here, no milliners or any other businesses that would denote it as a decent place to live, it was purely set up to service the crofters from the nearby estates.

There were more inns for passers- by than there were stores, and a bar rested on each corner and right in the middle was the place he dreaded the most. Hamish supposed it was the reason why a place like the *Red Scarlet* did so well here, nobody cared what went on. Hamish rode on until he came across the stables and, on entering, he handed his horse to a nearby groom who nodded in greeting.

"Och Lad, could ya tell me where the *Red Scarlet* be?" Hamish asked the young groom.

"Hell's bells gov'ner, ya sure ya wanna be goin there?" The lad asked him sheepishly.

Hamish cringed as he was once again referred to as governor. He couldn't wait until he was out of England. These Sassenachs were making him feel caged in. "Och for starters Lad, I am no governor, I am a Scot born and bred. Do no' be placing me in the same category as yer Sassenach lords. And secondly, aye I am sure I want to be going there."

It wasn't so much his words as it was the scowl on his face that had the boy hurrying with directions. Once the lad had explained to

Hamish where to go, he took off in the opposite direction to tend to Hamish's horse. Hamish let out a tired breath, the last thing he had wanted to do was scare the lad but he didn't have the time or the patience to calm him down, he needed answers. After hiding his weapons just inside the doors of the stables, Hamish headed in the direction the lad gave him, his only prayer was that Mel was indeed here.

It was getting late, and the sun had begun to set, unsavoury types were strolling the streets, loud and boisterous, drunk and flailing about. Ladies of the night giggled and laughed and occasionally a rat broke free of the shadows and darted down the street. The whole town made Hamish feel dirty and unclean, he couldn't wait to get out of here. Before long, the sounds of raucous laughter, screams and music spilled out of one particularly decrepit building. This had to be the *Red Scarlet* Hamish thought disgustedly.

Hamish approached cautiously, keeping an eye out for the Duke, or any other familiar face, the last thing he needed was to be made, especially when he was this close. Preparing to enter the establishment, Hamish took a deep breath to centre himself, the thought of entering a place such as this made his skin crawl. As his foot touched the front porch, a woman's pained scream from an upstairs bedroom echoed into the night and laughter followed.

Hamish's stomach knotted as fury like none he had ever felt raged through his veins, the thought of Mel in one of those rooms being tortured and subjected to who knew what sent a bloodlust coursing through his body. As another scream sounded thought the night, Hamish's eyes dimmed, and it took every ounce of warrior training he had to stop the power rising in him.

Hamish knew he had to gain control or he would end up murdering every soul in the place. When he finally got his racing heart under control Hamish squared his shoulders and entered the establishment as unperturbed as he could. He needed to portray himself as a man who held no feelings for the women who were captured here, he had to appear to fit in with this crowd of debauched animals, only then could he become inconspicuous enough to blend in and watch for any signs of Mel.

Mel couldn't believe that it had been three days since she had been dumped in this hellhole, she mused as she cleaned the floors of the empty rooms. She swore that Claudette gave her this job on purpose, and the stupid bitch seemed to gain pleasure in giving her the rooms with the most blood and fluid in them. Mel shouldn't be surprised; Claudette was determined to inflict as much pain and suffering on her as she could before the Duke came for her. The woman sure did know how to earn the money her clients paid her that was for sure.

The woman also gained pleasure in keeping Mel in the dark, especially when it came to the duke. Each day that he didn't return meant that it was day that Mel was spared from being molested under his orders. But the promise of his return set Mel on edge and each day that he was gone meant more torture for her at the hands of the demented woman downstairs. Mel shuddered with repulsion as she once again wiped over something wet and sticky.

Leaning back, Mel dipped the sponge into the bucket of water that had now turned the colour of rust from blood, and rinsed it clean once more. Mel tried not to think of all the diseases that were floating around in this room, or in the water that she had just had her hands in. Mel hated germs with a passion, and to make matters worse there was hair everywhere. Mel hated touching hair, it creeped her out, and yet here she was touching blood and hair, could her life get any worse.

As Mel wrung out the sponge with more vigour, her ribs protested, they were still bruised and battered from earlier this morning. Mel supposed she shouldn't have lashed out at Claudette yesterday, because no matter how gratifying that one punch was, it had cost her. Claudette had made sure of it; the brutality Mel had faced today only proved how vicious the woman could be. Mel smiled to herself, at least the bitch had a nice shiner to go with her gaudy dress.

Wincing in pain, Mel placed her hands over her ribs to try and ease the ache she wouldn't mind betting at least one of them was broken. Breathing as deeply as her ribs would allow, Mel prepared to finish the job she had been tasked with when the devil herself marched into the room, clicking her tongue. The smirk on her face sent chills down Mel's spine. *What did the woman have in store for her now?*

Thirty-Four

Damn he was tired; this was the third night he had been in this hellhole. The first two nights had produced nothing and, if he didn't make any headway tonight, he would have to come up with another plan so that the owner didn't get suspicious. The waitresses had already been giving him funny looks and encouraging him to purchase their wares. Up until know Hamish hadn't had to buy anything, but he couldn't sit idle for much longer before they threw him out, this was a business of disrepute after all. Men came her to buy one thing and one thing only.

Making his way through the crowd, Hamish found an empty table, he sat down in the rickety, uncomfortable chair and took on the same menacing facade he'd worn the last to night in hopes of deterring people from talking to him. It wasn't hard to do, the anger he as showing was as real as this place, it only added to his menacing look and, so far, most people had kept away.

The facade was working well until a busty brunette wandered over to him, she had not been here the last few night, but tonight she had been staring at him since he walked in. Hamish tried his best to keep his eyes off of her, but it didn't work. Out of the corner of his eye Hamish saw the wench fix herself up before making her way over to him. Hamish had hoped that she would take the hint and stay away, but unfortunately the thought of making a few coins overrode her fear of him.

"What be ya pleasure?" she purred as she rubbed her body along his arm. The smell of stale beer and her gaudy perfume made

Hamish sick to his stomach, and while she may have been a beauty in her day, years of working in the place had replaced that beauty with gauntness, despise and fatigue.

"Och, a scotch for now wench," He sneered at her. It felt unnatural and dirty and went against every fibre of his nature to be cruel, but Hamish had to play along. He didn't know whether the girl was a prisoner here either, but she wasn't his problem.

The woman pouted but didn't say anything more, instead she went back behind the bar to get him his drink. Hamish hated disrespecting women, but this situation called for him to put his morals aside for the night. Here he needed to portray himself as a man with despicable morals, a man that would do whatever he needed to do to get pleasure. It would raise suspicion to be any different. Once more alone Hamish sat with his back against the wall, watching and waiting. He studied everyone in the spacious downstairs bar area, looking for any clue that may lead him Mel's whereabouts.

Around him men were groping women roughly, some were even abusing them right in the bar area, and no one appeared to care. There were no boundaries or rules here, and that frightened Hamish to his core. It took all the training Hamish had not to break some of their necks, but Mel came first. As he continued to watch the horror's that were occurring, part of Hamish hoped that the young woman back at the estate had been wrong. While he wanted nothing more than to find Mel, Hamish prayed that this had been nothing but a waste of time because he did not want to think that Mel could be in a place like this.

No one deserved to be here, especially not a 21st century lass who probably just wanted to go home. As the night wore on Hamish hopes of not finding Mel increased, the young woman who had brought him his drink came back once more trying to gain his services. Sitting on his lap the wench pulled his face to hers, the stench of her breath made his nose curl in disgust. He slapped her hands away.

"Nay wench, ye have nothing I want." He growled, roughly pushing her off of him.

"What's your problem, mister?" She snapped angrily before she stumbled off to find another target when Hamish simply looked away and didn't answer. Thankfully his tactic had worked, the wench steered clear of him for the rest of the night, as did the other whores.

As the hours passed by, Hamish continued to observe the melee and remained alert, but he was becoming restless and despondent. *This was hopeless.* Hamish came to the conclusion that he was not going to find Mel here, three nights of no sightings told him that. While Hamish was relieved that Mel was not in this place, he was also out of options. This had been his last hope and now it looked like she had been moved on.

Hamish clenched his fist on the table and cursed under his breath, the duke could have gotten the warning in time and pulled her out. Hamish needed to get out of here and find out what happened to her, he needed to come up with another plan. Every minute he spent sitting here was another minute Mel was in danger. Hamish stood and downed the last of his drink preparing to leave when a commotion on the balcony drew his attention.

There she was!

Hamish couldn't believe what he was seeing, there on the balcony only a few feet from him was Mel. In true Mel style Hamish watched as she struggled and fought as she was dragged from one room to another by a large, buxom woman. Hamish was relieved to see that her spirit hadn't been broken, a small smile spread across his face as Mel launched into a tirade at the woman, that fire was still alive!

Hamish's humour faded however when the woman backhanded Mel so hard she stumbled. Hamish was about to rush forward but halted his action just in time. Balling his fists in anger once more he stayed standing but the table doing the only thing he could, watch. Hamish couldn't help a grin of pride cross his face when Mel lifted her head and spat at the woman. The woman screamed at Mel as another girl grabbed Mel by the hair and practically threw her into the room before she slammed the door shut and locked it. It seemed that the 12th Century England wasn't quite prepared for a 21st Century lass either, he thought wryly.

Hamish wanted to rush up the stairs and rescue Mel, but he knew that he wouldn't get anywhere near her before he was stopped. No Hamish's best bet was coming up with a solid plan, and that involved the buxom woman Mel had just spat hat. Hamish watched as the woman in question shoved the key to Mel's room down her top and proceeded to come down into the fray. No one else seemed bothered by the commotion he had just witnessed, almost as if it was a regular occurrence. It made him angry to think about Mel going through this each night, but at last there was hope. He had found her, and she was alive!

Sitting back down, Hamish took a deep breath and tried to calm his beating heart. He deduced that the woman he was watching had to be the owner of the *Red Scarlet*. No-one else in this place had the power to treat the women like she had, except the men of course. Now that Hamish knew that Mel was all right, he needed to clear his head and come up with a plan. Calling the waitress over Hamish ordered another drink and prepared for a long night, he knew this couldn't be rushed. Mel was okay for now, the best thing he could do for her was figure out a way in which he could get them both out of this alive.

As Hamish sat at his decrepit table, he calculated his options, and as he drunk drink after drink Hamish began to realise the only logical way to get Mel out of here was to pay for her. *"Cac."* Downing the last of his scotch Hamish swore once more. Both Mel and Ceana were going to have his balls when they found out that he had paid for her like a common whore. But there was nothing for it, he had to get her out of here before the duke came back and this was the only way he knew how without drawing unwanted attention to them.

The decision made Hamish rose, downed the last of his drink and went to see the owner. "How much for the wench in that room?" Hamish asked the buxom woman, he had watched for the last hour. Hamish had been right, she was the owner, he could tell that by the way the men and the wenches came to her throughout the night. Hamish recoiled inwardly as the old hag's eyes looked him up and down as if he were a morsel that she wanted to devour and he hoped and prayed that the price he was going to have to pay wasn't him.

"Now mister, wouldn't you prefer someone a little more experienced with handling men as big as you?" The woman purred as she ran her hand up under his kilt and unabashedly grabbed his cock. Bile rose in Hamish's throat as she continued to work him. Hamish had to force himself not to grab her hand and reef it away. He needed this woman on his side and offending her in such a manner would not gain him that aid.

"As much as I would like to sample ye, right now I would prefer taking that wild 'hoore up there for a ride," he whispered with faked pleasure. "I saw ya little spat and she has more fire in her than all ya other lifeless 'hoores and I want somethin' wild, ya ken."

The woman gave him one last wistful rub before she removed her hand. "I would love to accommodate you honey, but unfortunately someone has already paid for her exclusivity, and that customer I do not want to disappoint."

Swearing under his breath, Hamish tried to think of another plan. He had not counted on the duke keeping her for himself, but he should have. Scanning the room Hamish saw men spending their coin like they had an endless supply, then inspiration hit him. *How could he have been so daft?* There was only one thing that spoke in a place like this. "How 'bout I pay ya a triple of what he is payin'?" Hamish offered. With the amount of coin he had just offered, no bargain was off the table.

Hamish knew it was going to cost him a hefty purse, the Duke would have made sure that it was worth the madam's while to keep her here for him exclusively. Hamish could see the indecision play out on the madam's face, she looked at him suspiciously for a moment, but the woman's eyes glowed with greed as she considered his offer. He knew she was weighing up the benefit of upsetting the Duke against the profit she would make, and just as Hamish suspected, money won.

"Fine honey, if you're that keen to have her you can. Maybe you will have better luck at breaking her then we've had. Follow me!" she beckoned as she started up the stairs.

Hamish had to stop himself from showing any outward emotion at the mention of the torture Mel had been going through. Balling his fists up and calling forward his power, Hamish continued to play his role as he followed her all the way to the end of the corridor, where she showed him to an empty room. Exhilaration pulsed through his veins as he realised that it wouldn't be long until he had Mel back safely in his arms.

"Before I bring her to you, I want payment up front," the woman ordered, pausing mid-step turning to face him.

Hamish had been hoping that she would wait until after the deed had been done, but he should have known better. With that much gold on the line and the Duke's wrath, the madam would have made sure he was good for it before he got to sample the goods. Luckily, Hamish had brought a decent amount of coin with him and would have paid everything he had to get her back. Reaching inside his sporran, Hamish pulled out a handful of coins and paid the woman ten gold coins, hoping it was enough. It was an exuberant price but, for Mel, he would have paid more.

Hamish still had a few coins left, and it would be just enough to get them home, but if need be he would give them up as well. Hamish was not sure how much the woman expected, as she hadn't given him an exact price, but as the woman tucked the money into her corset and left, he assumed it was enough. Now all he had to do was wait and come up with a plan for their escape once he had her.

Thirty-Five

Mel cleaned the blood from her lip, cursing everyone and everything for the hell she was in, she winched as the rawness of her lip joined the pain in her ribs. Could this get any worse, Mel thought miserably, that was when the door opened. Mel turned and saw Claudette staring at her with a look of such satisfaction Mel knew instantly that her night was going to slide further into hell than it already had.

"What do you want?" Mel spat at her as she turned around and looked in the mirror once more. Mel couldn't bring herself to keep the venom from her tongue anymore, and she was through showing this bitch any type of respect. It didn't matter what she did, this woman was hell bent on making her as miserable as she could, so why should Mel make it easier for her than she had to.

"Oh love, I am so going to enjoy this. You want to know what I want, I want to watch you break and tonight that just may happen."

Mel furrowed her eyebrows together, before spitting. "What the hell are you blathering about now?"

Mel had expected the woman to go into a rage as she had every other time Mel had spoken to her rudely, but the smile that crossed the woman's face scared Mel. "It's your time to shine, sweetheart." Claudette sneered as she came forward and grabbed her arm roughly dragging her out of the room.

"Where are you taking me?" Mel demanded, trying too reef her arm free of the woman's grasp. But as Mel expected the woman chose to ignore her, it was her way of making Mel suffer a little more. Since she'd gotten here, Mel had pleaded and begged to be released, but to no avail and the only thing she had come to understand was that this woman got just as much pleasure out of torturing the girls as the men did.

Mel had finally had enough, "I said, where are you taking me?" Mel screeched, once again reefing her arm, this time gaining her freedom. Her ribs screamed in protest, but she didn't care. Now was her chance, Mel tried to find a way out but several men below had paused and were now watching her with way too much interest. There was no way she wanted to be down there, besides, the ridiculously gaudy outfit they had her in would only hinder her escape. Mel could barely breathe the corset was so tight, running was going to be near impossible. Mel was surprised that her boobs were staying in at all, they were pushed up so high.

Mel continued to look around, that was when she spotted the door at the end of the corridor, perhaps it led outside. It was worth a shot, Mel thought hopefully, but before she could make a move, Claudette grabbed her arm tighter and hauled her down the hallway again. Claudette still hadn't answered her question, and it didn't appear as though she would. *The least the bitch could do was warn her about what was going to happen*, Mel thought bitterly.

She was just about to give her a piece of her mind when they stopped in front of a bedroom door. Mel knew that this was one of the rooms that the men hired out when they wanted alone time with the girls, and she knew what went on inside. Mel had cleaned up the blood and semen enough now, and then the reality of what was happening came crashing down on her. It was finally time. She was being sold.

Bile rose up in the back of her throat, and her breath started coming out in short, sharp bursts as the screams of the girls next door rang in her ears. Grabbing Claudette's arm, Mel tried pleading once more. "Please, please don't do this. If you have any compassion at all, don't make me do this. I don't belong here and you know it. I just want to go home."

Anger welled up in Mel as she mentioned home, this was not how her life was meant to go – these people were insane. Looking into the woman's eyes, Mel searched for any trace of compassion and understanding, but the emotionless eyes that stared back at her told Mel she was wasting her breath. Claudette didn't care about human decency, she only cared about money, and when she opened the door and pushed Mel in she knew the woman meant what she had said. Claudette was going to get as much pleasure out of seeing her break as the duke would. Mel was well and truly fucked now.

As she stumbled into the room, Mel caught a glimpse of her smirking face as the door slammed shut behind her. Numb, Mel heard the key click in the lock as Claudette's footsteps went back down the hallway, away from the room. Mel pounded on the door, furiously screaming for her to come back, promising all kinds of hell if she didn't. Mel didn't care who was in the room with her bath moment, she was too afraid to look behind her and see what kind of monster had paid for her.

But as the minutes ticked on and no-one came, her terror rose. No-one was meant to touch her without Mowbray being here, she had heard him order it himself. Her stomach sunk, that could only mean one thing, the duke was here, and he was here for her. Hearing heavy footsteps behind her, Mel quickly glanced around trying to find any kind of weapon, but there was nothing. Apart from the bed, the room was almost as sparse as the dungeon had been. Between the locked door and empty rooms, the place was escape-free.

Mel closed her eyes and balled her fist by her side, she was ready to fight with every fibre of her being. If this man thought that she was like every other woman in this place he was in for a rude shock. This man was going to learn what 21st Century women were made of and Mel promised that it was not a lesson he would soon forget.

As the footsteps continued to come closer Mel took a deep breath, squared her shoulders, lifted her head a little higher and slowly turned around to meet her fate.

Blinking twice Mel tried to come to terms with what she was seeing. Her mind must have finally cracked, either that or she had already been knocked unconscious and was dreaming, that was the only plausible explanation for what was in front of her. Mel continued to stare as her eyes locked with the greens of Hamish's.

She was frozen, she even found it hard to breath. Mel was afraid that if she moved, if she even blinked he would disappear and the duke would be there instead. But the longer she started the more she began to believe what she was seeing. There he was, Hamish; with his legs braced apart, standing tall and strong – her magnificent warrior was there. Closing her eyes, Mel took a deep steady breath and slowly reopened them; praying that her eyes weren't playing tricks on her. But when they opened and he hadn't disappeared, her heart beat faster. Hamish was still there watching her carefully, her relief was so overwhelming her legs buckled and she fell backwards against the door.

"Och Lass, now didn't I warn ya to stay out of trouble?" he asked with a lopsided grin.

Mel's battered and bruised heart filled with joy, the reference to their battle on arriving at the keep not lost on her – it was his way of letting her know that he wasn't mad with her. Mel couldn't hold back the tears any longer, pushing herself from the door she fell into his open arms. Pain ripped through her body as he caught her and wrapped her in a bear hug with arms that she thought she would never feel around her again, arms that she'd dreamt about every night. As he continued to hold her Mel realised she was sobbing, great heart-wrenching sobs, sobs that intensified when he pulled her in tighter.

"Shh, doona fuss yaself. Ya safe now," he whispered as he kissed her forehead and rocked her gently.

Looking up at him through tear-filled eyes, Mel took in every plane of his beautiful face, she drunk him in like a drought-stricken land absorbing rain after a deluge. He had come, against all odds, and he had found her. As Mel stared into his eyes, she realised that she loved this man to the very depths of her soul. This wonderful man who both infuriated and melted her at the same time, had accomplished what no man had been able to in years. Hamish's hands cupped her face and he carefully wiped her tears away with his thumb. The love and gentleness in his touch was such a stark comfort after nothing but abuse and hate for weeks. Mel felt fresh tears brewing, and has her love for him grew she clung to him never wanting to let go.

"I can't believe you came for me." She hiccupped as the tears started to slow.

"Och Lass, now ya insult me. Did you honestly no' ken that I would?" He asked gently.

Mel shook her head. "No, it's not that, I didn't doubt you would try; truthfully, I didn't think anyone would be able to find out where I was taken. I assumed that, if anyone came, it would be Kessan, after all I am his guest." Talking about home brought the horror of seeing Alec lying in a pool of blood and the feeling of being alone and afraid crashing back down on her. Her whole body started trembling anew.

"Och Lass, that is one thing ya will never have to worry aboot. I would turn over every stone if I had to, to find ya." Hamish swore to her vehemently, as he one more drew her in for a hug. Mel winced as his strong arms pressed against her and her cracked rib protested; a small groan escaped her lips before she could recover.

She wasn't surprised that Hamish noticed her pain and dropped his arms away in horror, Hamish noticed everything. "Och, how badly are ya injured?" He asked softly, easing her away from himself to try to see for himself. Mel was surprised to see the anger flashing in his eyes.

"It's nothing but a few bruises." She lied as she looked up into his beautiful green eyes. The concern she saw in them was her final undoing. Placing her hand abasing his face Mel leant up and pulled his mouth down to meet hers in a fierce and almost desperate kiss. Hamish pulled her gently up against his body and returned her passion, but she could tell he was holding back.

The way he was kissing her now was nowhere near the passion he had shown her in the glen that day. Right now Mel needed him with a fierceness she had never felt before, she needed the same passion she had felt that day. Ignoring the pain that was now raging through her body, Mel deepened the kiss as she tightened her own arms around his neck, an overwhelming need to feel his strength filled her body and she sighed in relief when Hamish let go of his concern and took her like she needed to be taken.

Thirty-Six

Mowbray stormed into his estate, fury radiating through every pore of his body. He had been on his way home, looking forward to taking some of his denied lust out on the young maid Elise, when one of his guards found him and informed him that a group of Scotsmen had come into his home and stolen Elise right from under their noses. Two of his best guards had been killed in the battle while three more had been injured leaving his home defenceless.

Mowbray knew of only one Scotsman who would have dared enter his home and take what was his, MacDonnell. Slamming his fist down on the table, Mowbray swore loudly with impatience. *Where the hell were the Macintoshes?*

He had sent his guard to fetch them yesterday, after receiving the news and they still had not shown up. *MacDonnell was going to pay!* Mowbray shivered with anticipation as he thought about the pain he was going to inflict on the laird, who did he think he was. But before Mowbray could do anything he had to wait to speak to the Macintoshes. He had a plan and he needed his allies to help but the plan in motion. A smile spread over Mowbray's face as he thought about what he was going do. He was going to make sure that the MacDonnell Laird understood exactly what it meant to cross swords with Mowbray, and the Macintoshes were going to help him.

Mowbray needed to get back to the brothel quickly, before the Scot found out where he was hiding the girl. If he thought he could just come and take her home, the Scotsman was in for a rude shock.

No-one, and he meant no-one, was going to take the whore away from him without a fight. She was his and he wasn't done with her, he would never been done with her. Mowbray's frustration began to build as the minutes ticked by, but the frustration lessened a little when the door opened and Laird Macintosh waltzed into the room, as if he didn't have a care in the world. It was all Mowbray could do not to kill the bastard on sight.

"Och, what is the problem now, Mowbray?" Laird Macintosh hissed.

"MacDonnell." He snapped sharply, incensed at the brashness of the Laird's entrance.

Mowbray was appeased a little when the Laird missed a step his composure shaken. "What do ya mean MacDonnell?" Macintosh asked, surprise and a glimmer of fear flashing across his eyes.

Mowbray was pleased to see the smugness leave the Laird's face; finally, the stupid bastard understood the seriousness of the matter. "Well, my dear Laird, that bastard came into my home, killed my men and took my property and this is all your fault." The rage he had felt earlier, returned twice as strong, his face mottled red and he could feel his reserve starting to slip. Taking a deep breath, Mowbray tried to bring his emotions under control.

"Ya no' meaning the Lass?" The laird asked angrily.

"No, she is tucked away somewhere safe, for now. But, he did take one of my other girls. What this tells me though is that he will not give up trying to find that whore. We need to distract him."

Mowbray watched as the Laird's jaw tensed, he knew that Macintosh wanted to kill McDonnell, but Mowbray had just taken that right away from him. Nobody was going to kill the Scotsman but him, but before he did Mowbray wanted him to suffer.

"What do you need?" Macintosh finally asked.

A smile spread across Mowbray's face, what he had in plan for MacDonnell should give Macintosh some pleasure. "I want you to go back to the highlands, to the McKinnon keep to be exact, and destroy anyone that ever meant anything to MacDonnell." He ordered.

An evil smile spread across the Laird's face. "Och, aye it will be my pleasure. I will also destroy MacDonnell at the same time."

"No, *that* bastard is mine, do what you will with his family but leave the Laird for me," the Duke hissed.

He could see that the Laird wanted to argue further with him, but he took one look at the Duke's face and exited quickly, leaving to do Mowbray's bidding. With any luck, the Laird would hear of the battle and return home without the woman. Scotsmen were fiercely loyal to their kin and Mowbray knew that the Scot's blood in MacDonnell would not allow him to do anything other than leave his mission and go home and protect his family. Mowbray was sure that the laird would forget about the girl in the process, leaving her to his administrations once and for all.

Mowbray smiled his first smile since he had left the girl at the brothel. He knew the men would follow his orders and once he had moved the bitch to a more secure place he would turn all of his attention to capturing the bastard. Not only was Mowbray going to kill MacDonnell, he was going to make him watch as he broke the girl right before his eyes.

Thirty-Seven

Recognising that time was an issue, Hamish knew in the back of his consciousness that they needed to get out of here and quickly, but for now that didn't matter, all that mattered was the woman in his arms. Hamish had been surprised when Mel had deepened his kiss, and before he knew it they were making love. Now as they lay on the bed, naked he couldn't find the will to move. He knew Mel was afraid that he was going to disappear as she hadn't left his side since she saw him.

Hamish looked down at her bruised body and fresh anger rolled over him. Mel tried to kiss him once more but he gently refused. As he gazed down at her, the anger continued to build within him. He should have gotten here sooner, he should have been able to save her from the pain she had endured. Maybe if he hadn't left her in the glen, she wouldn't have been taken and then the marks that now marred her body could have been avoided. Hamish ran his eyes the length of her body and he wished that the duke or the madam were in the room so that he could rip their hearts out.

As Hamish's anger rose higher he took stock of her injuries, promising retribution later. Her lip was cracked, swollen and encrusted with dried blood, a reddened imprint of a hand burned on her cheek and he could see several small cuts in her hairline. He leant forward and kissed every mark on her face, before he sat up and continued his appraisal.

As Hamish moved the sheet out of the way so he could see her full body he was shocked at the number of bruises that blemished her beautiful skin. Her entire body was marred with them; her ribcage was blackened, and he wouldn't have doubted that she had at least a couple of broken ribs. The sharp, shallow breaths she was taking certainly suggested so. Welts that could only be from a leather belt formed thick ridges on her stomach and breasts. Hamish could see the welts trailing over her ribcage and he knew that if he turned her over, her back would look just as bad as the front.

Mel had gone through absolute hell while he had been trying to find her and he tried to keep the shock and anger from showing on his face. Moving to position himself over her to get a better look at her injuries, she once again tried to bring him lower, but he wouldn't be deterred. With determination Hamish took her hands in his and held them gently above her head. Leaning forward he continued to kiss each and every bruise until he reached the core of her womanhood. Releasing her arms, he lowered his head, and took her into his mouth, gently lapping her until he had her writhing underneath him.

"Please Hamish, I need to feel you inside me." She begged. Hamish couldn't deny her anymore, he was loath to hurt her, but he need her as much as she needed him. Positioning himself at her opening, Hamish gently traded places with her until she was straddling him. Mel looked down at him confused.

He offered her a small smile as he explained, "This way I wonnae hurt ya." Hamish gently raised her above him and then lowered her onto himself.

Hamish hissed with pleasure as he watched her eyes slowly close. Her head fell back on a moan that he felt deep in his soul. He was so deep inside her that he was almost undone then and there and, when she started to gently ride him, it took everything he had to let Mel find her pleasure first. It didn't take long before she cried out and he felt her clench around him. His name escaped her lips with emotional ecstasy in her husky voice and that was his final undoing. Hamish's body resonated with desire and hunger and, as he held her hips as gently as he could, he pushed upward one last time, spilling his seed into her.

Hamish closed his eyes as he felt the release of the tension and worry of the last few weeks melt away. Mel fell forward, kissing his chest as she did. Hamish gently wrapped her in his arms and held her close as they both floated back to Earth. He knew he should feel guilty for doing that to her, but he couldn't bring himself to feel anything but pure bliss.

They lay in each other's arms for several minutes, but Hamish knew they should move. They had already taken enough time, but right now he didn't have the energy nor the will. And from the way Mel was holding him, he was certain that she didn't want to either. He wanted to stay like this for eternity, but reality came crashing in on him when he heard a scream from somewhere in the building. He felt a shudder as Mel tensed and then groaned as her ribs protested the movement. Anger and guilt at everything she had endured mixed together, building in him a rage so pure that he could feel the magic in him pulsing. He knew he had to get it under control before the rage ignited the magic and it became unpredictable. When his power became unpredictable Hamish couldn't promise what would happen, and that he could not allow.

Hamish wasn't ready to show Mel that side of himself just yet. But as soon as he had Mel safe, he was going to unleash the magic on every one of the bastards who had laid a hand on her. "How did you find me?" Mel asked as she kissed his chest, bringing him out of his anger and cooling the power the was rising. It never ceased to amaze him how quickly she could build up his desire for her, while calming the madness inside. Just the touch of her lips on his skin sent him to the stars.

Closing his eyes, Hamish tried to will himself away from those thoughts. They didn't have time; they'd done enough not to arouse suspicion, but they needed to go soon. Hamish answered her, hoping that it would get her moving "we were able to get some answers out of one of the bastards who had been left to die in the glen. Then ya friend Elise sent me here."

Mel bolted upright in the bed, grabbing her ribs as they protested once more. A look of pure grief and pain entered her eyes and it had him worried. Hamish sat up and took her face in his hands, forcing her look at him. Softly he asked "och what is it Lass?" Ya can talk to me," The pain that radiated out of her eyes ricocheted through him.

Her body trembled as she looked at him, "they killed Alec, Hamish. Those men they just killed him and left him there to die. I tried to save him but...I....I and now I have also endangered Elise." Her words broke off as she buried her head into his chest and wept.

Hamish put his arm around her, "och, nay it is ok. Alec is fine."

Hamish soothed. Mel lifted her head, her eyes desperately seeking his for answers.

"Iain found him on the side of the road just outside of the village. He tried to make it back to us Lass, but he had lost too much blood to make it all the way back. He is still not fully recovered, but he is alive, I promise ya. Elise is also fine; I sent her back to Ceana with my Men." Hamish felt happiness at being able to offer her some good news. Mel's relief shone through her eyes and her sobs relaxed. She looked at him with hope on her face, "do you honestly believe he is going to be ok?" She asked softly.

"Aye Lass, I do." He nodded.

Through watery eyes, she smiled up at him as she reached out and took his face in her hand, moments later Mel touched her lips to his in a kiss that showed him just want this woman meant to him. Never in his life had Hamish considered falling in love, and now he couldn't imagine how he was going to let the lass go.

Thirty-Eight

Everything was going to be okay, as long as Hamish was here nothing bad would happen to her, Mel thought giddily. She still found it unbelievable that he had shown up and even though she knew they should be running, Mel didn't want to let him go. The immense relief at seeing him and not the duke was like no other feeling she'd ever had before and part of her was still afraid of waking up and realising it was a dream. Mel wanted to spend more time with him, holding him, touching him and kissing him, but deep down she knew Claudette would come back soon.

Their time was running out and Mel knew that Claudette ran a tight ship with her clients. Her clients only got what they paid for and nothing more, nothing less, and considering that Mel wasn't even supposed to be here she was sure Claudette would not give her a minute more. Neither would she want to miss the satisfaction of seeing her "broken."

The gleam that had been Claudette's eyes as she threw her into the room told Mel that the woman thought Hamish was going to be just the man to do that. Mel wondered exactly what Hamish had told the vile woman to make her think he would. Mel knew that the bitch wouldn't have given her to him if she had even an inclination that the duke was his enemy. Mel would have to remember to ask Hamish about it, but later, the sooner she put as much distance between herself and this place, the better. Reluctantly pulling herself out of her lover's arms, she whispered urgently, "Hamish we need to get out of here!"

"Aye, I ken Lass," he nodded as he swung his legs over the bed and picked up his kilt. Mel was grateful that this man was not one to take his time, he was already in warrior mode. As Mel went to pull herself up from the bed, she stopped, and admired him for a minute, she couldn't help it, unlike Hamish Mel was not disciplined at all when it came to him. She watched the way his muscles flexed as he wrapped his plaid around himself, and she continued to watch as he finished putting on his sporran. But as she continued watching it occurred to her that something wasn't right. Something was absent from this picture.

Then it hit her, Hamish didn't have any weapons on him! From the moment she had met him, he had never been without them, especially not his sword. Even that day down near the pond, he had had a small knife strapped to his leg, while his weapons lay off to the side near his clothes and yet here he stood with nothing, not even a knife.

"Where are your weapons?" Mel blurted without even thinking.

Hamish chuckled. "There's my blood thirsty wench." A smile spread across her face on its own accord. She knew that he was referring to the times that she had fought with him and she supposed that he was correct, she was a bit blood thirsty, but this was not time to joke.

Mel poked her tongue out at him, when he didn't answer, and knowing that he wouldn't, she rose to dress herself. Depression and humiliation struck her when Me looked down at the gaudy brothel clothes she had been wearing. She didn't want to put them back on, not in front of Hamish. The corset constantly crushed her abused ribs and the thought of putting them back on was too much to bear. Looking around the room in desperation, she tried to find something, anything else that she could use as a makeshift dress, but there was nothing. *Damn it.*

Fresh tears pricked her eyes, she was going to have to wear them unless she wanted to make her escape in the nude. Nausea erupted in the pit of her stomach as Mel glared at the offending garments, wishing that she could set them on fire. "Here," she heard Hamish say. Mel breathed a sigh of relief when he pulled out a shirt and an extra plaid from his bag. The shirt was miles too big on her and the opening came half way down her chest, but it was still better than the alternative. Tying the strings up as best she could, Mel wrapped the plaid around herself to form a makeshift skirt, it would have to do until she could get some decent clothes.

"How do I look?" She asked impishly, trying to lighten the mood. Hamish gave her a lopsided grin.

"Och Lass, perfect as always," he replied before kissing her. Calming her nerves, Mel readied herself for the next hurdle.

"Ok, my Highland Hero, how do you plan to get us out of here?" she asked in her best military voice.

Hamish didn't show any reaction to her statement. "Is there a back way out?" He enquired instead, the serious tone back.

"Yes, but that door and this one are locked." She informed him, wondering what they were going to do.

Hamish merely shrugged and grabbed her hand as he went.

"Be prepared to move Lass."

"But how are we going to get out?" Mel asked. He shrugged once more and was infuriatingly vague as he directed her beside the door at his back.

"Locked doors are nothing for a 'Highland Hero'." He winked right before he used his muscles to break the door free from its flimsy lock. Mel stood there stunned; he had just broken a locked door quicker than she could get the lid off a jam jar, he truly was a warrior.

"Do this often?" Mel asked, trying to ease her rising trepidation at the thought of what awaited them outside that door, there was no way someone didn't hear the door being broken open.

"Och, only when I need to save troublesome wenches." He winked.

Hamish gave her a purely masculine smile, shrugged his shoulders nonchalantly again for good measure, then stuck his head out of the door to check that the hallway was empty. Of course, it wasn't. Breaking down the door had earned them an audience, one of which was the woman that would stop them from leaving. Claudette stood with her hands on her hips, and two burly bouncers at her back.

"Where do you think you're goin' governor?" She fumed.

Masking the surprise in his face, Hamish recovered, "I was planning on taking the 'hoore downstairs for some drinks, afore I punished her some more." Hamish sneered as he let go of Mel's hand and leaned casually against the doorframe.

Mel cringed at hearing *that* word on his lips, she knew he was only role-playing, but it still hurt. When Claudette looked at her, Mel tried to put fear in her eyes and took an involuntary step back, hoping to give the impression that she was afraid. But it didn't work, Claudette wasn't fooled as the bouncer inspected the doorway.

"Nice try honey, but I cannot let you leave with my prize whore." she purred before she grabbed Mel's arm and dragged Mel to her side. Mel struggled to loosen the woman's iron grip as the bouncers rushed Hamish. The three men fell back into the room as their fighting broke out in earnest. Doors opened all the way down the hall as men and women poured out of their rooms to see what the commotion was. Some watched the fight, while others were openly leering at her. Mel became achingly aware that her shirt was showing more of her breasts than it was covering, and she tried to shield herself as best she could in Claudette's grip.

A loud thud as a body hit the wall hard, had Mel jumping. Hoping it wasn't Hamish, Mel stared at the door and was relieved and a little shocked when he strode out of the room, his shirt ripped, blood running down his arm and a fresh cut above his eye. Claudette gasped and pulled Mel in tighter, the woman knew they had her beat and yet she was still trying to gain the upper hand. Mel froze when Claudette's arm curled and tightened around her neck, holding her like a shield as Hamish angled one of the bouncer's weapons at Claudette's throat.

"I suggest you let her go," he said calmly, the threat hanging in the air.

The grip on Mel's arm tightened and she cried out as Claudette's nails pierced her flesh. Her cry was cut short as the pressure around her throat increased and she choked out his name. Hamish pushed the sword's point deeper into the woman's throat, drawing blood and letting the bitch know that he was not playing games. Claudette stood still, tense and angry as Mel struggled to breathe in her clutches. Neither one of them was giving up their stance until Hamish pushed the sword a little deeper.

Finally getting the message, Claudette slackened and loosened her grip on Mel's arm, while she removed her arm from around Mel's neck. Before she could gain her breath Mel was shoved forward, she stumbled into Hamish, gasping for the air that had been denied her.

"Fine take the whore, she has been nothing but trouble anyway. But know this, you had better enjoy every minute you have with her, because you won't get far before he finds you. I promise you that!" Claudette sneered

Hamish grabbed Mel's arm and without wasting any more time he headed for the back-door, sword raised, glaring, begging anyone who dared cross his path to challenge him. Luckily no-one did.

Mel wanted to pause to take a deep, relieved breath and recollect herself, but she knew there wasn't time to relax just yet. They kept moving, Hamish pushing past anyone who got in their way until they finally reached the back exit where, just like the bedroom door, Hamish broke the flimsy lock with little to no effort at all. They were almost out, only a few more minutes and they would be free. As they stepped out onto the back stoop, Mel inhaled her first real breath of freedom and she had never felt more alive than she did right then.

In no time at all, they were racing down the stairs and into the street that would take them to the stables, and then home. As they ran, Mel could hear Claudette screeching and ordering her men to go after them, while also screaming for someone to send for the duke. Panic tore through her, but Hamish had also heard it, and he picked up his speed.

Mel winced as her abused body rejected the fast movement, but she soon forgot about it when they reached the stables. As relief washed over her, an involuntary shiver ran through her as the enormity of what could have happened to her hit home. Looking back at Hamish, she was once again filled with love and thanked God he had shown up when he did, this man would hold her heart forever.

Thirty-Nine

Once they had reached the stables, Hamish dressed himself in the weapons that he had hidden, he then mounted his horse, lifted her in front of him and together they had ridden out of the town. That had been two days ago, two straight days of riding, never resting. Even though Mel was an experienced horse rider, every muscle of her already battered body hurt. She needed to stop.

Turning to Hamish, she pleaded, "Can we stop now please? I need to have a shower and rest. My backside has gone numb; my legs are aching, and my ribs feel like they are slowly breaking apart. I'm starving, I need to eat a decent meal before I collapse."

Mel knew she sounded like a petulant child, but she was so hungry her stomach had begun cramping and she couldn't remember the last time she'd had a decent meal. The crap they had forced her eat at the brothel was barely tolerable and she had often refused to eat it. *Where the hell were health and safety standards when you needed them?* To make matters worse in the last two days they'd been travelling, she had been chewing on nothing but the dried pieces of meat Hamish had packed, she needed something free and hot.

Mel probably would have continued on, despite the pain and hunger, but when she saw the little town up ahead, all she could think about was having a hot bath and a hot meal, and if fate was feeling generous, maybe she could even get a cup of coffee.

"Please?" She pleaded once more when Hamish didn't answer. Hamish was looking at her, the indecision warring in his eyes. She knew he was weighing up her need to stop with his need to keep her safe and moving, so she was grateful when he agreed.

"Aye alright Lass, we are in Scotland, so I suppose we could stop for a wee bit." He relented.

As Hamish kicked the horse into a faster speed, Mel almost yelped with anticipation for them to reach the town, she would gladly put up with the aches the faster pace was causing her knowing that she would soon be able to have a hot bath.

The relief was short lived. Right now, she should have been eating a nice warm meal, and maybe enjoying a warm bath, but instead they were standing in the foyer of an inn, where Hamish and the proprietor were arguing in Gaelic. Mel had heard enough Gaelic during her capture with the Macintoshes to sense that Hamish was frustrated.

Turning away from the two men, Mel allowed herself to relax for the first time since she could remember. She admired the inn, it was a quaint place. Long wooden tables were placed throughout the hall, while a bar stretched along the back wall and a kitchen could be seen through the back. A small fireplace had been built into the wall on the far side of the foyer and its warmth welcomed all who walked in the door. Sconces filled with flickering candles aligned the walls, giving the inn an almost romantic atmosphere.

The walls themselves had been decorated with paintings of horses and the Scottish landscape, while not an artist herself, Mel admired the skill in the artwork. You could almost feel the fog rolling in over the hills and smell the fresh heather filled fields. The art studios back home would pay a fortune for these pieces, she surmised. Heck, maybe they had! She thought wryly, remembering what year she was in. Turning towards the door, Mel noticed a wooden staircase to the left. A prominent feature of the room, it lined the entire wall leading to the rooms upstairs and looked well-built and taken care of. A far cry from the dilapidation of the *Red Scarlet*. Two maids were currently carrying buckets of water up the stairs, probably for a patron's bath.

Mel sighed, she longed to wash away the blood and grime of the last couple of weeks and to feel clean again, she would kill for a hot shower; but right now she would bathe in a bucket of hot water if she had to. Lost in thought, Mel hadn't realised Hamish and the owner had finished their argument. She flinched when Hamish grabbed her roughly by the arm and all but dragged her outside.

Something was wrong; it was so unlike him to be rough with her, especially since he knew of her injuries. Mel could not make out what Hamish was muttering under his breath, but he was clearly angry about whatever they'd been arguing about.

"Hamish! Take it easy!" She snapped, unable to handle the pain any longer.

Mel had expected her voice to break through his rant, instead he ignored her and continued to pull her away from the nice little inn. Mel was baffled on where they were going until she saw the stables and realised what Hamish was doing, "Please tell me we aren't leaving?" She demanded finally trying to wrestle free.

Mel could hear the desperation in her own voice, but she couldn't help it. The thought of getting back on the horse right now was too much. Hamish stopped and dropped her arm, she had finally broken through his speech. Running his hand through his hair, agitation clearly visible on his face. He answered, "Aye."

Mel opened her mouth to say something, but before the words could leave her lips, he raised his hand and continued to speak, "I'm sorry, but we cannae' stay here!" Hamish didn't give her time to respond before he grabbed her arm and pulled her towards the stables once more. Mel knew it was his way to stop her arguing, but she was through taking orders. It was about time something went her way, and she would be damned if she let anything stop her.

Forty

M el dug her feet in trying to stop him again as she grabbed his arm with her free hand, it was easier said than done. The man was a giant and she was no match for his strength. But that was not going to deter her, there was no way Mel was leaving here without a bath and a decent meal!

The man could ride on without her for all she cared. In the last two and half weeks, she had been dragged halfway across the land, tortured by a madman, sold to a brothel and travelled two days nonstop on a horse. Her nerves were shot, and to top it off, she had a cracking headache from coffee withdrawal.

At this moment, she would kill for a coffee, any kind of coffee, just to take the edge off. *Tristan was right, she should look at doing something about her addiction*, right now though she had bigger fish to fry. Thinking about everything that she had been through brought the anger she had been feeling boiling to the surface again.

"No!" She shouted forcefully. Reefing her arm backwards she tried to dislodge it from his grip. Her actions had finally broken through his thick little bubble and brought him to a stop. Hamish was looking at her now as though she had lost her mind. And perhaps she had.

"Och Lass, please ya doona ken the situation." He begged.

Mel glared furiously at him as all the emotion she had been storing inside let loose, "you know what, buster?" she yelled, poking her finger into his chest. Incensed by surprise that she saw in his eyes, she prodded him again as she launched into the rest of her tirade.

"I'm sick of people thinking that I will not understand what is going on. I have had enough of being dragged around and ordered about. I am dirty and I am hungry, so whatever you have to tell me had better be good. Shall I remind you that I am an intelligent, independent 21st Century woman, I run my own business so I'm sure I can get my brain around whatever it is you have to say. You had better start explaining why we can't stay here and it had better be a good excuse, like the threat of death. Otherwise, you can damn well leave without me." She inhaled sharply.

It felt good to release that tension. Mel knew she sounded bitchy right now but she didn't care. She was done. She was through following orders and if he didn't start speaking soon she was going to go hunting for a place to sleep herself. Hamish gave her a pleading look, but she was not going to budge. Mel stood there, arms crossed waiting for him to tell her what was going on, daring him to ignore her.

"Ya not goin' like it...." He started trying to dissuade her once more. Mel just stood there and glared him.

"Doona' say I dinna warn ya..." He sighed and shrugged, when she didn't respond. "Simply put, we cannot stay there unless we are married."

Mel gaped, momentarily stunned into silence. That was the last thing she had expected him to say. Of course, she should have expected it; after all he lived in a time where men and women did not travel alone unless they were married, it was a sin to do otherwise. Mel thought about what he told her for a moment more before speaking.

"O... kay, well that inn can't be the only place to stay." She reasoned.

Hamish shook his head letting her know that she was wrong in her assumption. "Aye Lass it is, that *is* the only inn in Greta Green and to make matters worse, the owner thinks I have stolen ya. He wants proof that ya are my wife or he is going to call the authorities, after all you seem more English than Scottish and the last thing this town wants or needs is trouble from the English."

Mel snorted at the irony, *now* someone wanted to call the authorities? Where had they been when she had *needed* them? Mel looked down at her now dirty makeshift clothing and realised that it probably did seem that way. They were obviously Hamish's and she wasn't exactly presenting as an independent woman. Mel stood there trying to think of another way around this mess, but the solution was simple. She grinned impishly.

"Just tell him we are married."

"Did ya no' hear me Lass? He wants proof, as in papers. Doona ya think I have no' tried telling him that ya are my wife?" His voice rose with anger.

Mel stood there watching after him as he strode towards the stables once more, fists clenched by his side. Deep down she knew the logical thing to do would be to leave and go home. But she was over everything. She was dirty, exhausted, hungry and suffering from an intense desire for caffeine. Mel was sick of having no control over her life and sick of being forced to obey others. For once, she was going to do something for herself. She wanted a bath and she wanted a hot meal, and by God, if she had to marry Hamish to get it, then that was what she was going to do.

There *was* a solution, and if she thought about the solution was not the worst thing in the world. Truth be told it was the only good thing that had happened to her in the last few weeks. Mel knew deep down that she shouldn't make any rash decisions while her emotions were running high, it had never ended well before, but at this point she didn't care.

Her father's logical voice echoed in her head, reminding her to think before she acted. But she dismissed it as quickly as she had her own concerns, Mel had no patience for rational thought, enough was enough. Clenching her hands into tight fists, she shouted at the stubborn man walking away from her.

"I. am. Not. Going. Anywhere!" She enunciated loud and clear and it got just the reaction she wanted.

Forty-One

Hamish stopped dead in his tracks, he couldn't have heard her right. Turning back, he looked at Mel, she was standing there defiantly, daring him to argue with her. *Was she mad? Didn't she understand what was at stake here?* Looking down the road towards the stable, Hamish tried to gather his thoughts, he took a deep breath preparing himself for the fight to come.

Hamish had his mind set, they were going home and there was nothing she could do or say that would make him change his mind. Hamish didn't want to act like the barbarian she thought he was, but when it came to keeping her safe Hamish would do anything.

Hamish's mind was made up, but when he looked back at her all he saw was Mel's back. Mel hadn't waited to see what he would say, his pause was all the answer she needed. Hamish could tell by her stride that she was mad, her hands were at her sides in tight balls and there was anger in her step. Mel had her mind set on getting what she wanted and Hamish knew this wasn't going to end well for them.

Hamish had to stop her before she got them arrested! What she didn't understand about his time was that she couldn't just go around demanding people do what she wanted. This was 12th Century Scotland and here, whether she liked it or not, the men were in charge. They didn't take well to a strange little English woman telling them what to do. Hamish ran at a sprint, trying to catch up to her, he needed to make her see sense.

"Mel, you have to understand," he said desperately as he grabbed her by the arm stopping her from entering the Inn.

Mel spun around on him so fast he couldn't maintain his hold. He wasn't surprised to see the anger in her eyes and braced himself for the storm. What she said next though, left him feeling as though the ground had shifted beneath his feet.

"Oh, I understand you all right. Now you understand me, if I have to marry you in order to get a fucking bath and a hot meal then that's what I plan to do! I. Am. Not. Going. Anywhere!" she yelled, striding angrily towards him.

Hamish backed away from her wrath, he couldn't help it. The woman had lost her ever-loving mind and he wasn't sure how to handle a crazy person. Looking at Mel, he attempted to discern if she was joking or not but what she said next told him that this was no joke at all.

"Now, either help me find the church or I will search this godforsaken town until I find it myself! I will be marrying someone today and if you want it to be you, you had best help me." She ordered.

Hamish tried to speak but all he could get out was a kind of pathetic 'wha?' noise. His mind raced to catch up with what she was shouting at him. *Was she really going to marry him just so they could spend the night here?*

"Och, Lass are ya daft?" He pleaded, finally finding his voice.

"I seriously hope you did not just call me stupid. But, if you are asking me in your own way if I am joking, does it look like I'm fucking joking? *Lad.*" She spat at him angrily.

Panic swelled in his chest. Mel was daft after all. Hamish couldn't marry her, even though he what to do so more than ever, it was too dangerous. Enemies abound wanted him dead, he had yet to deal with his powers, and Hamish had vowed never to marry.

But none of those problems compared to the fact that Hamish knew without a doubt Mel would never stay here, even if he wanted her to. No matter how much he wished it Mel wasn't from here, she had always planned to go home and Hamish knew that with everything that had happened it was more the than the day she had first arrived. *So why would she marry him?*

Staring at her, Hamish tried to imagine what it would be like to be married to her, but it wasn't hard to see it. As they stood there eye to eye, he realised how much he wanted to keep her. No one had ever stirred his blood as she did, and he knew instinctively that life with Mel would never be lonely or boring. Hamish could feel his well-constructed walls start to crumble as Mel dug herself deeper into his heart and he knew he was in serious trouble when he felt his objectives slowly start to fade away.

Mel relented and her face relaxed as she noticed his confusion. "Look Hamish, I'm not asking you to make this a lifelong commitment. Just marry me for now, we can figure the rest out when we get back to Ceana's. *Please?*"

He could hear the desperation in her voice and Hamish had to fight the urge to give in to her. He couldn't do it, not even for a little time, because he knew deep down in his heart that if he did marry her, he would never let her go, and that wouldn't be fair to either of them. Hamish had to make her understand how bad the idea was, he had to make her see sense. Placing his hands on her face, he brought her eyes up to meet his as he tried once more to make her see reason.

"Lass ya doona ken what ya asking of me."

The hurt and sadness that entered her eyes brought a lump to his throat, bringing with it the last of his resistance crashing down around them. Hamish knew that he shouldn't do this, it was pure madness, but he was running out of arguments to give her. Hamish searched his brain for one last reason to deny her.

"Hamish, please... I just need to stop, I need to relax and I need a true moment to feel safe again." She said on a cracked whisper.

Hamish swore under his breath as she cracked through the last of his reserve. Mel had managed to do what no other had, Mel had reached the far reaches of his heart and with that he gave in.

"Och, ok Lass." He said with a finality he felt to his core.

The relief that entered her eyes in that moment made every bit of suffering he would endure worth it. And Hamish would suffer, because in the end he knew that he would have to let her go and it was going to be the hardest thing he would ever have to do. Hamish knew without a doubt, that he loved the Las, he loved her more than he ever would have thought possible. Over the few weeks that she had been here, she had wormed her way into his heart, a heart he had tried so hard to shield.

Hamish wouldn't tell Mel any of that of course; not only wouldn't he force her to stay here, deep down he knew that he would never be worthy of someone as pure and good as Mel. His life was on a dangerous path, one that he was destined to travel alone and she was something he could never have. Taking her hand, Hamish spun her around and headed back towards the other end of town. Towards a life that he had only ever dreamed of having. A life that he would inevitably have to let go.

Forty-Two

Mowbray was furious. The little bitch had gotten away and there was only one person who could have helped her. Whirling around with fresh anger, he grabbed Claudette by her throat, lifting her off the ground.

"Who did you sell her to?" He roared. He could kill this woman, he had specifically told her that no-one was to touch the whore until he was ready and yet she had taken it upon herself to place Mel in the hands of the one person who could save her.

"I don't know, honestly." She choked. "I never asked for his name, the only thing I remember about him was that he was Scottish." She answered huskily through the tight grip he had on her throat.

"Scottish!" He screamed. "You stupid whore!" Mowbray roughly pushed her away, and stormed out of the office. Claudette had just confirmed what he already knew. *Damn MacDonnell!*

How dare he think he could come in here and steal what was his, *again*! More than ever now the Laird would be sorry he ever stepped foot into England, both him and that little bitch were going to pay. Slamming the door, Mowbray stormed out of the brothel and headed down to the stables to get his mount. Surely someone had to have seen something on the night that they left, it wasn't as though this town had a plethora of stable employees on hand. Storming into the stables, he summoned the first boy he saw.

"You! Come here now. I have questions for you!" He ordered. The groom stopped what he was doing and came over to where

Mowbray stood waiting. The young man was already cowering and there was nothing more Mowbray hated than a coward, well except for many the Scotsman.

"Can you tell me anything about a Scotsman and a woman who would have left here a night ago?"

He expected the boy to tell him everything he knew, but he just stood there shaking his head. Mowbray was quickly losing patience with all of them, useless bloody town.

"You had better not be lying boy, or I will gut you where you stand." He threatened.

The boy swallowed. "Aww, come to think of it governor, I do remember a man and woman leaving here quick smart a night ago. But he wasn't stealing her or nothing, she seemed more than willin' to go with him. In fact, I heard him say they were headed for Scotland, so they are probably hitched by now."

The boy was rambling, happy to give the duke any information he could and thought he'd done well. Fury erupted within Mowbray's body and it took all he had not to break the boy's neck.

"Which way did they go?" He cut in, stopping the lad from his incessant rambling.

He didn't have time to sit here and drag it out of him all night. He had to catch them. "Um, they went that way," the boy said pointing North-West.

Mowbray paid the boy for the information, mounted his horse and headed in the direction he had pointed them. Oh, they were going to pay all right, the highlander was going to die a slow, painful death; no-body stole what was his. But before he did, he planned on breaking the little whore right in front of him.

He would get great pleasure from it, and after he broke her Mowbray was going to watch as her lover died right before her eyes. She would watch as the lifeblood poured out of his body, and she would know that his death was her fault., Nobody made a fool out of Mowbray and got away with it. With any luck, the Macintoshes would be back in the highlands and hopefully every last member of the bastard's family would also be dead.

An evil smile spread across Mowbray's face as he continued after the pair. This was going to be glorious he thought as he left town. That little whore didn't know what she had just unleashed.

Forty-Three

"Laird, Laird, Laird!"

Kessan looked up from the accounts that he and Caelan were going over as young Robert came running breathlessly into the hall.

"Och, over here," he directed the lad. Kessan smiled as the young boy slid to halt and changed direction.

"Sorry to interrupt ya Laird, but Brodie sent me to fetch ya right away. He said to tell ya that the Macintoshes have been spied crossin' our land. He also said to let ya ken that they are prepared for battle!"

Cursing, Kessan forgot about the accounts and headed out to the gates where he knew Brodie and the others would be preparing the keep for battle. He could hear Caelan close behind him. *What the bloody hell was going on?* Hamish still wasn't back and now the Macintoshes were declaring war on his clan.

As he reached the gates, Kessan could see not only his men, but Hamish's as well taking their positions on the ramparts. The gates were being prepared to be sealed as soldiers brought the young and old up from the village. They would be safe within the keep walls.

"Brodie?" He barked.

Brodie didn't need any more prompting. "They're about a day's ride out Laird. Hamish's men are heading out to find out what's goin' on but our scout tells me that they ride in their battle colours."

Kessan cursed again. "Continue to prepare the keep for battle, I will go and secure the castle, and then I will return."

Kessan turned and headed for the caste, he had no need to worry that his men wouldn't do as he asked, and he planned to join them as soon as possible. But first he needed to make sure that his wife, children and brother's family were safe. Once they were Kessan promised that declaring war on him would be the last thing the Macintoshes ever did.

Forty-Four

They had risen early and headed home as neither one of them wanted to waste any more time. As they rode along in silence, Mel looked down at his ring on her finger. It was a simple gold band with a mixture of rubies and the MacDonnell crest evenly spaced out around it. It was simple, but it was beautiful. Mel had tried to tell Hamish that she didn't need a ring, but he had refused to marry her without one.

Tears sprung to Mel's eyes when he had removed the ring that was always present on his little finger and placed it on hers. Despite it being her idea, the enormity of what she'd done hadn't quite sunk in. She was married. *She was married.* That thought kept going round her head and it wasn't getting any clearer. It still sounded so strange to her, for years she had thought the moment would never come, and when it finally did it had happened in the middle of nowhere in a century far removed from her own.

What had she been thinking? Ceana and her parents were going to kill her.

Last night had been a blur; after their wedding, they had gone back to the inn with the proof the owner had wanted and then they had sat down to one of the best meals Mel had ever had. It was a humble meal of mashed potato, gravy and haggis. Never in her wildest dreams had she ever imagined herself eating haggis. But it was warm, honest and comforting and that alone made it wonderful after all the stodge she'd been fed over the last few weeks.

The ring wasn't the only thing Hamish had given her. After dinner, when they had gone back to the room, he had pulled a knife out from his weapons stash and handed it to her, telling her it was now hers to keep as a wedding gift. It was the most beautiful knife Mel had ever seen. She had no idea what it was made from, but it was heavy, and Hamish had told her that the pattern that wound its way up the handle was his family crest.

"I want ya to carry it for protection always." He had informed her. Mel had taken his words to heart, she felt the knife pushing against her upper thigh as they continued to ride north. Hamish had shown her how to tie the sheath to her thigh so that no-one would know she was wearing it, it had stirred up all her emotions once more. Once Hamish had taken the knife back from her, Mel could no longer deny her need for him. Mel had practically jumped Hamish and thankfully he did not deny her, instead he had spent the night making passionate love to her. For now they were in a bubble of passion and nothing and nobody could ruin it for them.

Everything seemed perfect. Until she had woken up this morning wrapped in Hamish's arms and the enormity of what she had done crept in on her, again. Mel didn't regret what she had done, she couldn't regret it, after all he was now hers. But now her mind had finally caught up with her heart, the consequences of her actions almost drowned her. Yes he was hers for now but deep in her heart Mel knew it wouldn't last for every.

In the very near future she was going to have to let him go, because as far as long-distance relationships went, this one would be impossible. It wasn't like they could Skype between her 21st Century office and his 12th Century keep. But as Mel lay there looking at the ceiling a new fear entered her, if anyone could make her stay here it was Hamish and she wasn't sure she could do that, she wasn't sure she was strong enough to live in the 12th century.

Mel rolled over and looked at the man lying beside her, her husband. When she saw his beautiful face, relaxed in sleep and bathed in sunlight, all the love she felt for him came crashing down on her and her heart broke. She *was* going to leave him. She had to; she couldn't stay in this time, but the thought of leaving him here was killing her inside. She had finally met the man of her dreams and now she was going to have to leave him.

As they rode on Mel wished there was something she could do, but after everything that had happened to her here she knew she couldn't stay in this world, and Mel knew he wouldn't come with her; but it was a moot point as she would never ask that of him. So where did that leave them?

Mel wanted desperately to make this work, so much so plans started to formulate in her mind. They could try and have a long-distance relationship; she could visit him every time the portal opened on the winter and summer solstice. And maybe when he was more comfortable he could come and see her.

But even as that thought crossed her mind, Mel knew it would never be enough. Her heart broke a little more as she continued to stare at the ring. Letting this man go was going to be the hardest thing she had ever had to do by far. But she had no choice any other option would only hurt them both. A cold chill blew around them and, as if sensing her mood, Mother Nature provided the ambiance. It wasn't long before the snow started falling, and she was taken back to the last time she had been stuck in a snow storm, only this time she had Hamish to keep her warm.

Thankfully, at Greta Green, Mel had been able to purchase some warm clothes to see her the rest of the way home. She had decided on a serviceable skirt and top, and as she sat in the ever-growing storm, Mel was grateful for their warmth. Before they had left, Hamish had wrapped the extra plaid he had around both of them, cocooning her in a sea of thick plaid and arms. But all too soon the snow was falling so fast and hard that even the plaid wasn't keeping the cold out and Mel was having trouble seeing five feet in front of her.

"We have to find somewhere to stop," she heard Hamish yell over the cold wind that was now howling around them as the storm picked up intensity.

Mel could do nothing but nod to let him know that she had heard him. Hamish must have known where they were, because they veered off the road and headed towards an outcropping of trees that lined the banks of a loch. As they broke through the trees, a small hut came into view, it wasn't much, but it would have to do. The part that Mel could see was derelict, but it still had a roof and most of its wall, so it would at least provide some shelter from the storm.

The little lean-to at the side of the cottage would offer his horse a little protection as well. It didn't take them long to settle the horse and get a makeshift fire going with the old pieces of furniture in the hut, and before long, the warmth of the fire started to penetrate the cold room. Hamish had barely said two words to her all day, and

Mel was starting to worry that he was furious with her. She couldn't blame him; she had practically shanghaied him into the marriage. But she didn't want her last moments with him to be filled with anger. They only had a little time left together and Mel needed these memories; they would be all she would have to hold on to once she was back in her own time.

"Look Hamish, I am really sorry about all this...." She began softly.

Her words were cut off when Hamish turned around to face her and her heart broke. He was back to being the warrior she had met on the day she had arrived. There was no emotion on his beautiful face and his simple reply had her mood sinking further into the gutter.

"Och Lass, doona fuss yaself, t'is naught that cannae be fixed in time." He said abruptly.

Hamish didn't give her a chance to reply, instead he strode out of the cabin to tend to his horse. *Well, screw you too, Mister,* Mel thought spitefully. He could have at least cared a little, but instead he went straight back to being their highland warrior she had met the first day. To be fair the marriage probably wasn't a big a deal to him, Hamish wouldn't have been stupid enough to fall in love, only Mel had done that. The truth was, Hamish probably helped her because of his loyalty to Ceana, a sister he *did* love.

A tear slid down her face as Mel removed the knife Hamish had given her for a wedding gift. She placed it under her pillow then curled up on the bed and tried to get some sleep. *How could she have been so stupid to fall in love with a barbaric highlander?*

She had wanted someone a little more masculine than the men she had dated back home, but this was pushing it too far in the other direction. Closing her eyes, Mel tried thinking about all the things she was going to do once she was home, there were so many things that she was never taking for granted again. But, as much as she tried, Mel couldn't get the man outside to leave her thoughts, and as the coming days dawned on her the tears began to fall again.

Laying on the bed in misery, with the warmth of the fire at her back and the weariness of her body making her feel heavy, Mel finally managed to drift off to sleep. Slowly, her mind began to sink into the realm of dreams but it was ripped out when the door was viciously thrown open, bringing with it the cold, freezing wind of the storm.

Forty-Five

The knife pressed sharply against his throat, warning him not to make any sudden movements. Hamish could feel the sharp blade tear at his skin with a pinch of pain. Although he wanted to fight, he obeyed the duke's orders as he propelled Hamish to the cabin and ordered him to kick open the door. Never in his life had Hamish been caught unawares and yet here he was. Hamish hadn't been the same since the lass had shown up. If he hadn't been trying to figure out his love Hamish would have been paying more attention to his surroundings, something he had been taught to do from a young age.

Mel was no excuse of course, it was not her fault that he was distracted. Hamish still couldn't believe that he had let the bastard get the better of him. *How had the bastard caught them so quickly?* Trying to quell his rising fear, Hamish kicked the door in with a crash, feeling utterly helpless in the duke's grip. His eyes immediately fell to the stirring form in the bed, frustrated at his inability to protect her. It was becoming a habit. Mel was again facing danger at his carelessness, but this time it could very well get her killed.

"Really, Hamish, now you decide to be pissed?" Mel hissed as she rolled over to face him. Her eyes were sleepy and half-closed, but the moment she saw Mowbray her eyes widened and she sat up in horror with a cry.

"Oh no, don't move bitch, or he *will* die." Mowbray jeered when Mel tried to stand. Mel stopped midway as if not knowing what to do. Hamish hoped that she wouldn't do anything stupid, she seemed to have a knack for disobedience, that 21st Century determination was not what they needed right now. Hamish needed the man distracted long enough so that he could get free and get his weapons from the corner of the hut, where he'd stashed them when they first arrived. But what Hamish didn't want was Mel putting herself in danger to accomplish it.

"How the hell did you find us?" Hamish asked the Duke, wincing as the blade scraped his neck in time with his speech. Not having any other option Hamish reached for his powers to calm the situation, but as usual, when he needed them, they were silent, his emotions and fear blocking their effect.

"Oh it was quite by chance, dear fellow, I do assure you. I was trying to get out of the bleed'n storm, when I happened upon this hut and, to my greatest pleasure, found *you*."

Hamish swore in Gaelic. He knew that he should have tried to push on if he had been by himself he would have. But the moment he had felt Mel shivering he knew that she would need the warmth of this hut to maintain her strength. Hamish had to be honest with himself though, his plan had been a little selfish on his part, the truth was Hamish was not ready see their time end.

Now they were in trouble for his selfishness. Standing there, doing nothing, was killing him; if Hamish had been by himself he would have just fought the duke. But he was not alone and he couldn't take the chance with Mel's life. Hamish wasn't at all certain that she wouldn't do something stupid, like try to save him. Hamish would have to bide his time, he would have to wait for the right moment for the bastard to make a mistake and, when he did, Hamish would relish killing him for the pain he had caused Mel.

The bastard had found them. "Why can't you just let me go?" Mel shrieked defeated and angry, fury and fear mingling through every cell of her aching tired body. Mel didn't expect him to answer, so when he merely stood there smirking at her she wasn't surprised.

Mel wanted nothing more than to walk up and slap that smirk right off his face, but while he had a knife to Hamish's throat, she couldn't do anything.

"Do not open that smart mouth of yours again." He demanded, pushing the knife a little deeper into Hamish's skin.

A shudder ran through her body as a small trickle of blood ran down Hamish's neck when the blade pierced through the surface. Mel waited for Hamish to react but he just stood there, blank and emotionless. God, she hated it when he did that. She wished just once he would let her know what he was feeling. Hamish had to be furious at her and she wouldn't blame him, after all it was her fault that he was in the predicament at all, if she had just listened to his dictate back at home she never would have gone into the glen to start with.

"Look just let him go; I will do whatever you want." Mel pleaded not knowing what else to do. While she never wanted to go back to that hellhole again, Mel knew that she would do just that if it meant saving Hamish's life. She now knew how Ceana felt, there was nothing Mel wouldn't do to keep the man she loved alive, even if it meant her dying.

The Duke laughed. "Oh *now* you beg, but no, while your offer does sound promising, I have no intention of letting him go. But make no mistake, I plan on doing whatever I want with you anyway, whore. And the first thing I am going to do is make this bastard pay for taking what is mine!"

Before Mel had a chance to comprehend what the bastard was telling her, Mowbray pulled the knife away from Hamish's throat and drove it into his side, all the way to the hilt. Shock rippled over Hamish's face as he dropped forward to his knees.

As she watched Hamish fall to the floor rage tore through her body. "You fucking bastard!" she screamed as she grabbed the knife from under her pillow.

Thankful for Hamish's gift, Mel sprung off the bed towards her enemy. Nothing was going to stop her from driving the dagger into the duke's black heart. She had almost reached him when he grabbed the hand with the knife and twisted it sharply, causing her to drop her only weapon in pain.

"You are going to pay for that." He snarled as he started walking her backwards towards the bed, the grip on her arm tightening and rendering it useless.

Mel spat in his face, she knew there would be consequences for her actions, but she didn't care. Everything had been taken from her when he had killed Hamish and no with nothing to lose she didn't hold back. With her free hand, Mel clawed at his face with the intent to cause as much pain as she could before he killed her. She wasn't going to die without a fight.

"YOU BITCH!" he roared and shoved her so that she fell backwards on to the bed.

Pain radiated up through her skull as he head hit the bar at the end of the bed and before she had regained her strength, he was on top of her, straddling her lower body and pinning her down.

Fear and panic began to fill Mel when she couldn't move, he had her pinned too well. Mel tried to squirm but her arms were trapped between her body and his legs.

"I should have done this the first time I met you," he hissed as he raised her blade above his head. Mel tried to close her eyes, but she couldn't take her eyes from the knife as pictures of her family and friends filled her mind. It was true; your life really did flash before your eyes when you were about to die she thought numbly.

"You will never get away with this. More people will come for us and when they do you will wish for a quick death." She promised. Mel was not sure if any of that was true, but she had to try something.

"I don't think so bitch, you see, by now all your friends and your lover's family will be nothing but a pile of ash and corpses. The Macintoshes should be arriving at their keep any day now, mutilating every last one of them!"

Mel felt sick, Hamish was badly injured and everyone else was most likely dead. She should never have come to the highlands, if she had just stayed at home none of this would be happing. Thinking about her best friends brought tears to her eyes. Tristan wouldn't even know what had happened to any of them, she realised weakly. *What would happen to him if no one came back?*

Time moved in slow motion as the knife descended on her and she knew that this was the end. Mel refused to let him see any emotion from her, his goal all along had been to break her and she refused to give him that even now. There she lay defiance in her eyes waiting for him to finally end her.

Then everything changed, as time stood still and Mel braced for her demise, an animalistic roar filled the room. To her shock and horror, blood started trickling from Mowbray's mouth as his eyes widened in surprise. Through the fog of the moment, Mel dimly noticed a sword tip protruding from the duke's stomach right before he was thrown away from her. Tears filled her eyes when Hamish grabbed her up into his arms.

"Is he dead?" She asked faintly.

"Aye Lass he is dead."

"Well that's nice," Mel replied, right before she fainted into Hamish's arms.

Forty-Six

Mel awoke sluggishly; at first she thought she had been dreaming, she was half expecting to wake up and find herself back in the brothel. Taking in the room around her the fog began to clear and it didn't take her long to remember where she was. Mel couldn't believe she had fainted again, it was a new record for her. Not normally one to faint, since being the highlanders she had done it three times. As Mel rubbed her eyes trying to remove the nightmare from her mind the ruined remains of the cabin came into focus.

It was no longer bitterly cold; the door had been shut and she was grateful for the sense of calm and warmth that radiated around from the fire. She could hear the fire crackling in the fireplace as the snow continued to fall outside the window on her left. Blinking she tried focusing her mind again and almost wished she hadn't. The duke's startled, shocked eyes as he realised his imminent death was near, flashed before her mind and she realised that what she had seen was no nightmare. The look on his face and the sight of blood had been too real, and Mel would never forget the expression that crossed his face.

But his expression was replaced quickly with another image, the one of Hamish being stabbed. Rising quickly at the memory, Mel surveyed the room, trying to find him, she prayed to God he hadn't died while she had been out of it. Feeling something sticky on her fingers, Mel looked down at her hands and realised with horror that they were covered in blood, the duke's blood. It must have spilled onto her when Hamish had driven his sword into the man's stomach. Mel felt sick and bile rose in her throat, trying not to think about it, she searched for Hamish, she wasn't sure how long he had.

A movement by the fire drew Mel's eyes there and she was immediately relieved to see Hamish. He had his back to her and he was unaware that she had woken. Mel was about to call out to him when he removed his shirt gingerly and exposed a deep gash that ran an inch across his ribs. Her own body went cold as she took in the steady trail of blood that oozed from the wound, down across his pale, sweating body, telling Mel that it wasn't just a simple injury.

The amount of blood he was losing had her worried. Wanting to make sure that he would live Mel lifted the sheet that had been placed over her and swung around. She was about to stand up when his words stopped her, he had placed his left hand over the wound and was reciting something that sounded like a chant, Mel was mesmerised by the words. She couldn't understand them, but the lyrical rhythm of them was beautiful and hypnotic.

Mel stared, hardly daring to breathe, as a white glow emanated around the wound, and before she could grasp what was going on the words stopped and the wound was gone. Hamish complexion had returned to a normal colour while his breathing sounded less shallow, Mel was stunned. *Magic? Magic was real?*

Falling back on the bed, she stared at him in wonder. "What the hell?" She finally stuttered.

Hamish shot to his feet, sword raised as if to fight, but the moment he saw her his eyes filled with a strange sadness and he lowered his sword facing the fire again. She didn't understand.

"Hamish, what was that?" She asked, walking over to him.

"'Tis naught to fess yaself with." He barked, making Mel flinch from his harshness.

"Hamish, please." She tried again as she placed her hand on his arm. The moment her hand touched his arm, he swung around to face her fury and sadness swirling in his beautiful green eyes.

"Och fine, ya wanna ken what that was Lass, it's a bloody curse is what it is." He snapped.

Mel didn't understand. How could anything that just happened be a curse? Curses were evil, set to hurt people, but she had never seen Hamish hurt anyone that didn't deserve it, and she had never seen him use magic to accomplish it.

"Hamish, you really can't believe that can you. Nothing of what I just saw is a curse, if anything it was a miracle."

Hamish snorted and turned away from her, "I am no miracle, I am a Druid, Lass, plain and simple."

Forty-Seven

❧✿❧

Mel couldn't have been more shocked if he had slapped her. Hamish was talking of the kind of power that wizards possessed. Ceana had told her a little about what a druid was when she had returned home two years ago, trying to explain how time travel worked. Despite experiencing the time travel herself, she still found it hard to believe that wizards existed, and she sure as hell didn't expect the man she loved to be one.

Christ, wizards belonged in fairy tales, not in real life and as every book and movie she had ever watched during her life flashed before her eyes it became even harder to believe. Besides, according to Ceana, druids received their powers through their ancestors, and as far as Mel knew, Ceana's real ancestors didn't possess that kind of magic, otherwise he would have been able to defeat Kendrick himself years ago.

"But how?" She asked trying to piece it together.

Hamish walked away from her and sat on the bed, Mel could see caution and hesitation in his eyes and it broke her heart that he didn't trust her with this. Ceana had never breathed a word of this to her, and she was starting to wonder if Ceana even knew herself.

Finally he spoke, "och, it happened after my da died. Ya see I knew there was power in my family, I just dinna ken how powerful. My Ma was killed for hers, and Ceana was chased to the edges of time for the same reason. We knew the women on my mother's side possessed powers, but I had no knowledge that any ran in my da's side. Premonition ran strong in the female bloodline, but there was no record of whether any male had ever possessed them, so no one ever suspected they would. I dinna come into mine until my father passed, it was the tragedy of his death that triggered my powers."

"Does Ceana know?" Mel asked trying to give herself time to work through what he had just told her.

"Nay, the only one who kens is the old druid who helped find Ceana. I went to him when I knew something was wrong. I doona have full control of my powers and he has been training me in secret. And now ya ken everything Lass." His eyes filled with desperation, sadness and loneliness.

"Why didn't you ever tell her?" Mel asked.

"Ya have to understand, I was afraid of putting those I loved in danger. Besides this is my cross to bear." He admitted, flatly.

"Hamish. You can't seriously believe that by them knowing this they would end up dead?" She tried reasoning with him as she went and sat on the bed beside him. Mel wanted nothing more than to reach out and comfort him, but she wasn't sure that he would allow it.

Hamish nodded his head, "Aye Lass I can. It's the very reason both of my parents are dead, and why Ceana was almost killed twice. The truth of it all is, in essence, I am cursed and will be 'til the day I die!"

His statement was said with such sadness and resignation Mel's heart broke. Here was a man that had so much love to give, and yet he felt obliged to hide himself away from the world. Suddenly, everything made sense; this was why he always seemed to keep himself at arm's length from everyone. He was so afraid of losing those he loved that he never gave them the chance to love him.

If it was the last thing Mel did before she went home, she would make sure that Ceana knew what was going on, and she would make sure that Hamish never felt alone in this world again, because she couldn't face her future knowing that this was his.

"Hamish, I don't believe that anyone who cares as much as you do about other people can be cursed." She took his hand in hers and he looked at her, dazed. "Now what do you say we head home and help the people we love?"

Mel knew that he didn't believe a word she was saying, but they didn't have the time to argue about it right now. Now they had to get home and make sure that everyone they loved was safe. She just hoped that weren't already too late.

Forty-Eight

Mel's eyes rounded as they rode up to the keep of Kessan's castle on the Isle of Sky. She couldn't believe what she was seeing. MacDonnell and McKinnon warriors were locked in battle with the Macintoshes and they were spread out across the land before them. Bodies from both clans lay strewn all over the ground and there was bloodshed everywhere. Some lay wounded, others dead, it was like a scene from a movie. Mel felt Hamish tense behind her, and before she could do anything, he dismounted and pulled her from the horse.

"Lass, promise me ya will wait here no' matter what happens." She could see the fear and induction playing in his eyes.

They were standing at the opening of the gate; she wanted nothing more than to run inside and find her friend, but Mel knew that she would only be endangering those around her and herself. There was no way she could battle these warriors, she needed to let Hamish do what he did best, and the only way she could do that was to follow his orders.

"I promise." She said as she raised up on her toes and kissed his cheeks.

A scream brought their attention back to the keep, Mel's eyes found her friend and realised with a panic that Ceana had put herself in danger. Ceana was running out of the castle, grabbing at Camden who had run into the melee. Mel watched with her heart in her throat until she caught him. Ceana tried desperately to shield him from the clashing swords and violence and Mel could only watch on in horror as she saw the moment the Macintosh realised who she was. With purposeful strides, he headed towards Ceana who backed away, holding her son tightly.

Mel shrieked as Macintosh slapped Ceana so hard she stumbled to the ground and struggled to rise again, at the same time, he tore Camden from her arms. Mel continued to watch in horror as the little boy wailed. The Laird raised a dagger to his throat, a sinister smile spreading across his face as he faced Kessan, who was desperately fighting off four other Macintoshes, trying to reach his wife and child.

Ceana was desperately trying to get back to her feet, struggling under the weight of her belly and Mel's heart felt heavy with grief as she heard the helplessness in Ceana's cries. Mel knew she had promised to stay away, but she had to help her friend. Making up her mind, she prepared to run to Ceana's aid when, from nowhere, a bright white ring of light burst through the air, knocking everyone within its range to the ground. Everyone except Hamish, she realised numbly as she lay on the dirt in shock. She guessed his powers were no longer a secret.

Hamish, stood arms clenched at his side, fury radiating from every pore of his body. He could feel the white glow of his power pulsating around him in tune with his anger. Nobody moved, nobody dare breath. He surveyed the battlefield making sure that his immediate family hadn't been hurt. Apart from everyone's stunned expression no one was hurt. Hamish sighed with relief, he hated that he couldn't control his powers, put it had been necessary to use them. He had only meant to knock out the laird but the minute he had directly threatened the life of his nephew, rage filled Hamish, rushing through every cell in his body and before he could rein it in, it exploded.

While Hamish was worried about what his sister would say, he couldn't stop now. Hamish strode towards Macintosh, grabbing one of the swords off the ground on the way. Once he was close enough, Hamish yanked Camden from his arms, shielded the little boy in his arms and then slit the Macintosh's throat in one smooth, deliberate movement, never taking his eyes off the man's own.

Emotionless, he watched the life drain out of them, and when the man lay on the ground, his blood flow slowing, he power pulsed excitedly with the pleasure of seeing the man dead at his feet. Hamish stood staring down at the twitching corpse before looking at his nephew, the boy had buried his head in Hamish's shoulder, his little arms wrapped tightly around Hamish's neck. Hamish's heart swelled with love as the little boy squeezed him tight. He was relieved there was no fear of him in the boy's heart, that he couldn't handle. He wasn't so sure that everyone else would feel the same, but there was nothing he could do about that now. Hamish turned towards the rest of his family and prepared himself for the questions that he knew was to come. But the only voice that greeted him was one filled with sarcasm, the voice of the woman he loved.

Forty-Nine

"So what should we call that one? The Giant Ring of Right? Or the Great White light?"

Mel smiled at the look on his face. She didn't think he appreciated her sarcasm, but everyone seemed tense and she needed something to break the ice. The fear she had felt when Macintosh had taken Camden, nothing to compare it to, and the adrenaline and shock of the moment hadn't worn off. Mel doubted she'd ever forget it, not even the fear she had felt at the hands of the duke could compare.

The bright white halo of light that had knocked everyone on their arses had come out of no-where, and then Hamish had casually strolled up and slit the bad guy's throat without blinking. Mel was not sure that she could forget the ease in which he did it, but it in no way changed how she felt about him. Things like this just didn't happen in her world, it was so far removed from reality that Mel was having a hard time believing what she had just witnessed.

Mel was trying to come to grips with the murder and mama that surrounded her, but when her eyes collided with Hamish's she knew everything would be all right. Neither one moved, they simply stood there staring at each other for a minute more, before everyone else sprang into action around them.

Ceana ran forward and snatched Camden from Hamish's arms and embraced him in a fierce hug, kissing him before passing him back to Hamish. Then before she could brace for it Mel found herself sandwiched as Ceana and Katie both threw themselves at her. Kessan and his men had quickly disarmed the rest of the stunned Macintoshes and in no time had them rounded up and headed for the dungeons.

Some members of the clan were helping the injured, while warriors removed the dead. Mel turned her attention back to her friends, her eyes filled with tears of relief and gratitude at being home and safe again. The three women started talking at once, each one trying to portray how much they meant to each other. Their conversation was cut short when a whistle pierced the air, bringing their noisy chatter to an abrupt halt. Mel wasn't surprised to see Hamish standing there, Camden still clinging to him, fingers poised to whistle again if need be.

"Was that really necessary?" She huffed.

Ceana laughed as she broke free from Mel's hold running over to hug her brother. "Thank you Ham. Thank you so much, you have no idea what this means to me." Mel heard her say softly as she laid a kiss on his cheek.

Hamish lowered his eyes from his sisters. "Think nothin' of it Lass, ya are my kin." He said earnestly.

"Why didn't you tell me about your powers?" Ceana asked him, hurt underlying the question.

Mel's heart broke as she watched Hamish shy away from Ceana's affection. It wasn't something that was obvious, but having gotten to know him she realised that Hamish never relaxed with anyone. He was pulling back into himself, just as he had before all of this happened.

"It was somethin' I felt that I had to deal with on my own, for everyone's sake." He answered Ceana.

Ceana slapped him, hard. No one had expected it least of all Hamish. Mel had to cover the laughter that bubble up inside of her when Hamish looked at his sister as though she had lost her mind.

"You great oaf, we are *kin* as you so kindly just reminded me and it's about time you started to realise what that means. It means that we deal with stuff like this together. I love you Hamish and nothing is ever going to change that."

Mel could see that Hamish wasn't yet convinced, but knowing her friend Mel knew that it wouldn't be long before Hamish caved. When Ceana didn't get the answer she wanted, she tried a new tactic. "Weren't you the one who told me that my power was something to be proud of?" Ceana reminded him. Hamish went to interrupt her, but she put her hand up and continued. "You don't see anyone treating me differently, or trying to kill me because of them. So, I think it's about time you take your own advice and let go of all the secrets."

Ceana leaned up and kissed him on the cheek once more, before grabbing him in a tight hug. Mel knew then that everything was going to be all right for Hamish. His family would make sure that he was no longer alone, she could go home and not have to worry about him.

Hamish was no longer looking at his sister, instead his eyes had her pinned to the spot. Her blood rippled, and her heart raced at the promise that they held. She knew it was going to be hard to get any time alone with him tonight, but Mel swore that, in the next couple of days, she would make sure she did, even if she had to sneak into his room after everyone had gone to sleep to get it.

Fifty

Just as she had suspected Mel didn't get any sleep that night, the first thing she had done, was demand to see Alec. Ceana had gladly taken her to his room, where he had almost recovered from his ordeal.

"Lady McKinnon will not let me go back my duties until she is one hundred percent sure that I am okay." Alec complained.

Mel winced when she saw the bruises that marred his face. His right hand was bandaged, and he had a bandage wrapped around his head. Mel's heart sank, knowing that she was the reason he was lying here, she was the reason he had almost lost his life. The pain that she had felt, while she lay awake at night thinking he was dead returned, but for a completely different reason. She owed this man her life.

Mel sat down on his bed and curled up beside him, shocking not only Alec but Ceana as well. "I am afraid I have to agree with her." Mel added, before whispering. "Thank you for trying to save my life." Mel leaned across and kissed the top of Alec's head.

When she pulled back a smile replaced Alec's frown. "Ya mean a lot to our laird ya ken; therefore, ya mean a lot to me. I would like you to know that I would do it all again. I just wished I had been able to stop them 'afore they took you."

Tears welled up in Mel's eyes. She was not so sure about what he said about Hamish, but she in no way blamed Alec for what had happened. Sitting up, Mel faced him with earnest eyes, "you did everything you could to save me, and it almost cost you your life. I never want you to feel like it was your fault." Once she had gotten his promise, Mel had sat with Alec for another hour discussing minor things until finally, she decided she needed some rest. Mel promised to check in on Alec again the next day before heading back to her own room.

On her way to her room Mel ran into Ceana, and now she sat next to Mel on her bed, gently tending to all her wounds while Mel filled her in on what had happened. Well most of it anyway. She didn't describe her humiliation and torture in detail, she spared her friend that. She also left out the bit about her and Hamish getting married and about their lovemaking. It wasn't that she was ashamed of it, it was just that she didn't want to have to explain her feelings to her friend just yet. If Mel was made to examine them too closely, she would be forced to admit that she loved him, and she was simply not ready to do that out loud.

Mel couldn't think about the pain that she was going to feel when she walked out of his life and went home, and she was going home. Mel had made up her mind the morning after the duke had been killed. She just couldn't stay here, this was not her time. She was a modern girl, she liked her modern conveniences and the predictability of the modern world and nothing was going to change that. She just wanted to put this whole thing behind her and get on with her life.

Unfortunately, that meant walking out on the only man that she had loved. "Oh Mel, I am so sorry. This is all my fault." Ceana sobbed as she hugged Mel close.

Mel pushed her friend back so she could look into her eyes. "How on earth do you perceive this as your fault Cee?" Mel commented shocked that her friend had even entertained that thought.

"I'm the one that sent you down to the glen that day. If I hadn't been trying to play matchmaker, then you wouldn't have been there in the first place, and they wouldn't have mistaken you for Hamish's woman!"

Mel sat and listened as her friend rambled, Ceana was no longer sitting on the bed, instead she was pacing back and forth in the room, agitated and upset. Mel felt dizzy, and then what Cee was admitting to finally dawned on her.

"Ha! So you admit that you *were* trying to set Hamish and I up." She accused.

Cee looked embarrassed, *good*, she should at least feel a little guilty over Mel's current predicament. Mel didn't blame Cee for Mowbray or the Macintoshes of course, but Ceana didn't yet know that her matchmaking had worked, she should have known better.

"Well of course I was. Come on Mel you're my best friend, and he's my brother. It was perfect. Don't you understand how much I miss you, and Hamish always seems so lonely. Was it wrong that I wanted two of my favourite people to be happy" She said as if the idea of them together was a natural thing. "But it didn't work." She added desolately, "all I managed to do was get you kidnapped and almost killed by a madman." Ceana sniffed and burst into tears again, Mel felt like a heel.

"I never meant for you to get hurt." Ceana said earnestly, taking Mel's hand in her own while searching her eyes for forgiveness.

Tears sprung to Mel's eyes. "I know that Cee! I never blamed you once for any of this; the idea of seeing you again was what helped keep me going." She hugged her friend.

Dejectedly, Ceana sat back on the bed. "Look at me; here you are giving me comfort when you're the one that has been through Hell. And what makes matters worse is that it was all for nothing. My plan didn't even work."

Mel walked over to the window, staring out over the green rolling hills. While she didn't want to tell Ceana about what had happened, Mel couldn't lie to her either. Ceana was the only person Mel couldn't lie to, she knew her too well. So Mel did the next best thing she said nothing, which in itself was a confession.

Mel could feel Cee's eyes boring into her back; the silence spoke for them. After a long drawn out silence, Mel relented, Cee was going to pry it out of her anyway. "Of course it worked." She finally replied with a sigh, trying to keep the bitterness out of her voice, but she couldn't do it.

"What?" Ceana screeched. "And you're only just now telling me?"

Mel flinched, and tears started to well up in her eyes again. *Gah, what was wrong with her?* She never cried this much. Crying just wasn't her. But ever since she had come to this godforsaken place her life had been turned upside down as had her emotions. Swiping at her eyes angrily, she turned around and faced her best friend. "What do you want me to tell you Cee?"

The rage was starting to come back. The injustice of it all was overwhelming. Why did her soulmate have to be born hundreds of years before her time? In a different country no less, and why did he have to be a laird? More importantly, why did she care so bloody much?

"You love him, don't you?" Ceana asked gently.

The tears were now running down her cheeks, Mel found she couldn't say the words so she simply nodded.

"Oh Mel." Ceana came forward and wrapped her in her arms. "You could stay you know." Ceana ventured.

Mel pulled back and gave her a look that said she was beyond crazy. "It was worth a try." Ceana shrugged.

Removing her arms from around her neck, she place one on Mel's shoulder and walked her back to the bed. "I was almost considering it at the beginning." Mel confessed. "But I can't stay here Cee, you of all people know that. This is not my world, it's his, and I don't belong here, any more than he belongs in mine. Besides, after everything that has happened I'm not sure I could stay even if I wanted to, it's too much. I wish it were otherwise, but you know what they say, if wishes were raindrops..." Mel didn't have the heart to finish her Grandma's favourite saying, right now she would do anything to make her wishes come true and the saying only reminded her that there was no other way.

As Ceana sat giving Mel a pitying look there was a quiet knock on the door, "come in," Mel called out and when the door opened it was to show Kessan standing outside, waiting for his wife. Ceana gave her one last hug, promising that everything would work out before she headed for the door, but, before she walked out, Ceana turned to face her, "Well, I for one am not going to give up. I still have two days until you go."

Mel shrugged tiredly. "You can try but it won't work." But as was normal Ceana hadn't heard her, she had already left with her husband leaving Mel alone to her thoughts once more. Now that she was by herself Mel lay down on her bed, wrapped herself into a ball and cried herself to sleep as her heart broke a little more.

Fifty-One

It had been a day and half since they returned and Hamish hadn't found time to be alone with Mel and time was running out. He was preparing to leave that very afternoon and Hamish needed to say goodbye. He had thought about asking her to stay and wait for him, but he knew that was not fair on her. He couldn't give her what she deserved, and he knew that she did not belong here, not after everything she'd been through. Still his heart screamed out for him to ask her, he didn't even know if she loved him, and he wasn't going to be the first one to say it.

Hamish saw that his men were almost ready to leave, he couldn't put it off any longer he had to find her. He headed for the stable doors and was almost there when they opened and Mel walked in. Hamish paused, waiting for her to notice him. "Are you leaving?" She when her eyes finally found him and she noticed his horse was saddled and ready to go.

"Aye." He answered her quietly.

Hamish wanted to say more, but he didn't trust his emotions. When she brought her eyes back to him, the hurt in them made his gut clench. "Were you going to say goodbye?" She asked.

Mel's voice sounded like that of a wounded child and it took everything he had to ignore the warrior within. Hamish took a step forward and placed his hand on the side of her face, lifting her head up until her eyes were level with his he hoped she could see the sincerity in them.

"Aye, I was. I was just on my way to find you."

Mel moistened her lips and it took all the will power he had not to bend down and kiss them. He needed to get this over without making it any harder on either one of them, and kissing her would lead to other things and that was not going to help the matter, if anything it would make it harder for him to let her go. "Oh," she said, stepping back out of his reach.

Hamish wanted nothing more than to grab her back and kiss her passionately, but he knew it was better this way. Hamish could handle her wrath, but what he couldn't handle was knowing that he had broken her heart.

"Well, I saved you the trip. I was just coming to find you so that I could give you these before I left tomorrow." She said, reaching out placing his mother's ring and the knife into his hand. "Don't worry I haven't told anyone, no one knows what happened, so it shouldn't be hard for you to annul the marriage."

Hamish couldn't move, not only was she giving him his gifts back he had just let him know that she was leaving tomorrow. This was the first time he had heard about it. Hamish had thought she would be staying for at least another week as Caelan and Katie weren't leaving 'til then.

She was going and she hadn't come to find him until now! If that's the way she wanted it, fine. Hamish shook his head. "These belong to you now, Lass." He said as he ran his thumb over the ring one last time. He took her hand, placed the ring and knife in her palm and gently closed her fingers around them.

Mel shook her head. "Hamish, I can't keep your mother's ring, you know that. We both know that this marriage isn't real and I cannot in good faith keep it." Mel opened her hadn't, picked up the ring and handed it back to him with force. Looking into her eyes, Hamish could see that they were glassed over, and he could have sworn that he heard regret in her tone.

Reluctantly sliding his mother's ring back on his pinkie, where it had been since the day she had died, Hamish forced all the emotions he was feeling down. He would not force her to take something she didn't want. "Och, thank ya, Lass." He acknowledged feigning politeness. They stared awkwardly at each other for a moment as he tried to decipher how he felt, and the truth was he loved her. Whatever else happened he knew the to be true and he wanted to leave her with something that would always remind her of him. "Please keep the knife though, Mel. Even if it's just for protection,

I'd like ya to have it. After all you've been through, it belongs with ya now."

At first he thought she was going to refuse, but to his relief Mel nodded, Hamish was pleased that she had accepted the knife because now, no matter where she was, she would have something of his. Mel stared down at the blade, absently running her fingers along the hilt before sheathing the knife. Hamish was not certain what she would do next but as she stood there silent and uncertain he couldn't stand what their relationship had become.

There was no more fire and passion; instead it had been replaced with awkward politeness and distance. They both realised what was coming and he did the only thing left to do. Turning around Hamish walked away heading back to his horse. He had to face the truth, whatever they had was over, she was leaving and their relationship never could have lasted. The only thing he could do now was get on with the rest of his life and let her do the same.

Hamish's resolve not to ask her stay almost came undone when her soft voice echoed around him. "Please be safe," she pleaded.

Hamish's heart swelled, he closed his eyes trying to get a hold of his emotions. Few people cared if he was safe or not, he knew that his kin loved him, and they didn't want him hurt, but they felt that way about everyone in their clan. This was different; this was love between two souls something he had never thought he'd have.

Damning the consequences Hamish turned around, planning to beg her not to go, but with a sinking heart, all he saw was the stable doors swinging shut. He was too late, she was gone. Fine, if that was what she wanted, he would leave, he would go home and be the laird his clan needed, and she would go home and go back to the life she'd had before coming here. Letting out a whistle, Hamish signalled his men that it was time to leave. He mounted his horse, kicked it into a gallop and rode out of the keep, refusing to look back behind him, unaware that Mel's tear-filled eyes followed his path from the garrets above.

Fifty-Two

Mel sat by the window of her office staring out across the Gold Coast Hinterlands, feeling nothing but numbness. Ever since she had come home five and half months ago, she had tried to get her life back to normal, but it was hard to determine what normal was anymore. She went out with friends, spent time with her family and even threw herself into her work with more vigour than she had before. In fact, she worked as much as she could, trying to keep her mind busy so that she wouldn't think about him.

At first it worked when she was at work or with others, keeping busy was the key; the minute she entered her empty apartment by herself however, the loneliness and sorrow that had become her life would creep back in. As the months had worn on, even work and friends couldn't keep it at bay. Now, nothing was working.

Looking down, Mel eyed the cause of her distraction – the ring Hamish had originally given her now sat on her right ring finger. She still couldn't believe she had it, after all she had given it back to him the day before she left. Mel had known that the ring had been his mother's and she couldn't, in good conscience keep it, but here it was on her finger, back in the 21st century. She couldn't wear it officially, that would raise too many unanswerable questions, and her heart just couldn't take that but there was no way she was going to leave it at home sitting in a jewellery box gathering dust either.

While Mel had denied the ring, she had thought to also deny the clan-crested knife he'd gifted to her, but as she'd looked down at the intricate scroll work in her hand she had decided to keep it on Hamish's insistence. She needed something of his that she could keep with her, and every night she slept with it under her pillow. It made her feel closer to him and it made her feel safe.

Mel couldn't take her eyes off the beautiful ring, she had been shocked when Katie had shown up here on her return, ring in hand. Mel knew she couldn't refuse it without explanation and awkward questions so she had taken it without comment.

Mel thought back on those last few days, part of her had been tempted to stay the extra week and come home with Katie and Caelan, but once Hamish had gone the highlands just seemed empty, and so the next day she said her own goodbyes.

"Mel, Hamish wanted me to give you this." Katie had explained when she came into the office. Mel couldn't believe what she was seeing.

"He came back before I left," she added, noting Mel's look of shock.

"Did he say anything." Mel asked not knowing if she was ready to hear about the man she loved.

Katie shook her head. "Only that I was to give you this. Then he left again. I assumed you would know what it meant." Katie had looked at Mel curiously, but Mel shrugged and had given her some vague answer about memories and the trials they went through. Katie hadn't been told of the significance of Hamish's family ring, so she couldn't have known what the gift had signified.

As Mel sat looking out over the town she tried to figure out why he had done it. He couldn't love her, otherwise he would have said so before she left, but he had. Heartbroken, Mel looked back to the mountains wishing she could see him one more time, even if for only a minute, there was so much that had been left unsaid. Logically, Mel knew that it didn't matter what the ring meant, she couldn't go back Hamish had probably moved on with his life. He was the laird of his clan and despite his misgivings that meant that he would eventually need an heir for his name to live on, and that would require a wife.

The thought of him with another woman sent a bolt of jealousy pulsing through Mel's veins but there was nothing she could do. She had given up any right to the man the moment she chose to leave. It wasn't his fault that she herself couldn't move on. It wasn't like Mel hadn't tried, she knew full well that this wasn't a long-distance relationship that could work. But every day she was plagued with one word. How? How did one move on when they felt like part of their soul was missing? How did someone stop loving their soul mate? But most importantly, how was Mel going to survive without him?

Unexpectedly, Mel was brought out of her musing when the door to her office opened. Not many people would enter her without knocking or at least without her receptionist announcing them and, as she faced the unexpected guest, Mel's misery deepened.

Before her stood Jack the Jerk, looking embarrassed and guilty. *What the hell did he want?* As Mel stared at him, she wondered what she had ever seen in him in the first place. He was just so average, that was the only way she could think to describe him. She knew she hadn't seen it before and it seeing him standing there she finally knew what she had wanted all along. Average wasn't it, no what she wanted was *extraordinary*. Ceana had been right, there was no way she was ever going to be truly happy with the man standing before her.

"Mel can we talk?" He asked cautiously as he stood at the door.

Mel could have laughed at how meek he was, it was as if he were expecting her to lash out. Mel looked down at her computer and typed in her password, she needed something to distract her. If he had come to her six months ago, she probably would have lashed out at him, now she just didn't care enough to want to. Too much had happened to her to consider Jack and the bullshit he had pulled as anything more than trivial.

"Why Jack? We have nothing to say to each other." Mel stated as she waited for her computer to boot up. She was hoping that by ignoring him he would get the picture and go away, no such luck. Mel could see that he was about to argue with her, but didn't have the energy to deal with his crap right now. All she wanted was to get him out of her office so she could go back to daydreaming about a man she did care about. "Look, if you have come here for some kind of closure, you have it okay. I'm good, you have my blessing. Now please leave."

Turning back to her work, Mel hoped that he would finally go. But, unfortunately, Jack being Jack seemed to have other things on his mind.

"Yes I have something to say." He started. "I have finally realised that I made a huge mistake. I was indecisive and confused, I thought someone like Clarissa was what I wanted in my life, but I now know that it is you I want. I miss you Mel." He said looking at her sheepishly and working in the practised charm that had always worked on her before.

Mel took a deep breath, closed her computer and gave him her full attention. She didn't give a rat's arse what had happened between the two of them, but she wasn't fooled by him coming here with is tale between his legs claiming to have seen the light. The truth was the bitch had probably dumped him.

"What happened?" Mel asked emotionlessly. She watched as Jack considered what to tell her. Moments later his whole body relaxed and a look of shame and anger crossed his face.

"She left me for her Yoga instructor." Jack stated miserably.

Mel snorted with laughter, she couldn't help it. The irony of it was too bloody funny. "Karma's a real bitch, isn't she?" Mel finally managed to get out between laughs.

Jack walked towards her desk. "Yes she is." He answered as he placed his hands on the seat in front of him. "Look, I know I shouldn't have let you go. We were made for each other; can't we give it one more try?" He pleaded and the pathetic hopefulness in his voice made her cringe. Even if Mel hadn't met Hamish, there was no way she was ever going to give this Jerk another chance. He had tried to destroy her once, he was not getting another run at it. Besides there was no room in her heart for anyone else anymore.

Standing up Mel raised her hand to stop him from sitting down. "Look Jack, thank you for finally seeing that what you did was wrong. But you and I are never going to happen." She said firmly.

"Oh come on Mel. Whatever happened to giving someone a second chance? We all make mistakes." He said annoyance tarnishing the wounded soldier look.

Shaking her head, Mel wondered for the second time what she had ever seen in him. "It's not that Jack. The truth is I don't want to give you another chance, not because you don't deserve it, which you don't by the way, but because I simply don't want to. Besides I'm married now." The shock on Jack's face said it all. She hadn't meant to blurt it out the way she had, but she knew it would be a sure-fire way to get him to leave.

"No you're not. How?" He asked dumbly.

"Yes I am." She said holding up her hand to show him her ring. Mel had inadvertently moved it to her left hand while he was stating his case. She watched in satisfaction as he sputtered and tried to process what he was hearing.

"Look, Jack, I think it's best if we just go our separate ways. Go and live your life, find someone who appreciates you for you, because that person isn't me, and it never will be me."

Mel sighed in relief when she saw resignation enter in his eyes, he finally realised that they were over for good. "Okay" He said sadly. "But I truly am sorry." He tried again, before he headed out the door.

"And I really don't care." Mel replied as he shut the door. For the rest of the day Mel buried her feelings in her work, trying once more to forget about the ache in her heart. But no matter what she did it wouldn't go away, something just weren't meant to be forgotten.

Fifty-Three

Two days later, she couldn't deal with it anymore, nothing and on-one mattered. Picking up the phone Mel did something she had never done before, she called in sick.

With her heart breaking Mel crawled back into bed and buried herself under the covers for the rest of the day. She couldn't believe that she had become one of *those* girls; the girls who pined over a man. She had always sworn that she would never do that, but here she was hiding in a fortress made from blankets, moping and eating tons of ice-cream. *What had her life become?*

A loud banging on her door drew her from her cocoon. "Hold ya bloody horses," she mumbled to herself as she made her from her room to the living area. She had yet to get dressed, but she didn't care.

"You had better be dying!" A gruff voice said as she opened the door to her Grandma G.G.

"No G.G I'm not dying." Mel replied rolling her eyes at the melodrama.

"Then why haven't you come to see me this week Pet, and why are you not at work?"

"G.G the week is not over, and I am entitled to one day off without being sick, you know, after all I am the boss." Mel thought about the last time someone had told her she could do whatever she wanted because she was the boss, and look how they had turned out.

Her grandmother looked at her, seeing straight through the sarcasm and the lies.

"Mmmhmm." She continued to stand there staring at Mel with a look that said she knew better.

The damn tears started again and before she knew it, Mel was running to her grandmother. She threw herself into her grandmother's arms and was immediately wrapped in a warm embrace. The woman may have been seventy-five years old, but she still had a strength about her that Mel envied.

"Hush Pet, it's all going to be alright." Her grandmother murmured gently.

"No, it isn't." Mel sobbed as her grandmother rubbed her back comfortingly .

"Why don't you tell me what's going on, and then we will see if we can fix it." G.G rationalised.

Mel's Grandmother had always been the cool-headed one in the family, if not a little kooky. If anyone could help her sort this mess out, it would be her. "Unless you can stop my heart from loving a man I can't have, we can't." Mel replied miserably.

Mel was shocked when her grandmother released Mel from her hold, stood back and placed her hands on her hips. "Oh child, do not tell me this is about that buffoon Jack what's his name. If it is I swear I will box your ears myself." Her grandmother admonished as she sat them down on the sofa.

Mel smiled, her grandmother always seemed to know the right thing to say to lighten her mood. She had never been subtle in her dislike of Jack. "No G.G. it's not about him." Mel answered with a heavy heart, wiping warm tears from her eyes.

"Then tell me what's going on Pet." G.G cooed and that's exactly what Mel did. For the next hour, she sat and explained everything that had happened between her and Hamish. Her grandmother absorbed it all without batting an eyelid, letting Mel pour out all her emotions and feelings that had been weighing her down. Her Grandmother offered her what no-one else had been able to, she offered her a warm safe place to admit what she felt. And what she felt was heartache.

Mel entered the Firefly Hideaway reception, when Caelan exited with the Samsons in tow.

"Mel?" He said with surprise in his voice. She leaned up and gave him a light kiss on his cheek. "Hey handsome." She said backing away from him with a smile.

"Is everything alright Lass?" He asked concern in his voice. She didn't blame him for that concern, for the last five months she had pretty much been MIA as far as going out and visiting her friends had been concerned. Katie had tried a few times to invite her to dinner, but the truth was Mel couldn't be around anyone that reminded her of Hamish.

"Yes, I just need to talk to you and Katie about something." Mel answered as she walked around him and greeted the Samsons with a hug. "How are you both?" She asked respectfully.

Mel had known the Samsons since her and Ceana were little girls. Every year, when they came up to the Firefly Hideaway they'd always given them candy and lollies whenever the girls had helped Cee's mum in the reception area, or if they had seen them playing around the cabins. She had fallen immediately in love with them as they reminded her a lot of her own grandparents.

"Oh, my dear, it's nice to see you again too. It has been far too long since we have seen your beautiful smile." Mr Samson answered. "You've grown even more beautiful since the last time we saw you." Mrs Samson added. Mel blushed; she never could handle

getting compliments from anyone.

"Thank you both, I hope you enjoy your stay." She said giving them one last hug.

"We always do my dear. You must promise that you will come and have a cuppa with us one afternoon," Mr Samson said giving her one last hug before he continued down the steps.

"I will try my best." She lied.

Mel watched them walk off with Calean chatting away with him telling him all about their ventures. She didn't realise how much she had truly missed them until now and while she would like nothing better than to enjoy a nice cuppa with the old couple catching up on what they had been doing with their lives, it was not going to be possible. If everything went to plan Mel wouldn't be here much longer .

"Katie is in the kitchen." Caelan stopped and yelled when he as half way across the yard, "I won't be long."

Mel nodded her head in recognition then opened the door to the reception area, her heart raced with the knowledge of what she was about to do and while she may have had some doubts she knew G.G was right.

It was now or never, and Mel was not prepared to accept never.

Fifty-Four

"Are you sure?" Katie was asking her for the fifth time as they stood outside the cave.

Mel laughed giddily. "Yes Katie. I'm sure." She was not sure who she trying to convince more, herself or Katie. Either way, come hell or high water Mel was determined to do this.

"Oookay." Katie answered, drawing the word out. "You do remember that there are no modern conveniences, right? Perhaps you might want to take a few cartons of coffee with you, I'm pretty sure you used up Cee's stash during your stay."

Mel groaned in annoyance. "Katie, I know you think you're being helpful, but seriously, just zip it."

Katie chuckled. "I'm sorry Mel; it's just that I'm still stunned that you're doing this."

"Don't worry, so am I," Mel retorted, before they both burst out laughing.

"I wish I could see the look on Cee's face when you rock up at her door." Katie said wistfully, grinning.

Mel smiled, she knew Katie desperately wanted to come with her, but the Firefly Hideaway was at full capacity and they needed all hands on deck. "I promise to send you a long letter describing it all." Mel pulled her friend into a final hug before she moved out of the way so she could talk to her husband.

"I won't be gone long love." Caelan informed his wife before he kissed her passionately. Feeling awkward, Mel turned away and waited until they had finished.

"You ready Lass?" He asked as he touched her shoulder.

"As ready as I'll ever be." Mel answered as she followed him into the cave. "I can't believe I'm going through this again." She said as the wind tore at her body. She vaguely heard Caelan's burst of laughter as everything around her went black and she once again asked herself if she was doing the right thing.

Even though it was her third time going through the portal, Mel still found it terrifying – it was even worse alone. As the wind quieted down and everything started to come back to normal she blinked the darkness away and took a deep breath to calm her nerves and racing heart. Stomach lurching from the journey, she again asked herself whether she was crazy. All of the memories, both good and bad, came flooding back and an involuntary shiver ran down her spine as images of the duke rushed to overwhelm her.

NO! She berated herself. She would not let those moments tarnish her happiness. Banishing the memories to the back of her mind, Mel focused on the reason she was here. Looking down at her finger she smiled at the ring still resting securely on her ring finger. *This* was the reason she was here. Mel had come to claim her man, just as her grandmother had suggested. Now she just needed to find him and tell him how she felt.

Mel wanted to spend the rest of her life with this man, she just hoped he felt the same. *Would he want her, after all that was left unsaid and the way that she'd left it? What if he had moved on?* These questions and more floated through her mind and Mel wouldn't blame Hamish if he had moved on, she was the one that had left.

"My God, I must be crazy to put myself through that again," she mumbled as her head spun, twisting the vision before her eyes. Blinking the dizziness away, Mel turned around towards the entrance of the cave.

At first she thought what she was seeing was a trick of her journey, but as she got closer, a light appeared. It was definitely not a hallucination. *Who had found her?* Images of the duke once more played in her mind, but she it couldn't be, he was dead, she reminded herself. Nobody knew she was going to be here, looking around she searched for Caelan to see what his reaction would be.

But when her eyes met his her heartbeat slowed a little, there was no fear in his gaze only acceptance. Maybe he hadn't seen the light, the effect of time travel took a while to calm down, maybe it was her own mind playing tricks. I mean come on, she thought to herself. How many times could someone go through that before it affected them permanently? Mel shook that thought from her head. She had more important things to worry about and she couldn't wait any longer. Mel started to make her way to the front of the antechamber, towards the light that was rapidly getting closer. It wasn't her imagination, there was definitely someone coming.

"Caelan!" She whispered urgently, but she didn't answer.

Mel had only taken three steps back towards her friend when her mind finally registered what she was seeing. *It couldn't be, could it? It was, But how?*

Hamish stood in the cave entrance, mouth hanging open, mirroring her own shocked expression. Slowly he smiled, and her heart sung with happiness, for the first time in six months her world finally felt like it was whole again. Not giving it a moment's thought Mel ran and threw herself at him. Hamish shook himself out of his stupor just in time to catch her in his muscular, warrior arms, the torch he had been holding dropped to the ground descending them into the shadows of the cave once more.

"Lass, what are ya doing here?" He asked her, hoarsely, disbelief evident in his voice before he kissed her deeply.

Mel pulled away and placed her hands on either side of his face, "I was just about to ask you the same question."

Hamish was about to say something to her but she shut him up before he could. She needed to get her speech out before she lost her nerve. "Hamish, I love you with all my heart and I can no longer live without you in my life. I have come here to claim my husband." She said with passion, before an unanswered question pushed its way to her mind.

Hamish shouldn't have been there. No one should have been; no-one knew she was coming, it was completely unplanned, so what was he doing here?

"Hang on. How are you here? Why are here? What were you planning on doing once you were here?" Mel fired at him in rapid succession. She knew she wasn't giving him time to answer but she had too many questions running around in her mind. Hamish laughed, Mel felt the rumble all the way through her body.

"Och Lass, has anyone ever told ya, ya ask too many questions. I was just aboot to do the same thing ya have don'. I was coming to yer time ta claim my wife."

Mel was stunned. "But why?" She managed to ask pathetically.

Again, he guffawed. "Och ya really are daft aren't ya Lass? Why else would I be coming to claim ya? I love ya with all my heart and I can no longer live without you in my life. You brought lightness and laughter into my life, when there was nothing but darkness. I know I should let you go and that it's unfair of me to demand it, but I just can't let ya go. I'm a selfish bastard, I know."

Mel saw the love in his eyes as he finished his confession and it filled her heart with joy. She even forgave him for calling her daft. No longer doubting her decision, Mel kissed him with all the passion she had been holding onto during their separation. "All right I'll stay." She said pulling back from him. "But I at least want some kind of plumbing installed."

Hamish burst out laughing and kissed her again. "I'm not joking Hamish." She informed him.

"Lass, for you, anything," he whispered against her lips.

"In that case, have you ever thought about growing coffee?" She asked, an edge of seriousness in her voice. Hamish chuckled and they began the journey out of the cave, towards their forever.

As they rode towards the Ceana's home on *Seodag*, Mel smiled blissfully at ease for the first time in months. With Hamish's warmth wrapped around her she realised that this was what she had longed for. She was glad that she had listened to her Grandmother. G.G had been right her heart was never going to mend until she was with the man who made it whole. After G.G. had informed Mel that home wouldn't be home until she had the whole of her heart, she had convinced her to come back here and claim what was hers, and that was exactly what she had done.

Mel was finally home. *Now* her heart was whole again, thanks to her highland hero.

Epilogue

Mel stood in her husband's arms as they looked out over the hinterlands from their two-storey house. She did not regret going back to the highlands, the man standing behind her was everything she had ever wanted and more. He had promised to make her move the highlands as easy as he could, and he even promised to spend one month twice a year in the 21st Century so that she could see her family.

That was where they were now, they were here for their official wedding. They still had two weeks left before the portal closed for another six months, Mel had made sure of that by going back to the 12th Century the first night it had re-opened. She knew that she would need time to bring Hamish home so her family could see her get married. She hadn't had the heart to deny them, especially since she was the last grandchild of G.G's to do so. Her grandmother would kill her if she didn't allow her to see Mel married.

After talking to her grandmother that fateful morning, Mel knew that she couldn't live her life without Hamish. After starting wedding preparations here in the 21st Century, she headed back to the 12th Century to get the groom; for a wedding which was now only four days away. Her grandmother and mother had done an amazing job organising the preparations in time and Hamish had been such a sport about the whole thing. He hadn't once complained about the fittings, or rehearsals or the crazy 21st Century wedding demands that had been dumped on him about a week ago when they returned.

Mel had explained about the modern wedding before they had come back to the 21st century and, like the hero he was, he just followed her lead, albeit somewhat overwhelmed. He didn't even complain when her brothers had grilled him for hours on end about what his intentions were. Mel's parents welcomed Hamish with open arms, they were finally happy that their last child was happy and of course G.G absolutely adored Hamish.

"If ya get sick of him Gal, I might just take him off ya hands." She had joked when Mel brought him home to meet them.

As a wedding gift, G.G had brought them this beautiful home close to the Firefly Hideaway so that they had somewhere private and close by to stay whenever they visited. It was her way of making sure that Mel came home, and often. After much deliberation Mel decided that she was going to keep her firm, she had hired two more accountants and made two of the senior accountants, associates. She had no doubt that they would keep it running and she would check in when she was home, and on the plus side, Mel had agreed to do the books for the Lairds she knew. I would keep her busy and now she wouldn't have to give up what she loved.

"Are ya happy Lass?" Hamish breathed in her ear as they stared out of the bay window.

"Aye." She replied mimicking his brogue.

Hamish chuckled and turned her so that she could see his face. "Are *you* happy?" She asked and was pleased when his eyes filled with all the love he possessed for her.

"I mean I know my family can be full on sometimes and this time is very different to what you're used to...." She left the window and rambled on. She didn't want him to feel out of place and it hadn't occurred to her until just now that this might be all too much for him and, after meeting her crazy family she wouldn't blame him if he ran for the hills. He was a very private man, after all.

"...and I completely understand if you are having second thoughts." She added breathlessly. Turning around she noticed the stunned look on his face.

"Are ya really worried that I am no' happy Lass?" He asked gently .

Mel took a deep breath. "It's just that all of this has been forced on you and I haven't really asked if you are okay with it. Hell, the ridiculous expectations of the modern world gets too much for us natives sometimes, I can only imagine how it must seem for you." She reasoned honestly, opening her arms indicating the house and the wedding chaos that lay around them.

Hamish took a step forward and drew her back into his arms. "Lass, as long as I am with you, nothing else matters. You are my heart and soul. You saved me from a life of loneliness, and for that you could ask for the moon and I would get it for you."

Mel's heart melted. "And you Sir are my hero. More than that, you are my everything. From the moment I saw you as I came down that mountain, I knew there was something about you. I have loved you from the moment I saw you in that brothel, knowing you were there to save me. It was then that you won my heart and soul. Without you I'm not whole."

Mel grabbed him and brought his lips down to meet hers, showing him just how much he meant to her. Soon their kiss turned hot, Hamish picked her up and started for the stairs that led to the bedroom. "I think 'tis time to try out the new bed, doona ya?" He asked her huskily.

She loved the way his brogue got thicker when his emotions were heightened. "Oh yes, I wholeheartedly concur!" She said breathlessly as he continued to nibble at her lips.

Heading towards the stairs, they continued kissing; he had barely touched the lowest step when her phone started ringing. Still unused to the little noisy box that constantly interrupted their lives, he waited to see what she wanted to do.

Mel shook her head, "not on your life am I answering that. Now take me upstairs so I can ravage your body!" She ordered as she kissed a path from his jaw to his neck. Hamish didn't need any more encouragement and she laughed as he took the stairs two at a time. Her mobile stopped ringing, but, just as quickly her home phone started. Mel couldn't care less, the world would have to wait because right now she was going to make passionate love to her highlander and nothing was going to stand in her way.

Mel and Hamish lay wrapped in each other's arms lovingly stroking one and other. Mel was debating if she should get up and make them something for dinner or better yet, *order* them something for dinner. All thoughts of dinner left her mind however, when the front door slammed open. Mel and Hamish sprung from the bed in horror and rushed to get dressed as Ceana's voice rang through the house.

"Mel, where are you?" She cried.

Mel hurried to get dressed, it was so unlike Ceana to just burst in. "Hang on, I'll be down in a minute." She yelled back.

Hamish, she realised with irritation, was getting dressed at a leisurely pace. She knew from experience however, that if she didn't get her butt down those stairs quickly, Cee would have no qualms about coming to look for them. Mel wondered how Hamish would handle his sister walking in on him naked, she didn't think he would be so calm then. Giving him a kiss, she hurried out the door closing it behind her to give him privacy. As she came down the stairs, she noticed Kessan was also there, closing the door more gently than Ceana had opened it. He was carrying their bags, while ushering the kids in.

The children ran forward giving her a big hug before they shot past her to Hamish, who had finally appeared behind her on the stairs. Hamish picked them up, kissing them as they begged him to let them go. He did, and they bolted off to explore the house. "Don't go too far." Ceana yelled after them, her two-month old son resting in his capsule that Ceana had placed on the kitchen bench.

Mel guessed that her friend was staying here which suited her just fine. She missed having her around, and nothing beat the sound of laughter and chaos that followed the children.

"I take it you're staying here?" She asked anyway, confirming her suspicions.

"Yeah, I knew you wouldn't mind." Ceana answered offhandedly. "The Firefly Hideaway is full and Katie and Caelan have a full house, with our friends staying with them." She offered up as explanation.

"Hi Ham," she added as Hamish joined them in the kitchen.

"Ceana what's going on?" Mel asked, as she picked up baby Sam, her intuition sensing that Ceana wasn't her usual self.

"Oh you're not going to believe it." Ceana answered, her voice raising an octave.

"Believe what?" Hamish asked. Ceana turned on them waving a

letter at them. Mel could not remember the last time she had seen Ceana so worked up.

"Believe what our stupid brother has done!" She retorted.

If it involved Tristan anything was possible. Mel waited, concerned, she had been so relieved when she had come home and heard that Tristan was still alive, but that was all that she knew. She hadn't had the chance to see him since she had come home and she was desperate to find out if everything was okay. With everything that had happened to her in the Highlands Mel still hadn't had the chance to tell Ceana what Tristan was doing, and once she'd come home and found Tristan alive, Mel decided not to cause Ceana any more worry.

Mel had kept tags on him though, she had even tried to call him a couple of times but she had never been able to get through. Grabbing the letter out of Ceana's hand, Mel started to read, she half expected the letter to detail what he had been up to. She was desperate to know if he had finished his mission and whether he was okay. But as Mel read on her astonishment mounted, and her face must have shown it.

"Lass, what is it?" Hamish asked wanting to know.

"He couldn't be that stupid, could he?" she asked the room, ignoring Hamish and turning towards Ceana and Kessan.

"Aye, they both could be." Kessan answered her in a calm and collective manner, but the anger lacing his voice was obvious to everyone.

"Och, would someone mind tellen' me what is goin' on?" Hamish asked once more.

Mel turned towards Hamish and wondered what she could say, perhaps she should just let him read the letter. She was just about to give him the page when Ceana answered his question.

"Well you know everyone has thought that Thora has been with her aunt for the last six months?"

"Aye" Hamish replied cautiously, trepidation entering his eyes.

"Well, turns out, she not missing so much as she's with Tristan, *here,* in the 21st Century. In the Amazon rainforest, no less."

Hamish stared at Ceana and Mel's eyes widened at the implications of what this meant. Tristan had taken Thora on his mission, the idiot was going to get them both killed.

"I'm going to kill him!" Ceana fumed as if reading her thoughts. "I'm going to kill them both!" Kessan snapped.

What was Tristan thinking?

"Och, I'm sure there is a rational explanation." Hamish tried reasoning and failed.

"Are you serious?" Ceana gaped at him. "There is no good reason to take Thora to the Amazon rainforest. Do you know how big that place is, and how dangerous?! There are not only snakes, and I mean big snakes, spiders and other dangerous animals, there are also *head hunters* for Christ sakes! Do you hear me *head hunters*."

With each word Cee spoke, Mel could see Kessan getting more upset. Tristan was going to be dead either way. "Look, the letter says that they will be back here in time for the wedding, how about we save the killing until after they have returned and they tell us their side of the story. Besides Cee, have you ever known Tristan to do anything willingly that would put another human being in danger?" Mel said logically.

"I suppose you're right." Ceana grudgingly agreed. "Alright, I will give him the benefit of the doubt, until he gets back. But, if he hasn't got a reasonable enough explanation I *am* going to gut him where he stands."

"Gee, Cee, have you been taking lessons from Kessan or something?" She joked, "You're really starting to sound like a true-blue highlander."

Mel laughed when she noticed the blush on her best friend's face and Kessan's stony expression. "Look, if he doesn't have a reasonable explanation I will help you gut him." She added for Kessan's benefit and it worked he relaxed slightly. Mel was glad that she wasn't in Tristan's shoes right now. Man, that boy had some explaining to do.

What on earth was he thinking?

"Well I guess the only thing left to do now is plan your bachelorette party." Ceana said slyly changing the subject.

Mel groaned, there was a little too much glee in her friend's voice for Mel's liking. And the mischievous look that entered Ceana's eyes didn't help the pit from forming in her stomach. "Oh come on Cee, I am technically married, so a bachelorette party is a bit redundant now don't you think?" She wheedled.

"What's a bacher'orette party?" Hamish asked Kessan, stumbling over the foreign word. Kessan just shrugged his shoulders. Mel blushed not knowing how to explain the ridiculous over-the-top wedding ritual of the 21st century. She didn't particularly want to explain strippers, penis straws and sparkly tiaras to the two protectively modest highlanders standing in her kitchen.

"It's a way for Cee to torture me that's all, and like I said, I am already married so it doesn't count. Technically bachelorette parties are for brides-to- be who want to celebrate their last night of freedom. That really doesn't fit my case." She tried once more.

"Ha! But this is your *official* 21st Century wedding. There's *no* way I'll let you out of this one, Mel." Ceana said, as she headed for the lounge room, pulling Mel with her. Hamish offered her a small smile as she pleaded with hi to help her, but it was of no use, Ceana was on a mission and what right did Mel have to deny her that pleasure.

Ceana and Mel spent the next couple of hours discussing the wedding, while Hamish and Kessan caught up on what was happening in the Highlands and as Mel sat listening to Ceana talk and the children off playing in the other room, she was once more grateful that she had listened to her heart. Never again would she feel as though her life wasn't exciting, nothing could ever make her feel more alive the man in the other room, nothing.

Later that night as Mel lay in Hamish's arms once more, she wondered for the millionth time how she had gotten so lucky. If she hadn't taken Tristan's advice she would never have met him. Thinking about Tristan brought back all her worry for him, she hoped that he was ok and that whatever was going on with him and Thora helped to bring the old Tristan back.

Thora had disappeared not long after Mel had gone missing, and as far as anyone knew she was staying with an Aunt down in the highlands. While that shouldn't have worried anyone, what did worry them was she had left without saying anything she had simply left her brothers a note and gone. It was so unlike Thora to do that. Kessan wanted to go after her but Ceana had talked him into giving her some space. Maybe if he had gone after her they may have been able to stop this madness.

But what was done was done and she couldn't wait to see Tristan worm his way out of this one. Mel smiled thinking about how Cee had reacted to the news that Thora was with Tristan. "What has ya smiling Lass?" Hamish asked as he ran his hands through her hair.

Mel looked up at him her playful smile widening. "Oh just how much shit Tristan will be in when he gets back." She laughed.

"Ya ken Lass, I'm starting to think that you have an evil side to ya."

"You had better believe it. Although it's nowhere near as evil as your sister's." She added and then Mel groaned at the thought of what Ceana had planned for her bachelorette party.

Hamish laughed. "Och ya may be right Lass."

"You don't mind that they are going to be staying here, do you?" She thought to ask.

"Lass, that is one thing ya will never have to worry aboot. I love having my family around, I have missed the children in these last few weeks."

The longing that entered his eyes brought forward a question that she had been meaning to ask him for weeks now. She knew they'd had the conversation before, but that had been before everything had gone wrong, and now that everything was right and Hamish was no longer afraid of his powers she had to know. "Hamish, how would you feel about starting a family?" She hadn't meant to just blurt it out like that, but now that she had, she waited with bated breath for his answer.

"Och Lass, I canno' think of anything better than starting a family with ya. For so long I believed the magic had to die with me, but being here with ya and ya kin has shown me that family is all that matters. Och an' with ya by my side, Lass there is nothin' I cannae' handle" He said as he kissed the end of her nose; he was so adorable at times.

"That's a relief." Mel said cheekily. She almost laughed at the look that entered his eyes.

"Lass?" he asked in a meaningful tone as he leaned back to look at her, a serious expression on his face. It wasn't so much what he said, but how he said it. It was the same tone he used on his men when he wanted answers and right now that was exactly what he wanted. Mel sat up and gave him her best impression of an innocent smile.

"What?" She said shrugging her shoulders.

Changing the subject, she tried even harder not to laugh at the exasperation on his face. "Now about this bachelorette party, what say you be my hero one more time and save me from a night of misery?" She tried.

Hamish gave her a knowing smile and decided to play along. "Och come on Lass, it can't be all that bad."

"Oh you have no idea, there will be dancing, and have I told you how much I *hate* dancing. And knowing Cee, there will be some kind of prank, like strippers or something even worse. You really will be doing me a great service."

"What are strippers?" Hamish asked confused once more. Mel smiled at Hamish's confused expression – the transition to the 21st Century wasn't going to be easy on Hamish. Just then she felt a little mischievous; she would leave this one up to Cee maybe she might think twice about hiring any.

"I think that one is best left to be described by your sister. You should ask her tomorrow." She said, feigning innocence.

Hamish laughed. "I think ye have just as much of an evil streak as Cee. But as for the other, I will be ya hero anytime, anywhere. Now is there something else ya would like to tell me?" He asked as he grabbed her and pulled her on top of him.

Mel couldn't make him wait any longer, "Aye," she replied bringing her mouth down to his, stopping just before she touched his lips. Taking a deep breath, she told him the news that she had confirmed this morning. "Well Laddie, I'm glad you want children, because in about seven and a half months you're going to have one, whether you want it or not!"

Hamish's eyes widened and the smile that lit his face was breathtaking. He quickly changed positions and before she knew it, he had her underneath him and was lying between her legs. "Are ya sure Lass?" he asked timidly.

Mel smiled at him and nodded. His smile spread wider and Hamish laughed joyfully, "och Lass, have I told you today how much I love you?" he queried passionately, touching her stomach in awe.

"I'm sure you have, but I never get sick of hearing it." She grinned.

"Well Lass, let me remind ye." He said mischievously, before he entered her. Mel sucked in her breath as she looked into his eyes at the love they emitted, and as they made careful, passionate, love, she once again wondered what she had done in her life to get this lucky. Whatever it was she hoped it lasted, because this man right here was all she had ever wanted. He was her heart, her soul, but more then that he was her hero. He was the one who had made all her dreams come true, and she would love him until the end of time.

The end

NOTE FROM AUTHOR

Hello to all my readers, I hope you have enjoyed the adventures of Mel and Hamish. I loved Hamish in Ceana's boo and I couldn't wait until he had his own story. For those of you who wondering what happened to Elise, I am happy to say she is happily married to a highlander, living the life she should have always had. And, yes Tristan and Thora will have their own story which is coming soon, Her Modern Day warrior may even have grandma G.G make another appearance. I want to take the time to thank you for your support. Below is a glossary of the words I have used throughout the book. Please feel free to send me your thoughts on my Facebook page YM Zachery.

Kin – Family
Doona – Don't
Ken – Know
Hoore – whore
Seodag – little Jewel
Cac – shit

www.ingramcontent.com/pod-product-compliance
Lightning Source LLC
Chambersburg PA
CBHW020125120726
47903CB00007B/2112